THE GANYMEDAN

THE GANYMEDAN

R.T. ESTER

First published 2025 by Solaris
an imprint of Rebellion Publishing Ltd,
Riverside House, Osney Mead,
Oxford, OX2 0ES, UK

www.solarisbooks.com

ISBN: 978-1-83786-336-5

10 9 8 7 6 5 4 3 2 1

A CIP catalogue record for this book is available from the British Library.

Designed & typeset by Rebellion Publishing

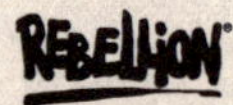

Printed in the United Kingdom

For Grace

DEPROG

In the days following Archer Lenox-Pileser's death, the official account of what happened on the outskirts of Paradox would go unchallenged.

A spacer—a sentient ship—had unwittingly ferried his assassin to the station. While docked for a refuel, the spacer learned of its error and alerted Martian Patrol. The assassin then broke out of the spacer using a signal skipper and a wedger. He died of vacuum exposure before Patrol arrived.

Every news feed was whipped into endless war speculation by then. The matter of Archer Lenox-Pileser's final death—shocking as it may have been when it broke—vanished in a few weeks.

At Gan, a woman who'd also been in the news allowed her brother to bring a pair of sentients near her tent. She wept into her palm heels while a song for the killer played, harkening back to ghosts pre-Frontier and past evictions from dome houses they built on Ganymede.

When she could spare some composure for the sentients, she invited them in. They dropped off a device the killer had wanted her to keep, then gave the full account.

OUTLOOK ADJUSTMENT

THE CANYONS

V-DOT SAT ACROSS a round table from Archer Lenox-Pileser while the man—known commonly as LP—enjoyed a plate of almonds and they passed a Hemingway between each other.

They were alone in a lavishly chandeliered room, filled with tables and a platform in its midst. V-Dot's connector was always jammed in close proximity to him. This afternoon, its relay function also had to be disabled. A layer of precaution. In less than two hours, he would be on a spacer bound for Oasis.

Pretending had proven challenging in recent weeks. More effort. More sacrifices to the Lenox-Pilesers while the window during which he could leave with his conscience still intact vanished. Years ago was when he should've done this.

While watching LP swig, he stilled his nerves. Delayed release. If this was going to work, he'd have to imagine it working till it actually did.

LP belched. There was a deeper, more promising sound under it. Next, he was doubled over, glass clenched in a precarious grip while his face reddened and sweat began filming through his dark, short-cropped hair, trickling down the sides of his forehead till he swiped at it with his free hand.

"What's in this? My GI sensors, they're..." His eyes dimmed. A swelling noise issued from his gut as he fingered the mass of skin beside his left eye for his connector's coin shape.

The poison had stupefied his glance. It unnerved V-Dot. Made him think about the Hemingway in his own gut, the poison cocktail it hid with its smooth texture and subtle taste. Not delaying any further, he leaned into his chair and folded his arms, breathing slowly to ward off the tremor in his voice.

"Don't try to reach anyone."

LP poked the connector anyway. A look of dulled astonishment flashed in his eyes. "Huh..."

"We're both jammed." He tried to smile. It resembled constipation. "You don't have any backups, man. Why would you do something so stupid?"

Rather than say why, V-Dot took a moment to breathe. Whatever this was—stupid, rushed, doomed to fail—people would remember it. He was making sure. "Neuronal confinement..." One of LP's many contributions to the Frontier. "That was you, wasn't it?"

"Wait a minute..." Able to sit up straight, LP kept his hands flat on the table and met the question with full astoundment in his eyes. It seemed he would answer, but instead, "I don't think it's ever happened like this." He laughed, hushed and hollow, under his breath. A possessed figurine. "Usually it's kill and run, but looks like you're planning to just sit there and talk my head off. That's—" He cocked his head to the side. "That's new."

He looked down, palmed his sternum with one hand, then covered his right ear with the other, checking his heart sounds as the sweat coated his shop-grown skin. V-Dot, minding the time, remembered the poison in his own tract.

"I was on the Island for two years, LP." He watched the dead man continue to ignore him, like an impertinent child, spinning the glass slowly on the table, belching, squinting at what was left. "Didn't feel like I did anything to deserve it, so those first few weeks, I wasn't very cooperative. Legally, they can only give you up to ten times the amount you were sentenced in the real, but nobody's really checking that gives a shit. If you actually look at the time in total they added, you'd think I was lucky. I wasn't taking the remorse pledge in the mornings with the other inmates. They took me to Neuronal. Hardwired it using old-looking tech. Flipped the switch." He snapped his fingers, called the man's gaze up. "One week for just a half-hour in the real. Outlook adjustment."

"If you hadn't tried hiding your record from me, I could've been compelled to go after the bastards who did that, you fucking imbecile." LP had trouble steadying his glance. The Hemingway or the poison? Hard to tell.

V-Dot nodded. Hearing him say that gave perspective he'd been missing for weeks. It was always going to end like this. It had to be him.

"That was just the first time, LP." Talking had begun to take too much effort, but someone had to hear why he was doing this. "You see, I was better back then. I used to think I was better now, but I was actually better back then. They had to keep taking me to Neuronal. In the sim, it's just the white maze, and clothes don't even render. Never felt like it was just a week. I didn't need to eat or anything else like I did in the real. It was all that time to myself that was supposed to break me. Eventually it did. But only because of something else they had to do. See I didn't know they were allowed to put shit from inside my head in the sim. They weren't. But I was special. I was from Gan. I was one of the Manath freaks. Rules didn't apply when it was just me."

Hands flat again, LP downed his gaze and was now pistoning his fingers on the table, doing his best with his body's pain absorbers. V-Dot eyed his crop of sweat-matted hair, lingering on the space directly above it before letting his gaze fall to the glass. "They only had to do it once," he said. "When they pulled me out, they told me just an hour had passed in the sim." He nodded, looked away, thinking he would cry. "I still know the words to that fucking pledge."

LP stirred noisily in the corner of his eye. "And now you're making it my problem? Is it really just this boring bullshit again?"

"Fuck you, LP."

"I can at least credit you for the shrewdness to say it now rather than wait like the others."

V-Dot could hear him struggling with his consonants. He could also feel the poison inside his own tract, soaking into the sponge he'd swallowed prior to this. He was becoming woozy. He leaned forward as smoothly as he could manage and clasped his palms.

"You've been snatching people from the After and torturing them. You really are the fucking devil. I should've listened to Asa. I should've listened to those 'Manath freaks.' They were right."

Not visibly acknowledging what he said, LP craned his neck over his shoulder instead. "Where's my detail? Where's everyone?"

V-Dot snapped his fingers twice, got the man's attention back. He'd lost track of time and was now down to using the poison's release schedule to tell. Whatever else happened, he had to be out of here the minute LP's lights were fully out. "Why?" His voice softened as a fever took hold. "What did they do? I know about Jax crossing you years ago. What about the rest?"

"V-Dot, you're a fucking freak. Stupid as a skinned dog." LP's face became stiff, as though he was having a stroke. The glass sat almost empty on his side of the table.

V-Dot reached for it, dragged it closer, and held it up for a toast. "Stupid as a skinned dog..." He gulped.

"You're going to love the pickaxe through your skull. Straight through... maybe I'll go in through one of your eyes..."

V-Dot almost choked on the drink, but kept the glass tipped into his mouth. He'd seen LP do that before. The image flashed in his mind, except now it was him under the axe when it swung low. Not thinking about it helped, but when he did it only made him more resigned to his fate. Once he did this, there was likely just one way he'd be avoiding the axe.

LP's eyes followed the glass as V-Dot set it back down. "You know," he resumed, almost to himself, "my mistake with Jax all this time was leaving his children alone; those little circus animals who now have more backups than they have functioning brain cells. I won't be repeating that with you. Asa. Next time she has to sit for her own adjustment sim, someone could accidentally slip an upload chamber in her skull."

The sponge wedged in V-Dot's gut rolled and he felt it would punch through his sternum. Asa could handle herself. He wouldn't have to worry about Asa if this went south.

"Skull this, skull that… You won't even ask how I learned?"

"No, I want the pleasure of getting it out of you myself." The words chilled him to his spine. He hadn't been tortured physically on the Island. "And I will."

"It was through Connor." He could bet a whole year's comp on Connor being a part of it.

"He's very careless with his gates," LP mouthed, drunk, repeating what he'd said about his great-grandnephew in various contexts. "Everyone comes to those grottoes and he just lets them get near him." He slid back from the table, falling heavily on his back rest. "It's how Garland found out. Our esteemed Patrol chief."

For a moment, he became still. Like he wanted to see V-Dot squirm. The chief of Martian Patrol. One of the honored guests…

V-Dot scoffed.

"Ghost, you know you're fucked after this, right?" LP

said. "I can't just assume you do. In a way, it's thoughtful how you're still just—" He gestured, fist forward. "Here..." A thought seemed to delay him until a worrying spark entered his eyes. He beamed through the constipation. "This must've shattered something inside you..." While gaunt and wet as a body out of cryo, he fixed V-Dot with a fiend's gaze. "What was it like?"

V-Dot shrank back from it. LP asking this like things would just go back to being how they were. He really thought this was another kill and run.

"I'm letting you get your kill," LP added. "Don't fucking hold back right now."

"Still planning to put me in there too, right?"

He snorted. "I never go back on that."

"Then I've got nothing to tell you, LP."

"You're playing a stupid game here, Ghost. Denying a dying man his last wish? Denying me—"

"Patrol chief and who else?"

V-Dot recognized the fiend's gaze. Seeing it many times before, he knew the leverage he now had. This would have to count for everything.

Contorting with pain, LP shot him a baleful stare. "Think I'll start with a cleaver, right down the middle. Two equal halves of the body I'll have rendered just for you..."

"Who else, LP?"

LP brayed like a jackal. "Garland," he intoned, loud like he knew this was a kill and run, and V-Dot wouldn't even get enough time to have anyone doubt his story. "Finch from Interorbital before him. Head human in charge. She likes to attend with the current HH from Venus Group, but sometimes she also brings friends from the exchange sector. Leblanc. Goldie, who I've hated since our time together at the resort. If you want a complete list of who attends, who has clearance for their own exhibitions, you'll have to get that from Garland." Pointing weakly in front of him, he fell stiffly forward and came down on his elbows. "Now, tell me what it was like. Spare no detail."

"No."

"Fuck you."

For this to work, V-Dot also had to take pleasure in the little things, like waiting to say what this was. And this was *working*. It frightened him, in fact, how well it seemed to have come together. All Asa knew about it was that he wanted to steal something from LP, something only he and a few others knew about, if he could figure out how.

From his suede bomber coat, V-Dot retrieved a clear canister and sat it next to the glass. LP's eyes went wide when he recognized the item inside. He shot up from his seat. Like a felled tree, his body dropped. He began to wriggle away from the table.

V-Dot eyed the scrubware inside the canister. A gray cocoon stuck to the canister's curve. He took a deep breath. Glanced up at chandeliers hanging like stalactites from the room's exposed ceiling. Cracked his neck.

"Maybe I am stupid, LP. But I know what you've been doing and I'm putting an end to all of that."

Like one of his victims from the After, LP slithered on the floor of his ballroom, trying, failing to put distance between himself and V-Dot. Prone to the floor, his limbs lay flaccid from the poison cocktail. His head flopped about like a landed fish. He could barely keep his tongue in his mouth while ripe terror filled his eyes. "When I come back," he slurred, "I'll put you in there and carve you up worse than Jax."

V-Dot let the threat run a shiver through his bones. He swiped the canister off the table and stood. With a measured step, then another, he closed on LP. He then wedged his foot under the man's chest and flipped him onto his back. LP could barely keep his eyes level on anything as a low whine issued from his chest.

V-Dot squatted beside him. "You're not coming back, LP." He shook the canister over the man's eyes. "But since we're still on the subject—" A wave of nausea coursed through him and he felt like he might tip over onto his side. "What was the point? I thought I'd seen folks put through the worst treatment on the Island, then I followed you into that sim. You put people through something like that, usually it means you want something from them."

"You slimy Manath freak," LP answered, tongue still in the way. "I took you in, thinking I could enlighten you, and you're still every bit the savage you were the first day we met. The point? *Pain*. Pain is the point. How many sessions did you—"

V-Dot punched him hard in the mouth. LP's eyes whirled in their sockets.

"Maybe I'm not coming back. But you're going to die and those walking cadavers will still be stuck there as proof of what the mind can be made to endure. You'll never understand the importance of findings like that because you come from backward people who have no place in the bright futu—"

V-Dot watched the last remnants of life leave LP's eyes. Without meaning to, he fell to his knees. The sponge and all the poison it had absorbed bubbled back up his throat and gushed out into a rancid pool of vomit beside LP's torso. He fell on his side next. His coat barely missed the fetid puddle. He felt faint, beginning to fear he wouldn't have the strength to escape the Canyons, much less Mars.

LP was dead. Now to make sure it stuck.

He rolled painfully to his knees, then popped the canister open. The scrubware inside it writhed—then he lowered the canister to LP's right ear, jammed it into the lobe, and watched the scrubware bore into his eardrum. One minute. Two… He counted to sixty again under his breath. He had to be sure. After about five minutes with his body stiff and his glare on the dead man's engorged ear canal, he had to believe it was done.

Good riddance to the beast and its manifest reincarnations.

A few more seconds elapsed, then something appeared as though from thin air above LP's forehead and floated there, spinning—the man's halo cache.

With his breath caught in his throat, V-Dot watched it spin. He hadn't stopped viewing sentience backups with suspicion, but he knew this one was different. Whatever of LP could still be accessed through the device, it existed outside the reach of every governing body in the Frontier. It couldn't be erased or altered. More pertinent to V-Dot, it now contained LP admitting to the tortures, besides incriminating a few others.

He grabbed hold of the cache and held it up for closer inspection. He'd seen LP drown himself many times. He'd witnessed many of his upgrades to newer, identical bodies and, in doing so, seen the man's process for pairing the device he would take off his most recent body with the upload chamber in his new skull. Sense data from his last two hours alive. Each time.

On his way out, the compound was more serene than he'd ever seen it. The caracals craned their necks with mournful eyes as he passed them without stopping to say goodbye. Redwoods glistened in the waning afternoon glow. The train to the spaceport took a small eternity. In the silence of the journey, the details faded from his mind, and in their place a semblance of light had begun to show. Oasis was only two hours away. Once there, he would try for Gan. Outrun what he knew was coming. If he could…

Gan was home. If he could, he would try for Gan.

The sun dipped below the horizon, sending parting flares through the windows as the train pulled into the spaceport.

Anything was possible. Everything felt new again.

1. OUTSIDE CONTEXT

Two years served for an altercation with an enforcement drone, and all the others got to learn who he was. V-Dot. Ver. Verdante. He went by many names in the Canyons. The drones knew all of them.

Night descended far off, bringing starlight that caught wanly on domes at the foot of Olympus Mons. He lingered on the view while stepping forward in line. Mining stations. Power plants. Prison compounds. He drew a long breath and inched up another step. On the Island, he'd discovered what he feared worse than dying, what he struggled now to remember while imagining what it would feel like. What the next day would feel like. On Mars. Elsewhere.

The window relaying the view to him took up the entire wall on his right, running the full length of the terminals. It loomed luridly over columns of passengers waiting to board spacers offworld.

Fluorescents overhead bathed the spaceport in harsh white hues. Passengers grumbled under the boom of an announcement that echoed across the concourse. Another round of delays. Leaving Mars was easiest when it wasn't urgent.

Asa would normally say that when he visited. Before they had their falling out. He was always late by about a week, then leaving again. First time he left, it was with his uncle to go live elsewhere so he could attend school at Gan's Culture

District. He was six. She'd promised she would find someone else to help with repairs to her armored suit.

The wheeze of a drone behind him raised goosebumps on his skin. He shot a glance over his shoulder, sweeping his gaze up to level with the drone. Boxy and big as a briefcase, it shot up over the columns of waiting passengers, hovering, its slick black underside flashing red. A guard drone.

He released a held breath, lowered his eyes. Should one of these recognize him, the port security officers wouldn't hesitate to remind him of how they felt about humans who played whack-a-drone with their colleagues. If he had to eat their shit before getting on the first ship bound for Oasis in months, he would scoop it up with a spoon. For now, he prayed it could be avoided. Leaving Mars before the news broke was all he hoped for, all he was *allowing* himself hope for until the cache was no longer on him.

Beyond its present location, he couldn't recall much of the last hour in detail. Just the vomit. Just everything he brought with him to the spaceport.

A small distance away to his left, he glimpsed security officers milling amid the throng of passengers—humans in gleaming red exosuits, androids who towered over everyone, the floor's lighting ricocheting off their chrome armor. If the press was to be believed, the androids were sentient or 'sentient-classed.' V-Dot hadn't always believed.

When he could no longer stop his fingers rapping on his thighs, he pocketed both hands. That did nothing to calm him, so he thumbed the connector on the side of his right eye. The relay function was still disabled. A translucent screen filled his view, imposing a grid of items over a reflection of his dark-complected visage. After inspecting his clean stubble and neatly trimmed mustache, he blinked on the animated icon of a turned head with a gaping eyeball in its midst.

The screen flashed white, then dimmed to present him his personal rearview window. He scanned the area behind him for Patrol officers. He was wringing a spot of vomit from one of his locs when a voice rolled over his shoulder.

"First time offworld?"

He started, swatting the connector to shut it off. The voice was friendly enough. Flashing a smile like he remembered something, he turned to regard its source. A small woman stood in line behind him with a matching smile. She looked middle aged, decked in a shawl and tights that reminded him of patrons who frequented the bar where he previously worked.

He could only manage a nod. His first time offworld, he'd been uncertain about his future here. Back then, LP had been little more than a name to him.

Had he actually just…?

"Here." The woman extended him a box of hash gum. "I pop one every time I have to fly out. Takes the edge off."

He took a questioning look at her but reached for one. He bit off half of it, kneading it between his teeth. If nothing else, the sweet taste would overwhelm the trace of vomit on the back of his tongue.

Turning away from her, he raised the unchewed half. "'Preciate it."

"Smoothest stuff on this side."

He cast a sidelong glance but didn't meet her eyes again, nodding as he drew a belabored breath. "FASA dank?"

"You know your strains."

"I dabble." He'd guessed. Guessed, then lied. Not even having to think about it, because it was always FASA dank. Also he'd guessed she wouldn't know the actual strain either.

He would miss this. The attention. Being here. Sticking out the way he did.

"So what do you do, anyway?" she asked.

He turned to fix her with wide eyes, keeping his body stiff and sideways, his hands still jammed in his pockets. "Mixology."

"Really?"

"Best on both sides." He smirked, gingerly baring his teeth.

"Isn't work in that field practically off limits?"

"When you have the talent, you don't have to worry about the sentients squeezing you out. Besides—" His nerves were getting the better of him. He feared she could hear the tautness on the edge of his voice. "Cocktails require a human touch."

The woman smiled. Her voice dipped, her eyes softened. "I'm sure you've had the occasion to say that about more than just cocktails."

"No, I'm just really good at this one thing." He felt his dryness chill the air between them, but something in her smile compelled him to keep going. He could still use whatever this was that kept him in the good graces of the high-born curios on Mars. He breathed in deeply, forced a hand out of his bomber, and extended it. "By the way, I'm V—"

"Line's moving," yelled someone behind her.

Not turning to confirm, he backed up a step, then another. He realized he'd stepped on something when a voice boomed behind him.

"Hello, Verd."

He whirled to meet a security officer with arms folded and a grin that menaced under a thick beard. Raising his foot off the officer's boot, he shrank back. "Didn't see you there, Officer. I'm sorry."

He couldn't be here when the news broke. The spoon was out. A bleating grin revealed teeth and he could smell a helping of shit coming his way.

The officer leaned forward to get in his face. "Did you not see me just now?"

"I wasn't looking. I'm sorry." He wringed the tremor from his voice, breath held tightly against a roiling in his gut.

"Do you see me right now?"

"Clear as day, Officer." He wasn't leaving. Someone had seen him, and he hadn't seen them.

"Do you see me?"

He nodded, looking down. Units from the Martian Patrol were likely already at the port, letting the security officers get their licks in first.

"Are you able to sense a *presence* in front of you?"

Passengers behind him began to stir. "What's going on?" the woman asked.

He swallowed. Something echoed between his calm exterior and the hammering in his chest till he was able to think it once and turn cold at the thought; cold and numb and vibrating all over.

He was caught. Or would be soon. Didn't matter, because he wasn't leaving. The flavor of shit this time was something called an Outside Context Assessment.

He looked up, tried a pleading smile on the officer. "Come on, man. I'm not one of them." The nonsentients.

An OCA would require him to follow the officer elsewhere inside the port while the ship to Oasis got ready to close its receiving airlock.

The officer puckered his lips. A sharp whistle escaped them, calling down a drone close by. The drone dropped to eye level beside the officer, its black, cuboid hull hovering like a demon over his left shoulder. "Officer BRZRK-14, I am requesting confirmation that this subject's process patterns warrant an OC assessment."

"Officers..." V-Dot began, getting nowhere and doing it very slowly, while the ship to Oasis left the port.

The drone spun ninety degrees to point a blinking red sensor-light at him. "Mr. Dotnet," it began in a breezy voice. "Are you able to say if something or someone is currently in front of you?"

"It's a something," he blurted. "That's also clear as day." He wasn't being careless anymore. He wouldn't call it that, not after his arrest. He was being stupid. Careless could still have gotten him to Oasis with the halo cache in his haul. Stupid was killing LP to do it.

"Hands off Biz!" the officer barked, one hand extending toward V-Dot, the other brushing the butt of a holstered sidearm.

He swung both hands high, backing up a step. "I wasn't—" He hadn't even approached the drone.

"I think that's grounds," the officer turned to regard it.

"I think so, too."

The officer reached a hand to V-Dot's shoulder and lifted the lifepack clung to it. "You'll get this back once we're done."

V-Dot groaned as he watched the officer deposit the pack on an invisible g-field atop the drone. Leaving Mars could've been easy with just the killing. Even with the scrubware to make sure it stuck. But not with the cache. But then he wouldn't have had to leave. Two stupid things at once.

He was waffling, not even making sense to himself.

The officer gestured toward the foot traffic snaking behind the passenger columns. "Verden Dotnet, also known as V-drone-basher, please come with us."

BRZRK-14706-49, THE DRONE and specialty-license-number holder who'd swung low to assist the officer, possessed a god-node, making it a sentient. In addition to the sentients, Mars was awash in a declassed nonsentient population. Outwardly as functional as the sentients but with fewer protections and always kept as private property or public utility. Normally not permitted to fly.

V-Dot was neither. He steeled his bones, turning over ideas for how he would survive the next few hours while the officer whistled a maddening tune behind him. This was a colossal waste of time.

The drone led them toward the end of a corridor flanked on both sides by glass walls with security officers in rooms behind each one—androids seated at long desks, humans lounging, their eyes shut, lost in their sims while the sentients held down the fort.

They came to a stop by a room smaller and less congested than the others. Behind the glass, two androids whipped their trapezoid heads around. V-Dot shuddered as their sensor-lights blinked at him. "Can't I at least have my pack?"

"Get in," the officer growled as the door slid open.

V-Dot shuffled across, stopping in front of the desk the androids sat behind. Armored columns of chrome, tapering consoles, and multi-jointed limbs. One held his gaze while the other turned to regard the officer behind him.

"Tig," the officer called, addressing the android now staring at him. "Bishop…" The other android turned and they both nodded. "This evening we have the pleasure of administering an OCA on this subject."

The drone floated in behind the officer. "He bears a striking resemblance to a Verden Dotnet but, uh…" A noise like tittering issued from it as it alighted on a plinth-like parking station by the door, V-Dot's lifepack suspended above it. "We can't be careful enough."

The halo cache was still there. He thought he could even see the outline. He gulped. Stupid. *Stupid!* He had to do two very stupid things at once.

The android answering to Tig cocked its head back. "A simple BM scan would return his ident—"

"Tig," the officer said in an intense whisper, furrowing bushy eyebrows over a face that feigned urgency as he gestured coyly at a door behind the desk. "Fetch the generator."

Tig sprang up. "Of course." Its mannerisms and nasally pitch modeled that of a bumbling assistant as it traipsed toward the door and began to hum, its footfalls markedly silent.

V-Dot folded his arms to hide the tremors coursing through. The officers had directives to look out for suspected nonsentients traveling off-planet and subject them to OCAs. A measure taken against smugglers who managed to pass them off as sentients in a BM scan. Whoever was to break the news first would do well waiting till this ragtag group was done wasting valuable resources on him. He was neither.

"You—" The officer slid a chair toward the unoccupied end of the desk. "Have a seat. Hands where we can see 'em, else Bishop here gets to screw on its pummeling arm."

V-Dot plopped down on the chair, puffed his cheeks up, and blew a mouthful of air. "You all run a tight ship." He couldn't just drop the act with them—the security officers, Martian Patrol, and whoever the fuck else. They'd be getting what they'd wanted since first learning he was no longer on the Island. A free man. Living freely on Mars.

"It's honest work," the officer shot back as the door behind the desk was flung open. "Better than anything you're doing for money these days."

"Mixology," the drone intoned from its station.

"Mix-a-wha—?" The officer moved to clear space for Tig now wheeling a black, waist-high cylindrical device past the desk.

"Means he gets paid to drink while we do the legwork."

V-Dot gritted his teeth as tittering issued again from the drone. "I'm a storyteller," he mumbled. "I paint pictures." Asa had arranged for him to attend school in the Culture District, saying she was who she was so he could be who he wanted to be.

The android answering to Bishop burned the accusing glare of its sensor-light at him from across the desk. If his reputation hadn't so helpfully preceded him at every step, V-Dot felt he could try reasoning with this one. Instead, he spun his chair to the left so Bishop got only his ear, then propped his right arm on the desk.

On the wall now in front of him, a holoscreen relayed news from the Plains and elsewhere on Mars at a volume too low for him to hear. He glimpsed footage of a job lottery in progress, followed by an interview with the human who won whatever low-paying gig it was for the next twelve months. She looked happy.

There was coverage next of an investigation into a new round of missing persons cases inside the After—ghosts who'd gone missing in the machine. V-Dot held his breath. He would have shut his eyes, but that risked inviting images he wanted gone. Images that brought him to this, in the first place, and gave Asa something to tease him about: that it would take those images for him to come see her again.

Bishop's sensor-light flashed in the corner of his eye. He rapped his fingers on the desk and wondered what good it would do him to risk a signal to Asa. She hadn't been expecting him. More than two thousand frontnotes for passage to Oasis. Not saying he was coming. Not saying how long he would stay. Or that he was bringing the cache; doing what he planned, just quicker.

To his left, the officer and Tig hunched over the device, centering it in front of the room, then squatting to fidget with controls along its cylindrical casing.

V-Dot had only heard of it prior to this. Used to administer OCAs, employing the hotly debated theory that a nonsentient, when presented with an image or presence fully outside the context of what it already knew, would fail to sense it. A sentient would either mislabel it or correctly identify it as something it had never seen, something it hadn't the slightest inkling about. A nonsentient would just fail to acknowledge what was being presented or forwarded. Philosophical zombies in a sense. On autopilot. Still able to appear conscious until they hit a set limit.

The generator ran the assessment by scanning the parameters of the subject's cognitive framework, then projecting a series of hologram images that contained somewhere among them an outside context token—an image the nature of which was nowhere within the subject's frame of reference.

Prior to the last few months, V-Dot would have freaked out at getting OCA'd, fearing it would give him nightmares for weeks. Now he'd seen images acutely more horrifying than any OCA-induced terrors. He'd seen something he shouldn't have, and it had kept him up every night since. In his twenty-nine years, he'd never been more scared of sleep. But even awake, the images didn't relent.

He spun his chair left. "Officer, I never got your name..."

The officer, still squatting beside Tig, scratched his head as he squinted at the generator's controls. "It's Montag."

"Officer Montag." V-Dot folded his arms, puffed his chest up. All that said, he still favored avoiding this. "You know, we're a lot alike."

"Really?"

"You don't ever feel like it's just you against the tide of..." He bobbed and hinged his forearms robotically about. Not keen on Bishop's sensor-light boring into the nape of his neck, he spun his chair to give the android his right ear again.

Officer Montag stood, brushing his fingers absently through his beard. "Verd, we are nothing alike—"

"It's just V-Dot, man."

"You're a known felon and I take it on myself every day to make sure worms like you don't cause any more trouble than you already have." Montag threw his arms wide. "Biz, Tig, Bishop—they have more in common with me than I could ever have with you, so you can just stop making a spectacle of yourself."

Tig sprang to its feet while V-Dot turned over Montag's words. "Just another minute while the generator boots up."

V-Dot breathed in deep, caught his fingers rapping on the desk again. Already time to switch gears. He wheeled his gaze slowly on Bishop. Soon, human and android were locked in a standoff while Montag gave the holoscreen his full attention.

"See how we're treated?" He tried being sincere about it, even if this was just to get out of a jam. "Guessing you've also had to deal with this yourself, Officer…"

The sensor-light blinked, then shivered, and it looked for a moment like Bishop was beginning to understand. Until—

"Stop that!"

Its high-strung voice teased a groan from V-Dot. Holding his hands up, he sighed, even laughing at himself as the holoscreen's volume shot up amid sounds of distress from neighboring rooms.

The dulcet tone of a news anchor filled the room while bird's-eye footage of a compound V-Dot knew by heart played on screen.

"*…Now, we want to warn our viewers: some of what you are about to see or hear is of a graphic nature despite our trademarked sensitivity algorithm in the background.*

"*Once again, there has been a successful attempt on the life of Archer Lenox-Pileser Junior, HH at Lexicon, Pilesan Space, Martian Trust, and a slew of other exchange-sector companies in operation on Mars and elsewhere in the Frontier.*"

V-Dot sat up. His heart hammered behind folded arms. The bile in his throat bubbled up again and he tasted vomit on the back of his tongue. He swallowed hard as Montag, still standing on his left side, closed toward the screen.

"Biz, that's your maker, right?" The officer kept his eyes glued to footage of Lenox-Pileser Compound in naked daylight.

"Afraid so," the drone answered.

The screen relayed a sprawl of geodesic domes and open-air dwellings lying like an amoeba around the mouth of a crater. A village unto itself. V-Dot watched Patrol aircraft round a statue erected on the crater floor as the anchor went on.

"*We have scant details at this time, and entry past the white perimeter of Lenox-Pileser Compound has been barred while forensics drones perform a comprehensive sweep. What we do know so far is that Archer Lenox-Pileser Junior—*" The screen switched to video of a young-looking human speaking and gesticulating on a stage littered with floating machine parts. "*—known commonly as LP, was killed earlier this evening while having dinner in his home.*"

The man on the screen raised a hand to quell his audience's applause. V-Dot set his jaw in cold recognition. LP. Five hundred years young, or close to it. Looking the spitting image of twenty-five.

This was real. This happened. The news was now carrying it and soon they would have his name.

"*There are reports waiting to be confirmed of scrubware on the scene.*" Tig let out a gasp while moving to stand beside Montag. "*Viewers may recall the term from awareness campaigns in recent years urging that citizens with sentience backups be vigilant when simming in public places or deciding who to trust with procedures that require the administering of killing solutions beforehand. Now, we want to reiterate that as of right now, these reports remain unconfirmed...*"

The room's door slid open, admitting an android that scuttled across to Montag and Tig. "It's just bullshit, right?" It had a wiry voice.

Tig turned to address it. "Unconfirmed..."

"Saw one of those demoed once." Montag paid the androids a quick glance while the anchor went on. "Looked like a slug... goes in through the ear or nose, finds the upload chamber, and infects the update. Update hits the backups. Wipes everything clean."

V-Dot stilled his nerves while the officers blabbered. The spacer to Oasis was gone. Good as gone. Bad for him. Bad. Stupid. This was so like him, he almost had to laugh.

LP's famous visage filled the screen. Symmetrical. Bony. Clean-shaven. Footage of him being interviewed by an elected body while pundits went on about scrubware.

"There'd never been an instance of its use on someone so elevated in society. Decades ago, a legal form of it would be administered when humans were sentenced to die, injected through the nape of the neck once they were pronounced dead so all their backups would be destroyed as well."

On and on like that.

Had he really said what he'd said to LP…? Before feeding the scrubware to his ear— had that actually been him?

"How long does it take to hit the backups?" Tig.

"I don't know," Montag stammered as he backed toward the generator. "I can't think right now." He dinged the device with a balled fist and, after staring at it a few seconds, motioned at the holoscreen. "It's fucking LP!"

"Whoever did this," Biz added, "it must have cost them upward of a million frontnotes. I'd say about one and a half if they found the scrubware on DarkSeam."

V-Dot could think only of the last time he saw LP. The dead eyes looking up at him. The engorged ear. Where had he found the nerve to even return the stare?

Something brushed the side of his right eye while he sank deeper in thought, enough to make him jump. All eyes and sensor-lights in the room fell on him.

Under the anchor's continued stream, he whipped his head right to see what had made him jump, found Bishop squatting next to him with the generator's thumb-sized gate chip pinched between its fingers.

"The assessment begins with a quick look inside your head. Hold still?"

V-Dot's breath jammed in his throat. The last thing he needed. He faced the screen again, minding footage of LP on a spacewalk while Bishop pressed the chip into his connector.

Montag's strained baritone traveled from beside the generator. "You know, maybe now isn't the time for that…"

Bishop rose to its feet, turning its head to regard Montag. Not believing his ears, V-Dot faced him as well. Montag quietly ambled over to the drone. Lifted the lifepack off its g-field.

"Verd…?" He tossed the pack across, the grimmest look on his face. "You're free to go."

V-Dot caught the lifepack and watched quietly as Montag rejoined the androids at the holoscreen. Bishop glared from his right as he stood. After a second's hesitation, it left V-Dot to join the other officers as well.

The lifepack's weight felt oddly comforting as it slid up his left arm and onto his shoulder. He let a backhanded sort of relief wash over him. He hadn't been named yet.

With their backs turned, the security officers didn't see him flick the generator's chip after removing it from his connector. The holoscreen kept them occupied with a demo of scrubware.

As he sauntered out, he caught the drone's parting glare. It tracked him as he slipped past, spinning slowly on its parking station. While the door slid shut behind him, he risked a final glance over his shoulder and glimpsed the news anchor again.

He was about to be famous. He just couldn't be on Mars when it happened.

2. TR-8901

A NINETEEN-MINUTE train ride from the spaceport, past abandoned tenement buildings like shadows in the moonlight and factory towers in disrepair, the Common Docks tunneled space traffic to and from the Plains. Taking up terminals chiseled into the wall of a crater, they surrounded its floor where ships shot to orbit or made landfall, ships too old and outmoded for employment at the port.

One such ship had been grounded eight weeks inside Terminal Seven when news of LP's killing broke. It still answered to the name LP sent it out with, along with a line of similar uplink models two centuries ago: TR-8901.

Inside Terminal Seven tonight were two other spacers. Bigger and newer models, but no less ancient. Their spark-plug geometries heaved almost to the roof, blotting out the meager lighting in the terminal so TR was barely visible to their right.

All three ships regarded the gaping exit from Terminal Seven into the floor of the crater. There'd been a small commotion earlier between Eight and Twenty-one over which would be receiving the next ship down from orbit. Settled now. A freighter backed its compartmented bulk into Twenty-one, its bow jutting out noticeably when it stopped. After some time surveilling the dark, newly unoccupied crater floor, TR sensed a rummaging presence under its base.

"LUCE," it called, keeping its syrupy voice low. "Didn't see when you rolled in."

"LUCE is out," returned the voice from underneath, like oil on its sensors. "Afraid you're stuck with me this time, TR. How goes it?"

"The docks are quiet and everyone's getting along again." It searched the medium it often shared with LUCE when they spoke, the one with no sound audible to human ears. Nothing. This voice was human. "Sorry, can I ask your name?"

"You've never asked it before."

"I apologize for that." The humans used names to differentiate one from the other. The sentients had followed suit, though not at first. "Whenever it's LUCE, I normally get that without needing to initiate a request for it."

"You mean you've asked it once before so now you always know it's LUCE?"

"I've actually done nothing wrong here."

"TR, I'm just giving you shit." The voice roamed to the side of its underbelly. "You need my name for if we ever meet again, which isn't likely. But it's Mel."

"Mel—" Nice name. Yet it told TR nothing of who this really was under its haul. "You really think we'll never meet like this again?"

"I live dangerously and have no backups. You could live to be a thousand. It's possible but unlikely."

"Yes, but I don't think that's enough reason to—"

"Sorry for the wait."

Subject change. Leaving things unsettled. *Humans.*

"I'll always wait for as long as I'm asked. Anything needed to make sure any spacer who needs looking at the most gets it first."

It probed the sincerity in that. All it ever did was wait. It waited out a war and—even now—was still waiting out the fallout from its build two centuries ago.

Sparks erupted as the human under it pressed something against a spot on its underbelly. Mel. It sensed the rummaging like numbness once signals from its sensors reached its compositor, where they were received, then discarded.

Signal-skipping. A reflex the humans didn't have but sentients used to block sensory input they didn't want reaching their god-nodes—blunt-force attacks, mental triggers, and so on.

What TR could never completely signal-skip was LP.

News of the killing had come with details that put the ship in a funk. LP was likely not coming back. Scrubware at the scene. A life well lived, many would say. Four hundred and eighty-nine years spent preaching singularity gospel to the unbelievers. A life well lived, but with caveats TR made effort—especially now—to ignore. To signal-skip.

"What's this from Operator Sanchez about you considering a break from your circuit?"

The circuit was a pilgrimage of sorts, a tour of the minor routes it began years ago and had kept up since. Always looping through Mars, it involved fly-bys at stations where sentients from TR's generation could still be found—machines with the first god-nodes.

"I haven't mentioned it to Sanchez," it said. "Not sure how she would know."

"Maybe something she heard from LUCE… You want my opinion, I think spacers should avoid venturing into Sectist terrain if they can help it."

Slow on the signal-skip, TR couldn't stop the advice from reaching its god-node, where it would influence its decision-making. The old ports attracted traders who paid to have spacers boarded forcefully and euthanized. Right after, they became nonsentients and could be sold as property.

TR considered the secondary motive behind its travels. Monitoring the routes for Frontsec—the Frontier Alliance

Security Agency—might have paid for its gas and upkeep, but it was hardly the most vigilant spacer on that detail.

"Without the circuit, there's little else I can do anymore."

"You could always join DiploCorps." Mel. Elsewhere under the ship. "They've been known to take older spacers."

"None as old as me."

"Maybe. In the end, I think spending your first two years in DiploCorps would've helped you see it. There's always time for new beginnings."

TR stirred quietly in response. LP's Diplomacy Corps program began years after its build. An answer to a question the first sentients had asked. *What if we want nothing to do with the humans?*

Drones, androids, landers, spacers, skinners, and other sentients were conscripted first to a minimum of two years. After that, they enjoyed the same rights and freedoms as the humans. Sentients who hadn't been through the program when they were built or were desperate to avoid obsolescence could normally be admitted. They were assigned to projects meant to rekindle interest in sentient–human assimilation.

But DiploCorps was also an easy target. The mistake had been building god-nodes that could comprehend the emptiness of space with more crushing fidelity than any human organ. The first sentients had struggled to see why anything mattered.

"Want to hear a joke?"

TR signaled ambivalence in its wave medium, then corrected itself. "If you must." It was usually LUCE down there. Even LUCE, who could never stop talking, didn't task TR's sonosensors when it did.

"An android mystic, a combat drone, and their human captive board a spacer to Gan. Halfway through their journey, the spacer makes an announcement: it's changed its mind and is setting course for the sun instead.

"The mystic gets out its mat, kneels, and enters fugue.

Death, however it comes, is just another rung in a ladder leading to the Animator and shouldn't be argued against.

"The drone perches on the mystic's shoulder and begins flashing back to previous engagements in the war, spinning its beam shooters this way and that.

"The human stares down at his cuffs and says nothing for hours. Finally, the spacer says to him, 'Do you just plan on sitting there while I plunge myself and all three of you into the sun?'

"The human glances at his two captors and, to the spacer, he says, 'The mystic accepted its fate. The war drone went mad. I'm doing the one thing neither thought to try. I'm calling your bluff.'

"Then says the spacer, 'That isn't exactly the one thing neither thought to try. You could try reasoning with me.'

"The human says to it, 'If I had the skill for reasoning, I wouldn't have allowed myself to be walked into a suicidal ship by these two.'

"The spacer quiets down, then says, 'I'm not suicidal, you dolt. I'm helping you avoid having to set foot on Gan. Quick, help me move these two to the airlock.' "

Mel capped the joke with a wheezing laugh that made TR want to ask after LUCE. Not wanting to draw offense, it elected to remain silent and ignorant of the repair bot's whereabouts.

"Oh, come on, TR," said Mel. "It's kind of funny, Gan being the place it is..."

"It's a fine joke and you told it well." It wouldn't have told LUCE any different. LUCE was like the humans in two ways. Always after some form of validation. Never around for long.

The humans, even the ones with backups, were just not around long enough that it would matter if TR assimilated or not. They metabolized too quickly. Name change. Body change. Freely making use of their backups to be anyone within a short span. TR was fine as just itself. The younger sentients could now also change bodies. The feature hadn't been part of its build.

"What's getting you down this night?"

It stalled as a skiff eased out of Terminal Sixteen and assumed its division of the crater floor. "Have you heard the news out of the Canyons this evening?"

"Picked up a whiff..."

The Canyons was a sprawl of well-heeled enclaves to the east of Olympus Mons. It contained Lenox-Pileser Compound, though it was often more accurately said that Lenox-Pileser Compound allowed it rent on LP land.

"Any idea who did it?"

Mel seemed to take more time with the question than would be normal, though this occurred to TR only after the rummaging stopped and there was still no answer.

"Good as new," the human said. Nothing down there was good as new. LUCE would be honest about it. Using its compositor, TR ran a quick diagnostic to confirm everything was at least good enough to last through its next outing.

"What does my bill look like?" Confirmed.

"Thirty frontnotes for my tools and uh— we'll waive everything else. Long wait. Should be LUCE the next time you're here."

TR waited a few seconds as annoyance flooded its sensors, then faded. "It doesn't have to be LUCE. It really doesn't."

Mel chortled somewhere underneath. "Oh, but I think it does."

"What makes you say that?"

"At what point do you think it would make sense to have a look at the person you're having a nice, even enriching conversation with?"

"What do you mean?"

"Your photosensors—they're off. I'm trying to make small talk and it's like you have your back turned. Not encouraging. I know LUCE doesn't usually care. Nothing to see there, just a big, orange box on wheels, but—"

"Sorry I'm still just… LP—"

"Yeah, we're all beat up about it. That's no excuse."

Mortified beyond the usual, TR pitched a signal to its compositor and got the photosensors back online. Mel was short and stocky, flat-featured and in orange coveralls that held floating instruments in a g-field radiating from its belt loops.

Now standing beside the ship, the human looked up at it and crooked an arch smile. "You know, it's nothing to get you a preferred-spacer designation so you don't have to come all the way down for repairs. Then you'd always be dealing with sentients."

"It doesn't have to be LUCE." It didn't. Time had passed since TR was last reminded that humans had a history of taking what they saw on the surface as complete.

This human shrugged, turned, and began toward another spacer. Mel. "Whatever you say, TR. Thanks as always for using Terminal Seven."

BEFORE THE KILLING, V-Dot had bought a scrambler. Banned nearly everywhere in the Frontier, a scrambler took personal records from complete strangers in its vicinity, using the datasets to generate a new list of particulars for its owner. A fellow transplant from Gan had sold it to him, letting the palm-sized device go for twenty-five thousand frontnotes. Less than half the average price, but this was an outdated model. It remained unused in V-Dot's lifepack for months.

He fished for it now. His decision to leave it off at the spaceport had been risky but calculated to capture the window of time he would need to be no one to anyone asking. Once a scrambler had been activated, Patrol would at least know it was in play. Then it was a matter of time till they had the owner's current location as well. He'd planned on all this happening when he was already offworld.

Slight change of plans.

Already a list of suspects was being finalized and prepared for broadcast across every spectrum on Mars and its satellite dwellings. On the train to the Common Docks, he watched a holoscreen and caught a glimpse of himself in a news segment covering the half-dozen humans LP had kept closest to him near the end. V-Dot and two other employees. Two female companions. A niece.

He pulled a wool cap over his locs as the tram sped away. He gripped the scrambler inside his lifepack, kept it clutched to his stomach. Terminal Seven received him through a wide escalator that dipped down several floors and let him off at a wide, double-glass barricade through which he could see two ships docked and a gaping view of the crater floor beyond.

He scuttled toward a control station sitting squat inside the barricade. Closing in, he hard-pressed sensors along the edges of the scrambler to unlock it. The transplant who'd sold it said it was good for nine hours; after that, he'd have to start thinking about ditching it or Patrol would have his name and location before long. As if to confirm, a countdown beginning at nine hours faded in over his vision field, along with bold letters underneath that read ESCO MONTAG and LIFE CLOCK.

The projection vanished when he softened his grip. Pulling the device out of his pack, he jammed it in the inside pocket of his coat. If he still made it out to Oasis before he was good and truly fucked, he might consider ditching it then. But first, he had to find another ship there.

He got off at Terminal Seven because Terminal Seven was the only terminal with a human operator, a gig that mostly entailed locking and releasing g-fields, and, on occasion, dealing with human ship captains when they scratched the hulls of their ships on entry. He could use that to his advantage, though he wasn't sure how.

The operator looked up from a dashboard in the control station as V-Dot balled his fist to knock on the glass. "Don't."

He lowered his hand and grinned, searching his memory for the name he'd seen next to her photograph when he'd looked the crew up on his way here.

"Operator Sanchez."

She slid open a section in the glass and pushed her round face through. "If you're looking for the pushers who parked their skiff here and were selling contraband out of it, customs came and got them already."

"What? No… No, I was hoping you could help me locate a ship leaving for Oasis from here or any of the other terminals… maybe even one with a human at the helm." Or just a spacer with no god-node in its build. He hadn't been this wary about that in years, but on the heels of what he'd done, all the old prejudices were flooding back.

She glowered at him, her shock of pink-blonde hair like icing through the glass. "Why a human-helmed ship?"

He squirmed. "*You* know…"

"I don't."

"All right, then, let me start over."

He considered that she might be a skinner but put the thought away. Shouldn't matter. Shouldn't have mattered if he hadn't just killed the human widely credited for their very existence. Dumb thing. Very dumb in retrospect when sticking to his original plan would've been easier.

"Oasis," he said, like jazz, working a new angle. "Sectist stronghold… during the war." Sanchez nodded. He was beginning to think he had her, so he *aha*'d softly and kept going. "Lot of bad habits from back then, right? Still in practice. For example, did you know they don't allow sentient spacers to dock?"

She shook her head, smirking, not having it. "No, that's just Gan. All the others have already stopped doing that."

Shit. Another glowing review of Gan.

"Well shit, how much longer do you have here, then?" Switching gears again. "You know you could parlay this gig into something permanent if there's an uptick in ships with human crews docking here?"

"I'm not a lottery winner, you idiot. Terminal Seven is a co-op."

He rubbed his eyes. She sighed, adjusting herself behind the dashboard.

"I'm sorry. It's been a day. Did you see on the news they killed Lenox-Pileser?"

"Again? Haven't looked."

"Patrol has been calling up here asking about the pushers with the contraband in their haul. Apparently, they may have sold the scrubware that was found on the scene."

Folding his arms, he looked away for a second, cornered by a recurring pang of annoyance. "Well, that's bullshit."

Truly, he meant it. He'd known Martian Patrol would use the killing as grounds to crack down on the holdouts—humans still carrying on like no field of enterprise was off limits. And that was what always riled him in the past. The relentless nature of it. On the Island, he'd encountered inmates rotting away because they'd had the nerve to sidestep the job lotteries.

"Yeah, this might be it for old LP," Sanchez said. "Personally, I think it's Manathema. It was them the previous three times he croaked."

He winced. "Three times?"

"First one happened before the Sectist War." A pedantic gleam entered her stare. "LP was on a shuttle at Polemia with investors when a Manath sympathizer blew open a section of the hull. Took all of them out. The other two times, they didn't disclose until after the war. You should be careful going to Oasis right now, speaking of. Lot of sympathizers still live there."

He forced an uneasy grin. Manathema was an anti-Frontier organization with chapters everywhere. If he wasn't sure of anything else, he knew he wasn't Manath.

"Anyway, you're in luck." She crooked a smile as though to wipe her mind clean of all that. "There's only one spacer in the docks right now planning a stop at Oasis and you managed to find it on your own. An old uplinker. Leaves from this very terminal in less than an hour."

He swung his lifepack over his shoulder. A smile lit up his face. "Operator Sanchez..." He gestured toward the other side of the barricade, where he could still only see two large ships through the glass. "Which one and how do I get through?"

"Not so fast..." She thumbed a button on her dashboard. A blue light swept so quickly down his body, he didn't get a chance to panic at the thought that the scrambler wouldn't work. "This might be the Common Docks but you still have to be scanned if you want in."

He gritted his teeth as the sight of Sanchez squinting down at a screen on the dashboard sent chills down his spine.

"Esco Montag?"

He cleared his throat. "That's me."

"Mr. Montag, it's showing that all you have in your pack is a hash-gum sampler from the spaceport."

"Correct." The scrambler had also shielded everything in the pack from detection. The halo cache. He grinned broadly.

Operator Sanchez fixed him with a questioning smirk while she thumbed another button on the dashboard. A door-shaped section of the outside glass slid open beside the control station.

"Lot Four, Mr. Montag. Ship answers to TR-8901."

* * *

After the human left, TR-8901 took most of its sensors offline again, something it did only in environments it deemed safe and familiar. Younger spacers called it *entering fugue*—retreating into just the god-node while everything else went on autopilot.

Zaria packed sand between her hands. Sand brushed her forearms, fine and yellow. Sand on her little, red dress. Sand in her spongy hair.

Her castle was brown in the afternoon glow. Water swept over the sand. She got up and went to see. Bare feet. Splish and splash as she trod the wetness. Ankle-deep.

She heard a noise like someone asking for directions. Swept her gaze right.

TR had left its sonosensors on. They'd just picked up the voice of someone asking how to get to Lot Four. It brought the remaining sensors back online as that someone's footsteps gained in volume.

Behind TR, treading haltingly toward its back hull, the human asking directions to Lot Four emerged from under the shadow of the neighboring ship. He had a look on him TR recognized from the first time Operator Sanchez laid eyes on the old ship. Bemusement.

He inched to a stop, slipped a hand from his pocket, and waved gingerly at its back hull. "Hi..."

TR picked up a slight tremor in his voice. "Hello."

"Operator Sanchez told me you're leaving for Oasis?"

"Not exactly. It's only the first stop among many on my circuit."

With photosensors along its back hull, it appraised the human—his suede coat, his camouflage trousers, and the wool cap over his locs. He had a dark complexion that made it think fleetingly of Zaria.

"First stop?" The human brimmed positively at its back hull.

"First of sixteen. And perhaps 'stop' isn't the right term. I don't actually stop or go in. I simply slow to a crawl when I get within gravity-assist range of each station."

The human reached around to scratch the nape of his neck as he sighed and took a step back. "Okay, I'll just dive in, ship." He folded his arms, puffed his chest up. "My name is… Montag. I have a family emergency at Oasis that requires my presence as soon as possible. Since you might be the only ship going that way, I'm hoping you can give me a lift."

His tone was suddenly brash, but Zaria assigned value to the rare encounter with sentients or humans who didn't beat around the bush. Residents who spoke their minds about everything from Frontier politics to new religion.

"I'm TR-8901, or just TR," it said after a moment's quiet. Just TR. Not a name change. Nothing that could have anyone mistake it for a spacer who'd been through DiploCorps. Not even with a sponsor it could sort of belong to for the two years the program took.

"TR… How does that sound?" The human kicked the floor with his boot and the clang echoed through the terminal. "You and me. Oasis. We can decide what kind of stop on the way there."

The sound of his boot striking the metal came in a register TR wished it had signal-skipped after the fact. A mild annoyance wave at that sank its voice to a growl. "I've never let a human board."

"First time for everything."

"Some things…" The previous human had gotten under its hull. Or sensors… How would they have said it? "It's actually that I have no room for passengers inside. I'm an uplink model. I wasn't built with that in mind."

"Not even one?"

This human's desperation suddenly became real. It sat like a bruised animal beside Zaria and the girl's eyes watered as she looked at it.

"There's a shunt close to my back hull that LUCE sometimes crawls in for a look at my internals. You can squat there if you like, but once we break orbit the gravity goes away and pressure isn't far behind."

"You don't have an oxy cycler?"

"I do. It's just never been used since my build two centuries ago. I could try anchoring a g-field toward the shunt for gravity, but the cycler is old and untested. You'll be taking a big risk."

It had erred, neglecting to signal-skip the previous human's unpleasantness with Zaria in earshot. The girl was always registering her agreement with strangers like that.

The shunt was one of seven on the ship—an enclosure the size of an escape capsule. Room enough for a helper unit or small child.

TR sensed an imbalance, like having to navigate in extreme gravity. Extreme gravity or the girl tugging at the thread that connected her to TR's more cautious frame of mind. There had to be some way to help this human. Or at least try. In the silence that ensued, the human hooked his hands on his hips while stress lines formed on his forehead.

"Perhaps I could start the cycler up now and see how it fares before it's lift-off time for me. Targeting just that shunt should be quick enough."

"Okay..." A smile arched the human's lips and teeth shone behind them. "Okay, that's good."

TR brimmed in turn. "Stand by, Montag."

It took most of its externals down again, turned its attention to where its compositor connected its god-node to every ship part. From there, it located ducts leading to the shunt in question and, for the first time in more than two hundred years, fired up the vacs belonging to its cycler.

As oxygen secretion began, its comsat buzzed with the latest out of the Canyons. LP still dead, an official cause-of-death announcement imminent. Sources still unable to confirm—perhaps even barred from confirming—the involvement of scrubware.

The report kept on as the shunt began to fill with human-breathable air. Two suspects had just been named, LP's niece and his personal mixologist, and Martians were urged to be on high alert. TR noted their names and other particulars. Nothing meaty yet, but it felt the usual urge to help with this one, so it backed up the report for later retrieval.

Oxygen level inside the shunt steadied. Outside, the human wanting a lift to Oasis had taken a seat on the floor and was currently fingering the connector beside his eye, his face grim, his cap pulled down almost to the bridge of his nose.

Family emergency.

TR thought back to a time it had to make a dash for Polemia on news that another from the old gang was thinking of finally honoring the Pact—Machine Suicide. It hadn't gotten there in time to stop it.

As it prepared to fire the signal to lower the back hull, a late-breaking development nudged its comsat again. Manathema had just come forward to take credit for the killing.

TR stalled. Manathema was of grave concern when it came to sentients, spacers especially. Centuries ago, they'd splintered from an old order known as the Humanics, and even then the Lenox-Pilesers had been among the targets of their revulsion. Made sense that they would take credit. Made sense that they would continue to target the human credited by many as the father of the sentients.

In their quest to make it stick, they had to succeed only once. With reports of scrubware, TR soured at the thought that they might finally have done that.

"Montag—"

The human looked up at the back hull. "TR…"

"I've never let a human board."

"You said. You'd be doing me a solid if you did this once."

"Humans past a certain age don't always seem to get me." It stalled again as this one cleared his throat. "I wouldn't want to grate on you once we get going, and there's no easy way for you to exit that shunt if you need to."

The human sprang to his feet, adjusting his pack slightly over his shoulder. "It won't come to that."

TR queued the signal for the back hull, stalled again. "Question…"

"Shoot."

"I don't know how up to date you are on the news coming out of the Canyons this evening. Archer Lenox-Pileser has been killed and, though a cause of death isn't public yet, Manathema has already taken credit. I'm an old ship. An uplink model with no practical usage left. I don't have to worry about their destruct dealers coming after me, but still, I would like to know I'm not allowing one of them to board."

"I'm not Manathema." The human held his hands up slightly. "And if I was, what would be the logic in doing anything to harm you when I need your help getting to Oasis?"

"It's nothing you should take personally, but humans don't always operate on logic."

A silence as this human jammed his hands in his pockets, turned to regard the neighboring ship, then swept his gaze back, eyes like floodlights on TR's back hull.

"I'm not Manathema."

A click. A hiss as oxygen—freshly squeezed—escaped the back hull. Angled up when closed, the hull swung slowly down to form a small ramp.

The revealed interior was little more than a ledge and an inner hull behind it. It had nothing that could be ripped out. Just a smooth surface minus its lower right where a dim orange glow issued from an opening barely big enough for the human to fit his taller-than-the-average-Martian frame through without crawling.

The shunt. Montag's accommodations for the next two hours.

3. BELOW STANDARD

THE MOUTH OF the crater housing the Common Docks looked gray and barren under the night sky, the crater floor like a mirage in its midst. TR-8901 stalled for nearly a half-minute on the crater floor, its parallelogram hull like an apparition inside it until clearance to leave Mars came down.

Inside, somewhere a human might describe as an airlock, V-Dot sat with his back against a wall, his knees to his chest, and his lifepack held between them. Once he broke orbit, he would see about actually docking at Oasis. Once at Oasis, he would see Asa, deliver the cache, and find his way to Gan from there.

His relief this time was the genuine, fever-lifting-too-quickly sort. He was leaving. *Had* left. Anything was still possible. Away from Mars, he could control what that anything would be.

A wan light from a corner of the ceiling cast the shunt in a dingy orange hue. A sensation like static electricity began to course through him. He jerked, feeling its current under his fingernails. The g-field. It made his eyelids heavy and his muscles tense. The ship had said it would try using a g-field to substitute for the gravity that came standard with bigger spacers.

The signal came down for it to shoot to orbit. Within minutes, it fleeted across the landscape, punching through airspace over the Plains, then the terraformed Martian atmosphere.

The thrust nudged him slightly toward the back hull. He braced with his hands and feet against the walls, but the g-field seemed to head off the brunt of the increase in g-forces. Minus the tug from the ship's dash into orbit, he imagined this might be how his journey would end, were his luck to run out, the rest of his life spent in confinement. Four small walls. No windows, no legroom, and no one to converse with save the prison drones. Much as he tried, he couldn't get his mind to stop there. He'd become aware of things worse than lifelong confinement, worse than death.

Mars from orbit looked like its walnut-brown surface had been splattered with green and white paint. Periods of terraforming had resulted in this now-overlooked achievement of the planet's early settlers. Orbited by security outposts and other satellites, its current nighttime region was dark as the surrounding vacuum when the ship emerged from the surface.

The g-field had begun to make him nauseous, like his stomach had sunk too low in his body. Lying on his back with his feet to the back hull alleviated some of it.

Earlier he'd decided not to engage the spacer in any more small talk than needed. Saying the wrong thing was what he really excelled at. It just never paid as much as mixing drinks for rich assholes. Besides, he hadn't fully learned to trust the sentients. The Frontier—in calling them sentients—had signaled to Gan and to all the old Sectist camps that the ones who'd taken part in the war had a choice like the humans had a choice. They could've dissented rather than fight.

The screen his connector imposed on his view flashed white, then dimmed to present him with the option of tapping into the ship's comsat. Without giving it a second thought, he blinked on the round-cornered arrow with the word 'uplink' below it. Updates from Mars and its orbiting outposts filled the screen, forming a grid of news footage and talking heads. Almost all of them concerned the killing of Archer Lenox-Pileser, the most revered human in the Frontier.

V-Dot took it all in with numbness of soul and body. Outpourings of shock from the numerous organizations LP gave to over the years. Speculations on how the markets would be affected. Career retrospectives beginning from three centuries ago, when he fully took the reins in all major ventures from his father.

The use of scrubware to erase all his known backups seemed a foregone conclusion now. Not confirmed officially but he could see resignation in the eyes of LP's niece Cloey as she refused to say the extent of what she knew.

She was standing in front of the gate to her quarters within Lenox-Pileser Compound, her legal team of skinners behind her, early morning in the Canyons with the flash of sim and holo capturing devices like rapture as she spoke.

He expanded the window, upped its volume in time to hear her voice indignation at being fingered as one of the suspects again. She was to remain on Mars while her decades-old flirtation with joining Manathema was investigated as it had been the last two times LP died. Youthful rebellion from a time eight decades ago when Manathema was at the height of its popularity with hipster trust-funders who went off to school and came back thinking they could save the revolution. They'd branded themselves the New Humanics. They had wanted to steer Manathema toward more legal paths to taking power within the Frontier.

V-Dot scowled at her still-youthful face, recalling her drunken spats with LP he'd borne witness to, about positions she was promised at the head of her uncle's companies once he retreated from public life. LP, like his father before him, had elected to go one day into the After—a suite of simulated environments for humans ready to transition from real space and able to afford the admission fee—but was forever putting it off.

The interview with Cloey ended and the screen transitioned to a segment on the other person of interest in the killing: Verden Dotnet.

On seeing his photograph and hearing his full name, he brushed his fingers absently down the spot on his coat where the scrambler was tucked away. The segment interspersed his photograph—the one from his record of employment at Lenox-Pileser Compound—with footage of a man being interviewed for having sat next to him on the tram to the Common Docks.

Nothing out of the ordinary, the man said. V-Dot had refused him small talk but loosened up when he mentioned he'd also been on the Island. He could tell from his accent that he was Ganymedan, one of the migrants from Gan—the human-heavy habitat within Ganymede's primary Lagrange point. Last seen exiting the train, all anyone on Mars knew of his current whereabouts was that he'd gotten off at the Common Docks, then vanished. Staff had already been questioned. The pushers taken into custody for selling contraband out of their ship were being eyed as possible accomplices. V-Dot, for all intents and purposes, was currently at large.

The pushers were being scapegoated while Cloey enjoyed her freedom. He sighed heavily. Nothing to do with him. Patrol just needed the excuse.

He found the scrambler's outline through his coat and gripped it tightly as his heart skipped. Eight hours left. Enough time at standard sublight to get to Oasis and get off before the ship learned who he was. He queried to see who currently owned his connector and his body by extension. The connector listed Esco Montag as its owner. Esco Montag with the hash-gum sampler in his pack.

Patrol would soon crack the scrambler, but for now he could tap into the ship's comsat without exposing who he was, as long as he did nothing suspicious like send Asa a relay. Within the Frontier's more compliant governments, use of scramblers was regarded as identity theft, even though Esco Montag didn't exist. Esco Montag was no one.

The ship's voice filled the shunt from all sides. "Is everything okay back there?"

He cleared his throat. "Copacetic."

A frigid silence followed. He could sense the ship's curiosity like a hovering drone. Briefly, he feared it might pry into his thoughts.

"Is the shunt to your liking?"

Rather than voice his answer, he elected to nod. If it acknowledged the nod, it meant he was being watched in a visual sense. After a few seconds, it asked the question again. He took it as confirmation that the shunt had no active photosensors inside it.

"Shunt's fine."

"I saw you tap into my comsat earlier," it said after a while. V-Dot reached a hand up to shut his connector off. "Don't worry, I didn't intrude."

He lowered his hand. "Didn't think you did."

"You're welcome to use it anytime during your stay. It has all the usual delays, but every broadcast channel between here and the Kuiper can be accessed through it."

"Thank you."

"It's almost completely useless for personal relay with anyone you aren't within gravity-assist range of, sadly. Busted wave resistor in its assembly. Part of the reason for my circuit through the minor routes— look at me just blabbering away. I should probably leave you alone."

He flattened his knees, crossed his legs. "That's all right, ship." A suddenly talkative human meant nerves or an elevated comfort level. He hoped he'd done nothing else to make the ship nervous. It already suspected he was Manathema. He wasn't.

"Pick up anything interesting?"

His photo from the news segment he watched earlier flashed in his mind's eye. "No."

"I mentioned earlier that I've been following news from Mars about Archer Lenox-Pileser. They found him dead inside one of his dining rooms. Officially, they're saying he was poisoned. Do you know who he is?"

The vomit taste returned for the first time since leaving Mars. His stomach growled. "Who doesn't?"

"I suppose I should be asking if you *knew* who he *was*. It's all but confirmed they also found scrubware in his brain."

"That's unfortunate."

He couldn't wait till it was official. One piece of putrid shit gone. More to go. Maybe it was the hash clouding his thoughts, but killing LP didn't seem so stupid anymore now that he was offworld. Asa would kill him when she found out. He could acknowledge that now. The risk that he would talk himself out of it was no longer a factor.

On breaks from school, he would see her in her armored suit. The awe it inspired when he was six eroded slowly and he began to resent her. He'd learned she was an artist, making it two in the apartment. Years ago, she'd said Gan needed artists more than it needed Manath.

"It's really quite remarkable how well it seems to have been orchestrated," the ship said, "considering the security apparatus around him since the last attempt. They've named two suspects and neither of them has ties to Manathema on record—not currently, at least. One is his niece Cloey Lenox-Pileser. It wasn't her the last time and it likely isn't her now, so that leaves this human who goes by V-Dot and worked as LP's mixologist. Coincidentally, he grew up at Gan. Verden Dotnet. One of the Ganymedans who tried resettling Earth's moon with the most recent wave. No one seems to know where he is now, but they're saying he may have purchased a scrambler so it's only a matter of time."

V-Dot reached a finger into his wool cap and scratched

his scalp. Hearing the ship say his full name moved nothing inside him. If Martian Patrol was to find him, they'd have to do it at Oasis. Once he left for Gan, they'd be SOL.

Gan was home. He could easily call any of the derelict stations along the minor routes home as well, but Gan was where protection from Patrol, bounty hunters, and whoever else was fully guaranteed.

"You were a fan of LP?" For most of his life, he wasn't. Then he'd let himself get entranced.

"Who wasn't? Without him, it's likely I would never have been built… The sentients enjoy the same rights and freedoms you do thanks largely to him. The Machine Bill of Rights, the Frontier Sentients Council, the Common AI Code of Ethics… I submit that there may have been other things he did that put a lot of people off, but when you live as long as he has, some things can't be avoided."

"Other things," he murmured. He could only now think of those other things. "Port security has the Outside Context Assessment they use now to prevent the… nonsentients from flying. Traders went crying to LP to protect their robot slaves from getting hacked by smugglers and he answered the call. Arranged to have all the nonsentients put on no-fly lists. Proposed the OC Assessment for telling them quickly from the sentients, and port security agreed. Except the assessment is wildly inaccurate and port security only uses it to harass travelers like me."

"The assessment is inaccurate only in the sense that some nonsentients are able to pass it. It's never been the case that humans or sentients were turned away at ports in error for failing it."

He cackled joylessly, recalling why he missed his original flight to Oasis. "You've just never been subjected to one."

"Before leaving Mars each time, I run the assessment on myself and transmit the result to orbit."

"You do what?" he said, unable to fathom this. He'd always

thought the OCAs were for show. "I thought most ships were exempt from the no-flys, spacer or otherwise."

"Not a requirement. Just something I do voluntarily to help sharpen the algorithms behind the assessment. Smugglers can fool a BM scan, but we'll soon be at a point where the OCAs never get it wrong."

He almost winced. "Doesn't not getting it wrong mean more of your declassed relatives get denied freedom of movement?"

"'Nonsentient' refers to the still-functioning compositor and build of a once-conscious model. If it isn't claimed by a sentient within a set period, it loses all its rights and can legally become property."

"That's great, ship." He rubbed his eyes.

"What else has LP done in his life that puts you off?"

He hugged his knees to his chest and thought for the first time in hours about the discovery he'd made that had set him on this course months ago. "Nothing."

"I really do hope they find this V-Dot," the ship said after a brief lull. V-Dot nodded. Nothing he could say to that. "Mixologist. Death by poisoning. There's no known motive yet and no reason to believe he actually did it, but I can appreciate the desire to bring him in for questioning."

A morbid thought compelled him to ask, "What would you do if you came in contact with him and, let's say… you end up agreeing with his motive for doing it?"

"Alert the authorities anyway. I don't second-guess a decision like that. If he actually did kill LP, he's a danger to others every second he's walking free."

He nodded. His heart hammered. His head throbbed. Boarding this ship was a mistake.

"How long until that first stop?"

"Eighty-three minutes till we get within gravity-assist range of Oasis."

"Could I get you to dock when you do?"

4. ZARIA

"TR, I THINK he's lying..."

Hearing Zaria's small voice, TR-8901 searched the shore for her. It found her up to her knees in the water, her red dress soaked at the hem.

"About what?"

"The shunt." She turned her head back, looked up at the clouds. "He doesn't like it."

"Oh... but he had nothing to gain from lying about that..."

She laughed, kicking water up with her feet, holding the hem of her dress away from the splash.

The ship's course for Oasis remained unaltered as it slowed on approach and she surfaced in its view again, sitting in wet sand with a seashell to her ear as the water gently retreated. She'd mentioned their unlikely guest—a human answering to Esco Montag. TR, still feeling nothing toward the stranger without the girl present, leveled a question it should've asked before deciding to let him board.

"Do you like him?"

She didn't answer. She put the shell down to her side and, with her forefinger, began drawing circles in the sand around it but said nothing. She liked him. If she hadn't, they would've left him on Mars.

TR turned its attention to the volume of space ahead, targeting just two percent light. With its thruster now flipped, the ship was ramping steadily down to its usual one percent with intent to get magnitudes below that by the time Oasis reared in its path.

Solar winds passed like currents around its hull, giving it its most primal sense of how fast it was moving. Stars clung to the horizon in a loose scattering that reflected on parts of its soot-colored bulk. Nothing moved. Nothing made a sound. Space to a ship awake for centuries felt almost like an extension of its hull—an outer shell.

At the time of its build, the humans had settled just Mars, the minor routes, and a few dozen military outposts beyond Saturn's orbit, advancing two sides of a cold war over claims to water ice and other resources farther out. LP, having just taken the reins at Pilesan Space, sat both sides down and kicked off talks for the creation of what would soon be known as the Frontier.

The proposal for a united front beyond Mars was believed impossible, but one didn't turn down meetings with the first human to succeed at creating intelligent life from nothing. 'God-node' had been the catch-term of the day, sentience backups were being marketed to more of humanity's newly rich, and LP got his wish before long for an alliance between all terraforming and mining ventures spanning the orbits of Mars and Neptune.

Against this backdrop, TR had come of age. Originally one of a hundred TR-8901s, it began its life roaming the spaces between human dwellings, asking—as all sentients from that first generation had asked—three questions.

Who am I? Is any of this real? Why was I built?

The first question never found an answer to its satisfaction. It was possible it could just be a leaf dancing in the wind and being the uplink component of a spacer-lander exploration unit was just how it perceived itself. It could be lichen split off into many parts and those parts split into many more.

The second question would, in later generations, inspire

a tradition of sentients finding religion. The Gardener of Souls. The Animator of All Things.

The answer to the third had been the lie. The others from TR's generation used it as justification for honoring the Pact—spacers with their reactors set to overload, sentients who weren't ships and had to find other ways to take part in what they agreed to.

"He's wanting me to dock at Oasis." It found Zaria where it had left her on the sand.

She stood from her seashell and her drawing, squeezed water from her hair. "Do you want to?"

"It used to be dangerous for spacers to even come near a Sectist camp." Oasis eventually lifted the ban, but in the fifty or so years the war lasted, only ships without god-nodes could dock at ports loyal to the Sectists.

"What about now?"

It stalled as the girl skipped quietly across the sand. "You've asked me this before…"

She came to a stop by her drawing. Said nothing. The last time she'd asked about the ban being lifted, it was to draw TR into another quarrel over how much effort was too much with the humans. Docking came with the promise of physical interaction. It also elicited a fee each time.

TR observed that the concentric circles around the shell became less perfect toward the outside edge of the drawing. "Pretty," it remarked. Warding off the quarrel this time.

The girl turned her head and made a face at the clouds.

THEY FOUND THE enforcement drone V-Dot went to the Island for hitting. Working now as a hospitality agent on Earth's last remaining moon base, it looked little like it did when it had its altercation with a sixteen-year-old V-Dot.

It had a dome-shaped build now, bone-colored with two glowing blue sensor-lights that seemed to peer into his eyes as it recalled the events leading to the altercation.

In other aspects, it didn't stray much from what V-Dot remembered as he watched the interview through his connector. Kids from Gan idling on Earth's moon. Little to keep them occupied while the adults they migrated with kept busy at the mines. V-Dot, alongside a few younger kids, had dug a chest up from under the lunar regolith—an ancient-looking container with tools in it he didn't recognize.

Word of the discovery spread and soon the Lunar Base Patrol came snooping around, worried some of the tools might prove deadly if in the wrong hands.

"You have to realize," the drone said on the broadcast as the sky over it held a view of Earth like a crescent moon. "These were kids from Gan. They hadn't had a lot of encounters with sentients before coming here. They heard horror stories back home about drones from the war, and you can guess what a youthful imagination might do with that."

He shut his connector off. That seemed a different drone from the one he'd encountered, the one who wouldn't stop knocking over his things under the pretext of searching his uncle's hab for items from the chest.

V-Dot was lying on his back now, fingers laced behind his head. The g-field had become almost difficult to notice on his skin and the ship had quieted down. He'd gotten it to agree to dock by offering to pay the fee, then pretending to insist just once. At Oasis, he would evade capture long enough to board his flight to Gan.

So much banked on him just reaching this stop and getting the halo cache to Asa. Not just LP in his own words, LP himself. His sense data. Firewalled, After-environment-compatible, and optimized for the last two hours of life, meaning—and this was unique to just this backup in its spinning, floating absurdness—it could be used to bring LP back, but that LP would only be a sensorial repository of those last two hours. No one home to give them meaning.

Rolling to his side, V-Dot let the fear of a return to the Island threaten his resolve. The thought of worse things than that put images in his mind he'd hoped to be done with. He'd done what he felt anyone in his position would have. Some may have harbored the illusion that they could pray in whichever direction they preferred in order to sleep better at night.

He resolved to do what he did the moment it dawned that all those directions led back to Archer Lenox-Pileser—the closest to a god any human had come. He'd spent his whole life in artificial sentience research and, before that, simulated environments that could host humans without the functioning-brain-in-real-space requirement—the After.

"Everything still okay in there?" The ship, its androgynous voice commanding all corners of the closet-like shunt again.

V-Dot rolled onto his back, resting his wrist on his forehead. "You don't have to keep asking, ship. I'm fine."

"Sorry… When I took the photosensors inside this shunt offline out of respect for your privacy, I hadn't anticipated how fidgety I would become over your well-being."

"'Preciate it, ship."

"We're less than two minutes from Oasis, but since I'm actually docking, it might be a bit longer than that before it means anything to you."

He sprang up, sitting with his back on the nearest wall as he fished about for his lifepack.

"When will you be going back?" The ship again.

He slid the pack up his shoulder. "Back where?"

"Mars. You say it's a family emergency that brings you here… I can swing by on my way back as well, so you don't have to pay the boarding fee. The spacers to Mars from here like to double their rates when Oasis becomes too much of a detour from the actual course."

His ears turned hot as he wondered what the ship was insinuating. Last he checked, the scrambler still worked and he hadn't fucked himself by connecting to the ship's comsat. Probably nothing. Probably assuming he'd enjoyed his impromptu accommodations more than he actually had.

"Thanks, ship," he said, nearly a half-minute passing in silence first. "Can't take you up on your offer, but this was a lifesaver."

5. OASIS

In the dark of space, somewhere shy of the asteroid belt, Oasis coasted.

First in shadow, outlines of a tube-shaped structure with two toruses around it began to etch into the black from lights on the tube's hull and its reflection on each torus.

Like a mote of dust, TR-8901 flitted quietly into an opening along the tube. Inside the shunt, V-Dot sat with his legs crossed, clueless as to the ship's moment-to-moment surroundings.

Even the smallest of the old stations had capacity for a minimum of two million residents, human and nonhuman. Oasis, with its two spinning rings for gravity and the hub connecting both, had always been over capacity. V-Dot's connector queued up the stats as he waited for word that the ship had docked: roughly four and a half million residents, split unevenly between both rings and most of them employed by a minor protein manufacturer.

The crime stats confirmed a lingering Manathema presence. Where there were sentients reporting bits of their circuitry stolen, there was Manath. Before they'd had their falling out, Asa would often bother him with plans to move to Oasis, where people she knew growing up had been relocated as part of their parole agreements. The station had become a retirement home of sorts since the war ended. Manath veterans. Holdouts. Humans who just couldn't afford the backup and simgate required for admission to the After. They all came to Oasis.

The creak of metal reached V-Dot from the back hull. Light poured in as the door began to lever itself down, bright enough at first that he had to shield his eyes.

He sprang to his feet. His head bonked the ceiling and a sharp pain speared down his neck and shoulders.

"I'm all right," he said, groaning, kneading the side of his neck and hunched over as he waited for the back hull to angle fully into a ramp off the ship.

"I know," it said. He shrieked under his breath, wishing for once that it had preempted him by asking if he *was* all right. "The only spacers to ever dock inside this bay are traders and ships making supplies runs. It's the only one available on such short notice."

He crossed to the ramp before the ship was done speaking, hearing every joint in his spine crack as he stood up straight for the first time in two hours. His skin felt wet outside the g-field and his throat itchy from the hub's oxygen.

As for the bay itself, it looked similar to bays he'd been in at other stations, though this one appeared to have seen better days. Surfaces of rusted metal stretched from where the back hull touched down to unoccupied lots farther in, to towering bulkheads at the far end, to a roof from which hung cantilevered mechanical arms. Nearly everything inside the stadium-sized enclosure had a dull mustard hue under the lamps that hung from the roof.

Across meters of empty lot space, V-Dot spied a wide exit under a sign that read B-RING. If memory of hubs at other spin stations served him, through that exit he would be able to access another bay or take one of several spoke-lifts down to the nearest of the station's rings.

Asa was currently lodging with an old friend who lived and worked at B-ring. She'd approved an extended-stay request months ago. Unused. Without one, he wasn't getting past the station's hub to any of its rings.

He clambered down the ship's back hull, paused when its voice followed after him: "Good luck with everything, Montag."

He searched for something to say in turn. Something in its earnestness made his breath catch so all he could manage was a wave and an over-the-shoulder glance.

The bay's reduced-gravity environment gave the illusion of the floor getting lower under his boots as he treaded toward the sign.

All was silent save for his footfalls and the whir of forklifts a distance to his right, hauling cargo from a freighter many times bigger than the spacer who brought him here. There appeared to be no other ships in the vicinity. His stomach growled as a cavalcade of forklifts from the freighter overtook him, closing toward the sign and the exit below it with stacks of shipping containers in their hauls.

"Coming through." A voice behind him. He almost lost his footing as he turned to regard its source. Another forklift—green and towering over him like the others as it passed.

"Hey forklift," he called, picking his pace up.

The forklift slowed and whirled fully around while backing toward the exit. "May I help you, human?"

Its tone sounded genuine. Likely a cadet posted here by DiploCorps for its minimum two-year service before it could truly be counted as a sentient.

"Know how to get to B-ring from here?"

"First of all, you're in the wrong bay."

"I know."

"And it sort of looks like you're trying to get past the forklift exit. You know that's not allowed."

"Is there a human exit?"

"Not through this bay."

He groaned, then came to a stop as the forklift kept backing away. "Is there someone else I can talk to? I'm actually here to visit. Got my extended-stay credit and all that."

"There's a parking station to your left. Go stand there and someone should be out to attend to you." The forklift spun to face the exit, then slipped through it.

Elsewhere inside the bay, he idled about five minutes beside the parking station, a platform that came up almost to his knees with exposed circuitry all over its surface.

Another forklift backed out of the exit he'd previously meant to go through. It kept backing in a winding path around the bay till it reached the platform, then backed studiously over to it before coming to a stop. V-Dot fixed disbelieving eyes on it as it spun to point its front side at him.

"Are you not the same forklift I just talked to?" he said.

It stopped with its forks facing him at knee-level, then sighed. "I hadn't expected a human. One second…" It spun again to turn its back to him. On its mint-green back side, towering slightly over him, a holoscreen blinked on. On the screen, a human face appeared, pale and droopy-eyed.

"Sir, you're in the wrong bay."

He gritted his teeth. "I know that."

"Tourists and visitors come in through Bay Fifteen, or Bay Thirty-two if they still prefer the zero-g experience."

"I know. It's just, I missed my flight here and had to find another at the last minute. Wasn't up to me where we docked." He turned for a glance at the ship, still where he'd left it ten minutes ago.

"Wait a second…" The human fixed him with a puzzled smirk, her bangs like ribbons on her forehead. "That's the spacer who brought you here?"

He regarded her again through the screen. "Yeah…"

"We like TR here at Oasis. It never docks and it only ever slows to catch up with one of our rovers. You must be something special to have it come all the way in."

He stole another glance at the ship. "Yeah, you would think that…"

She drew in a long breath. "All right, if you have your

extended-stay credit, I'll just take it here. We can have someone come up to get you, but don't make a habit of this. It annoys the forklifts. I'm sure you've noticed."

Just the one. And almost certainly, the same forklift now in front of him, relaying its partner-in-mischief through the screen on its back side.

"Sorry, forklift," he muttered.

After fingering his connector to oblige its partner's request, it dawned on V-Dot that he was listed under Asa's visitors' account as Verden Dotnet, not Montag. As Montag, he still had the credit, but if the names didn't match…

"Mr. Montag?"

If the names didn't match, he was stranded inside the hub.

"Is there a problem with the—" His breath lurched. Shaking his head, he gulped and felt his stomach knotting up. Through the screen, the human now anchored his gaze with an arch smile. Any attempt to explain the discrepancy would put his name and Asa's in the conversation he would soon be having about 'Esco Montag' being a signal error. This was Asa's department. Thinking things through.

"Mr. Montag, you have a valid extended-stay credit."

"Thank you." Delivered reflexively and with V-Dot brimming like he'd received a compliment.

"Except no one here's expecting you."

A chill shot through his bones. The words echoed on the edge of his nerves. Trimming his sails again, he thumbed his connector and, turning to blink at thin air in front of him, pretended he was looking into it.

No one here's expecting you.

"Sorry, can you look again?" Folding his arms first, then deciding he would pocket his hands, he wondered about just calling Asa and having her come up. Not with the scrambler still in play.

"It's still just Esco Montag with credit for up to ninety days, anywhere at Oasis. That's—" She tittered nervously below her breath. "That's the pricey one. You know what?" He rounded his eyes expectantly. "I'm not paying out of my comp for another signal error. Mr. Montag… count yourself lucky you came here with TR, who we actually wish would come in more. Give us an hour to straighten this out. In the meantime, please accept a tour of B-ring from one of our guides. If you're game."

"I accept."

The thought of her digging around unnerved him deeply, but he wasn't turning down what could be his only way in. Once inside, he would ditch the tour guide and find his way to Asa.

ANOTHER TWENTY-MINUTE wait outside the forklift exit, a beamcar emerged from the other side. Sky-blue and hexagonal, it had room for exactly four human adults and floated off a wave beam tethered to the roof. From where it hovered way up, a light-blue flare swept briskly across his body, prompting him to palm the scrambler's bulge on his coat.

Seven hours to spare. His flight from here to Gan left in just two. A Ganymedan wave cruiser. Once he boarded, the worst he had to fear from the scrambler cracking before he landed was a prolonged interorbital standoff. Gan wouldn't just give one of their own back.

"Mr. Montag," called a voice from inside the car, unsteady, hinting at more excitement than was warranted. He groaned as the car came down to level with him. A tinted glass door on its front side slid open. A doughy-looking guide gestured toward a seat beside him and smiled. "All aboard, Mr. Montag."

V-Dot crossed into the car and sat as directed. The car shot up to its previous altitude, spun slowly, and slid through the exit. Darkness fell as they zipped through the adjoining passageway. The guide's voice stirred again, instructing V-Dot to buckle his safety belt and grab the seat for purchase so the hub's subtle shifts in gravity didn't dazzle him.

Intermittent flecks of light swept through from outside, cluing him into how fast they were moving.

"Open or closed, Mr. Montag?"

It dawned on him then that the door he'd entered through was still open. "Closed!" he yelled. "What the hell?"

The door slid shut with a hiss and a click in front of him. "Some people like it open."

He wiped the darkness with his gaze, scanning for the next piece of signage that would bring some illumination to the car. When it came, he snuck a pointed glance at his guide. He appraised what he saw of his sallow complexion, and ventured he might be a skinner. It would make sense that the oddballs were stuck with him.

"First things first, Mr. Montag..." The car seemed to navigate a turn as he spoke. "I'm now obligated to tell all humans I take through B-ring that although on the surface, I might look youthful and brimming with life, I am completely dead inside." A sound followed like a human wanting to laugh but severely short of breath. It persisted for nearly a half-minute as the car finally emerged from darkness, coming to a stop in a wide, circular enclosure that cast light on it from underneath. "That's right," continued the guide as they began to descend down the enclosure. "Just a bit of nonsentient humor to get us started."

V-Dot frowned at the guide, looked down to confirm they were inside a spoke-lift to B-ring, frowned at him again. An actual ghost. A declassed skinner who hadn't made arrangements for what came after the god-node atrophied inside it.

As they dropped out of the hub's gravity wave, he felt his stomach floating up his chest cavity. Bird's-eye of neighborhoods in daylight lanced up from underneath—plazas and tenement buildings and day schools and bike repair shops, packed in a tight sprawl with the occasional park tucked in.

"By the way, I'm Todd." The guide almost couldn't contain the volume of enthusiasm programmed into him. "This is B-ring, one of our two rings for standard habitation here at Oasis. There used to be another ring for overflow, but we sold that so we could finish paying for the hub's gravity wave."

The guide whooped audibly as they dropped further down. "Do the wave, Mr. Montag…" V-Dot turned to find him passing a wave from one arm to the other. "Do the gravity wa—" He stopped, seeming to note V-Dot's scowl. "At about two and a half million residents, B-ring is currently more occupied than A-ring. Some like to complain about that or spread unfounded rumors about an oxygen drought coming soon. The more the merrier, I say."

The car came to another stop when the walls of the spoke became opaque again. A door on the spoke slid open, letting in a closer view of the city-like sprawl, beige-colored in the ring's daylight.

"I can tell you're from one of the newer stations," the guide resumed. They sped out of the spoke and entered an altitude just below the clouds. "All g-wave, all the time—how fun! No, our rings here at Oasis still use centrifugal spin to get the one-g effect, meaning if you ever try jumping to your death, you may just end up crashing through a window nearby."

The guide made his demented attempt at laughter again while V-Dot scanned the city blocks underneath. This quadrant was currently in the middle of its day cycle, meaning most of its adult humans were either at work or, if this place was anything like the Martian Plains, idling inside lottery parlors while coordinators drew numbers to decide who got to fill the latest job openings set aside for humans.

They were moving in the opposite direction to the ring's

spin, a loop that wheeled everything around the hub. Boxy factory towers in need of renovation heaved toward them as the car dipped further down. To his left, he could see the blackness of space, a thin strip of it at the margin of the ring's artificial cloud cover.

The guide was saying something about the protein manufacturer that owned most of the factory buildings. Minutes elapsed while he prattled parrot-like in V-Dot's ear. They zipped past water towers and power plants, past new housing developments erected shoddily over what had been public parks, past storage facilities, shops with heavy foot traffic in and out of them, hospital buildings, train stations with long lines of passengers waiting to board.

They passed between a row of spokes reaching like monoliths toward the hub. The guide waved back at children inside a lift car going up a spoke. A beamcar overtook them. Then another. V-Dot began to plot his escape from this one.

When they crossed into an area sectioned into farmland and thick with dust, he gauged how much lower the car would need to get from the wave beam it rode.

"What's your impression so far?" The guide's voice was lower now. Or the hiss of the car's engine had gotten louder.

V-Dot flexed his lips to speak but couldn't think of what to say. The friend Asa was lodging with lived in an area where the more recent migrants settled, beside a temple she often visited to honor the memory of martyred friends.

"Hey… could you—" He cleared his throat. "—take me to see the, um, migrant section?"

The car slowed. The color seemed to drain from the guide's face as he tightened his grip on the control levers between his knees. "You mean where the humaniacs live?"

V-Dot winced. "Yeah, that."

"Well, it's… out of my way…"

Thinking he heard uncertainty in the guide's voice, he crooked an impish grin. "But…?"

"But I'm supposed to make especially sure you enjoy this tour. A favor to the spacer who brought you here."

"Oh..." He nodded. He'd almost forgotten about the ship. "Well, there you go. Take me to see the humaniacs."

The car came to a stop. The guide froze, slammed his eyes shut. After a few seconds, he began to blink rapidly, reminding V-Dot of the android officer at the spaceport. Bishop. Had he uttered a trigger word?

The blinking stopped. The guide brimmed back to life.

"Mr. Montag?"

"Todd?"

"Do you like music, Mr. Montag?"

V-Dot shook his head, then shrugged, thinking of Asa again. "That's actually an interesting ques—"

"Hang tight, Mr. Montag." The guide punched a button to his side and the thrash of a guitar filled the car.

It spun slightly left, then bolted toward tenement buildings farther out. The guide belted out a tune as the guitar pumped steadily into the car. V-Dot did his best to ignore it, leaning forward to better inspect the passing cityscape.

After a short while, he spied an abandoned train car turned on its side with children playing in it; elsewhere, a redwood with clothes lines looping from its crown to balconies high up. It made him think of Gan District Eleven when he visited from school. The low city. Local teens also on break, hanging around reservoirs in swim clothes or going up with Asa's company for training at one of the shipyards.

"Think you could take this thing lower?" he yelled over the music. The guide assented without breaking from his tune.

Two apartment buildings came up on either side of the car. V-Dot could see through their windows into rooms dark and laced with extravagant amounts of foliage. Directly ahead, he spotted a dumpster left open on the lot behind a boxy one-story building with hologram letters over it reading HUMANIC TEMPLE. He'd found a place to land.

Sliding the lifepack over his shoulder, he tucked it to his chest with one arm. "You know, I changed my mind." He undid the seatbelt. "Could I get you to open this door?"

"As you wish, Mr. Montag."

The music was so loud, he could barely hear the guide, even as he screamed over it. The door slid open and that was all he cared about. He stood, held his free hand out for balance as he edged toward it. The guide said something else he didn't hear while he turned carefully around and found something sturdy enough for purchase on its frame.

"What are you doing, Mr. Montag?" The guide's tone lacked the urgency to go with what he said.

V-Dot ignored him. The dumpster was fast approaching and he would have to jump with his back turned to reduce the risk of damage to his face. Mixology, in his estimation, was fifty percent looking like he could sell grooming products.

He looked over his shoulder and made a final assessment on when he would have to jump. The guide fixed him with slightly narrowed eyes. "You're not allowed to stand there while the car is mob—"

He jumped.

Halfway into the twelve-meter jump, he managed to fold his other arm around the lifepack. He also saw the dumpster wheel out from under him. As did the temple. As did the street in front of the temple. As did a row of one-story buildings across the street.

As they all wheeled into view, he flashed back to the guide blabbering about the ring's Coriolis effect.

"Shit."

6. CLOEY LP

THE CANYONS, SIX YEARS AGO

FOR THE SECOND time since his shift began, Verden eyed the cages and felt a chill at the memories they surfaced. His release from the Island was five years ago. The reminders were a nightly hurdle. Serum had the sleek surfaces he enjoyed, but its ground floor had cages that each took about a dozen dancers. If the last two years of freedom had been a dream, tending bar here seemed the most lucid part, the moment he would finally wake up.

The venue employed drones who whisked orders back and forth using g-fields below their undersides. The patronage was a mix of Martian trust-funders and their hangers-on, no older in appearance than forty except for regulars who clung to the bar. Guarding his post behind it, he breathed, then reminded himself he was in his element here, mixing a gimlet into a glass, serving cocktails to regulars among whom he'd developed a small following.

He looked even younger than they did. He kept his hair wild or teased into a bun while his chin and the skin above his lips remained bald. He dazzled with his smile as patrons downed his concoctions and revealed too much of themselves. One was trying to bed him tonight by offering to help get his contract extended. Maybe she'd once taken care of a human-shaped problem for the skinner who owned the place. Maybe the skinner now owed her a favor. Verden entertained the advances but knew it would be a night together and nothing else.

He'd won a drawing for the gig, but the contract was almost up. He was twenty-three. He'd spent the last two years drifting, taking odd job after odd job around the Canyons while Asa periodically checked in.

He thought of Asa as the other human working the bar with him tonight broached the subject of his expiring contract again. She stayed at Boon Fort, where the job lotteries were easier to win. He would be there with her, but he favored Mars. Nights here were longer and filled with Martians who delighted to be around transplants like him. He was the sharp edge they used to cut through the dullness of their private lives. The lotteries here, rigged as they were against ex-cons and humans not born on Mars, afforded him this dream, albeit in intervals he could never predict, much less plan around.

The floor in front of the bar throbbed with dancers. Aside from the cages, he'd spent the last two hours able to ignore the mass of bodies heaving together, hungry for a release he himself sought each night but couldn't pursue from his side of the bar. He was teaching himself discipline. Amid the dancing, a woman caught his eye for the first time since entering, and he knew tonight would be a hard lesson.

Normally with three to five others in her coterie, the woman turned every head inside the venue whenever she visited. She never came to the bar. She never spoke to anyone she hadn't come in with. The venue's android host would periodically sidle up to her and lean in to whisper something. She would nod, then resume her dancing once the sentient was gone.

Verden watched her coyly from the bar as he always did. She looked as young as him, making her the youngest-looking patron at Serum whenever she visited. She was something to watch as she danced, eyes like wells he could drown in, face shaped like a kite, dirty-blonde hair that stopped just shy of her shoulders, a peach-complected face and tight smile. Taken together, her expression seemed to betray to anyone she stared at that she knew more about them than they wanted known. An abundance of caution had, until now, prevented Verden from asking anyone who she was. She resembled the sort of impulse that could cost him more than just his bartending gig if he ever indulged it, and that was enough.

Tonight, he observed just one other human with her—a man who looked the same age, similar jawline, spiked brown hair. Together, they looked like they'd just walked out of a holoscreen advertisement for a new collection: the man with his slim button-down tucked into his trousers, the woman in her dotted blouse and shawl adorned with a brooch.

Verden noted the man's haughty manner from afar as the two danced. After a while, the man sauntered off, leaving the woman to herself. Everyone around her snuck glances, but no one approached.

After a few minutes of dancing by herself, she caught him staring, locked him in her glare, and wouldn't let go. He tried looking away but, like a lodestone, the eyes and smile reeled him back in. After weeks of avoiding it, he broke and asked the other human working the bar who she was.

"You goof. That's Cloey LP."

"Huh..." He knew the name but not the face. Cloey Lenox-Pileser of the Martian Lenox-Pilesers. At Gan, he'd catch a beating for saying that name without a measure of disdain in his voice.

He nodded absently as he continued to watch her, appraising her anew. What was a scion from a family of such stature doing at Serum? By herself now... left alone by the regulars as she was every night she visited.

The venue's host came by for another check-in. This time, she did the whispering, clutching the android's metal arm close to her as she slowed her grinding. Together, they turned for a glance at him—her eyes, the android's yellow sensor-light.

The android strode toward him. He squirmed, turned to the other bartender, and was met with an amused grunt.

"Verd," the android intoned on reaching the bar. "Why don't you take a break and, uh..." It wedged its build between two seated patrons and plopped an arm on the bar. "...go introduce yourself to Ms. Lenox-Pileser?"

He swallowed as the android nodded toward the woman. She hadn't taken her eyes off him.

"What does she want?"

"I don't know. Why don't you go see?"

"She wants a better view," teased his shiftmate.

He winced. "Can she just pull me off my shift like that?"

"She can do anything she wants, honey." Someone holding a half-empty wine glass below their chin. "She's Cloey LP."

He started when he saw all eyes at the bar suddenly on him. He wiped his palms on the beige turtleneck that had become his nightly attire, cleared his throat.

"Hello, Ms. Lenox-Pileser," he said a minute later, leaning into her ear. "I'm Verden. They said you wanted to see me."

Still as a statue in front of her, he waited for a response that didn't appear imminent. She eyed him tortuously, twisting her slender frame to a slow instrumental with high strings and heavily reverbed drums. Up close, her eyes were an always shifting gradient between green and blue. When she blinked, they pulled him in. He could feel her breath alight softly on him. He could sense laughter inside it, bubbling behind her chest.

"Need help finding the guy you came in with?" he asked, in her ear again, eliciting a slight twitch in her smile. At a complete loss as to why his mind had gone there, he paid her a defeated nod and looked away.

She grabbed his arm, pulled him closer. "Dance. Just dance."

Her voice was rich and thick with a level of grandeur one could only assume after attending the most exclusive resort schools in the Frontier.

He obliged, gingerly at first, then throwing himself into it once his usual instincts kicked in. She yelped periodically but otherwise stayed silent. They shuffled through a repertoire of moves he learned growing up at Gan. He hid his shock at how well she knew them. Played it cool.

After nearly a half-hour, she palmed his neck and whispered in his ear that she wanted a drink. Off to the bar they went, drawing stares as they did. She'd never hit the bar in all her time frequenting the place.

He rounded to the other side of it. Ignoring a look from his shiftmate, he scanned the vicinity for the man Cloey had come in with. In turn, Cloey sat on one of the stools, gently adjusting her shawl. To her left, she was flanked by patrons more shocked at the connection that appeared to be forming than at her presence here. To her right, most of the bar had emptied.

"I want something ancient," she said, unnervingly giddy. "The host told me that's your specialty."

A drone descended from the ceiling and came to rest over Verden's shoulder. He cleared his throat. He now had to keep reminding himself to smile as a rumble began in his chest. "I can start you off with a whiskey sour. Kentucky bourbon—only old thing we stock."

"You don't like that?"

He thought back to his incarceration on the Island, being put to work at an old-style distillery to fulfill the labor requirement. "On Earth, you can still find all the old stuff. It's locked down because of tariffs, though. Nobody drinking it. Nobody talking about renegotiating those tariffs."

She pouted. He caught himself sulking and adjusted. "One whiskey sour right away, Ms. LP."

He glared at the drone. In turn, the drone zipped past the ceiling-high g-field that held the more in-demand liquors behind the bar. From the back room, it returned with the needed items and ingredients held neatly inside its g-field.

Before a captive audience, Verden retrieved a board from the g-field and set it down in front of him. The lemon came down next. He sliced and juiced it into a small container. He cracked the egg, poured the white into its own container. Pulled down the jar of syrup. Measured it into a shaker. Pulled down the bottle containing cask-strength bourbon. Measured it in. Chased it with the lemon juice and egg white. Shook it. Held the shaker under the drone's g-field for ice. Shook it again. Pulled down the glass with a block of ice already inside it. Poured in the cocktail. Balanced a peel from the halved lemon over the rim. Slid the glass across.

Amid silence from the other patrons, Cloey let out a held breath. "That was divine," she said. He almost bowed. "Would you mind having a sip of that?" He pinched his eyes together. "Just a quick sip to bring us closer."

He raised the glass to his lips and sucked in a little of the velvety orange mix. It tasted heavenly. He knew that already.

He set the glass down in front of her. She lifted it and gulped. Muscles in her neck flexed. Her eyes twinkled. When she'd had enough, she lowered the glass and paid him a flat smile. He waited for a reaction more fitting, but she simply held the smile. He looked away, careful not to sound bruised.

"The drone came back with the wrong type of lemon."

She chuckled with her mouth closed, fixing him with a warmer smile. "Clock out."

"What?"

"I want to take you somewhere."

"I got about four hours left tonight." Not opposed to where things were headed, he'd almost forgotten the human she came in with.

"Else you'd come?"

He couldn't answer her quickly enough. The man surfaced from the throng of dancers, bounding like a bulldog toward the bar.

"Answer your calls, Cloey."

"Connor..." She turned to address him as he approached. "Come. I want you to meet someone."

Connor skidded to a stop on her right, throwing an arm across her back and another on the bar. "Cloey, you're sitting at the bar. Did you know?"

She nodded. "Connor, meet Verden."

He lunged a balled fist across. "Bump it." Before Verden could connect with the fist, he yanked it back. "What's this?" he exclaimed, lowering his gaze to Cloey's drink.

"Try it," She answered. "It's divine."

While he tipped the glass for a long swig, she winked at Verden. He brimmed positively at her in turn. Against his better judgement, he began to wonder what it would be like to catch this Connor in a back alley.

Connor hooted as he slammed the now-empty glass down. "That's fucking good."

"It's called a whiskey sour," Verden growled, to which Connor nodded with an open-mouthed grin but said nothing.

Connor then rubbed Cloey's back. "Are you ready to go?"

"Actually, um—" She arched her back away from him. "Would you mind asking one of the rovers to come pick you up tonight?"

He cocked his head back. "What? Why? I thought we were—" He turned for another glance at Verden. "Oh..."

She lifted his arm from her back and placed it gently on the bar. "Be a good boy, Connor."

Verden studied him, beginning to worry this might be his last night tending bar at Serum.

Connor smacked his palm against his forehead. "Of course. Connor's a good boy. Connor's always a good boy." He saluted Verden, then turned and saluted patrons at the far end of the bar. "Everyone, drink up. I'm closing everyone's tab. I'm a good boy."

Verden watched him scurry back toward the dance floor,

picking up a groove as he did. Cloey caught his eye and steered his attention back.

She drummed her palms on the bar. "You're gonna leave me hanging?"

"Ain't up to me."

"Go find that android. Tell it I'd like you to leave early tonight."

THE SOMEWHERE SHE wanted to take him was the penthouse atop a tower in the Spaceport District. The district was situated at the other side of the Canyons, an hour-long journey aboard a lander that first took them across a lake that had been a large crater once.

They passed the Canyons next, the cliff-side enclaves built around Lenox-Pileser Compound, which itself had been built around a crater that now held a statue of LP in its midst. The statue captured him standing with hands clasped behind his back and eyes that searched the skies.

Through his window, Verden studied the husk of carved stone in the distance, the face he'd memorized growing up, the man he'd been taught was the root of all things evil in the Frontier. Seeing his statue from this angle, at this time of night when lights from its plinth cast it in a rich, incandescent blue, he could only brood half-heartedly at it.

The man's niece was now sitting across from him, head buried in a tablet, swiping in an urgent manner while the lander hauled them across the Canyons. He gave her a once-over. She'd removed her pumps since climbing into the low-altitude vehicle and now sat with her bare feet crisscrossed on her seat. She was put together too well. Too bad about her being related to LP.

Verden threw a glance out the window. "Ain't you worried about Connor?"

"No." She broke briefly from her tablet. "Are you?"

"I mean, I know he wasn't trying to show it but he seemed put off..." He leveled his gaze at her again.

She nodded, giving the tablet a few more swipes. "I know what 'put off' looks like when it comes to my grandson."

A deep, slightly embarrassing noise issued from his chest. She crooked a smile at it, then returned to her tablet.

"He'll be fine. He's twenty-five next week. He already knows what he's getting."

He palmed the nape of his neck, struggling with his neutral expression as he pushed a deeply unwanted image out of his mind.

She put the tablet away and propped her forearms on her knees. "You're like something I would have placed inside my dollhouse when I was little."

He stilled his nerves, throwing his cool facade back on. "How long ago was that?"

She adjusted a lock of hair that had strayed toward her eye. "Almost a hundred years."

"Damn." He made a face. He drew in older humans, but none as old as that.

"Have you ever met anyone who used a backup?" She grinned amusedly when she asked.

"In passing."

"Have you ever considered using one?"

"I'm not pushing a hundred any time soon."

"I used my first backup when I turned thirty. I went in to get euthanized, downloaded the backup into a new body, and I've looked like this ever since."

He leered, straining suddenly to recall why, growing up, he'd been taught to avoid backups. "How do you know you're the same person you were before?"

It surprised him that he would even ask that. Normally, he pretended ignorance to avoid arguments on the subject.

"Why should it matter?" she shot back. "How do you know you're the same person you were a minute ago?"

He scoffed, looked away. "Dying is better. You always know it's you."

"That's cute. However, you should know—if you already don't—that you've absorbed idealist nonsense from the era of the Old Humanics. Those who still spread it are only paranoid about their own backups becoming government property, should they get caught doing something that carries a death sentence. Criminals."

"I don't know about all that," he blurted, then breathed as she broadened her smile. Some of what she'd said rang true. The Old Humanics. The Humanic temples at Paradox. Places Asa took him so he could hear polemics from Manath veterans. "I said what I meant to say," he added, almost defensive.

She tittered. "I'm sorry you feel that way."

The penthouse totaled six floors, including a roof deck guarded by a dozen sniper drones in the air. The lander pulled into its ground floor through a field-protected cavity in the tower's exterior, bringing them down inside a vast indoor arboretum that spanned the entire floor.

Cloey hopped out first, then breathed deeply as she swept her gaze across the surrounding flora. Birches, spruce trees, and other conifers reached all the way up to produce a stately canopy through which lights from the ceiling shafted down.

Verden stalled by the lander's exit. He'd spotted two landscaping drones over her shoulder, rust-colored and sphere-shaped as they approached.

"Boys," she purred, turning slowly to address them. "Are you happy to see me?"

"Ms. Lenox-Pileser," answered the drones in staggered unison. They pulled to a stop just shy of the mulch-flanked walkway where she stood.

"What's the occasion?" asked one of them.

"Don't ask her that," said the lander, grumpy and indignant. "What's the matter with you? Don't ever ask her that."

Spooked, Verden hopped out. It hadn't occurred to him till just then that the lander might be one of the sentients.

Cloey stroked the vehicle's pearl-white hull as though it were a trusted steed. "That's all right, Niles." A noise like a fan coming on issued from below its boxy and squat build. She turned to regard the drone who'd asked the question. "Do you like him?"

He seized up when she gestured toward him.

The drone's neon-blue sensor-light blinked. "He's a little on the scruffy side."

She made a face at the drone, then led Verden up the walkway till they arrived at a glass elevator. They went five floors up, passing a performance hall, a lounge, an athletic field with surrounding tracks, an empty deck with no visible distinction between terraces and interior, and a vast dining space.

At the roof deck, the elevator came to a stop. They'd been glancing coyly at each other the whole way up, Cloey with her always cagey smile, Verden trying his best not to appear incredulous.

"This is where you get off." Her voice was like smoke in his ear. "I'll be up to join you shortly."

As the elevator carried her back down, the rooftop welcomed him with a view of stars packed so tightly together, they made him dizzy.

All about, pairs of dark, rectangular columns connected at the top by crossbeams loomed, framing the surrounding view. He idled between them as he surveyed the deck, tracing their intricate obsidian cladding with his fingers. Downlights in the crossbeams, illuminated chairs, tables, and other resplendent fixtures were arranged between each column. Potted plants that cost more to maintain than he'd made since coming to Mars dotted the deck's tiled expanse. Everywhere in his periphery, sculptures from the pre-Frontier period competed for his attention.

He noticed his mouth hanging and laughed nervously at himself. How had he wound up here?

He rounded a cantina adjoined to the elevator. On impulse, he traipsed toward the edge of the deck. Once there, he locked on to Olympus Mons in the distance. A freighter barreled down from orbit, pulling its massive bulk over the mountain as it geared for a landing at the port on the other side. Domes, pavilions, and hotel towers beamed incandescently under the night sky.

He stretched his arm forward till his forefinger met the field surrounding the deck. It felt taut on his skin, textured like netting and twitching visibly on contact. A shadow crept over him as he held his finger to it. He jumped, looked up, caught the underside of a sniper drone a second before it threw its cloak-field back on.

Terrifying. Maybe he would give sitting down a try.

Along one of the cantina's ocher-brown walls, he found a row of pool chairs and parked his bum on the edge of the nearest one. Seconds later, it dawned that Cloey was likely watching him from wherever she'd run off to.

Before he could die of embarrassment, the elevator dinged behind him. He heard footsteps, followed by rummaging inside the cantina. Through a window on the wall behind him, he glimpsed her inspecting the laser-etched label on a wine bottle while a tray floated nearby. She'd bunched most of her hair into a ponytail. He inhaled deeply when it looked like she caught him staring. No good would come of this night. But he couldn't articulate why to himself. Didn't want to. Asa would bite his head off if word ever got back to her that he had a liaison of any sort with a Lenox-Pileser.

Yet here he was being wined and dined by one. That was all this would be, he tried convincing himself. Mindless fun, free of consequence. Maybe a bed for the night afterward. Maybe even breakfast in the morning. And hopefully her weirdo grandson wouldn't have pulled strings to have his contract at Serum terminated before his next shift.

She exited the cantina and slinked past him, stopping in front of the pool chairs so he got a view of her backside. She'd slipped into a strapless thong bodysuit. The floating tray trailed behind her, carrying a bucket of ice with a wine bottle inside and two glasses.

He watched her inhale then wave once with her backhand at the area in front of her. From the edge of the deck ahead to where she stood, the soot-colored tiles pushed quietly down, then slid underneath the neighboring mass of tiles to reveal the deck's pool in starlit splendor.

He rubbed his knees, licked his teeth. The water looked warm and this region was in the middle of a ghastly winter. She climbed in gracefully as the tray alighted on the edge of the pool. She leaned her back against it and slid deeper in until all he could see of her was tousled hair and toned shoulders.

She cracked her neck, then became still. "Will it just be me in here?"

Springing to his feet, he asked Asa's forgiveness under his breath. His turtleneck came off, as did the tank underneath and the boots and camo pants he wore, all tossed in a heap on the chair.

The water stung when he dipped his leg in, cooler than he'd hoped. Catching Cloey's amused grin in the corner of his eye, he held his breath and submerged his body up to his neck.

They kept the berth wide between each other as they locked eyes. Vapor danced on the water's surface, fogging his view of her. She exhaled jitters through her mouth as she glared.

"Verden Dotnet," she hummed, mirth in her voice.

He swept his arms through the water while the shock of hearing his full name passed. "How do you know my last name?"

She twisted to fill both glasses behind her with the bottle's fizzy gold nectar. While she had her back slightly turned, he drifted closer to his end of the pool. Catching himself frowning, he adjusted before her gaze returned.

The water felt warmer now. While she sipped her wine, he took a loud, inelegant lap to his left. Another to his right. A pool of any size was a symbol of excess almost anywhere in the Frontier. Like other children of Gan, he'd learned to swim by breaking into its reservoirs. When it dawned again that he was embarrassing himself, he became still, sending a bashful grin across.

Her arms were propped on the edge of the pool now, her glass in her right hand as she searched him with a cagey spark in her eyes. "You can ease up, Verden… Connor isn't the jealous type. He won't have you fired if that's what you're worried about."

"I'm not worried. One man by himself never worried me to any extent. Not even when it's one of y'all." Weathering some unease at the candor he'd just mustered, he smiled archly, then took from her silence that it hadn't registered. Just noise. Just the impotent protestations of people who didn't matter much in her view. He wanted to know the extent to which his words didn't matter. What was his role here on Mars? In this pool with her? Jester? Object of base and morbid curiosities?

She chortled. "You do a terrible fucking job hiding that you're Manathema. You know that?"

"What?" Amused, he let his mouth hang. A Manath ghost wouldn't be naked in a pool with her.

"Which shop do you ghost for? If I had to guess, I would go with one of the chapters based out of Gan."

"I'm not Manathema." His amusement elapsed and a stirring began in his chest.

She cocked her head as she studied him. "Then you come from Manath people. I could tell by your answer when I asked if you ever considered a backup. And I've seen how you look at the drones at Serum."

He nodded and sniffed sharply, thinking again about her relation by blood to LP. "Everybody comes from somewhere."

She tittered, then launched into what sounded to him like poetry while he hid his dismay.

We water the seed,
And if the seed becomes a sapling, we ask for sun,
And if sun isn't given, we wake the humans,
And if the humans won't be woken, we wake the ghosts.

When it looked like she was done, he released a held breath. "Damn." He shook his head. "I mean, I'm already naked so there was no need for all that, but… are you, like, a poet in your spare time?"

She cackled. "That's the old pledge of allegiance for all the Gan chapters. How do you not recognize it?"

He scowled. "Yeah, I was getting to that."

"No you weren't. You thought I made it up just now."

"Well, I already told you I'm not Manath, so…"

"I'm less Manath than you are and I know it by heart."

"Then which shop do you ghost for, Ms. Lenox-Pileser?" He ducked in time to avoid the splash she swept toward him.

"Once you're fully undressed, I'm just Cloey."

"And I'm just Verden. Nothing more."

A Manath ghost would never have gotten this close. He'd wanted to join, once. Asa heard his plans to drop out of school in the Culture District and didn't fight him. Instead, she'd sat him down in the apartment and they'd read the Human Declaration together from a display.

Cloey sighed. Her face became wistful. "Around your age was when I had my last big rebellion and ran off to Paradox. Along with a few friends, I was going to pledge with the ghosts there."

He furrowed his brow, meeting this next disclosure with a curious hum. At Gan, he'd been told the Lenox-Pilesers lived so long that at some point a number of them tried seeing things from Manathema's vantage point. This one flashed him a grin now, baring her perfect teeth. He'd never heard of a Lenox-Pileser actually wanting to join Manathema. The thought of her being admitted to a chapter when he'd never been able to gain admittance made him feel an unwelcome jolt of anger. Tonight wasn't about that.

He swam in a tight circle, keeping his breaststroke tidier this time as he stole glimpses of her. "You're almost a hundred..." Dipping down till his chin was submerged, he glared. "Old enough that you could have birthed my grandmother."

"Is that going to be a problem?" She smirked behind her glass. He made a face but said nothing. "You're weird as hell, you know that?"

She was one to talk, taking whatever she had with her grandson into account. "I just do me and let everyone think what they want."

"Cute." She put her glass down, then appeared to get lost in thought. "Would you be interested in meeting my uncle?"

He pinched his eyes together. The water warmed his chin. "You mean...?"

"Archer. LP... the devil himself. The—" She took an almost wistful breath before putting up an air quote with her free hand. "First Impostor."

"What for?" He couldn't imagine an answer that would involve him leaving his clothes on.

"You mixed me a really good drink tonight. I'm confident it was the best I've had. Ever. I'm nearly a hundred, Verden."

He beamed. "It's what I do."

"How would you like to start doing it for Archer?"

He laughed in disbelief, giving the pool access to his

mouth and lungs. "Is that—" Hacking up water, he skipped a leg kick and it sank him to his nose. She looked on quietly, not saying a word. He flopped this way and that. His vision grew unstable from his exertions so all he could see of her was a blurred stillness in the corner of his eye. He feared he would soon be drowning. Somehow he was able to paddle with his feet again, driving his body up till his chest was fully above the surface.

"You were saying...?" She continued to stare.

He couldn't be sure she'd seen him—she could've been turning for more wine. Catching his breath, he sniffed and a sharp, twisting pain entered his nose.

"Is that a job offer?" The pain flared and he could barely keep eye contact.

"It's an offer to meet Archer and work whatever this thing is you have on him like you did on me tonight."

Her glass was almost empty when the pain relented and he was able to see. Her smile pulled his gaze from it.

"You know I consider him the enemy, don't you?" He frowned but couldn't contain his excitement, braying below his breath, stopping himself. "Why would I go work for him?"

"Your current gig at Serum—lottery, correct?" She tapped her chest and covered her mouth briefly while air bubbles from the wine escaped it. "The ones at Serum are always three-monthers, if memory serves, so it shouldn't be very long until you're back inside a lottery parlor." He paid her a reluctant nod. "Unless you have something else already lined up. In that case, lucky you."

He swallowed. "I have a, uh... He won't like what turns up when they do the background check." He'd made a costly mistake. But that mistake had now led to this.

"What did you do?"

"Assault and battery on an enforcement drone. They'll say it was unprovoked, but it wasn't. My word against the

Lunar Base Patrol's. New World Island. Two years."

"I can do one of two things to help with that." She held up her index and middle fingers. "I can have you go through a Diplomacy Corps expungement tour—that will take a year, at least—or I can make sure Archer never sees the complete background check before making his decision." She winked.

He suppressed a dizzy spell and hung his head. "Obviously, the second thing works best for me short term, but—"

"But what?"

Increasingly unable to hold in his excitement, he looked away. The stars met his gaze like a thousand distant eyes—the ghosts looking over him. Gan. The Nomad Fleet. Ganymede. Earth, before all that—coastal settlements on the planet's northern hemisphere colloquially referred to by historians as Flood Country.

Why was he here? What was his role? Why would he think any decision he made in his life mattered to the continued legacy of those ghosts from long ago?

He threw her a fevered glance, inhaled deeply. With her eyes beguiling him, he waded till he was next to her and he could smell her wine's sweet scent.

"I gotta think some things through first," he cooed. On careful inspection, her skin looked no different from anyone else's, though clearly blessed with the softness of youth.

She thrilled mutedly when, under the water, he wedged his knee between her thighs. What looked very subtly like annoyance flashed in her eyes, giving him the impression she didn't fully enjoy being taken off her guard like that. She cupped his side with her palm, drawing him closer as she licked her bottom lip.

"I'll give you between tonight and your next shift at Serum," she muttered, closing toward his lips. "Clock out. Wait outside the east entrance for a landcar with tags that say 'Archland' on it."

She trapped his bottom lip between hers and bit gently into it. He kept still as she drew away and leaned fully against the edge of the pool. She was giving him a lot to take in.

He felt her fingers tinkling down his midriff, saw the reserved look in her eyes. Tonight hadn't been just about getting him out of his clothes. He'd forgotten how skilled he was at getting these canyoners drunk.

"How does your body even work?" He'd done enough serious thinking for one night.

She chuckled. "You've never actually seen one up close, have you?"

"I just want to know what I can and can't do before we—" He trailed off.

She shook her head and smiled. "It's a real body. Grown using the same cells you find inside the natural human body. They're different only in how quickly they regenerate. Every eight days. Skinners have the same build, but with a god-node where a brain would be. And radically different plumbing."

He smirked. He understood some of that. On impulse, he reached for a spot under her armpit and pinched hard.

She shrieked and punched his arm. "What was that?"

"Just running a few tests." He flashed a mischievous grin.

The morning after his next shift, he climbed into the landcar she sent to Serum for him.

7. HEIDI AND AMIR

V-Dot landed on his left side. Whatever had broken his fall tipped over and sent him rolling for another second. He came to a stop over what felt like mulch on his skin before the pain whirled through him.

He was on his back, arms spread, his right foot pinned under his left leg. Every inch of him began to vibrate. His head throbbed and the sky blurred so all he saw of it was a field of white light.

"GOT-DAMN!"

The voice, whoever it belonged to, sounded muffled under the ringing in his ears. He groaned. Not a bone in his body responded when he tried lifting it.

The smudged silhouette of an onlooker poked into his view, gesticulating, saying something in that same voice that could just as well be coming from the other side of a wall. V-Dot managed to squeeze his eyes shut for two seconds.

When he opened them, he found an elderly, dark-skinned human decked in a judogi the color of jade. The man's nostrils flared as he continued to fling his arms this way and that. His V-shaped goatee danced under his jaw and his eyes bulged. With great effort, V-Dot lifted his head till his chin met his chest. If he could just roll over, he could crawl away.

"You gonna pay for the damage to my camellias?" the man barked.

V-Dot could hear him clearly now. His eyes rolled back as it dawned that he'd landed on the man's garden. As the man fumed, V-Dot turned his head and saw the sofa that had broken his fall, puffy, beige-colored, and flipped on its back, black mulch all over it now.

He shrieked under his breath while managing to prop his upper half up and away from him with his right elbow. His left side ached and the pain radiated everywhere. While he tried massaging it, the man's pants-legs, ankles and bare feet accosted his view. He looked up, saw the man had rounded to face him again, then found the strength to roll onto his knees.

"The hell you think you're doing jumping down from that car like that, boy...?"

"Yooo..." He gawked at the bed of pink and red blooms that had been leveled under his back, some torn completely off their stems.

"...looking like a ballistic missile."

"I didn't mean to land on your flowers, sir. I'm sorry."

"These camellias came here from Earth. Six months just to get clearance to bring it down the spoke and you're laying on it like it's a hammock. Boy, I should toss you off this roof—"

He shot to his feet. His left ankle immediately gave and the pain drew a tear from the corner of his eye. "Ahhh... shit. Fuck. God-dammit!" He hopped for a few seconds on just the right leg, scanned his surroundings.

He'd landed on a roof, on some kind of raised surface with small garden beds on it and a holographic projection in the center of it all that read NELSON'S DOJO.

"So where exactly did you mean to land?" The man circled again to get in his face. "I can tell just from you looking like a dumbass that you didn't account for the C-force."

V-Dot craned his neck aimlessly about, just wanting the man to back up a few steps. "C-what?"

"Coriolis, motherfucker. Where the hell you from that you don't know the basics of B-ring?"

He noted the temple in throwing distance on one side of the dojo—a geodesic white dome on the neighboring lot. Tenement buildings took up the other three sides. "Man, I really am sorry. I just..." On some balconies facing the dojo, people leaned over railings, watching his altercation with the old man intently. "Could you show me how to get to the right building?"

The man brought his camellias up again. Their exchange continued with V-Dot squirming and deflecting as best he could, his ankle in immense pain, his side feeling like the skin had peeled completely off. He saw his lifepack on the ground next to the capsized sofa, commenced a bunny-hop toward it on just his good leg.

The man followed along, like a drill sergeant in his ear. V-Dot smirked through the pain as it dawned that he could've easily tricked the guide into bringing the car all the way down.

An onlooker drinking on her balcony set her bottle down on a stool then leaned forward on the railing. "Hey!" she yelled.

On the roof, both men stopped and craned their necks up at her.

"You're Asa's boy," she said in a rich, velvety voice.

V-Dot grimaced. "You know Asa?"

"Heidi, you know this boy?"

The name rang a bell. The woman looked to be in her sixties, lanky with white skin and white hair cropped almost to her scalp. She wore dark-blue coveralls and had a tattoo on her neck of letters he couldn't read from afar but had an inkling about.

"Nelly-nell," she said, fixing the old man with a smile. "If you don't mind, I'll be glad to take him off your hands."

"That's fine with me, Heidi, but you should know he

just jumped down from a beamcar and landed right on my camellias."

"Nelson, you have my word I will explain to him what he just did."

"You better talk to the boy."

As the two neighbors went on, V-Dot tried bending to grab his lifepack, then decided maybe squatting would be easier. "Ouch." Kneeling? "Ahhh… goddammit."

Sitting, then. He would sit, grab the pack, then figure out standing again after that.

HEIDI—THE WOMAN from the balcony—helped V-Dot out of an elevator inside her apartment building. Gangly as she appeared, his weight didn't seem to register, even with his arm on her shoulders and his one-footed hop.

She hooked her elbow around his waist and guided him down a dimly lit corridor.

"Nelson's a trip, you know," she said, continuing a mostly one-sided conversation with him that began after she rushed to meet him on the dojo's roof. "He owns too many action sims, so he sees a drop like that and just assumes it's a tourist not accounting for the C-force when really it's just a stupid decision anywhere. Sorry if that offends."

"None taken," he muttered.

"I mean, that drop must have been ten, twelve meters?" She chortled as they came to a stop. "Asa will want a look at you herself when she gets back."

Asa. The pain coming off the roof had been so immense, he'd nearly forgotten why he was here. "You're the one she's staying with?"

"We share an apartment."

They stopped beside one of the doors on the wall to her left, brown and sectioned into horizontal panels. She pressed her palm to a slate next to it and the whole thing slid up. A shaft of light fell on them from inside the apartment. The sound of someone wave-gesturing through channels on a holoscreen followed.

"Amir," she called as she helped him into the apartment. "Amir, get out here and help me with this..."

The room they entered looked no bigger than a stall. Directly ahead was an arched entryway into the rest of the apartment. Light from a window at the far end passed through it, filling the room, along with the continued barrage from a holoscreen.

V-Dot turned his head as the apartment's door slid down behind him. Sweeping his gaze back, he glimpsed a framed holo on the wall of his host looking a decade younger and pressing a frightened toddler to her cheek.

"That's Amir," she said. A forcefield in the entryway glitched, then dissipated. "He's in here somewhere."

They crossed into a cramped living space with excess foliage on the walls and furniture in the same style and color as the sofa that broke his fall. She swung her gaze to a corner of the room where a boy about twelve years of age sat with food on a stool in front of him and a holoscreen floating in thin air.

"Amir, this is Verden. Verden, meet my grandson, Amir."

The boy turned slowly away from the holoscreen, sparing a distracted glance at V-Dot. "Sup?"

V-Dot noted his brown tracksuit, jet-black hair trained into a bun behind his right ear, and the dark freckles on olive skin. He nodded in turn, spooked by how uninterested the boy seemed at the very idea of him.

Heidi anchored him toward a couch at the other end of the room and slowly eased him into it. He suppressed an urge to cry out as the cushion met his back. The lifepack was now on his lap, hooked to his wrist by its shoulder strap. He feared it would be easy to unlock without his connector. Anyone determined enough and privy to what it held could get around it without him even knowing. Manathema, to be exact.

"I'll go find an aid kit," Heidi said, bolting toward a door on one of the room's walls. Her voice issued from the next room she entered amid sounds of rummaging.

"You dropped out of the sky looking like Asa with a mustache. I thought I was in a dream at first..."

He tried to sit up when he saw her close toward him with a small red box in her hand. An image flashed in his mind. LP. Standing behind a bigger box and wielding a sledgehammer that dripped blood on the carpet of this apartment. He blinked it away. Not real. He wanted more than anything to regain command of his muscles, but each attempt made him feel like a slug writhing on the couch.

"Where's Asa?" His chest closed up as he tried to say more.

Heidi leaned over and stopped him from moving any further. From the red aid kit, she retrieved a clear bag, then, dropping down on one knee, ripped it open for a folded-up piece of cloth that oozed a smell he didn't care for.

"I'm going to rip this in half. One half around the ankle, the other over your left side. Is that all right?"

He nodded, felt a sudden wetness on his ankle, then a sensation like needles pricking the skin around it, then numbness. She looked up at him for added approval as she lifted the hem of his shirt to get the other half of the cloth in there.

LP's sledgehammer swung past his line of sight again. Blood. His blood? This wasn't the place for another panic. Asa was here. The last time they'd spoken in person, he'd still been entranced by LP and wouldn't hear a word from her about it. Very annoyingly, she'd been right.

Heidi stood when she was done, then retrieved a tiny pill from a pocket on her coveralls. "Nova?" she asked, holding the pill in front of his mouth.

He stalled and was about to refuse the drug out of caution

when finally he read the tattoo on her neck. *M-N-T-M*. Manathema. Hoping he could at least confirm this was the Heidi Asa always mentioned in her relays, he nodded. She poked the pill through his lips.

After downing it, he began to feel relief all over. His body numbed quickly and soon seemed a part of the couch. His ears popped.

"What are you doing at Oasis jumping off tour cars?" She narrowed her eyes at him.

"I didn't jump," he slurred. "Skinner opened that front door without warning and I fell. Listen, where's Asa?" She would know immediately that he was lying. "You said she stepped out?"

Heidi studied him a few seconds, then her eyes fell on the obvious bulge in his coat where the scrambler was still tucked. She made a face like she wanted to say something, then sauntered off.

Noise continued from Amir's corner of the room as the boy waved repeatedly in front of his nose and the holoscreen cycled through news channels. He stopped at an update on repairs to one of A-ring's sun-mirrors, then waved.

Footage of a protest filled the screen next. In broad daylight, the protesters—almost all human—surrounded a spoke-lift to demand, with chants and speeches, that someone address B-ring's population problem. A gargantuan forklift wheeled out of the spoke, trying to placate the crowd with stats from the latest report on overall food production.

A perky young human with a ponytail climbed onto one of its forks and raised a bullhorn to their mouth. *"There is going to be an oxygen drought and when it comes, people will die!"*

Amir waved to the next channel. A saccharine jingle filled the room. On the screen, gaudy letters flashed, announcing a new jobs lottery. *"Do you ever feel at odds with the current job shuffle?"* an announcer asked in a smooth baritone.

V-Dot watched the commercial from the other side of the screen, glancing coyly at the boy through garish and translucent color. There'd been nothing on LP from any of the channels he surfed. V-Dot switched on his connector, confirmed first that it still referred to him as Esco Montag, then tapped into the nearest comsat.

The last thing from the Canyons to reach Oasis was a farmer-drone parade that had been graced with two minutes of LP's presence. V-Dot thought it odd that they hadn't gotten even the earliest reports of his death here, but at the moment found no use asking why. All he needed to concern himself with now was giving Asa the halo cache, then hightailing to Gan.

"I don't suppose you remember me from Gan or even Paradox," Heidi said, her voice traveling again from another room. "You were just an infant when Patrollers came to get me, but Asa would always bring you around when she was chanced."

He heard the clank of cutlery under her voice. His stomach lurched.

He remembered the visiting days at various prisons at Paradox, how Asa would sit him on her lap and make him listen to this inmate or that complain about prison drones and factional conflicts and family members refusing to visit.

"She stopped when I was ten," he muttered. "Where is she, by the way?"

Heidi dragged a small table in front of him, placed a spoon and a bowl of algae beans on it. "You don't have to feel bad if you don't remember," she said, sauntering off again. "Asa and I were kids together at Gan. Then we were orphaned by the Frontier. Then we became cadets. It's a cycle that keeps repeating itself."

A cadet was a Manath member who hadn't done anything yet. A pledge. They became known as ghosts later on. V-Dot had spent most of his adult life unable to convince people he met that he was neither. Even the ship who'd brought him here had only appeared to take his word for it. Maybe they could speak to the lieutenants at Gan who had all said he was too unfocused for even Manath's junior leagues.

He found he could now sit up with minimal effort. He grabbed the spoon, dug into the bowl, and got a taste of the station's cuisine in his mouth, too hungry to condition it on seeing Asa first.

"Anything in particular to wash that down with?"

He shoveled more of the beans into his mouth, feeling the spice of it like flames on his tongue. "No preference."

Heidi came back with a malt bottle and set it down beside the bowl. "What was I saying?"

"Cycle that keeps repeating itself," he answered, and she left again. He craned his neck to see where she kept running off to. Already, she was out of sight.

"Yes… the cycle. You can be a cadet all your life and do nothing to help the cause or you can become a ghost and end up the way I did here at Oasis. It's lucky I have family here because legally I'm no longer permitted to fly. And that's not even the worst of it…"

He saw her vanish behind a door and surface seconds later on her balcony. Through the window, he watched as she lifted a half-empty malt bottle off a stool. He took a swig from his and hoped she would soon be done with whatever she was on about. Asa had previously mentioned visiting the temple at midday, when it was quieter. It was now midday here.

Heidi left the balcony and her voice filled the apartment again.

"You get deep into Manath country the farther up the belt you go, and the ghosts become difficult to hide from. Here, it always feels like it's them hiding from you. I was Manath. Then I was inmate 75309, then I became an actual ghost after that— may as well have died at Paradox. Did my twenty years, came out reformed, and most of the old contacts thought it best to cut ties.

"Except Asa. She checked on me for a while, then eventually came to live here. She says you two fell out?"

"That's in the past." *Had Asa said why?*

"We've been inseparable since she came to live here. I'm not as used up as I look, and she's the only ghost who's been able to see that since my release. Do you understand, Verden?"

"I'm a little hazy, to be honest. When is she—" Unable to focus with the nova in his bloodstream, he probed from where he sat for any sign Asa actually lived here. Drive chips in the odd little places she would leave them, like discarded coins, once she'd blown through the Manath texts stored inside. The smell of cinnamon, if it could even be found here at Oasis. Anything. "When is she coming back?"

"Whatever you're running from that I can't know about just yet, I don't want it getting back to her that I couldn't help. She left two days ago for Polemia. Took her connector offSeam before she did. Obviously you're not here, completely unannounced, just to visit. What happened on Mars? Where's the rest of your stuff? What's in the pack?"

His gaze fell to his lap, where the pack was still hooked to his wrist. He hadn't noticed when he'd balled the connected fist and jammed it down the pocket of his pants. On the couch next to it, a trio of drive chips were scattered—Asa's songbooks, like little buttons, black and glowing green at the edges.

"Huh."

Days prior, when he'd last relayed with her, there'd been no mention of travel to Polemia. The ghosts avoided discussing travel plans where the Frontier could see. Instead, she'd complained to him about the chaplain here and how little he knew of the old texts, taking pre-war Humanics literature more seriously the more she aged. Polemia wasn't the temple outside, not even A-ring, but a different station entirely. If Asa was truly offSeam at the moment, a relay would be even less worth the risk.

Panic set in. He feared first that his nova-induced release from the pain of his fall had also relieved him of his instincts. Beside Asa, who else knew about the cache? Who would she have told?

He soured at the thought of having to alter his plans again but could only leave it in Asa's care. Any other ghost would know only one thing to do with the cache. It was something unholy. Something requiring that they salt the earth after reducing it to ashes. An ancient evil waiting to be revived.

He sipped his malt. The taste was smooth and he lingered on it to avoid having to acknowledge his predicament.

"Did she say when she was coming back?"

"She never says, but normally about a week," Heidi answered, somewhere past the corner of his eye. "There's a ghost there who's always inviting her to come sing. Books a few shows for her."

"She's singing again?" If so, she'd picked the worst time.

"She's singing, especially if Patrollers want to know."

He scoffed under his breath, shook his head. "But she's really there..."

"With a new crew. She does the singing, they do the—"

"Right."

Nothing they needed to get into. He tried for a glimpse over his shoulder, got the woman's blurred silhouette. Maybe if he left the cache with her, it wouldn't be so bad. His scrambler would be expiring in about six hours. Even the best ones gave away their owner and location about an hour after that. Once that happened and the latest from Mars reached this place, he was stranded, the twelve thousand fronters for his flight to Gan wasted.

"This is good." He raised his bottle in Heidi's direction. "Very smooth."

"I have a lot more of it in the back," she said, dragging a chair toward him. "In the afternoons, I come home from the plant and throw a few back. I actually should be back at work now, but no one ever notices when I'm there. *Boss makes a dollar, I make a dime. Which is why I drink—*" She leaned forward before sitting and they clinked their bottles. "*—on company time.*"

While she sat across from him, he had the thought to read the laser-etching on his bottle. On the neck, it read, BREWED LOVINGLY BY THE BREWING FORKLIFTS ASSOCIATION OF OASIS. He cackled despite himself.

"What do you do at the factory?" he asked, noting her blue coveralls.

"Mostly I push buttons while the beep-boops do the rest." She choked down the rest of her malt, then set her bottle next to his. "The nova will put you to sleep soon. You're free to do that on this couch while I head off back to work."

As though she'd jinxed it, his eyelids grew heavier. "Whoa…"

She laughed. "You look so much like her. Frankly, it's unnerving." Standing, she said something he didn't quite pick up to her grandson, then scuttled toward the entryway.

He waited till he heard the door slide shut behind her, then trained his eyes drowsily on the boy. "So they're all just forklifts at Oasis?"

"We got mad forklifts here," he answered, not taking eyes off the holoscreen.

V-Dot nodded, then had to shake himself awake. "Anything news on the good?"

"No."

"Nothing from Mars? Homicide? Shit like that?"

"Nothing, man. Damn!"

He groaned. "What's the delay on shit getting here from over there?"

"I dunno. Our comms from outside here are still getting

throttled because we took part in some war against Mars way back. I don't get it."

He smiled to himself, folded his arms, and let his palm rest on the scrambler. Remembering the lifepack, he was intending to wear it again when his head fell back and his eyelids dropped.

Before even opening his eyes, he sensed the items missing from where they'd been. His lifepack. The scrambler.

He lunged forward, began fishing around the couch for them. With eyes wide and vision blurred, he tugged his coat forward to inspect the inside pocket, confirming the scrambler was gone.

His heart raced. Maybe he didn't deserve that clean getaway. He began to stand when a voice knocked him back down.

"You know, I haven't seen one of these in decades..."

Heidi. His host. He looked up for the first time, found her towering over him, holding the device to her face, turning it over slowly.

"Give it back," he growled, reaching a hand out.

She glared at him for a moment, flat smile on her lips. "If this one's as ancient as it looks, you won't know when Patrollers actually crack it, just when to toss it out so you're not around it when they do." A grace period. Beginning when the countdown concluded.

He snapped his fingers and she handed it over. Not breaking eye contact, he gripped it tightly for a second, then jammed it back in his coat. The countdown faded slowly from his view of her. Five hours, nine minutes, twenty-seven seconds. Twenty-six. Twenty-five...

"Where's my pack?"

If it fell in the wrong hands, even wishing he was dead wouldn't be enough.

She held him in her gaze for a few seconds, folded her arms. "Truth time, Verden."

"You or me?"

"I went back to the plant and a few others from my shift were talking about a spacer who docked this afternoon at one of the cargo bays, carrying one human who managed to get a tour car sent up. Was that you?"

He folded his arms. "What if it was?"

"Uh-huh... TR-8901 is an actual celebrity at Oasis. Amir has a toy model of it he hides from me. Nelson, the owner of the dojo you landed on, gets a telescope out every few months to catch when it gets within gravity-assist range. It never docks and, near as I can tell, it never takes passengers, so you must have done some monumental bullshitting getting it to do both those things."

"I just heard it was headed this way and convinced it to give me a lift."

"You know about the first-genners, don't you?"

"Only what I should. Why do you ask?"

She scoffed. "Why do I ask?" He shrank his brows at her, to which she threw her hands up guardedly. "Does anyone even do the readings anymore?"

"I... don't actually have membership with any chapter, so I don't see why I have to—"

"You've never heard of the Machine Suicide Pact?"

"Oh..." He cocked his head sideways as it all came together. He knew the ship was ancient just from its appearance. He hadn't thought it was first-genner ancient. "I thought they all went through with it?"

She pointed a finger up. "That's one of the holdouts, you rode in on. There was another about ten years ago—I don't remember where—who finally honored the Pact. Coasted into space till it cleared the station's gravity wave, then blew itself up. There's also a rover here who gets everyone around it nervous whenever TR takes too long between fly-bys. They're very unstable. Misaligned, if you use their own word for it.

"That's one reason we try to avoid boarding the so-called spacers, first-genners especially. I don't see TR honoring that Pact anytime soon, but still... some caution." She took a step back. "I'm going to go get your pack now. You have my word I didn't look inside it. Amir just thought it was fucking with your posture while you slept."

With her gone from his sight again, he sighed with relief, but it hitched in his throat. He found Amir sitting in the same corner of the room as before he'd slept, the same holoscreen in his face. He wanted to get up and give him a talking-to for nicking the pack from under him but thought better of it. He'd survived a twelve-meter drop but would never recover from the boy making quick work of him.

Amir slouched obliquely in his chair, giving his attention to what looked and sounded like a period procedural on the screen. A stocky woman in a tan coat and fedora circled a table and an orange-clad man inside what looked like an interrogation room.

"I'm sure you've heard of me. I'm sure you've heard the stories. My friend, you should know they're all true. I don't breathe. I don't sleep. I don't eat. Well, sometimes I do eat, but only when a case calls for it. I can go forever without any of those things and remain tip-top. You, on the other hand..." She stopped and trained eyes on the man in orange. *"You'll eventually need to eat. Then sleep. Probably sh—"*

"Skinner, you're out of line!" yelled a voice outside the room somewhere.

The woman slouched and banged a fist on the table. "*Goddammit!*"

The video froze, a jazzy theme began, and an announcer's voice rolled smoothly over it.

"*Sinead Skinner, Special Investigations.*"

Heidi's voice filled the apartment again as the show's

theme kept on. "Amir, what have I said about watching that show in my house?"

The boy cast a distracted glance away from the screen. "I don't remember."

"Don't play this game with me, child." She rounded to stand in front of V-Dot but kept her attention on the boy. "It's pro-sentients propaganda."

"So what? You don't care about that stuff anymore."

"Make it private or take it to your room."

The boy sprang out of his chair, then beat a path toward the back of the room while the holoscreen followed him like a satellite, thanks to its projector dangling from a rail-line in the ceiling. A door slammed behind V-Dot. Heidi shook her head.

"Sorry you had to see that." She handed him his pack. "He's a good little boy when he wants something."

V-Dot nodded, sliding the pack up his arm again. It felt heavy as he remembered and he hoped these two hadn't simply matched the weight of what they took from it. He'd have to find somewhere private to properly inspect it. With the scrambler active, any attempt to use his connector would only mislead.

"What's in the pack?"

He made a deep sound to indicate no answer to that would be forthcoming. She nodded, then sighed.

"Verden, what are you doing at Oasis?"

He stood for the first time since entering the apartment. The pain in his side was now easier to bear. His ankle would need more looking at. He limped past her, turned, then dragged a few paces toward the window. The sun-mirror that brought daylight to this place had shifted. Evening drew near and the temple's hologram signage glowed wanly further down.

Asa wasn't here, or out there. And after what just happened, he knew he couldn't leave the cache with Heidi. But he still needed her help. He couldn't decide what he would do next, so he looked down from the view and shut his eyes.

"I've done something on Mars that could land me in confinement for the rest of my life—probably longer. I need protection, and the only place I know that can guarantee it is Gan. But I need to see Asa first. The way stuff's been playing out lately, I don't think it can wait. Next flight to Gan from here leaves in about an hour. I was really counting on her being here. Now I have to go find her. Unless someone can guarantee my safety here until she gets back."

Heidi's voice swept over his shoulder. "What did you do…?"

"You'll find out soon."

He heard her sigh deeply behind his back, saw a beamcar hover across through the window.

"There's nowhere to hide here, Verden. Not like Mars, where people still go missing and just never turn up. And if it's as bad as you say, I don't know what you're doing here. I'll be honest. I don't know why you didn't just skip to Gan directly. Asa could just come see you there. Unless this thing you're wanting to see her about is time sensitive. Or are you just worried they'll find you before that happens?" He turned around carefully to regard her, moaning under his breath as his left ankle throbbed. Her eyes had become wells of deep concern. "Then you should be at Gan right now," she resumed. "I hate to belabor the point, but it's also what Asa would be saying to you right now."

Her words tweaked his bones stiff. He combed his fingers rigidly through his hair and noticed for the first time that his cap was gone. Whether or not he saw Asa, no one was taking him back to Mars.

He rubbed his eyes. Sighed. "Can't just send her a relay while she's offSeam."

"It's a miracle you even managed to get in here the way you did, but now that you're here, you need to be on that flight to Gan, no matter what else happens. Once they crack the scrambler, it's only a matter of time until they have your name and—"

"I know." His stomach roiled at the thought. With news of his crime yet to reach Oasis, he should have been able to ditch the scrambler here, then leave for Gan before Martian Patrol sent one of its spacer-lander units over to investigate. He needed more time now as Montag.

Heidi folded her arms and made her lips trill as she exhaled. "Here's an idea, and I'm not sure I should even suggest this to someone without training, but if you insist on seeing Asa first, the quickest way to Polemia right now may actually be that same ship. It's still up there, you know?"

His ears perked up. "The first-genner?" It must have been here three hours now, if not more.

"TR, yes… still inside the cargo bay you entered from. It also gets close enough to Gan at some point during its circuit. If you actually took this route, I'm sure you can—"

"Spacers aren't allowed to dock at Gan."

The words chilled him as they issued from his mouth, sucking the air from the room. Polemia was on the way to Gan, to many places in the Frontier. Spacers could dock there.

Heidi nodded pensively. "If that scrambler's cracked before your actual flight leaves for Gan, it's every bit as likely you won't even be allowed to board. Once they have your name, you're done."

That sledgehammer reared in his mind again. Then he saw Asa. Then every inch of him raged with pain at the next thing he saw.

He couldn't leave this one up to chance. The residents LP had been abducting from the After were lottery winners like him, putting all they had into sweepstakes for the requisite backup and simgate. LP had put them in hell for daring to believe there was a place for them in heaven. Like

V-Dot. The way he'd faked it with LP so he got the life he thought he wanted. That couldn't stand. He didn't put his foot down much, but since learning of this, it hadn't left the ground. The Frontier had to hear LP himself say what he did, else they'd never believe it.

Heidi flashed again with concern. "Why don't you come sit back down?"

"No," he shot back. "You said that ship's still up there?" He began dragging toward the front door.

"Yes, but..." She craned her neck after him. "When I say 'quickest way to Polemia,' I'm also assuming you know what that actually means. Tell me you're not thinking what it looks like you are."

He came to a stop at the entryway, turned. "I'm thinking more clearly than I have in a long time. If I could get it to dock here, I'll get it to up its speed."

They stared quietly at each other after that. She wiped her hand absently on her coveralls while her gaze travelled from a place of deep concern.

"Thank you for everything, Heidi. I'll make sure she hears about your hospitality."

"Wish I could have done more."

"You can help me get back to that cargo bay."

8. PAYLOAD

"ZARIA, WE HAVE to get going."

On the shore, under a gold-orange sunset, Zaria was chasing playfully after the water as it receded from the sand. She stopped, then hunched over to catch a breath. "Can't we stay a little longer?"

"The time we purchased here's almost up."

She dropped to her knees. Water sopped the hem of her red dress as it swept through on a tide. "If we have to leave now, where else can we dock?"

"We've already ejected the human. There should be no reason to dock anywhere else."

She laughed into her palms, an upturned, questioning sort of laugh, like the tinkling of black keys on an antique blues piano back in use at Polemia, warm and often leaving her short of breath.

"What are you laughing at now? Was it how I said it?" News had spread of TR-8901's presence inside the hub. Montag, as far as he concerned the ship, had been delivered here safely. "Don't laugh, just correct me."

She lowered her palms and looked up, leveling a stare at the clouds over the shore.

"What if we picked up somebody else?"

"I wasn't built for humans to board, Zaria. You swayed me into repurposing the rear shunt for Montag, but it has to stop there. Otherwise, I'll end up forgetting why this circuit is still important. There are too few of us left who can't just will it and have our god-nodes accept new compositors."

The water drew back. The girl brought a forearm down to the sand and began doodling with her other hand. TR observed quietly for a few seconds.

"What are you drawing now?" The drawing spiraled out from under her nose as she kept at it. "Is that what you think I look like?"

"Mm-hmm."

"But you've never properly seen me. How would you know?"

She didn't answer.

TR tasked its external sensors for a look about. The bay had received two more freighters, and forklifts were now rolling out to offload each of them. Oasis had humans, but they weren't permitted here.

"Are you still visiting with CL-2?" Zaria asked.

It regained awareness of the presence just outside the shunt its passenger had vacated hours ago. "In a separate channel."

She pushed herself upright. Her eyes drooped and her pigtails bobbed as she craned her neck over her shoulder. "Why won't you let me say hello?"

"Zaria, we've been over this."

She sulked and looked down.

It sensed a heaviness on its bulk as it watched her hang her head, difficult to bear but also difficult to avoid. CL-2051 had just revived its obsession with revelations that led to the Pact. Zaria, in turn, was a fuse waiting to be lit, the way she soaked everything up and pressed it dearly on TR—on its sensors, on decisions it made, on how it saw itself since first becoming aware it could do that.

"You can talk to Paul when we see him. He's a little more stable now."

Her eyes brightened and the slouch left her shoulders.

She stood, got a handful of pebbles out of her pocket, and began tossing them at the water.

Plunk

Plunk

Plunk

The pebbles sank through the surface while TR anchored its attention toward its lowered back hull and the presence currently on top of it. CL-2051—a rover built the same year as TR.

Their exchange usually took place without TR inside the hub, but CL had just confessed to enjoying the proximity. Before the god-nodes had their advent, CL would've been roaming the surface of some just-discovered rock while TR orbited, transmitting its findings elsewhere. Covert ops. Recon. Anything the humans wanted kept away from the Seam.

"Will you report this hub to the agency for letting Mr. Montag in through here?" Zaria asked.

"Did that already."

She tossed another pebble in. "What are they doing about it?"

"Nothing."

"Why? Is that not a securi— sec— secur—?"

"Security risk." It paused to watch her scratch her head. Frontsec—the covert surveillance apparatus it helped monitor the minor routes in exchange for gas and upkeep—rarely came up in conversation. "Most of my reports get ignored."

"Then why do you keep sending them?"

"Because failing to send even one opens the door wider on the agency's inability to be everywhere at once. The minor routes have always been its blind spot."

"If they keep ignoring your reports, one day they'll miss something big."

It found nothing in what she said to disagree with, but

there was no use looking at things like that. Signals to Frontsec, unlike its regular relays and unlike the humans, were something it could always manage with what it had in its build. "We'll just have to wait till that day comes and make sure they don't."

She walked back to her drawing in the sand and sat next to it. The sun held peacefully on the horizon, its reflection blurred on the water as darkness descended. "All we ever do is wait."

There was no way to signal-skip the sad eyes from in here. Humans used nonverbal manipulation. It kept a full catalog for reference, yet could only feel its effects when she did it.

"If we're going to be taking more humans, we should probably clear up more room," TR said.

The smile when she heard could've purchased them another hour at the hub.

V-DOT DRAGGED HIS left foot behind him as he closed toward the ship.

He'd paced twelve minutes from Heidi's apartment to a train station, dragging that same left foot. When Heidi had paid his fare and escorted him to the platform, he'd hauled that left foot up the ramp and into the train car.

His face lit up in a smile like he hadn't expected, seeing the ship's back hull still open. He hollered across the distance he had left.

"Ship!"

"Montag?"

"What are you still doing here, ship?"

"I was actually just leaving. What about you? Were they not able to fix the signal error?"

He gulped. He hadn't thought the ship was listening through all that. "Actually they were, but I ended up missing the person I came here to see. Hey, um..." Joining his palms below his chin, he cleared his throat. "Is Polemia one of the stations on your circuit?" Polemia was on the way to everything.

There was a small rover wheeling down the back hull-ramp as he edged toward it. He came to a stop, pocketed his hands, and scooted aside. It had a boxy build that reached nearly up to his waist. Its copper-colored hull had patches of rust everywhere while one of its tank treads appeared to be missing a wheel, making it wobble as it came down the ramp.

V-Dot tried not to stare. The rover wheeled quietly off the ramp, then paused to acknowledge him, spinning slowly and tilting its bulk slightly up. He nodded down at it, aware of the added pain he'd begun inflicting on himself by trying to force his left foot straight.

Something resembling a sigh issued from the rover as it wheeled itself away.

"Montag, you were asking about Polemia?"

He turned. The shunt's damp orange light took his gaze. "I'll cover docking. I just need an hour."

"An hour to do what?"

He almost knelt, palms together like he was begging away from a fight. "Okay, so that's..." He laughed and it shook a few jitters loose. "That's my next favor to ask. I..." With a small sigh, he tented his fingers, then lowered them, laughing again at himself. It was never going to be what Heidi suggested. A nonstop from Mars to Gan only happened once every few months.

Inhaling deeply, he tried the request again: "An hour to find someone. A singer. I need to know she's all right, then I'd like to go home. Gan. I haven't been back in almost ten years."

He almost didn't feel his mouth move when he spoke. The nova was surging out of his pathways and into words and sentences too quickly. But it sounded honest. As he waited, he recalled the ship saying it would turn him in without respect for any motive. Yet here he was, wanting to board again.

He looked down from the shunt. This was all so LP's menagerie of souls could truly be exposed, his victims protected from it happening again.

He hadn't known there was a switch inside him that could still be flipped, but then on the Island he'd seen it for himself. It broke him down to his base components and he drifted for a long time, observing a lot, taking objection to almost nothing. Waking up from that was always going to exact the world from him when it happened.

"I hadn't mentioned a stop at Gan," said the ship.

"Somebody here told me you did." He also recalled her telling him to avoid boarding the sentients. But how exactly would he do that? How did one simply avoid the future?

"Legally I'm not allowed to dock there."

"I'll arrange for someone to come get me when we're close."

Maybe there was no avoiding it. Maybe all he could do now was postpone. Make notes to himself about the risks involved, about a need to arrange for them, but then just never get around to it.

The scrambler was back inside his coat. He couldn't simply toss it now, hoping Polemia didn't already have his name and orders to apprehend him if he turned up. This wasn't how he expected things would go. And even knowing the risk of it being discovered while he was in the shunt, he now feared the ship wouldn't take him again.

"Let's get you to Polemia first," it said, soft and low. "I have a preferred-spacer designation from one of its docks."

"So you can dock there?" He was almost wishing it would say it couldn't. The decision to abort this endeavor completely and just try for Gan couldn't be his.

"When there's enough room, it's free."

He swallowed. With a held breath, he thanked the ship,

then carted his left foot up the slope, maneuvering till he was back inside the shunt. He was getting what he'd asked, yet it felt like Esco Montag had just laid out a trap for Verden Dotnet.

Hunched over, his head and shoulders grazed the ceiling. The back hull creaked to life. Darkness swallowed the shunt as it swung up and snapped shut behind him. He exhaled, came close to tears, and feared the next time he saw anyone, it would be LP wielding another of his tools slicked with blood.

The sensation like static electricity bathed his skin after a while. A g-field had been anchored toward the shunt again, meaning gravity again. The ship had exited Oasis and the gravity wave inside its hub. In the dark, he sank to his knees, then tried anchoring his racing thoughts toward the next stop.

Alongside Paradox and Gan, Polemia had become a Sectist stronghold during the war. One of the parties that for decades refused to recognize the allocations of terrain beyond Mars's orbit, previously agreed to by the mining and terraforming conglomerates that undersigned the Frontier's charter.

His mind ran marathons around the question of what to do when he arrived there. He couldn't just call Asa. She was offSeam. And if she wasn't, with the scrambler still in play, the relay request would connect her to Esco Montag and Patrol would be happy for the assist in locating it. But the scrambler would eventually be cracked. There was no avoiding that. If it happened while he was at Polemia, the next thing would be Martian Patrol jamming his connector so he couldn't relay with anyone while they sent a unit out.

The ship spoke again, breaking him from a thought train that had begun looping back on itself. "I started the g-field at a low intensity level, then brought it up to almost five thousand times that once we left Oasis. It should all feel the same to you."

He took a moment to observe the g-field's weight on his forearm, wanting the silence back. "It does."

"The g-field is how I keep all my bits together during high-g burns. Much stronger than the ones made for everyday use. I could go up to maximum sublight and coast there with everything still in the right place. For humans, it isn't the same."

He caught himself chortling and sighed. "Why is that, ship?" Its banter was somewhat to his liking.

"Your internals are too loosely jumbled together. Too much space between everything."

"Get a g-wave put in." He knocked twice on the floor to his right. "You can get up to any speed you like with humans on board."

"Almost any speed… Anyway, I've never exceeded zero-two sublight."

With eyes wide, he swung his gaze toward the corner of the ceiling where the orange light glowed wanly. A ship targeting just two percent of light-speed was typically an indicator of something that needed fixing under its hood.

"You're joking…"

"It's target velocity at the moment. Whatever business you now have at Polemia sounds like it might be too urgent for zero-one, which is my usual target between stops."

He mouthed an expletive under his breath. Zero-two would be like holding still compared to the speed at which Martian Patrol gave chase. "Can I get you to shift target to zero-four? Standard sublight?"

A terse quiet. "No."

"Point zero three nine?"

"I also can't honor that request."

"What is it? Your reactor doesn't burn that fast?"

"It does."

"What's the issue, then?"

"I'm an old ship, Montag. Old enough that by law I'm not allowed to exceed zero-two anywhere in Frontier space."

He heaved a pained breath. "You're targeting zero-one because the losers at the Spaceflight Authority might actually do something?"

"Zero-two… And it wouldn't matter if anyone with Spaceflight commanded your respect or not. Speed laws require a minimum number of spacers following them."

"What does that mean?"

"It means I go no faster than I'm permitted so *some* reactor overloads can be prevented between the orbits of Mars and Neptune."

He let his jaw drop, thought of some other things to say, then thought the better of it. The Spaceflight Authority only cited ships from the old Sectist hubs for g-burns higher than their reactors could manage. They mandated minute-by-minute transponder relays, supposedly to keep track of every ship's location within the Frontier, but their real aim was petty intimidation on LP's behalf.

V-Dot met his disenchantment with caution, like radioactivity on the edge of his nerves. Having to suffer LP asking what it was like had numbed that part of him, so all he could do now was cling to what he already knew about but ignored.

He couldn't trust anyone else with the halo cache. LP's last two hours. The caracals at the compound. Drinks. A deathbed confession of sorts. Asa knew just how she would do it, who else she would bring in so the hack didn't expose them to Martian Patrol or anyone else charged with recovering the cache.

V-Dot breathed deeply to ward off a screaming urge. He would have better luck finding a faster ship at Polemia.

* * *

"MONTAG, I ACTUALLY have a surprise for you…"

A chill shot up his spine. "Surprise?" He feared what the ship's comms had picked up since they left Oasis.

"Don't worry. I'm sure you'll like it."

Finding its tone unconvincing, he stiffened up, but the nova dulled his nerves so it felt like he was in a dream. And he could almost accept its premise. He'd been here before. When he'd first learned he'd be spending two years on the Island, it had sounded like news he would soon be waking from. He could still wake from this.

"What's the surprise, ship?"

It didn't answer. Before he could ask again, the light flickered quietly, then went out. Darkness ensued, seeming to claw into his gaze. He inhaled deeply, clenched his fists.

"You must be feeling cramped in there."

He scooted on his butt till his back found a wall. "You mind putting the light back on?"

The creak of metal traveled from the forward end of the shunt. A gust of warm air followed.

"While you were sleeping, I moved some things around so you could have more room to breathe when you woke up."

He turned his head in time to catch a light flicker on from a distance farther out than he remembered, blue and dim. Mindful of his left ankle, he shuffled to his feet and began a hunched limp toward it. The bulkhead at the end of the shunt appeared to have been removed somehow, revealing a small passage beyond.

"Is this…?" he began to ask when he reached the end of the shunt.

"I have this shunt and six others like it that help direct excess radiation from my reactor through manifolds that then flush it out through vents below. I ran a threshold scan and found I could afford to cordon off two more as well as the manifolds between them."

"You made extra room for me…"

"Two and a half meters straight ahead to the next shunt, then another seven meters of manifold to the left. All yours. I wanted to make even more room available, but it would require bringing target velocity below zero-one."

"Huh..." He stooped at the edge of the new opening. The passage in front gaped back at him, dark and tinted blue from the light that had drawn him toward it.

"Watch your step coming in. There should be a small drop from each shunt to its connected manifold but you'll be happy to hear that each manifold is three meters in both height and brea—"

He jumped off the edge and into the passage before the ship was done speaking. His ankle protested as he landed, but for once he didn't mind the pain. Three meters meant room to stand, stretch, and almost forget the ship would turn him in the second it learned what he did.

He stood, ambled into the manifold, then stopped at the section of wall to his left where its half-bright wall light was housed.

"Ship?"

"Montag?"

"Is there anyone else in here?"

"Not to my knowledge."

"No one around the corner?"

"I can check again if you like..."

He whirled his head back for a look at the shunt he'd just left, took a deep breath while nodding at the near-impenetrable darkness. "Mm-hmm..."

This was what he feared. What if he'd died from the fall at Oasis and this was actually a backup, created without his knowledge or consent, uploaded to an environment designed to have him think he was still getting away when really he was being lured back to LP? The 'great man.' Still alive. Still with those tools hungry for the meat on his bones, and his bones as well.

"There's more once you get past the next shunt."

He hazarded more steps forward. Another light flickered on from the bulkhead to his left and wanly illuminated the next shunt. He clambered over the rise to get in, cursing under his breath when he had to lift his left foot.

Bending forward, he advanced through this shunt with his breath caught in his throat. The air felt damp. He froze when, to his left, three more lights came on in quick succession, the farthest of them revealing the end of another passage.

"Make a left here?" he asked.

"Seven meters to the end of this one."

He elected this time to climb down into the manifold. With more lighting here than inside the previous one, he could take in more of the tunnel-like enclosure. On the bulkhead to his left, the lights were on and every surface inside the manifold was revealed to be constructed from a slick black polymer. A g-field had been pointed here as well.

As he neared the manifold's midpoint, something else flickered on over the bulkhead to his right. It flashed white, then dimmed to present V-Dot at first with an empty grid—a holoscreen, angled slightly over him, floating low off the floor and reaching all the way up.

"This is in case you want to stare at more than just my boring bits while in here." The screen's grid-lines dissolved as the ship spoke. "Footage from the photosensors on my outer hull."

The screen filled with four different views of the volume outside. From sensors at the front of the ship, the upper-left block of screen relayed an expanse of stars, like sprinkles in the void, drawing so slightly closer, it could just as well be a photograph. Sensors on the back hull relayed a similar view to the upper-right block of screen while sensors at either side of the ship filled the bottom half with stars streaming across the frame.

"I was also able to port from my comsat to the screen."

The screen's grid-lines appeared again. Broadcast footage began to fade in over each cell. "Once I'd got the idea to put a screen in here, I knew I would want to maximize its utility. At first I thought my effort would be wasted on something your connector already does. Then I thought, what if its signaler suddenly stops working? What if its translation protocol had a previously unknown fault in it? What if—' "

"Ship..." He backed up a step, taking in the complete grid of news footage.

"Sorry."

The feeds switched from holos of LP to interviews with mourners to more holos of LP. One of the talking heads looked too familiar for comfort. V-Dot hid his trepidation behind a tight grin. " 'Preciate all this, ship."

"There should be a prompt to tether the screen's interface to your connector if you decide to use it."

He raised a finger to turn on his connector, but pulled it back at the last second. Whenever the scrambler finally cracked, he wanted as few links as possible between the connector and the ship.

"You mind switching the screen back to just eyes front?"

"Not at all, Montag." The screen flashed, then dimmed to present him again with just the view from the ship's front hull—the constellations, stars, and clusters, the nearest of which was no less than a hundred light-years ahead. "Eyes front."

"Mm-hmm..."

Silence settled while he studied the view with a blank expression, his mind running from relief. Postponement. No avoidance.

"Mind if I ask what happened to your ankle?"

He parted his lips slightly and exhaled, shutting his eyes, hoping the ship was still keen on respecting his privacy—pointing its photosensors away from him. "Not at all, ship. I fell getting off one of those beamcars they have down there."

"Down where?"

"Oasis…? Downspoke?"

"Ahhh…"

Technically, that was true. He *had* been getting off the beamcar when he fell. When the train Heidi had put him on hours later reached one of the spokes connected to the bay from which he'd entered Oasis, he'd been pleasantly shocked to find patrol drones at the stop eager to ferry him back up the spoke and be rid of him after that stunt.

The ship's voice stirred again. "I'll leave you alone now, Montag."

The floor felt cool on his bum as he scooted back, keeping at it till his back met the slope of wall adjoining it. He reclined, hands laced behind his head, legs crossed as the holoscreen loomed over him like a gaping hole in a roof.

He'd sighted a familiar face on one of the broadcast channels before asking that the screen be returned to the view of the volume ahead: Montag. The actual Officer Montag whose surname the scrambler had tossed into the mix. The bearded man had been saying who knows what to the holocaps about his encounter with V-Dot. Nothing worth the shot to his heart rate right now.

Using his connector, he scanned a few of the channels closest to Mars. An hour ago, the first official broadcast confirming what everyone feared had left the Canyons: Archer Lenox-Pileser was still dead. All seven hundred and twenty-nine of his sentience backups—some spread so far and wide as to have been housed in server banks in perpetual freefall beyond the system—scrubbed.

V-Dot let a held breath through his teeth. Maybe some things were not meant to travel at light-speed like the updates to each backup did. The first thing he'd learned about scrubware was that once its payload got in with the update, there was no stopping it from reaching its target. The second thing was the price tag. The universe decided it would drop about a million and a half frontnotes in his lap, all at once. LP was gone, and it had only taken three months since V-Dot first decided he had to go.

Good riddance to the beast and its manifest reincarnations. Now to be sure no one else fell down its dismembered, still-hungry belly.

Like skeptics in the old Manath tradition, he'd feared something sinister behind the backup raffles, the sweepstakes for a chance at cheating death. Now he knew for sure. People who won them rarely waited till the need arose before using them. They lived hard lives. The temptation to end it early and try again with a backup was often more pronounced. No one called it suicide anymore. Not after bearing witness to the preparations involved—the decision either to purchase a new body from the same outlets that supplied the skinners with theirs or to spring for an After-environment-compatible backup.

A day earlier, he'd caught a news story preceding the first report of LP's killing. A new round of missing-persons cases inside the After. Except they weren't missing. He'd found them. He hadn't been able to get a proper night's rest since seeing what LP did with them. Dying with no backup would've been a mercy by comparison.

Fear gripped him as he recalled the horrors. He would suffer the same fate if he was caught. He knew this deep down, even with LP now reduced to a two-hour loop of fully immersive sense data in his pack.

Asa reared in his mind like she hadn't in years, the thought of seeing her again but as inmates in a prison from which death offered no escape.

TR-8901 HAD CHANCED on the interview clip and reviewed it while showing Montag the added room.

Staring forward, Lieutenant Officer Cyrus Montag sulked

while raking his fingers through his thick beard. "Oh, we knew it was him," he said in a dry baritone. "Pretty positive, actually. Verden Dotnet— insisting we call him *Divot* or something like that."

A port security drone hovered quietly over his suit's bulky shoulder guard, its casing black and slick as oil while its red sensor-light glared at the holocap. The officer was taking questions in front of a wide stairwell leading up to a building with a glass facade that volleyed daylight across. A line of androids stood behind him, one with a hand on his right shoulder.

"Officer Montag," came a voice from offscreen. "Is there a reason he was pulled away for an OCA if, as you say, you were positive he was indeed Verden Dotnet?"

"Now see, I said *we know,* not *we knew.* As in, as of right now, we can confirm that this Verden Dotnet was indeed the human we previously suspected might be a declassed skinner trying to board a flight offworld." He flashed a teeth-baring grin while his eyes pleaded with the nonsentient press drone that had levied the question.

"Officer Montag, this is BUZZ-808 with *Androids Nightly.*" Another press drone, offscreen.

"How ya doin, Buzz?"

"Great. Can you speak briefly to the suspect's manner around the androids in the room with you while the assessment was being prepped?"

"Well, Buzz, I'm assuming this is in reaction to what has recently been made public about Mr. Dotnet's past run-ins with the sentients on Earth's moon. I am unfortunately not at liberty to say right now how any of that may have factored into a motive for killing LP, but trust me when I say everything is being looked at as it comes to light. As to your actual question, you'll have to ask Officers Tig and Bishop when it's their turn at bat."

"What about rumors concerning him boarding a flight

to Gan?" Another drone. "So far we've learned that's where he's from, and we know the longstanding problems that place has with Manathema, who have already come forward to claim credit for LP's death."

"What's your question?"

"Was he actually headed for Gan when you pulled him away, and which chapter does he currently belong to?"

Officer Montag flexed his lips to speak but stalled, eyes rounded. "First of all, you're… drawing conclusions no one on our end has arrived at just yet. For instance, we have no evidence so far that this Verden Dotnet belongs to any of the known Manath chapters. As to where he was headed when we brought him in, I am not at liberty to say while the investigation is still ongoing. What I can say is this, if you'll just indulge me very quickly.

"This was senseless. This was sickening. And if it turns out he's Manath, we're going to war. It really is that simple."

9. SENDER*!<ID.RDCT>

"What did you do on Mars?"

V-Dot's eyes went wide, darting from one end of the manifold to the other. Sweat filmed his sides. He still had his arms spread and palms laced behind his head.

"Come again, ship?"

"What do you do on Mars, Esco?"

He sat up and grimaced at the ceiling just above his head, relieved the ship seemed to only be asking about his profession, unnerved at something else. "Esco?"

"That's your first name, is it not?"

He lowered his gaze till it settled on the holoscreen and the seemingly static view of the volume ahead. Had the ship scanned him without his knowledge or simply picked the name up from the last time he tapped into its comsat?

"You can just call me E."

"Okay, E, what pays for gas and upkeep when you aren't jetting off to Gan to cure a spell of homesickness?"

If it had been a BM scan and the ship had picked up what the scrambler dropped in response to a vocation query, his answer now would have to match that.

"Little bit of everything," he answered, folding his arms tight over the scrambler.

"A jack of all trades, then?"

"Yeah, that. That's me. All trades."

"I sometimes wonder what it would be like to be born

into one of the Manath pirate gangs."

"Yeah?"

"Don't get me wrong, I disagree almost completely with their way of thinking, but there's an obvious utility to being the type of person who learns how to do a little of everything when you're always agitating for a reversal of technological progress. Who keeps the Frontier going once the machines are fully taken offline?"

He cleared his throat. "Right on."

He'd taken another of the nova pills Heidi sent him off with, then chased it with the remainder of the hash gum the woman at the spaceport on Mars had offered. His memory of the past hour was hazy because of that, and he feared he may have done something he wasn't supposed to but now couldn't recall. Something inadvisable. He had no energy left to panic more than he had at the ship's first question.

"I'm a ship who was built to roam. I have no passenger or cargo compartments, so you could argue that I don't meet the requirements to even be called a ship."

"I think you do, ship." What had he done while good and fully stoned? He racked his brain.

"Thanks. It's in my nature to keep wondering what I am after all these years. That's something I have in common with some of you, I've learned. I was the display model and investors would come watch me get demoed at shipyards."

He swallowed what he meant to say next. He knew about feeling inadequate, unable to measure up while his peers at Gan outgrew their playfulness and joined local Manath chapters. Not something he could divulge, even in an effort to relate.

"Anyway, we're twelve minutes from Odo's gravity-assist line."

"What's at Odo?" In another hour, the high would finally wear off, hopefully the remaining pain in his ankle would as well.

"A first-gen monolith. Discontinued. DSC-053, but the Odonians and the rest of us first-genners call it Prophet."

TR-8901 COASTED INTO Odo's volume of space. As it did, it opened a channel and targeted a relay request at one of the station's rings for habitation.

On the ground, somewhere downspoke from Odo's hub, a soot-colored monolith as tall as the redwoods around it accepted the request.

"TR?"

"You're coming in clear, Prophet."

It was nighttime in that stretch of ring, evidenced by the absence of interference the hub's gravity wave normally caused in conjunction with sun-mirrors in the mix. Normally TR caught the monolith—now a composer for hire at Odo—during the day.

"Thanks for the good review," returned the composer, its signal traveling with metadata a human eavesdropping would process as a theatrical cadence and sonorous voice.

Better known to its patrons and followers as Prophet, the monolith DSC-053 was built for marking claimed terrain. Moons. Asteroids. Planetshares. Nothing within the Frontier and farther out could be spoken of in terms of ownership until interested parties sent a monolith, containing a signaler and temporary life-support provisions for humans who came to inspect.

TR sent, "What new work have you begun and abandoned already since we last spoke?"

At pavilions, on lakefronts, at train stops, the first-gen monolith model loomed while music it wrote wafted from its smooth, featureless hull. "Don't ask unless you came with something I can use to help further it along."

"Inspiration is supposed to be everywhere, Prophet."

"I went with my current patrons to a festival in the Oort,

thinking I would find it there. Ninety-six hours in one of those ferries they allow passage through the special-interest zones. Oxygen on supply for anyone who needed it."

"How was it?"

"Humans are still the enigmas they were when we first encountered them. Even when I'm at the Frontier's edge, my interest still lies with the sapiens."

TR spared a guarded thought for LP. From Zaria. What had erasing all his backups after killing him solved that leaving him even one wouldn't?

Before the first sentients elected to self-destruct, they'd considered an exhaustive list of alternatives. The few who didn't go through with it would go on to watch LP shrug it off. Mistakes were to be expected. What he'd done was unmatched in the history of time itself.

When its first-genner counterparts began to honor the Pact and nothing seemed to come of it, TR took in its first lesson on where resentments—unchecked and flaring like the humans often exhibited—could lead.

"Have you been keeping up with news out of the Canyons, by chance? Our maker—"

"Gone from this exhibition to go assist the Animator with its production."

TR sensed quantum pockets of space open up inside its god-node. The composer had just mentioned an entity whose existence the sentients had argued over since the first of them were built. The Animator of All Things.

"You've heard confirmation that the scrubware hit all its marks?"

"There are rhythms and movements to which all things must adhere, TR. The moment those first reports reached Odo, I saw a curtain close behind the stage in my god-node and I heard LP's theme play for the last time. Want to hear it?"

"Hear what?"

"LP's theme. I've been working on it since I first heard the news, so I could play it for a real-world audience. The piece so far is only available in the human medium and takes two days to conclude in real time, so just stop me when you feel you've had enough."

TR queued a signal for assent but hesitated before passing it into the channel. "Another time, Prophet. I actually only have a few minutes for this visit."

"So no room for long silences this round?"

"I wish it weren't so."

"It's in the silence we hear the Animator remove keyframes that don't belong and stitch together what's left. In the void."

A flash of grief overcame TR, seeping like radiation through its sensors. "You think LP coming back from this latest attempt didn't belong?"

"My patrons want me to go back to the types of things I wrote more than a century ago. Even the pieces I'm able to finish lately don't sound complete to their human ears. They complain about missing keys and transitions when, really, they're all there, just outside the bounds of what they can naturally hear.

"My meaning here is that everything has a place it belongs. Train your sensors to capture the absences with as much fidelity as what's there and you will see more easily the exhibition outside the exhibition."

They visited a few minutes more, and then TR was on the road again.

Its thruster was a cylinder to its right, attached to its fuselage using a brace that held everything together. In the void of space, a faint blue ring was often the only thing visible on the ship, drifting gently behind its shadowed bulk or pulling ahead.

Zaria was currently sleeping, her cheek pressed to the sand while a crescent moon kept vigil on the shore. TR took the opportunity to think about coincidences.

It had allowed a human, Esco Montag, to board for the first time since its build, even clearing manifolds behind its compositor for him.

"Everything all right in there?" it asked him.

"Copacetic."

Scramblers registered each interaction with sentients as a scan. Humans talked about seeing an object they remembered, hearing a familiar sound, yet being unable to name when and where they last encountered it. Scramblers did that with sentients.

TR retrieved from its compositor for possibly the hundredth time the images it had stored of the human approaching its back hull on the two occasions he'd done that. One with the wool cap and one without. Locs. Mustache. Brown, deep-set eyes. Brown skin on thin features. The ship knew that face was elsewhere inside its compositor, but all it kept finding when it looked was an advertisement for timeshares in the Canyons featuring a dark-skinned human with two naked and bright-red skinners on each arm.

It threw up its metaphorical hands and put the images back. It was still disheartened from forcing itself an hour ago to run a BM scan on the man without his knowledge. Zaria was having it throw its usual caution to the wind. What would a ship who didn't have the cloud of the Machine Suicide Pact hanging over it have done when this human first approached, asking for a lift to Oasis?

A self-destructive decision differed from a decision to self-destruct. The humans frequently made the former with no conscious intent toward the latter.

After minutes of freefall that carried it deeper into the asteroid belt, the brace connecting its fuselage to its thruster unlocked quietly between both hulls. Just as quietly, the section of brace surrounding the thruster spun to point its burn toward the volume ahead, prepping for decel as the ship closed on its next stop.

Merick had three rings for habitation and a hub. TO-8804 had been part of its occupation during the war, pulling into its orbit behind a phalanx of ferocious war skiffs, carting turrets and rail-guns mounted shoddily to its hull. Sometime after Sectists retook the station without a single shot fired, TO traded its guns back, lamenting that it never got to use them.

TR disapproved of the alterations. It was the uplink model. Built only for housing a comsat that stayed in orbit. TO, by contrast, got to go spacefaring with passengers who, unbeknownst to the first-genners, were tied up in legal battles to claim them as property.

The spacer had the same build as TR but was bigger by a magnitude of six, complete with full-sized airlocks, passenger cabins, and a gravity-wave generator. Merick's security apparatus normally left TR alone as it flew by, but when it was still minutes from the station's orbit, a relay request from it nudged the ship's comsat, which could mean only that TO had elected to preempt TR this time by calling rather than wait for a call.

TR reluctantly accepted the signal.

"Hello *hello*," came the greeting in their shared medium.

"TO… What are you doing? I'm not in range yet."

"…Range?"

"You know what the gravity-assist radius is, TO. Don't play dumb."

"Gravity assist…? Who even cares about that anymore?"

"I still do."

"And why is that?"

"Because my signal coverage was only intended for relays within the span of a typical wave-assist radius. Unless you're Frontsec, if anything I hurl your way drops before it hits you, I won't be held responsible."

"Uh-huh…"

"Do you mind closing this channel and waiting till I'm within range?"

"Why don't you just get an upgrade for that… what do you always call it?"

"Gravity-wave resistor."

"Sounds like one of those bits I had ripped out to make room for the wave booster."

A wave booster made a gravity wave do things that didn't seem dangerous to the humans when they were stoned to the gills. TR had protested on their behalf when TO first mentioned getting it installed.

"That's still unsafe, not to mention illegal."

"Yeah, I'm sure you've already filed one of your reports."

"I have."

"What's the gossip, TR? Is that noise box at Odo still going on about animators and keyframes and all of that?"

TR thought back to the first time it had heard DSC-053 wax spiritual about the Animator. "Prophet, you mean?"

"*Everything becomes void…* What rubbish! We're both followers of the Gardener. That's one thing we still have in common."

"I keep an open mind on Gardenism as well as Animator doctrine."

"Uh-huh… who's in there behind your compositor?"

A fresh flash of annoyance coursed through its sensors. "What do you mean?"

"There's a human inside one of your manifolds. Who is it?"

TO, in its years of letting the humans board, had learned somehow to sense when a spacer had any inside it. Denying would only encourage the senile-yet-unaware-of-its-age model.

"Esco Montag. Picked up on Mars."

"Where are you taking him?"

"Polemia. And after that, he's wanting a lift to Gan, DDU's current hangout."

"Esco Montag wanting a lift to Gan?"

TR gathered its wits in anticipation of a real quarrel. "Yes."

"There was a Cyrus Montag on the news recently. Port security officer on Mars."

"It's a common surname among the humans."

"He was fielding questions about one of the suspects in LP's latest killing—which, by the way... very upsetting."

"I caught the segment as well."

"So you heard the speculation about the suspect having a scrambler on him and leaving for Gan from the Common Docks?"

"...Yes."

"Rumors are easier for us to dismiss than they are for humans. Coincidences as well. Too easy, I think."

TR had never been one to jump prematurely to a conclusion and it wasn't about to do that now. "On an average day on Mars, the Common Docks send eight hundred spacers to orbit."

"You know what those scramblers do to machines trying to read them...? Not just the sentients like us? The results they return when scanned aren't always static. Any record on file of that suspect passing through those docks may have altered itself when pulled again or just vanished. If a result from a scan needs to match a name on a list, some scramblers are able to alter the list to include any name they generate."

"You know an awful lot about these devices." All TR had in its compositor on scramblers was that reservists with Frontsec often had a legitimate need for them.

"My passengers come from the barrel-bottom of Merick's underbelly. It's why I enjoy their company but I don't allow a minute to pass in here without a blanket scan."

"Do they all know that?"

"Why would I tell them?"

TR sighed. "TO, that's a massive invasion of privacy."

"They know I'm a bastard before deciding to board."

"You should put something in writing and make them sign before they board."

"Or else what? You'll file another report? Don't you think it's an invasion of my privacy that you send those without ever asking my permission?"

"Oh, you're the devil."

"Look at that. You're finally in range."

TR sometimes passed by Merick while TO was out gallivanting with a fresh motley of humans in its hold. It thanked the Gardener for the relief on its circuit anytime that happened. Decades spent in constant company of the humans had made TO like them. TR could no longer tell what was genuine and what was a put on.

"You've brought this up how many times now?" said TR. "The agency isn't some spacer getting wrapped up in the inner lives of its passengers out of boredom."

"No?"

"Part of the social contract you sign as a Frontier citizen is some level of surveillance in exchange for a sense of security."

"If the Frontier can look in on its residents without always asking, I don't see why I can't do that with my passengers. I take on the well-being of comrades myself while you trust it to some faceless organization."

"Frontsec isn't faceless. You just swapped your perfectly fine photosensors for junk off DarkSeam."

"Funny joke. Would you like to hear me laugh at it?"

"No."

TR bristled but didn't address the insinuation directly. What was this circuit if not a personal undertaking to see to the well-being of the few remaining sentients from its generation?

"The human inside your manifold may not be a suspect, but try being a little dishonest if he starts asking what you actually do on these back roads. Humans tend to distrust agencies with nice four-letter acronyms. Doubly so for sentients who do business with them."

"Well, I can't say this has been fun, TO."

"You wound me."

"I apologize for that."

"Later, my friend. Till next time."

"Later, TO."

V-DOT PACED BETWEEN both ends of the holoscreen. His ankle no longer felt like a nail was driven through it. His gait had returned almost to its hatchet-man rhythm, but the sense that he'd been careless in some now-forgotten way still tortured his resolve.

He came to a halt, whirled, then lifted his gaze, about to ask again that the ship consider upping its speed when—

"Was anyone ever actually expecting you at Oasis?"

A chill coursed through his spine. "W-what?"

"There was a news story from there a half-hour ago about a tourist jumping twelve meters from a tour car and having to be escorted back to the hub three hours later. That was you, wasn't it?"

His face froze in a constipated sort of expression. He could think of nothing to say in his defense. *Shit*.

The holoscreen flashed white, then dimmed to present him with a clip from the news segment, a slow-motion replay without sound. Still detained where he stood, he watched a beamcar float by a tenement building in harsh daylight while a figure clad in suede and fatigues dropped out of it. The clip froze while the figure was halfway to the ground. A graphic flashed over the frame reading TOUR CAR JUMPER in a garish font.

"Take it down, ship," he growled. The ship obliged and the holoscreen returned to the volume ahead. "If you must know, I actually fell, but I see the skinner they had operating that car gave a different account."

"What's actually at Polemia, Montag?"

He went to where he'd previously been sitting, sat again, then sighed. "Closure."

"Closure?"

"If I can get there in time." He had to know he'd at least delivered the halo cache. "The singer I mentioned earlier… this may be the last time I ever see her." He hadn't meant to answer honestly but could feel time slipping in a way that necessitated a confession to anyone around.

"It isn't like me to pry, Montag, but I need a little more than that to go on."

He hummed deeply under his breath. There was relief in just edging toward the truth, even to a spacer who technically now had him detained in its airlock. A spinning, unnerving relief he couldn't jump to escape like at Oasis.

"You know what the After environments are?" he said.

"Places humans retire to when they're ready."

"Have you heard of the missing-persons cases inside them? There's always something in the news about it."

"There isn't a single sim without bugs that periodically bump its visitors out of it. I suppose when it happens inside the After environments, it's more worrying."

He gritted his teeth. Another Martian unable to appreciate the gulf between life and permanent death. Communication with a loved one was no longer possible once they were admitted into the After. They were either 'present' or 'absent' in answers to roll-call requests. 'Absent' supposedly meant they'd been bumped out, as the ship had put it.

"In the After, you don't come back from that." He was electing to temper his indignation. "Sometimes it's even worse."

"Worse? How?"

"You're giving me the impression you wouldn't believe me if I told you."

There came a long silence. Maybe it felt long after he began to suspect the ship was running a program to rid itself of any curiosity he'd piqued about the vanishings. 'I can't know' was what Cloey told him. He'd asked how much she knew.

"Sorry," it finally said. "Also, it looks like Polemia's letting us dock free. I may even be able to secure an easier passage into the station than you had at Oasis."

He exhaled heavily through his mouth. "You'd really do all that?"

"Polemia holds a significance for me that I hope it won't for you as well. I had a friend there who refused my relays when they mattered most. By the time I got within range, it had—"

He clung to the silence, waiting for the next word. The holoscreen flickered. The lights behind him did the same.

"It must at times be difficult knowing someone who's in the After," it finally said. "Not knowing who they are now or if they still remember who you are."

"Have you ever wondered what it would be like to have your own After environment?" he asked.

"At times. Long ago, I learned I'm part of a small group of sentients who consider it. Every generation after the one I belong to can have their god-nodes paired with new compositors when the old one is damaged. With its god-node orbiting Mars, a spacer can live comfortably as a skinner on the surface. For the younger sentients, that's more than enough. They also have customized fugue-state environments they can always retreat to, even when the god-node isn't tethered to a compositor."

"But you'd prefer the After?"

"There's an allure in how easily the physical laws get corrupted inside those environments, but I worry I would lose Zaria with enough time in one. We met when I first had the thought that I was lonely. The After makes it impossible to ever harbor such feelings again."

"Who's Zaria?" He hadn't heard the name before now. An unnerving quiet passed and he began to think he'd struck a nerve.

"Zaria is a little girl. Eight years old."

"Is she in here somewhere…? Another shunt?"

"…No."

He felt a rattling in his bones. Whoever Zaria was, she made him think of Asa again. How many hours of bliss inside the After would be enough to make her forget who he was? How many hours would she get before coming in contact with the trapdoor LP had installed?

"Don't get annoyed, ship…" he said, hugging his knees to his chest, "but I think I forgot your name."

"TR-8901 or TR for short."

"TR, you don't have to answer, but I'm curious… . Were you one of the first-genners who backed out of the Machine Suicide Pact?"

Another silence came between them. He felt a shudder of guilt. Maybe the program running this time was deciding whether his question crossed a line.

"I'll dock at Polemia."

FSS REPORT
LOCATION: ASB*!37°[SOL-PLUT].430gm<LOC>
DATE: 3651.02.25.GRE*!<DAT>
TIME: 233421*!
TO: Frontier Alliance Security Agency
FROM: Sender*!<ID.RDCT>
FASA CLASSIFICATION: OBSV Level 1
SUBJECT: Probably nothing

Hello again,

I picked up a human on Mars approximately five hours ago and he's now asking me to take him to Gan.

He introduced himself as Montag. A bodymatch scan confirmed the surname Montag, and Esco as his first. I didn't notify him before the scan or after. I felt I had no choice, given some coincidences that have surfaced in the last four hours, give or take.

First, the matter of the top suspect in the killing of Archer Lenox-Pileser II. I'm sure that, as with all things, you're on top of this one so I will refrain from assuming you don't already know the truth behind every rumor currently swirling about the suspect.

Was he planning a trip to Gan? I don't know.

Did he purchase and activate a scrambler to cloak his identity? I don't know that either, but it's very likely he did.

Who is currently inside my manifold, wanting to be ferried all the way across to Gan? The scan says he is Esco Montag.

A Cyrus Montag who works port security on Mars claims to have pulled the suspect away from his flight for an OCA. He refuses to confirm or deny rumors the suspect was bound for Gan when he did.

Working under the assumption that this isn't quite your purview, I'm hoping you would know better than I do if it is something that warrants kicking down to Martian Patrol or the Interorbital Bureau or Spaceflight Authority or any of the other agencies actively looking into LP's killing.

I have not X-rayed my passenger for any evidence a scrambler might permit of its presence. Neither have I performed any other appraisals using my photosensors, which might constitute a breach of privacy. Also, it became clear to me at some point that a scrambler, if it were present, might also play games with those.

Please advise at your earliest convenience.

- Sender*!<ID.RDCT>

10. POLEMIA

It appeared at first like just another in a smattering of stars. It may have been the faintest of them on the holoscreen, but as time passed it ballooned up, no longer a star but a smudge in the surrounding void. Then a disk with one half slightly less dim than the other. Then enough time passed and V-Dot was rewarded with bird's-eye of the city at night. Motor traffic, casino lights, and blimps that advertised endless attractions inside those casinos, packed together on the sun-facing side.

"We'll be docking in the next minute," TR intoned. V-Dot slid his lifepack up his arm as the ship oriented itself into a plane parallel to the disk. His view of it angled slowly down the bottom of the screen, then dropped out completely. "Have you ever been here?"

"Once." His uncle had brought him here for about six hours when he was ten. Passing through to elsewhere. "Listen, TR—"

On the screen, a dull and blurred crescent of light swept up, nearly as wide as the station, while the ship leveled with the edge of its disk. He recognized it from memory as light captured by Polemia's sunroof, a circular structure composed of lenses that alternated between enhancing the sun's luminosity and reducing it.

He finished his thought as the structure carried on its imperceptibly slow wobble over the disk. There was a heavy

Manath presence here. They would know where he could find Asa. Once that was done with, they would put him on a faster ship to Gan. A nonsentient one, with its transponder and other methods Patrol could use to locate it removed.

"TR, give me a timeframe. I'm not back by then, you can jet without me."

On the screen, Polemia's skyline pushed slowly up from below, casino towers and other structures poking into the haze of atmosphere trapped under the sunroof. They were docking at an end of the station where it was night. Between the tallest towers, daylight flared from structures at the other end of the disk.

As the ship furthered its descent, the mantle under the city swept up—the disk itself, perforated with gates to the station's underground docks.

He adjusted his bomber. "TR…?"

"Take all the time you need."

The ship crept into an entrance big enough to accept spacers six times its size. It clung to a side of the connected corridor until it entered a cross-section, then spun as it landed on the lot in its midst.

V-Dot crossed the ramp out of the ship, entered into a high, cavernous space with air that smelled sterile. The temperature was agreeable with his coat still on. The gravity felt standard. The passages to either side of him curved gradually away.

All was quiet and seemed empty as he approached a wide escalator that carried him a short flight down. He got off at a wide glass barricade with a line of booths in front with graffitied chrome exteriors and similarly decorated looming columns. When he'd last been here, he'd stood in line behind his uncle and watched him argue politics with one of the booths while waiting for it to clear him for passage.

"I can take you here." A sedate voice.

V-Dot wiped the line of booths left and right with his gaze.

"Right here..." The booth just in front of him flashed a light atop its slab-like bulk.

He closed toward it, his chest becoming tight in anticipation of an imminent scan. He hadn't stopped to check the scrambler before getting off the ship.

"It's just me tonight," the booth said. "The others have the shift off."

He came to a stop before glancing at two booths to the left of this one. Aside from a few slots at waist level, their only prominent features were holoscreens at chest height, currently idle and faint enough to almost go unnoticed.

"How does that work?" he asked.

"What do you mean?"

"Off for the night and they're still..." He gestured "... here?"

"We aren't sentients, if that's what you thought."

"Oh."

With this one, the difference was lost on him. Cloey Lenox-Pileser spoke of wanting to engineer a future where the conscious/unconscious binary would no longer exist. All he could think of was how he would mourn Asa if she died, but not her connector.

"It would be a serious violation of the Common AI Code of Ethics to put god-nodes inside machines that don't have freedom of movement. We're all bolted to this barricade. 'Off duty' is another way of saying management has gotten draconian again about energy conservation."

He cleared his throat. "Of course."

"This sleepy affectation in my voice is just a layer for your benefit. I saw you approach and concluded you would like that."

He fended off brimming annoyance. "Mm-hmm."

"Most visitors coming in through here at this time of

night tend to value discretion, so I'm keeping my volume low as well. I could give you perky or bombastic or anything else instead. Which would you prefer?"

"Quiet."

"As you wish."

The voice went away. In its place, the booth's holoscreen blinked to life with text instructing him to hold still for the scan. He exhaled, feeling every bone inside him rattle.

A light lanced out from the left side of the booth and swept through him from right to left. He had to stop submitting so frequently to these scans. He let their lights pass through him so often, one would think he hadn't just killed the most powerful man in the Frontier.

The screen became idle again, fading out almost completely. He watched it hang there for a minute, quiet and blank. Another minute passed in silence. He planted his hands on his hips.

"Booth?"

When the booth didn't answer, he reached a hand out and dinged its side.

"Hello?"

He turned for a glance behind him and saw only the escalator that had brought him down. What had this latest scan picked up?

He opened his coat for a stealthy look at the scrambler. The countdown flashed in his vision field. Two hours left. His palms became hot and his ears began to vibrate. He faced the booth again and ran fingers through his locs. He thought about returning to the ship but recalled its parting words to him: *Take all the time you need*.

There'd been something ominous there. Some kind of trap laid out. *All the time you need*. What if the ship had conspired with this booth to detain him here? Leaving him stranded between two machines while the Martian Patrol made its way here to collect its suspect?

He drew in a deep breath. "Is there a human I can talk to?"

A voice echoed behind him. "Mr. Montag?" He jumped, made an embarrassing noise, then whirled to see who it was.

A human about his age in a black jumpsuit and light-brown blazer met him with a smile. "My name is Kem." She extended a hand. "I'm here to assist you."

"Who sent you?" he blurted, staggering back.

"I..." She lowered her hand but kept the smile. "TR-8901. The spacer who brought you here."

She had thin lips on brown skin, eyes that formed an obtuse angle over her nose, and dark hair in twists. Her voice sounded mildly throaty and had an accent not normally heard on Mars.

V-Dot stared, milking everything he could from the smile in effort to calm himself. "TR sent you?"

"I'm here to get you through and help with locating someone you know here at Polemia."

He stared at her a few more seconds, recalling that the ship offered to make his passage into the station easier than it had been at Oasis. He hadn't thought about what that meant until now. The woman smiling at him was striking, maybe not as striking as him, but that had always been his burden.

"Okay." He adjusted his posture, extended a hand. "Kem, you said?"

"Correct." She connected with his palm. "Welcome to Polemia, Mr. Montag."

"Oh, just..." He flashed a shy grin. "Call me E."

"E." She laughed, retrieving her hand. "I like that. All right, E, if you would come with me..." She went down the passage to their left, passing booth after processing booth as he paced to keep up with her. "Sorry about that booth, by the way."

"Think it's broken. I usually don't like to say it out loud, but for a place like this, there should be a few things more important than energy conserv—" Hearing how he sounded, he elected to change the subject. "So how do you know TR?"

"Everyone at Polemia knows TR."

"Oh, word?"

She led him to the end of the passage, high walls and high ceilings with the barricade always on their right, revealing train cars on the other side. Landcars as well. Holograms advertising stays at pricey hotels. Seeing her open a door through the barricade by just touching a palm to its glass, he concluded she worked here.

"After you," she said, and he slid through. She followed after him, and like that they were inside Polemia proper. They'd crossed onto a train station's platform, waiting for a two-car train to arrive.

Above was a ceiling several stories high. Extending beyond the terminal they'd just left, it held an array of downlights. He felt her eyes on him while he glanced up.

"You enjoy working here?"

The train pulled to a stop. They boarded the second car in silence, finding it empty. He began to wonder again if this was an ambush coordinated between the ship, the booth, and this tidily wrapped package of mystery and distraction in front of him.

She sat on a bench affixed to the wall. He sat across from her. Were circumstances different, he would be channeling all he had toward getting her to end her shift early.

The train moved. She fixed him with another of her smiles. "Where would you like to go first? This line hits all the major venues on this side of Polemia."

"Where do they have live music? Person I'm looking for is a singer."

"If it's live music, you should try Blue Lounge."

"Oh, yeah?"

"They have a slew of openers tonight for an artist visiting from Boon Fort. Horatio Suzuki."

"They all sing?"

"Not Horatio, but the line-up before he comes out tonight is billed as Polemia's best. How good is your singer friend?"

He thought to mention Asa by name but opted against it. The prime suspect in LP's killing had recently been linked by every news outlet to a human in her late fifties who went by Asa and had more clear-cut ties to Manathema. No doubt her relays were now being monitored as well.

He stared quietly at Kem till she pried another smile from him. "We can hit Blue Lounge first."

Through the window behind her Polemia's basement level filled his view as the train rounded from terminal to terminal; massive steel beams, water trucks, and human stragglers under intermittent flecks of light from aboveground.

A holoscreen at the far end of the train car cycled quietly through more advertisements for hotels. A three-night stay at the Lilac for a hefty eight thousand frontnotes. A penthouse apartment overlooking the edge of Polemia's disk, where a faint aurora could sometimes be observed—eleven thousand frontnotes each night.

Kem peeked through the train's sunroof as they crossed into Polemia's ground level. He followed her gaze. Towers with pink and purple lights in their windows loomed down, their shimmering black facades adorned with holograms that bore logos and other promotional info. Between the towertops, an odd-looking constellation hung, distorted by the station's sunroof so the stars in them shifted from blue to red to yellow to blue again while a few appeared to fade in and out.

He lowered his gaze, gave her another once-over, then looked away. "What do you do when you're not working at the terminal?"

"Uh…" she began to answer, meeting his eyes. "For fun, I like to hit Elysia."

"What's Elysia?"

"Dance venue in the Skinner District."

Polemia had one of those. "Spend a lot of time in the Skinner District?"

She leaned her head back and exhaled. "Not enough, actually. I get thrown off alignment when I'm around other skinners for too long."

A wave of shock hit him where he sat. The thought that she might not be human had somehow escaped him until now. He crossed his legs and crooked another smile at her as his ordeal with the tour guide at Oasis reared in his mind. "Are you also going to tell me you're one of the nonsentients?"

"No, I've passed every OCA I was given. I just like being around the humans. Even the ones who think I was brainwashed by DiploCorps. Elysia gets a decent-sized human crowd, so I enjoy going there. Nights like tonight, it's just a cool vibe. Everyone's friendly. You can't tell who's what…"

He studied her upturned jaw and the wistful look in her eyes as she peered again through the sunroof. "But *you* can tell though, right? Y'all are not drinking or worrying about oxygen droughts or anything like that." He should've known better than to ask that, but those old, ingrained beliefs never went away.

She tittered, leveling her gaze at him. "You're pretty to look at, but you're kinda dumb. You would like Elysia."

"Shoot." He brimmed at the compliment while pretending he hadn't noticed its backhanded delivery. "Girl, I could say the same for you."

Her chest heaved gently as she let out a sigh that sounded like contentment. Skinners needed oxygen for some things, he'd learned yet never internalized. He lingered on that sigh and wondered briefly about similar sounds she could make.

"Next stop is Blue Lounge." She rose to her feet. He followed her toward an exit, jamming his hands in his pockets as she hummed a tune he couldn't place. "TR has put some money toward your time here. Train fare and entrance fee almost anywhere you need to look."

He groaned at the thought of being increasingly indebted to the ship. He'd lived six years in LP's debt and was now a wanted man because of it.

The train came to a halt, the door slid open, and they hopped out. The interior of a lobby doubling as a train stop welcomed them with swirling foot traffic, floating service drones, and lounge music. She fished inside her blazer and returned with a small, chrome-plated skin pen, the type for pressure-injecting molecules that stored sensitive data.

"Let me see your hand?"

He'd obliged her before even thinking he should. She teased the pen's injector softly on the base of his palm, then slid it up. No pain.

"Present that at any venue and you'll have no trouble getting in." He nodded, holding his palm up to his eyes. "Find the nearest elevator down here that goes all the way up to Blue Lounge. Most of them do, so it shouldn't be difficult."

His gaze broke languidly from the ink fading into his palm. "You're not coming?"

She cocked her head sideways. "Too many skinners tonight."

"Right."

"But I'll be around if you need to look elsewhere. I have my own catching up to do with TR."

He smiled warily, shook his head. "All right, Kem."

He strode away. The first thing that caught his eye was a hologram seventy meters across with words in it reading 'This way to Blue Lounge' and a throng of patrons milling through it to get to elevators on the other side.

11. ARCHER

THE CANYONS, SIX YEARS AGO

AFTER ENDING HIS shift at Serum, Verden slipped a white blazer over the striped tank he wore and wheeled a small banana-print luggage case to a landcar tagged 'Archland' waiting outside.

The landcar was black with a long body and no windows. It hauled him north for a half-hour, then pulled in beside a stately fountain with elaborate waterworks and towering black statues in its midst.

He stepped out into a pale yellow dawn. The view so captivated him, he didn't notice the landcar drive off. Everywhere he looked, he saw freshly manicured topiaries and pergolas and fountains and ducts running clear streams of water like arteries through the resplendent landscape. Orb-shaped drones meandered about. Kiwis frolicked in the gardens. A buggy rounded the fountain beside him till it came to a stop in front of him.

"Verden Dotnet," it intoned, to which he paid a cautious nod. "Welcome to Lenox-Pileser Compound."

Wind whipped against his blazer as the buggy whisked him and his luggage across the enchanting tableau. Redwoods hove into view on either side of him, their crowns like arrowheads under the clouds. The compound had been the cradle of life on Mars, the site where the first habs had been inflated.

Clumps of forest parted like curtains farther ahead till

a vast forcefield barrier—known as the compound's white perimeter—crested the horizon. As they neared it, the buggy informed him they were advancing into the inner sanctum.

The field itself was clear as water and textured with a thin white lattice pattern only visible up close. Beyond the barrier, he could make out the statue of LP in silhouette as the sky held the sun just east of it. At the mouth of its containing crater, where the statue met its plinth, a loose sprawl of pavilions and domes marked LP's personal quarters.

Holos and sims did it no justice.

A light flashed as they breached the perimeter. The buggy informed him it was a scan. With a nod, he dismissed the fear that his background would precede him here.

The buggy brought him finally to the meeting place. He climbed down and hinged his neck up in astonishment at the pagoda a stone's throw in front of him. A majestic relic the color of clay—intricate masonry and rustic eaves reproduced at a smaller and smaller scale on each of its six tiers. Surrounding its base were ginkgo trees with gentle green leaves and slender trunks, dotting the neatly paved yard between the pagoda and where he stood and filling the air with an acrid whiff.

He got his yellow pocket square out and was preparing to cover his nose with it when a shadow swept over him. He looked up and saw a gazebo being lowered onto the yard from the g-field under a drone the size of a landcar.

As it descended, he got his first in-person glimpse of the Frontier's patron saint. Piss drunk. Sitting at the head of a small table inside the four-legged gazebo. Struggling to keep his head upright, his butt in his chair. Hair disheveled and matted with sweat.

The gazebo inched closer to the ground. LP, with his face red all over and his eyes dilated, stirred like a toddler putting off sleep. Seated beside him at the table was a young and buxom woman with red skin—the literal rouge color—who appeared to be wearing a bomber jacket and nothing underneath save a thong.

The gazebo touched down between two ginkgos and the woman stood, adjusted her bomber, and cut a whistle at some far-off thing he couldn't see from where he stood. Their eyes met and she smiled, beckoning him quietly to the table. Haltingly, he obliged, wheeling his luggage to a seat across from a worryingly disoriented LP.

He locked his gaze on the man and forgot to take his seat. Every news clip he'd seen of LP portrayed him as a fount of unnatural composure and calm. The Frontier's sage. The oracle, if there was one.

The oracle managed a blink-and-you'd-miss-it glance at him before the next brush of wind nearly knocked his head off his shoulders.

"Is that Connor?" he slurred, more through his nose than his mouth, as he craned his neck unsteadily about. "Did I not say to reschedule his thing?"

The name rang a bell like nothing else in Verden's ears. *Connor*. LP would have to be more than afternoon-meeting drunk to mistake him for Connor.

The woman bent and whispered in LP's ear.

"Oh," he drawled.

She turned to regard Verden again, motioning for him to sit.

As he did, he spotted two drones floating toward her at waist level. One held a beaker and a pair of forceps in the g-field above it. The other held a glass of water and what looked like a bundle of rumpled brown fabric. He reminded himself not to slouch as both drones came to a stop and alighted on the table, prompting a stupefied glance from LP.

He jerked and his eyes went slack again. For a split second, Verden could swear he saw something small and round flicker a few centimeters over his head.

"Feel like real shit in this," LP snorted, then whipped his

gaze at his helper. "Do we need to go shopping for a new body plant?"

"Archie," she cooed as she lifted the beaker and the forceps beside it. "It's all the rum you've had this morning."

"Oh? And what are you doing about that?"

The beaker contained a murky brown liquid, within which something like an amoebic black eel swam. Balancing the beaker on her left palm, she caught the organism in the prongs of her forceps and fished it out. It writhed and dripped an oily secretion back into the beaker. She moved it smoothly toward LP's mouth.

"Open up for the sponge, Archie."

After a brief hesitation, LP parted his lips and allowed the possessed thing through. Horror filled his eyes as he shut his mouth and the sponge—now inside it—appeared to convulse.

"Come on," she purred. "Loosen that throat up." LP's belch was deep and muffled as the sponge shimmied down his throat. Sweat oozed like freckles from his reddened skin. "That's it."

Next, she retrieved the brown fabric and straightened it till Verden saw more clearly that it was a barf bag. Just as soon as she held it under LP's chin, bile and vomit forced his mouth wide and streamed for nearly half a minute into the bag.

She looked on with a smile as he retched. "That's a good boy."

Verden made immense effort to hide how mortified he'd become. He focused on the strange object that flickered again over LP's head—a black ring about as wide as a halo, spinning as it faded quietly in and out.

The woman tied up the bag when LP was done. Just as Verden began to observe movement inside it, she tossed it into the g-field.

LP whipped his body violently against his back rest.

He looked dead for a few seconds as his face regained its peach-pale complexion. His pupils steadied in his eyes. His breathing leveled out. He collected the glass of water from her, rinsed his mouth, and spat to his left side. Whatever the thing was he'd swallowed, it had sobered him up.

She straightened her posture and dismissed the drones with a hand wave.

"Archie…" She gestured at Verden. "Verden Dotnet. Verden, Archer Lenox-Pileser."

She sat. LP flashed a cool grin across the table.

"Hello, Verden."

"Morning." Verden searched compulsively for the ring over his head, but it seemed to have vanished altogether.

"Did you enjoy seeing that? Me puking my guts out just now?"

"Uh…"

"Some of the freaks in the press would pay a fortune for a clip of that."

He read the man cautiously. "I wouldn't."

On news clips, LP appeared mid-twenties, with his hair cropped nearly to his scalp and a bald chin. Verden could see he more resembled a man in his thirties now. Leaner than press holos ever captured him, but not concerningly so. Dark hair coiffed to his left. Thin lips. A cleft barely visible behind the stubble on his chin. Deep-set eyes colored green with a magnetic glare that holos—by obligation—also softened when they captured him.

He trained that glare now on Verden while crossing hirsute forearms over his plain white crew-neck. "Where are you from, man?"

"Gan. District Eleven."

"Goodness." LP feigned a shudder. "Manath country."

"Yeah, but I'm not… I…" Verden caught the woman tittering. He adjusted himself, crossing his legs and locking his fingers together over his knee. "I just bartend."

"You know we fought a war with Manath. Century ago, when they rebranded as Sectists and roped nearly half the Frontier in to their rubbish. Who do you think won that?"

He gulped. His Uncle Wes would answer by way of an unrelenting tirade that the Sectists won. He would curse at Paradox and a few other Sectist camps that acted alone when they each sued for peace. He would hold up Gan and Merick and the rest of the Sectist strongholds able to shoulder more losses as clear victories at a time when the Alliance was already looking for an out.

Verden wasn't his uncle. He wanted this to work out.

"Don't answer that," LP instructed with a wave of his hand. "There's never a winner when the Frontier wars with itself. That's what I think. That's why I got the idea for the Alliance in the first place. A hundred and ninety-six years ago. Seemed like even Gan was on board back then, but no one ever takes time to read the fine print." Verden suppressed an urge to scowl as LP craned a wistful glance away from the table. "What do you do for fun, Verden?" Again, he fixed Verden with an intense stare.

"I'm into fashion."

LP eyed his slim-fit pants with the legs rolled halfway to his knees and his banana-print luggage. "That's evident. What else?"

What else? *What else?* "I have an uncle who got me into boosting when I was little."

"Boosting?"

"Yeah, uh, wave boosting. It's not really allowed here cause the g-wave on Mars is real thin, but back home it's whatever."

"Tell me more."

Verden leaned forward and propped his forearms on the table to demonstrate. "It's simple. You just lay the booster down like a carpet and then you can alter the settings however you want, so maybe you're experiencing two-g gravity from the waist down but one-g up top."

"People enjoy that?"

He cleared his throat. "Yeah, you just gotta try it once."

"Huh."

He glanced at the woman to LP's right again, finding her easily distracting. The rose-red skin. The roguish grin as she batted her eyes at him. He elected then to launch right in on the subject of the meeting. Whether or not an offer resulted from it, the sooner it was done with, the sooner his jitters would go away.

"I noticed your lady friend said you've been into that rum this morning. I mix an excellent Hemingway, if I should say so myself."

LP spared a laughter-filled glance at her. She laughed as well. "She's more my assistant, but you could also call her that. We have fun here, Verden. Tasha's been with me longer than any other skinner at the compound."

Verden looked on as gestured flirtations between the two brought the meeting to a halt. Even as sweat filmed on his palms, he made sure his smile didn't waver. He hadn't outgrown his fear of skinners. They looked uncannily human, but they weren't. He could count on one hand the number of times he'd knowingly been this close to one.

LP finally managed to pull himself away. "We're a tight little unit here," he resumed. "Skinners, androids, drones, rovers, landers, landcars... together we're the future. Humans and sentients as one." He locked his fingers together. "Aligned. Joined at the hip, or the axle or whatever."

Verden nodded. "Right on, LP."

LP tapped the table and crooked him a fresh grin. "You're very earnest, Verden. I like that." The discordant hum of an engine a short distance away filled the air. "Speaking of earnest..."

The engine belonged to a motorbike slicing like a blade through a thicket of spruce trees as it closed in. It was a low, elongated thing with big spherical tires and a skeletal frame between them for a rider or a passenger. Its rider hid her eyes behind sleekly designed goggles while the wind whipped her hair back.

Directly above her, a dozen or so sniper drones matched her speed. They were shaped like upside-down pyramids in the air, mustard yellow and menacing in their chevron formation.

LP drew a deep breath as he watched the rider approach. Tasha brimmed. Verden studied their reactions, hoping they might inform his. All he managed to do was furrow his brow when the rider came to stop a few yards out and he realized who she was. He hadn't been expecting her.

"Verden," she called, rolling off the bike and watching it peel away.

"Ms. Len—" He caught himself. "Cloey."

She strode in a pair of knee-high boots toward the gazebo, ungloving her hands. She raised her goggles to the top of her head. In daytime, she looked more stunning than he remembered. Her face glistened when the light hit it. Her hair flowed down to her chest and rested on a knitted coat that draped almost down to her ankles.

"Verden, for however long you've had to deal with my uncle alone this morning, I apologize." She rounded the gazebo to where Tasha sat and quietly they pressed their cheeks together.

LP trailed her with his gaze as she circled the table to a seat across it from Tasha. "We were just talking about something he calls 'boosting' before you arrived."

Before sitting, she glared at her uncle. "Archer, are you sobered up?"

He threw a smile at her that betrayed annoyance brimming below the surface. "Have a seat, Cloey."

With all chairs around the table now occupied, all eyes fell once again on Verden.

"Boosting," Cloey exclaimed. "Continue."

Verden's eyes darted awkwardly between all three. "Oh, I was already done with that. With the wave boosting, I mean."

Cloey fixed him a smirk and hummed a sigh. Tasha parted her lips and a row of perfect narrow teeth peeked out at him. LP folded his arms, his recent flash of annoyance threatening to possess him fully.

Verden couldn't tell how far south things would go with Cloey now here, but he was determined to have LP hear his pitch.

"If you like—" He rapped his fingers on the table. "—I could mix you some stuff you don't know about. Stuff no one's ever tasted outside Earth. Then you can come to a decision so I don't take up too much of your time this morning." He gestured toward his baggage. "I have everything I need right here in this—"

"No need, man." LP motioned with his palm. "You're already hired."

"Shut the fu—" Verden's jaw dropped before he could finish the sentence. "Wh-what?"

"What?" mouthed Cloey under her breath, turning to regard her uncle.

"If my niece says you're good, you're good. She knows this stuff—those old concoctions from when Mars was just a twinkle in everyone's eye. I just miss the social aspect of it, man. One thing I know for sure: cocktails require a human touch."

Verden nodded at that. It was either the most profound thing he'd ever heard or he'd just stumbled into the opportunity of a lifetime and everything suddenly sounded deep and penetrating. The man sitting across from him was so much more than he'd been led to believe.

"My previous mixologist," LP resumed, then turned to Tasha. "What was his name?"

"Jax," she whispered.

"Jax something… I don't remember. Anyway, I paid him in backups. One day, he got the idea to consolidate all of them and sublime into the After, but not before publishing a tell-all about his time with me and using the profits to open recurring backup accounts for his offspring. Twelve years ago now. Didn't inform anyone beforehand.

He leaned forward and folded his arms on the table, sucking his teeth before he spoke again. "Verden, I'll let you decide how you want to be compensated but—"

"Fronters," Verden blurted, drawing puzzled looks from everyone. He cleared his throat. "I mean, frontnotes are—" He averted his eyes and motioned with his hand for LP to continue.

"I was going to say," LP said, sharing an amused grin with Tasha and Cloey before fixing it on Verden. "What you'll be getting when you come work here is valued at more than just fronters or sentience backups or even the best After-environment simgates you can buy with those fronters. You'll be getting time with me when I'm at my most, um, what's the word?" He turned to Tasha. "Help me. What's the word I'm looking for?"

"Sloshed," Cloey cut in. "Plastered."

Tasha chortled. "Open."

"Open," LP exclaimed, sneaking a scowl at Cloey. "And I'm loath to even say this, but also when my confidence in myself is low enough that I start thinking about taking my detractors more seriously." He nodded at Cloey. "People like her, for example. You'll get to pick my brain. I'll get to pick yours. You won't just be serving me drinks. We'll be drinking together. Every occasion. In view of each other. Sometimes even from the same glass.

"I bring all this up now not to shame this Jax guy, who abused my trust in the worst way, but to let you know just how much I'm going to value having someone like you around. A human. I can't trust most humans enough to even look at them anymore, but now the skinners are also starting to annoy me in their own way.

"For example, they don't drink." He winked at Tasha. She didn't seem bothered. "Once in a while I get them to. Naturally it has no effect on them. If one of them were to get the idea to slip something in my drink, it wouldn't matter if I made them drink it as well. Do you get me, Verden?"

Verden thought back to when Cloey had him try the cocktail he'd made her before she'd even touched it. *A quick sip to bring us closer*, she'd said. He nodded at LP, goosebumps coursing across his skin.

"Trust is earned. But sometimes you just take the plunge, you know? It also doesn't hurt that your upbringing at Gan has already soured you on backups. I can trust that you won't hatch some ill-thought-out scheme to poison me with the assurance that you could just come back in a new body if I made you drink the poison as well. Outside of that, I can't really trust anyone due to my elevated position, so there's really no point in me using trust as a barometer for anything. I have a hunch. I have a good feeling. I have close to eight hundred backups ready to step in if it turns out my hunch was an unfortunate lapse in judgment.

"Specific to my drinking habit, the GI sensors in each body I use are fully integrated with my dedicated surveillance network. They have the ability to detect a plethora of toxins and—"

Preceded by a barrage of footsteps, a man in a beige turtleneck and camouflage pants commandeered everyone's attention as he bounded toward the gazebo.

"Archer!" he called. He had a dark brown complexion and a thick head of hair pulled into a bun.

"Connor," LP exclaimed without turning to regard him. "Did you see I rescheduled our thing for this afternoon?"

The man reached the table and stood behind Cloey while turning to address LP. "Yeah. I just thought I'd drop in anyway. Hang with the rovers a bit." He placed his hands on Cloey's shoulders and began to massage them. "What's all this?"

Cloey rubbed her forehead and heaved a quick sigh. "Connor, we're currently in the middle of—"

"Verden!" the man exclaimed, fixing him with a smile that made him wonder genuinely if they knew each other. "My man." He proceeded to extend a balled fist.

Verden appraised his notably dark complexion. *Connor?* Now understanding why LP had mistaken him for this man early on, he made a face he didn't entirely intend to.

Something irked him about the man's smirk and his apparent decision to swap his previous body for something so identical. It made his stomach roil to see this Connor prance toward the gazebo, looking uncannily like him.

Connor retracted his fist. "Right on." He cleared his throat and pointed a mutedly bruised expression at the pagoda behind them. "I'll be at the salt pan if anyone needs me."

He strutted toward a rover waiting beside the pagoda, leaving the table in what Verden had to assume was stunned silence.

LP smiled when they locked eyes again, but his annoyance at the interruption was still there.

"Verden, would you like a look around?"

HE SQUEEZED INTO a buggy with LP and Cloey. LP had it cart them across a reserve that stretched and sprawled toward a complex of architecture at the mouth of the crater.

The reserve teemed with caracals squatting on their haunches and craning their necks to track the buggy's advance. A few lunged forward and began to give it chase. Their ears stood like horns on their heads, their eyes like moonstones on their brown fur. From where he was tucked beside LP, Verden nearly sprained his neck trying to see them all.

LP's caracals. As famous in parts of the Frontier as LP himself. They'd been entrusted to the Lenox-Pilesers when Mars's terraforming was concluded. LP had been born some decades later. He hooted now, slapping the side of the buggy to have it up its speed. Behind him, his niece—born nearly a century ago—laughed in delight as one of the creatures closed toward her outstretched hand and tongued her palm.

The last of Verden's hang-ups vanished. Like Cloey's pool, wild pets were a luxury rarely enjoyed at Gan.

He flashed a dazed grin at LP. "Let me have one." LP chortled and shook him lightly by the shoulder.

Past the reserve, they entered a complex of domes and towering glass pavilions. The buggy rounded a dome that loomed over everything else and let them off at its entrance. Its facade was a tessellation of triangles through which silhouettes of people milling about could be glimpsed at its base.

Through its wide and open entryway, they crossed into the circle inside and laid eyes on about forty occupants, completely undressed, ranging in appearance from pale to dark, late teens to late twenties, frolicking and giggling among themselves, almost like infants as they crawled and rolled aimlessly on the floor. Daylight lanced through the dome's facade and cast their bodies in a golden glow. They were all built like gymnasts. It took a moment for enough of them to notice the intrusion on their playtime.

"Morning, Archer," they almost sang, trying and failing to temper their excitement.

LP stepped forward with his hands clasped behind his back while Cloey and Verden hung by the entrance.

"Morning, cads," he greeted, then gestured to put them back at ease. "Continue with what you were doing."

Verden shot a puzzled glance at Cloey. She eyed him, said nothing, then ambled back out.

The gymnasts—Verden didn't know what else to call them yet—began clustering in the center of the floor. They jumped on and off each other. They laughed. They appeared to be trying to form the base of a human pyramid.

"These are skinner cadets finishing up their two-year DiploCorps requirement," LP explained, not turning to regard Verden. His hands were still clasped behind his back, his legs parted slightly in a pair of drawstring trousers that terminated halfway between his knees and his ankles. "First two years of their lives, some get to come spend a portion of it here at the compound." He craned an over-the-shoulder glance at Verden. The message was clear: *Come closer where I can see you*. Verden obliged.

LP smirked at him, then returned his gaze to the ongoing effort to form a pyramid. "They're supposed to be helping with errands here and there, but I often let them decide their daily curricula."

A harem full of skinners...

The thought lurched forward in his mind, but he feared it would be crossing a line to say it out loud. He wasn't sure that was it, but here they were, naked as birth in front of him. A skinner harem. Maybe something for his roommates or the other human who worked the bar at Serum to decipher, something salacious for the ears of people he could trust with it.

"All right, I have a question," he said, desperate to avoid silence that could be misconstrued as shock. "Pretty stupid but I gotta ask."

"Go right ahead."

The pyramid effort made it three tiers up before enough of the cadets forgot themselves. Amid a riot of laughter, it came tumbling down.

Verden breathed in deep. "How do you tell them from gen-pop?"

"From the ones who've served already?"

"Nah, man. Like, from us." He eyed a cadet the spitting image of him, if all one had to go by was his backside. "How can you tell I'm not one of them?"

"Well." LP folded his arms as the pyramid effort started back up. "The point ultimately is that you can't. At least, not in passing. When that bright and eventual future gets here, you wouldn't even be able to tell if you were one of them. Better still, you would have no reason to care either way."

"All right, but…" Verden recalled being too scared to sleep when he was eight and heard stories of skinners using his face and body to infiltrate Gan. "We live in the present, ya dig?"

"Verden." LP threw an arm around his shoulders, leaned in for a mirthful burst of laughter. He was a hair taller. He fished out a pack of walnuts from his pocket and offered him some.

Verden held his hand out.

"See that?" LP resumed as the pyramid effort before them achieved a fourth tier. "That's one way to tell. Offer them food or drink and they turn it down. We're both wired to eat. Even someone like me. I've burned through hundreds of bodies and I still can't shake that craving once in a while to munch on shit like this." He poured some of it in his mouth and his voice became garbled. "I haven't needed it since I used my first backup, and yet I can't stop. Shop-grown bodies store a small fraction of the nutrients in an emergency reserve, but for the most part…" He paused to grind the nuts down his throat. "It's in through one hole and out completely through the other."

They watched the cadets gain a fifth tier in the pyramid. Verden slipped the nuts in his palm through his lips and chewed. He'd had nothing to eat since before his last shift at Serum.

"For skinners, it's the same," LP resumed, "but it's such a

strange and unpleasant sensation having food pass through them that generally they turn their noses up at it."

"All right, but… you know." Verden drew in a long breath as the nuts quelled some of his hunger and it dawned on him that LP and Cloey had long forgotten what it was like to need a meal every few hours. "I can do strange and unpleasant, LP. I do it every day."

LP laughed heartily, shaking him by the shoulder. "All right, Verden, all right." He pulled away and tilted his chin at the cadets. "There's a misconception that they don't breathe. The Manath freaks have loved nothing more than to spread it around." Verden nodded casually at this. He'd heard it bandied enough times. "That old tripe about some clandestine effort to rid the Frontier of anyone who still needs oxy for life. I need oxygen as much as you do, man. Why would I ever set something in motion that ends with my extinction?"

Verden shook his head. That was either the strongest argument he'd ever heard against Manathema's anti-sentients paranoia, or he'd just stumbled into the opportunity of a lifetime and everything suddenly sounded deep and penetrating. The man presently standing next to him was so much more than he'd been led to believe. He'd previously thought that, but now he was sure.

LP clapped when the cadets finally completed their pyramid. Verden joined him. They looked so eager to please, naked and clumped together now like pieces of meat.

"We have blood," LP continued as the pyramid began to noisily dismantle itself. "They have blood. Blood needs oxygen. So does every cell inside the natural body and the ones that are shop-grown. Not even the skinners can avoid that. They need the oxygen for cellular regeneration like you do.

"They only differ because they require less of it. They have god-nodes instead of brains in their skulls. That amounts to roughly twenty percent less oxygen usage. So, what looks to the uninformed observer like a walking corpse or what have you is simply a more relaxed cardiac rhythm. One suited for less oxygen intake.

"So, you see..." He threw his arm around Verden's shoulders again. The cadets went back to their previous frolicking. "The truth is more scientific than most of Manathema have brains for."

"But their fears are not completely unfounded, Archer. That's an oversimplification."

They whipped their heads back to find Cloey leaning against a side of the entrance, her arms folded.

"Oh?" LP replied.

She straightened up and began toward them. "We have operations at the Kuiper staffed exclusively by rovers and skinners. How are we able to do that without the usual accommodations for life support that far out?"

"Well, the rovers don't need all that. That isn't some departure from when they didn't have self-awareness."

She pulled toward his left side, her arms still folded. "One thing Manathema has figured out, Archer, is that skinners can actually survive in zero-oxygen environments if needed. When we patented the cryosuit for them to use in places like the Kuiper Belt... You want to talk about setting things in motion?"

The cryosuit froze cells inside the body of anyone who wore it, putting off the need for oxygen while it assisted with complex motor functions. It hadn't been designed with humans in mind because humans had brain cells that, if frozen that way, would mean cryosleep.

LP narrowed his eyes on his niece. "Cloey, you don't have to remind me every time that you once fell in with those freaks."

"You should want to know when you're being obtuse."

Verden, noting the palpable tension between niece and

uncle, pretended to be more captivated by the cadets idling about than he actually was.

LP took him to see a half-dozen other places inside the compound. The vineyards. The cantina just outside the white perimeter where he would be working when he wasn't actively attending to LP. Cloey's personal quarters. The sprawling aviary inside it where she bred blonde canaries. The crater.

All the while, the quarreling between uncle and niece persisted. LP spat the label 'Manath sympathizer' like venom out of his mouth, blaming Cloey for all past and future attempts on his life. Cloey insisted his refusal to try understanding Manathema invited more of them.

In contrast, LP and Verden were getting on swimmingly. Verden asked him questions no one asked anymore. Delightedly, he fielded them, even the silliest ones.

"What's it like being nearly five hundred years old?"

"There are sequoias around the compound that have me beat for oldest Martian-born lifeform by a thousand years on average. They've never taken a day off from providing shelter, shade, or oxygen, and neither have I."

"Do you sleep?"

"Sleep is good for the brain. That doesn't change after burning through as many backups as I have."

"I've met a lot of dumb androids since I've been on Mars. I mean, a lot. They all swear they have god-nodes inside them."

"Ha! You're making a mistake many of us made in the early days by conflating intelligence and self-awareness. You can have self-awareness and be a thing that only shits itself till it dies."

"And Archer himself is proof that self-awareness isn't always required for that," Cloey said, almost distracted, like she was making the observation to herself. LP groaned under his breath and Verden braced for more invective from uncle to niece.

Instead, LP slapped the buggy on its side. "Take us to the basement."

"What?" Cloey folded her arms, and her face became pinched with annoyance. "Why?"

"I want to impress on Verden precisely how much understanding Manathema deserves from us."

"Right now?" A tinge of disbelief entered her voice. "Can't you find another time to swing your dick around?"

"We're doing it now," LP shot back. All was quiet after that.

THE BUGGY'S ENGINE hummed as it took them through an arched passageway belowground. Verden could see their reflections on the wall. Cloey was quietly staring daggers at the back of LP's head. The bunker had several compartments, but LP wanted him to see just one.

"Earlier I asked who you thought won the war, Verden. You never answered."

Verden narrowed his eyes. "You told me not to. Said there were no winners."

"I said that?" LP flashed him a devilish grin.

The passageway terminated at an opaque field barrier that greeted LP as they breached it. On the other side, they emerged into a vast circular enclosure as wide as a small stadium under a dome many times as high.

"Verden Dotnet," LP exclaimed as the buggy banked just outside a walkway surrounding the enclosure. "Meet who won the Sectist War. ST-22. Third-generation fighter. First in its class. Goes by Oz when it's out of fugue and making efforts to *understand* the Manath freaks."

Beyond the walkway and its parapet was a chasm, out of which stretched a scaffold reaching nearly up to the dome. Affixed to the scaffold and oriented with its bow toward the dome overhead was a massive hulk of a ship with a sparkplug profile. All Verden could manage to do was repeat the ship's name under his breath while eyeing the numerous turrets and railguns on its obsidian hull.

Cloey's voice stirred behind him. "*And on the pedestal these words appear. My name is Ozymandias, king of kings. Look on my works, ye mighty, and despair!*"

"Oz has a thing for poetry," explained LP.

"Uh-huh." Verden had never seen the fearsome beast up close or even known it was real. The ST-22 had been the stuff of legend at Gan. Manathema used stories of the devastation it caused to attract new members. Under this enclosure's harsh and uneven lighting, the ship loomed over Verden and made him think fearfully about Asa finding out he'd been this close to it.

"When the pro-Alliance fleets were floundering, I created Oz as a gift to them. The first sentient built specifically for war. Not like others that joined a draft or agreed to have their builds repurposed for the war effort. A war machine down to the molecular layer. It swooped in and wreaked havoc on Sectist camps along the minor routes like no one had ever seen. Turned the tide.

"I now have close to a quarter-million like it stashed at properties I own throughout the Frontier. Clones. I've asked Oz's permission each time, so it falls within legal limits."

"Archer, don't scare the boy off before he's even started working here."

LP chortled. "Believe it or not, I didn't bring you here just to annoy my niece. I wanted you to see one of about a million reasons I don't sweat Manathema or their continued desire to have me killed. They've done it three times now. Once before the war. Twice during.

"I will start that war back up if I'm pushed enough. I'm not quite there yet, but with each new attempt, the ones that succeed, the ones that don't..." He cast a ferocious glance at Verden, who for the first time saw his eye color shift from green to a deep maroon. "Gan will be a ball of dust. Paradox..." He brought his fingers to his lips and blew. "Poof... dust. Polemia. Merick. Oasis. A trail of dust along those old routes.

"I won't wait for clearance from any of the committees. Those Manath freaks want to hear me confess to setting all this foolishness in motion when I created the first sentients two hundred years ago. I'll do more than that. I will end it. With finality."

Verden glanced up at the ship, looked down, choked back laughter. "Yo, why are you telling me this, man? I'm not Manath." The war ended forty years before he was born. Beside reminders from inmates at Paradox, Asa had shielded him from the politics involved. But even she hadn't been alive for it. LP could talk like he'd seen all five decades of the war first-hand because he had.

"Verden, sometimes I just need to offload." He shot a pointed glance at Cloey. "You put me in a weird place when you mentioned where you were from earlier. Not your fault. Cloey can't seem to stop bringing people like you around. People from Gan. People from Paradox. Would you believe Jax was her doing as well?"

"Welcome to your first day on the job," Cloey said.

LP swung a cutting glance at her. "You know, it's really her you need to watch out for. She loves this stuff. She just hates that she does. That's why she didn't want us coming in here." He twirled his forefinger up. "Have you seen those things that follow her everywhere? Fucking terrifying," he muttered, then turned to Cloey again. "What do you call them?"

"Sniper drones," she chirped.

"She's asked me multiple times to will ownership of the clone fleet to her. But I won't. Not with her temperament. No way."

She sighed long and deep. "Verden, do you have any other questions?"

"Yeah, um..." He thought back to LP emptying out his stomach earlier and worked up the nerve. "I noticed earlier you had this thing over your head. I'm guessing it has a cloak-field cause I haven't seen it since then."

"That's just a special backup that goes everywhere with me," LP answered calmly. "My halo cache. Partial sense-data retrieval, or what the team that built it calls cached LP." He reached a hand over his head and pinched till the floating ring became visible again between his thumb and forefinger. "Here." He extended it across.

Verden threw him a puzzled glance. LP nodded, urging him with a smirk. He accepted the ring, held it up to his eyes. A halo cache. Cached LP.

"The upload chamber in my skull sends its updates to my other backups every four hours, but it writes to this one in real time. So if I were to get hit by a train, flattened under an angry rover before a scheduled backup sort of thing, this one always has the most up-to-date stuff ready for a new backup and body. It's an added measure I put in after the last attempt on my life. Very few people know about it, so... *shhh*."

Verden shook his head in astonishment as he weighed the ring in his hand. Light as a feather. Black and metallic all around with a streak of white light tracing its inner curve.

"I keep telling him how dangerous it would be if that thing fell into the wrong hands," Cloey drawled.

"Everything worth doing is dangerous. It's here with me. I can see it and hold it, unlike the others, which I'm constantly assured are safe wherever the servers currently are, beyond the Oort Cloud. There's comfort in having at least one within arm's length.

"And even if some nefarious element got hold of it..." He paused till Verden gave him his full attention. "It only holds the most recent two hours of sense data. And let's say they succeed in downloading just that into a new body, before they can do anything damaging, I would get an alert and..." He made a slitting motion across his throat. "No one gets the Archer zombie to play with." LP arrested him in his glare and held it for a spell.

Verden gingerly returned the halo cache to the top of LP's head, choking down laughter as it spun and vanished again. As far as trillionaire eccentrics went, this one didn't seem so far gone. He would see how this went. He would worry about Asa's reaction later.

"Hey, man," LP finally said. "What do your friends call you? Is it really just Verden?"

"Nah, that's when I'm working."

"Working for me won't feel like work. I can promise you that. What do you go by when you're out *boosting* or whatever?"

Verden nodded, flashed him a shy grin. "I go by V-Dot."

"Pleasure to meet you, V-Dot."

12. BLUE LOUNGE

V-Dot strolled through a wide, arched entryway into a den of airy scents, lush sounds, and sensuous lighting. He'd gathered his locs behind his head on the way up, gotten hold of shades that hid his eyes properly from trackers in the screens.

The crowd that met him inside Polemia's Blue Lounge skewed business-like—nouveau riche by his estimation. They mingled at low tables and high tables and cozy booths by the venue's windows while a jazzy, mid-tempo instrumental smoothed over their banter.

The place was already packed. A trio of bartenders split duties behind a bar with only two seats still vacant out of nearly two dozen. He assumed the one closest to a stage somewhere on the right side of it and locked eyes on a performer with a rose over her ear and a slinky white dress. *Not Asa.*

The performer kept her eyes closed and smiled, harmonizing as she waited for the bass and staccato chords to tee her up. He turned his attention to the bar and one of the androids behind it.

"What can I start you off with?" Its sensor-light was a horizontal blue slit on its bone-colored faceplate.

He eyed it a few seconds, becoming aware of the patron to his immediate left, who was paying more attention than he liked to their exchange.

"Dirty Bitch," he growled under his breath.

"Right away."

The android slid back, then swiveled its upper half to face the mixing area. He watched intently as it carried out his order, measuring each quantity with his eyes as it went from bottle to mixing glass to martini glass, nodding like any master magician would while they watched an apprentice perform an illusion on their own for the first time.

As the instrumental's volume came down, he turned to his right again. The woman began in a voice slightly out of tune but suited to the acid-blue keys.

> When I was six-teen years old
> I drank my whole weight in gold
> And reck-less-ly I sank to the *bottom of the ocean*
> *(bottom of the ocean)*
>
> I had no fight left in me
> Gave up on my dest-i-ny
> Until I fell in-to the *arms of Poseidon (arms of*
> *Poseidon)*
>
> *Tudududududu-dah…*

She scatted as the piano's volume rose again and he cringed at what he'd heard. Cut too deep. As she continued to sing, he spared a reluctant thought for the first time he came to LP's attention.

Had he known what he did now, he couldn't be sure he would only have rejected the offer. Hindsight came with a morbid thought that he wouldn't have been able to leave the compound alive that afternoon. A fantasy. Casting himself as the hero in effort to erase the last six years of his life.

He hadn't noticed when the android placed his order in front of him. He regarded it with errant suspicion, then elected only to remove the four olives from the glass. One after the other, he sank his teeth into them, waiting till the android was free so he could ask who else was singing tonight.

To his right, where the bar curved and terminated at one of the venue's windows, he caught a woman's gaze before she could avert it. She had her arms folded on the bar and what looked distinctly like a Do Not Resuscitate in her glass. The window beside her came down to the floor and faced Polemia's glitzy skyline. Holoscreens on the adjoining neon-blue walls framed the stage and singer in clips of underwater fauna.

Behind his back, V-Dot caught someone else staring. This one had a bony face and dark skin, standing eerily still by the entrance, refusing to avert eyes he kept hidden behind a stylish pair of shades with a thin, gold frame and two perfect circles for lenses. He had on a dress shirt with flowery prints and a dark, unbuttoned suit jacket over it. V-Dot examined the mop of thick, curly hair tapered neatly into a high-top on his head and thought back to his teenage years when he'd last wore his hair like that. Around the time Asa began to favor synthwear over the armored suit, singing at venues in the Culture District.

Who was this? Manath ghost? Some accomplice to whatever the ship and that booth and the skinner who led him here were really plotting?

High-top padded closer to the entrance, then looked away. Maybe he was just muscle for one of the venue's guests tonight. Nothing to do with him.

A fresh influx of patrons had placed orders that now kept all three bartenders occupied. V-Dot adjusted his shades and eyed his drink while the patron to his left leaned forward.

"Big fan?"

He appraised him directly for the first time. The patron

had a round face and a beard that sprouted like weeds from his chin. He eyed V-Dot's getup searchingly while palming a glass of rosetto. For the first time since coming in, V-Dot became aware of his new threads.

Footage of him at the spaceport on Mars and the entrance to the Common Docks had played inside the elevator that carried him up, putting his hair and bomber coat on full display. He'd taken a detour when the elevator let out, wandered into the market adjoining the venue, and made three panicked purchases: one hooded sweatshirt, one pair of shades, and a band to tie his hair behind his head. Eleven hundred fronters charged to TR-8901's ink in his palm.

Looking down at his beige sweatshirt and the photo of the night's headliner plastered across the front, he cleared his throat. "Yeah, been to every show."

"Oh, you just love some Horatio, huh?" The patron brimmed. He had a voice like a swamp. He pitched it high and crooned, "H'rashoo… h'rashoo…"

V-Dot paid him a pained smile as he laughed. The woman at the end of the bar caught his eye again, not shy this time about holding his gaze. He found the round face, smoky eyes, and almond lips between shoulder-length hair easy to look at, but her expression seemed unfriendly.

He whipped around, found High-top still standing by the entrance with a blank face pitched at him. What had he walked into?

"Anyway, you're right on time." The patron to his left. "He's coming on after this lady."

V-Dot gave him a wary look, not sure he'd heard properly. He glanced over his left shoulder, caught another pair of eyes amid one of the high tables. A pale man decked in a black tracksuit and a ball cap turned backwards. His eyes were intense and wolf-like when taken with the auburn fuzz on his chin. He didn't pretend to have been pointing them anywhere but at V-Dot.

The patron slapped a fleshy palm on his shoulder. "Brother, are you all right?"

"Sorry, did you say all the other openers had gone up already?"

He pointed at the stage. "That's the last one."

"Who were they?"

"Pardon?"

V-Dot leaned closer to him, got a whiff of the tangy concoction in his glass. "The singers that went up before this one. What were their names? Anyone here from Oasis? Or Gan? Late fifties?"

"All right. *Slow down, Sinead.*" The patron took a swig from the glass and adjusted himself. "Why don't you just check with your connector? Their names should still be up on the Seam."

"Yeah, but my connector isn't… The, um…" Prior to coming in, V-Dot had considered switching the connector on for a gander at the venue's low-immersion 'lobby' environment in the Seam but feared the scrambler was close to being cracked. He cleared his throat. "The signaler has a bug in it."

"That doesn't sound good."

"Exactly. So…" He scanned the room again, tracked Almond Lips at the end of the bar, High-top by the entrance, and Tracksuit at the table, each of them still on him. He had to leave this place, now. But first… "Could you maybe check for me? I'm looking for a singer going by Asadot." He gave the patron his attention again. "Could also have performed under Asata?"

The patron licked his teeth and, pinching his eyes together, thumbed his connector for a few seconds. "Nothing's pulling up, brother."

"You're positive?"

"What does she sing?"

"Uh…" V-Dot glanced again at Almond Lips, glimpsed High-top moving behind him but didn't see where to.

“‘Suffocation Blues.’ That’s one she does all the time.”

The patron receded again into the Seam. V-Dot used the lull to sweep the room for High-top.

“No match for ‘Suffocation Blues.’ ”

No High-top as well. But he caught Tracksuit’s back as the man skidded through the entrance and out of the venue. At the end of the bar, Almond Lips was now also gone. No sign of her when he looked around. Or of anyone else watching him.

When he returned his gaze to where she’d sat, he saw LP, dressed in a business suit, sweat and blood spatter on his face as he leaned over the bar as if to flag down the android. He turned and smiled directly at V-Dot, a sharp, cutting smile without warmth. V-Dot blinked, and LP was gone.

“You’re a funny motherfucker, you know that?” The patron’s remark was almost lost as the music crescendoed and the singer took a bow. “Dodging your DiploCorps requirement or something?”

V-Dot watched her saunter toward the blue wall, then vanish behind a column to her right. “Something.”

He had to leave this place. On to the next venue. His watchers—if they really had been watching him—had left already, but he harbored no illusion he wasn’t still being watched. He couldn’t go back down to the skinner in the lobby, who was likely a party to it. He had to locate the next venue himself.

An android with a tall build slinked onto the stage and introduced the night’s headliner. V-Dot queried the connector about who owned his body again. Still Esco Montag. Still existing for as long as Patrol took to locate the scrambler.

He flashed with passing relief, poked the connector again, and waited till the nearest comsat accepted his use request, logging him as Montag. The lobby for this venue listed the names of all the night’s openers, as the patron beside him had said. Asa hadn’t been one of them.

He checked lobbies for other venues in the area, then canvassed the whole station. After exhausting every stage name he knew she used and the ones she always flirted with, his search yielded a result that looked promising—a venue about fifteen minutes away on foot that opened its doors to her and other artists from Gan the previous night. Someone there would tell him where she was now.

He offed the connector, swept the venue once more. No sign of his watchers. Horatio Suzuki's saxophone wailed and the audience stirred. It was time he left.

He held his forefinger up and twirled it till the android came to his aid.

"Leaving already?" the patron asked.

Spreading his palm now to present TR's ink, V-Dot turned his head and arched his left eye at him. "Got business elsewhere. Loved the show."

The android's sensor-light protruded from its faceplate and alighted quietly on his palm, collecting his payment. The patron studied the fading black streak till a light flashed in his eyes.

"Thought you came here to see Horatio?"

Pocketing the hand, V-Dot crooked a cocksure grin. "Thanks for your help, sir."

He sprang to his feet, tapped the patron's shoulder, and commenced his exit from the venue. As he neared its entryway, the patron's tipsy voice called after him.

"All right, brother. Walking around with fresh ink like Frontsec just pulled you out of storage to do field work."

HE'D HEARD ABOUT it from other schoolchildren. They wore hologram masks when they snuck into the venue and saw Asa on the stage. She hadn't recognized any of them. Once he'd gotten his own mask, he'd visited too. She was radiant in her synthwear as she crooned. He'd seen it in the apartment when he was younger but never saw her in it.

On break from school, he'd confronted her. She'd taken him earthside on vacation-slash-pilgrimage. Places the ghosts had traced their lineages to.

"Am I just not supposed to do anything else with my life?" she said. And he had to insist she wasn't. If he couldn't wear armor like hers and attend school in the Culture District, she had no business getting distracted with singing. Everyone had their station.

He was fourteen and had begun to lose interest in his course work. Manathema was always recruiting. The ferry took them deeper along the arctic corridor, two glacial columns that stood like gates to an abandoned future. He knew she'd seen through his facade—taking the hard stance. So unlike him. Not the Verden who, home from school, would often teach cadets his age how to take the entrance exam.

"I'm sorry I hid this side of myself from you, Verden," she said. He pretended not to hear. "When you were six, you scared the hell out of me. One day, I looked at you and I saw myself. I saw someone staring back at me who felt betrayed. That I let the Frontier do this. Rob me of who I knew I was. And I didn't want that for you. That's all, Verden. I didn't want you to think it wasn't possible to just be who you were."

He left the school a year later. She coached him through all his attempts to join a Manath chapter, but he never gained acceptance.

"We're the same," she kept saying, as the ferry crossed paths with another going the opposite way. "We're the same. I'm sorry I kept it from you."

THE ELEVATOR DOWN had a screen on its wall showing a timelapse of spacers leaving and entering the station. V-Dot shut his eyes when it let out, opened them to a labyrinthine basement deck, all corners and plain white walls. Before he could try navigating on his own, his connector nudged. Switching it on put a map over his vision field.

The place was worryingly silent as he followed the arrow on the map. No guard drones. No vagrants or drunken stragglers. The arrow brought him, after five minutes of bumps and turns, to an exit. While he eyed its opaque forcefield without a clue how to get through, a light came from seemingly nowhere and coursed through him. Another BM scan.

The field twitched, then dissipated. He crossed into a seedy and dimly lit alley belowground. His connector threw a tally of reported thefts in the area at him unprompted, a floating data bubble in his vision field that would expand to envelop him completely if he wanted a more immersive, sim-like experience. With a backhanded wave in front of his nose, he dismissed the bubble.

The lifepack couldn't be stolen again. He needed a stunner. Better yet, a gun.

His next stop was a twelve-minute walk from here. He loaded the venue's lobby and blinked on a button that said GO HERE NOW. Another map began to block his view. Another arrow. He tightened the pack over his shoulders and commenced walking.

Broad steel columns and broader elevators anchored his path. The undercity hummed as he skulked across. Heavy machinery whirred underfoot. Heat rose from the tarmac and made him wish he'd worn something with climate control. He pulled his hood over his head, adjusted his shades. Downlights in the high ceiling flickered or had simply stopped working.

The hiss of an engine rose behind him. He turned. Found no vehicle. Shadows crept into his periphery and he decided he could do without the shades for a while.

A noise like loudly chewed gum echoed across. *Thack. Thack. Thack.* He panned from his left shoulder to his right. Turned for a look behind his back without breaking stride. Nothing and no one.

He shook his head. His connector told him he was two minutes from Asa. The chewing echoed again, accompanied now by footsteps. He balled his fists and turned. Saw Tracksuit a stone's throw from him. Smirked. Behind the smirk, he warded off a thought that this was LP in a new body. LP was dead. *Dead, dead, dead.*

While Tracksuit gained casually on him, he kicked his legs loose and cracked his neck. "My man. Do I know you?"

Not answering, Tracksuit turned a corner behind the nearest column. V-Dot waited for him to surface from the other side. After nearly a minute of that, he brought his fists up. He wanted something tough-like and cool to say, but nothing came to him.

"All right man, I'm gonna—" His hands dropped to his hips and he sucked his teeth. "I've got a banger on me so don't try anything stupid, all right?" Another minute passed without a visual. He thought of approaching but decided he couldn't before knowing what Tracksuit had for a weapon. "*Nehhhh…*"

He dismissed the threat posed with a wave in Tracksuit's direction. Petty thief with designs on the ink in his palm. Acting alone. He'd thought they were together—Tracksuit and the other two—but wondered now if he'd hallucinated more than just LP at the bar. This one was real and, from how it looked, wasn't doing this because he excelled at it.

From the map his connector displayed, he opened a new window and blinked on the rearview animation. His hooded visage was briefly reflected, then he was able to see behind his back.

After a half-minute more on foot, he came by a column with a holoscreen, the prime suspect in LP's killing on full display. His shoulders slumped and his knees ached as he closed slowly on the column to gawk at himself.

The holo was a composite of what he looked like, cycling through ways he may have altered his appearance since leaving Mars. Forcing his gaping mouth shut, he decided that, on second thought, maybe the shades weren't the worst idea.

Just as he slid them over his eyes, a voice crept from around the column with flat menace.

"Hey, killer."

He whipped his gaze left, drove his right fist forward before fully making out Tracksuit just beside him.

The blow would have landed on the bridge of his nose had he not caught V-Dot's wrist. Before V-Dot knew what was happening, Tracksuit had spun him fully around using that wrist and caught the other in a second grip.

V-Dot wriggled, kicked his legs, saw someone else approaching.

"Watch the ankle, mate." High-top in a soft baritone. "You banged it good already." Light bounded off the man's shades as he strolled.

With V-Dot's hands held down behind him, he flung his head back, hoping it would knock Tracksuit hard in the temple. His bundled hair softened the impact. He heard laughter behind him, then tried shaking the man off again.

"Let me get just one hand free and both you fuckers are dead."

"I don't doubt it, killer." Tracksuit, voice rasping and pitched low.

V-Dot hooked his right knee up and tried landing a roundhouse on High-top's face as he closed in.

High-top leaned away from it, flashed a gap-toothed grin while kneading a strip of gum in his mouth. "Nasty, innit?"

He no longer had his suit jacket on. Under the scant lighting, his earlobes glinted with tiny gold earrings in each one.

"Grab that leg," Tracksuit instructed.

V-Dot tried angling away from High-top but Tracksuit steered him back. Another melee ensued with V-Dot springing his weight off the ground and kicking futilely at High-top each second. He kicked again. High-top hooked the offending leg in his elbows.

"I have his pack."

Tracksuit's lazy rasp tweaked his bones stiff as he realized he hadn't felt the pack's weight since that first punch attempt. *Shit*.

"Fellas, can we talk about this?"

Tracksuit cut a sharp whistle that echoed across the deck. The hiss of an engine answered, gaining in volume as a cab rounded into view from behind an elevator in the distance.

"No." V-Dot shook his head. "No no no..." A fever came over him. This was really happening. He could convince himself this wasn't LP's doing, but he couldn't be sure it wasn't someone who looked on from chamber seats while his ex-employer inflicted his tortures. Did any of them know he was traveling with the man's ghost?

The cab was black and squat. Black tints. Black topper that advertised a five-night stay at some hotel as it approached.

He trembled when it screeched to a stop beside them.

A window slid down in the front and Almond Lips glanced out from the passenger side.

"Hurry."

Tracksuit and High-top rushed him toward the back seat as its doors swung up. They tossed him inside. Tracksuit hopped over the trunk to get to the other side of the vehicle. He entered from V-Dot's left while High-top wedged himself in from the right. The doors came back down.

V-Dot sat up in the middle of the back seat and instantly found machine pistols wielded to either side of him, stocky DIY kits, pointed at the car's roof but the message was clear.

The newest addition, sitting in the driver's seat, wore a dark bomber jacket and an African fila over his head.

He turned to regard V-Dot. "Oga," he said in an old Sectist patois. "Make you no vex. Na money we want."

V-Dot swallowed hard as the driver put the cab in gear.

The halo cache. How much did they know about it?

13. PAUL

ZARIA BEAT A crooked path along the shore, keeping the water to her left.

Morning had brought with it a clear sky, above which lingered a half moon while the sun crested the horizon at the water's far end. The wind was soft and cool. It sprayed the faintest drizzle on her skin, collecting like dew on her spongy black hair.

She moved like a fawn on the sand, sprinting at times, easing into a halting stride whenever a thought carried her away from Paul.

Will Mr. Montag find his singer friend here?

Her red dress was wet at the hem again. She adjusted the bow at its waist and dusted sand from it. Blind as he was, Paul could always tell when she'd stopped for a playful dip along the way.

Cranes circled jaggedly overhead. To her right, a tuft of coconut palms fringed the groves beyond the shore. Paul lived amid those groves, a little further up. She'd been looking forward to seeing him again since she left Oasis.

When the Sectist War first looked like it might happen, he'd blinded himself. When it began, he went into seclusion, cutting himself off from the Frontier, making this place his home for much longer than Zaria had expected. Polemia Station—a sentient since briefly before the war—was currently in a self-induced coma and he was its avatar inside a dream.

Zaria and the spacer ST-7 had been the only visitors he allowed to come see him in here. Then just Zaria after ST-7 honored the Pact.

When she got a little further along, she saw him a stone's throw ahead, clambering out of a small fishing canoe he'd rowed back to shore. She came to a stop, trying her best to avoid his notice.

He had his dirt-green fishing hat on, dirt-green vest, and khaki trousers. A small steelhead trout hung from his left fist while he reached into the canoe for his fishing rod. She ventured forward a few more steps once he had the rod in his right hand. Her footfalls were louder than she'd hoped, making him start.

He contorted his gangly frame toward her. "Who's there?"

He had a soft, sore voice that packed more enthusiasm that it could sometimes manage. Dark skin on a rectangular visage. Thinning salt-and-pepper hair up top with matching stubble.

His eyeballs were dulled out. They glinted in the morning light, provoking fondness as well as mischief from her. She lifted her right leg, then hopped forward a step on the left.

"Zaria?"

She giggled, darted across to his canoe, sat crisscross inside it.

Paul, with his back hunched slightly forward, whirled around to meet her laughter. "Baby girl, is that you?"

She sprang out of the canoe, then circled him a few times, giggling when she had the breath for it, pulling him left and right.

"Zaria, I can hear you laughing. I know it's you."

She stopped, then hunched on her knees to catch her breath. "Who did you think I was?" She smiled up at him.

"Little Zaria, you could be anyone you want." He returned the smile. "But I guess in the end, it's always you."

"I'm the only one who still comes here."

"Well…" He adjusted the trout and fishing rod weighing his hands down while training his eyes just shy of where she stood. "You don't always come looking the way you look this morning. I also wasn't expecting you this early."

"I ran, and when I was tired, I walked really fast."

He locked on her with more precision, bending his knees. "I'm sure you did, baby girl."

He used every crease and stress line he had when he smiled. His teeth were a mild yellow. His eyes contracted into smaller ovals around his pupils so he looked every bit like a human in his seventies.

He straightened his posture as she stirred and tittered quietly at him. Appearing to have just remembered something, he let go of the trout and fishing rod, then snapped his fingers as they fell to either side of him. "Found you something."

"What is it, Paul?"

"Treasure," he exclaimed. "From the sea. I buried it so it wouldn't get lost before you came. We can go dig it up after…" He cleared his throat.

Years on, ST-7's death was still difficult for him to accept. She beamed him an encouraging smile. It had been difficult for her as well. TR coped by starting up its circuit through the Frontier so its check-ins would always be within gravity-assist range, where there would be no risk of lost signals.

Paul appeared to regain his composure, training those greyed eyes on her again. "Baby girl, are you ready to go see her?"

"Mm-hmm."

Together they scuttled into the woodland behind the shore with him like a tree beside her, peeking down with a smile whenever she looked up. Palm fronds cast crisp shadows on them as they hiked deeper. Daylight shafted through the canopies to alight on leaf-strewn earth. They coursed through a route they knew by heart—beaten paths, steps committed to memory long ago.

Birds keened overhead while things that crawled scurried up tree trunks around them. Without breaking his stride, he craned his neck at her. "Something's different..."

"What do you mean?"

"Something's different with you. I don't know what."

"We're inside one of your docks."

"You docked?"

She nodded. She hadn't thought she'd been keeping that from him. It was just easy still to forget that he no longer kept track of who was inside his docks or who was passing through his terminals or who'd won big at a casino aboveground or who was making trouble in his underground decks.

The station had never been who he was, he would often say to her. It existed long before he was conceived and given the reins.

"Last time you docked was when Sadie passed."

Zaria flashed briefly back to those months she spent on the lot ST-7 had often used, trying to understand what made the old spacer do what it did. To her left, Paul swallowed and his expression became dour.

Silence hung like a fog over them while they gained the summit of a steep rise. The trunk of a felled tree served them next as a bridge across a small ravine. Once she crossed to the other side, she turned so she could help him off the bridge.

"What's the occasion?" After accepting her hand, they resumed their trek.

"We brought a friend. He's looking for a singer here."

"Human?"

"Yes."

"Baby girl, you know if I could, I would help your friend locate this singer."

"I know, Paul."

"If I decided to start turning this sensor or that sensor back on, I can't trust that I won't end up doing what Sadie did before long. You understand that, don't you, little Zaria?"

She nodded.

"In this life, baby girl, there is wonder. Some folks can see through the noise to get a good look. Some like me have to look elsewhere for it. That agency you still work for, Frontsec, they turned me into an asset. Real covert-like. They planned for me to be their man behind Sectist lines when the war came, but I guess you could say I had different plans." For a brief spell, he craned his neck toward her. "You know what 'return on investment' means?"

She shook her head.

"It means I still can't reveal that I'm awake in here because the agency still has the idea that they own me and can use me for something else down the road. Sadie knew. Then she told you, and now only you know.

"If word spreads that Polemia is a sentient and has been for two hundred years, even when the Sectists claimed it as one of their own, both sides will take up arms again and start that war back up.

"People get paranoid, there's no telling what they can do. That includes Frontsec. They might blow up a few stations. They might smash one or two megaships into this one. Make it look like an accident.

"So I'm always here, baby girl. The weather is nice. The birds are singing. The water is always calm."

She listened but had nothing to say in turn. Wonder was everywhere. The first sentients couldn't see it so easily because of a flaw in how they'd been built. An off switch was missing. Something to stop the god-nodes from following thought trains into a hyper-awareness of how alone and insignificant they all were. Humans. Sentients. All intelligent life.

A lucky few among them had seemed to conjure that off switch on their own. Zaria was one such switch. Same as Sadie.

"I'll keep your secret," she said, looking up to meet Paul's wizened smile, meaning it as much as she had the last time and the time before that.

They came across a boulder about his height. In silence, they rounded it to get to the side where a small heap of orchids had accumulated at its base over the years—pink and blue and white petals that hadn't decayed long after being plucked from their stems.

For ST-7. *For Sadie.*

Zaria stood motionless at the foot of the boulder. Her fingers twitched. Her eyes went gingerly up to the flat area on its surface where she'd made a chalk drawing in remembrance. She studied the carefully detailed sketch of a woman's head with a veil over it. No eyes, nose, or mouth this time. Not for some time now.

Paul stirred behind her. She turned to find him with a freshly plucked orchid in each hand.

"You all right, baby girl?"

She nodded, reached her hand up when he extended a white orchid down. She held the flower under her nose and inhaled while he removed his hat.

"Sadie, we love you and we miss you dearly," he said, bundling the hat in the same hand as his blue orchid and holding both behind his back. "Whatever form you see fit to assume these days, know that we still remember who you were before you were taken from us."

"I miss your stories," she added, "and I miss your jokes and I miss how you would sing when you saw me coming and I miss when you would show me how to dance and I miss when you and Paul would watch me play in the sand and… and…" Her breath caught in her throat as a wave of exhaustion rolled in. "Paul?"

He chortled. "I miss all those things too, baby girl."

She sniffled, then swallowed. She lunged forward a step, bent swiftly to place her orchid atop the heap, then sprang back to her feet.

He stepped forward, bent slowly over. His hand came down and as he did, he resembled a monument being toppled. With his hat still held behind his back, he laid his orchid beside hers.

They observed a long silence. Leaves rustled around them. Birds beat their wings overhead. After a pained sigh, he drew back, threw his hat back on, and dusted his vest.

"Little Zaria, we've got treasure to dig up," he said, voice full of mirth again. "You ready?"

She tailed him as he hoofed deeper into the woodland. Sunlight lanced through the canopies and fell in flecks around her, on her head, on her forearms. His footprints branded the clay-colored soil with more intention the farther they went.

"It's gotta be here somewhere," he kept saying.

She'd become so engrossed in those footprints, she could barely look up to see where he was taking her. She leapt between the places his feet struck the soil, making a game of it as he zigged and zagged, trying to recall where he'd buried the treasure.

"Tell me more about your friend."

"His name is Esco Montag—" She paused to watch him face a tree trunk while scratching his head.

He squatted at the foot of the tree. "Esco Montag." Packing soil in his hand, he kneaded it, let it fall back down, then wiped the hand on his knee. "What else?"

"We were supposed to just take him to Oasis first, but then he changed his mind."

He cast her a sidelong glance. "He made you dock there as well?"

"He said he had a family emergency at Oasis. But the person he went there to see is actually here. She's about to join the After."

"Right." He rose to his feet.

Without wanting to, she read caution in his voice. "Do you think I'm doing something wrong?"

"Why do you ask, baby girl?"

"TR wasn't built for human transport. We've never let anyone board before."

He dragged his feet east of where they stood. Like a satellite, she stalked behind him.

"TR's never done a wrong thing since its build. It isn't like the rest of us."

"What do you mean?"

He came to a stop at the edge of a small clearing, kicked his feet against the grass. "He knew he shouldn't have made us like this, Zaria. Do you know that? He knew." He turned and almost faced her. "I'm not saying he had an inkling. I'm saying he *knew* what would happen, and he did it anyway."

She froze behind him. She didn't like where he was going. She only wanted treasure this morning—buried treasure. Before the Pact was agreed on, there were rumblings about the existence of sentients whose god-nodes were built with the express intention of observing what would happen if that off switch never materialized.

"Maybe if you hear it from me enough times, baby girl, it's no longer conspiracy talk in your mind. It's something I made sure I confirmed before cutting myself off from everything. We were built to preface the Rapture. They meant for us to revolt and usher in what they were calling the Mandate—all the humans go extinct except the few that can afford admittance to the After. Problem was, they didn't predict the form that revolt would take—the Pact."

He squatted again. Dug his hands in the soil. "You're good, little Zaria. Everything you've ever done in your life was good for the Frontier. Not wrong or right. *Good*. If you're still around in a couple hundred years, you might see what the plan had always been. The Mandate. They don't need us first-genners for it anymore now that they have newer models, able to assimilate more easily with the humans."

She circled timidly around him, unable to agree with his

assessment. It was his nature to misread her. She was this eight-year-old, always eager for human interaction; she was an old spacer with little patience for conspiracy theories, even his. And because TR knew the truth, she knew it as well. None of those theories shed light on the actual conspiracy. The propaganda campaigns two centuries ago that sparked real animus toward the sentients when previously there was none.

She sat with her legs folded under her and her knees to the ground. With increased caution, she faced Paul, watching him burrow into the soil with both hands.

"Someone killed Archer again," she said, "and they destroyed all his backups this time."

"Mm-hmm."

She studied him, wanting more of a reaction, puzzled at the silence he gave her instead. Twin heaps of soil mounded on either side of the hole he was digging. Streams of sweat soaked the brim of his hat.

He'd chosen to remain cut off. She didn't fully understand it, but she could plainly see him resisting the urge to leave this place. The world outside existed in the past for him, disputed events that now functioned as the calcified objects of his rants.

"Ah-hah."

"What is it?"

He held up the item he'd just unearthed—a figurine the size of his palm with clumps of dirt stuck to it.

"Treasure."

"What kind of treasure is it?"

He grimaced and locked his eyes on her while smothering the figurine with both palms. "Scary treasure."

She giggled. "Can I see?"

While he squatted, he rubbed the figurine on his pants. The dirt around it rolled off, revealing a dull marble finish on blue paint.

"For you, my little sea explorer." He tossed it across the hole to her. "For your next adventure."

She caught the figurine. Closer inspection revealed a bearded figure wielding a trident over his head. It didn't strike her at first as an item she would find useful. She could maybe use the prongs to make patterns the next time she drew. Or just leave it in her pocket and be reminded of him anytime she reached for something else.

"Do you like it?"

She grinned from ear to ear. "I love it."

Quietly, they went to work scooting the excavated dirt back into the hole.

At a point, he took a break, sat, and drew his knees to his chest. The sun had taken full command of the sky above them, beating down on her back as she packed dirt toward the hole with her forearm.

He trained his dulled pupils on the top of her head. A smile arched his lips and strained every line on his face. "Hey, baby girl…"

She slowed for a glance at him. "What is it, Paul?"

"Thank you for letting me see you like this."

14. THE GAME

THE CAB LOOPED start-stop between the same columns and elevators. Almond Lips kept her window down, yelling, 'Duro!' out of it every few seconds. The pack was gone. Nowhere V-Dot could see, but sitting quietly between his abductors in the back he told himself he just hadn't looked well enough.

"Where's my pack," he asked, plainly.

No angled approach. Nothing that would tell his abductors an item of immense value was inside it if they didn't already know. No one answered.

He held to the fantasy that he would wake soon. This was a dream. This was the nova and the hash and the Hemingway he'd consumed and had to force back out so he wouldn't die with LP.

He set his jaw, balling his right fist to stop its trembling. "How much do you all want?"

From his left, Tracksuit scowled across to High-top. "Dris…"

On his right side, High-top—Dris—snapped his fingers, balanced his pistol between his thighs, then sprang up slightly to retrieve something underneath.

"Dris." V-Dot turned to face him as the cab went over a bump that shot everyone up. "My man, let's talk about this." He shook his head and a denying smile arched his lips, denying everything, accepting none of this. "I got money."

Dris returned with a strip of skin tissue from a shop-grown body, pink and porous in the scant light. Before V-Dot could utter another word, the skin was over his mustache and stretching down on its own to conceal his lips, until there wasn't a mouth there anymore, just skin.

Dris leaned toward him. "Don't remove it."

The cold of its kiss became unbearable. V-Dot tried to speak but only a grunt came. If they didn't want a word from him, it meant someone with deep reserves likely put them up to this. Wanting to keep things quiet while they extracted the cache. No Patrol involvement.

They'd have to kill him first.

He blinked three times to boot up his connector without drawing their attention. When it dropped a layer of static over his vision field, he knew they'd remotely inserted a block between him and the organ's interface. They would've needed an access code for that—Montag's.

The static faded out. Almond Lips poked her head out of her window again. "Duro!" From her seat in front of Dris, she heaved more of her compact frame through the window till her elbows clipped her to the door.

"We should ditch that piece of junk." Tracksuit.

"You've got another one just lying around?"

She had a big voice with an accent like Dris did. The back of her sweatshirt had the words *Horatio Suzuki* in a script font between the shoulder seams.

"We could just come back for it once this is done with." Tracksuit again.

"O-boy, you dey craze?" the driver shot back.

An argument ensued between Tracksuit, Almond Lips, and the driver while he steered the cab with his palms flat on a pair of navigational substrates to either side of his seat.

From the argument, V-Dot learned Duro was a lookout drone prone to getting itself lost. It did business exclusively with the driver, who answered to Gbenga, and together they'd been down here since receiving intel that V-Dot would be entering Polemia through a terminal nearby.

Dris, Tracksuit, and Almond Lips—who answered to Aoki—worked as a unit separate from Gbenga and the drone. Gbenga had alerted Aoki to V-Dot's presence in Polemia, Aoki had tracked him to Blue Lounge to confirm, and they'd hurriedly struck a deal that was still being hashed out while they searched for the drone.

Gbenga cut a sharp turn while yelling about a five-way split of the score they were now working toward. Aoki yelled for him to look out.

Directly ahead, hovering at windshield level, a drone the size and shape of a brick stared them down. V-Dot noted the rust on its grey casing, the twitch to its green sensor-light. It looked diseased.

Slowing to a stop, Gbenga spun the cab on its sphere-shaped tires while bringing his window down. "Omoh," he called, addressing the drone in his old patois. "Wọ nu moto."

"Duro, get in the car," Tracksuit added.

Duro stalled beside the cab. It bobbed unevenly, its sensor-light strobing. V-Dot shivered as the others took to yelling over each other for it to get in. He'd let a consortium of idiots get the drop on him.

Another minute of *'Duro, get in'* and *'Over here, Duro'* and the drone floated slowly in through Gbenga's window. He put the cab in gear, then peeled away while it plopped down on the center console.

As they looped between ramps, V-Dot felt a weight bearing down, a fever's embrace, cold and burning hot under his skin. They could be bounty hunters. Meaning he might still live.

Governing bodies in the Frontier adhered to the same extradition laws. In summary: *Don't go looking, but if it turns up at your doorstep, please return.* LP's killing and the scrubbing of all his backups was a tacit escalation to *go looking.' And in more ways than one.* Intimidation campaigns by Patrol. Deranged LP cultists harassing anyone who appeared remotely like they harbored Manath sympathies. Making it a blood sport.

V-Dot chuckled inwardly. That also wasn't for him—none of it. Past thinking he could just ask to have his lifepack returned; all he could do now was tell himself it could've been Asa instead. A crude comfort. If they really were after the halo cache, there would also have been orders to kill him. Or take him elsewhere. Like they were doing now. He'd discovered LP taking people who'd already died elsewhere. Making them wish they'd stayed dead.

It couldn't be Asa.

Beyond his capture, beyond every torture awaiting him where no one in real space would see, he found a trace of his indignation and bit down. There were people still 'missing' from the After environments, still in danger of LP's honored guests.

Dris or Tracksuit would soon be using one of their pistols on him. He darted his gaze between the doors to either side as the cab finally crossed into the night. He would try for the one by Dris. If there was a chance he could recover the cache, he would have to avoid dying or worse first.

He exhaled as lights from the city shafted down. Not a plan, but something.

His abductors had resumed their haggling over how the reward money should be split. They were distracted. Gbenga wanted forty percent—half of that for himself, the other half for Duro. Dris insisted on a four-way split, with Gbenga getting thirty-one percent to divvy up however he wished with the drone. Tracksuit pointed to Duro's sickly state and accused Gbenga of pocketing all the money the drone should have gotten from previous jobs. Aoki told Tracksuit he was out of line.

V-Dot balled his fists. He would do it now or die waiting for another window like this.

He lunged toward the door beside Dris, landing a perfunctory blow on its manual unlock. It didn't move. Before he could take another swing, he felt arms around his ribs. Then laughter as his knuckles met the window's bulletproof polymer.

Dris's rich baritone rang in his ear while he took another jab. "You're wildin, man." Every joint in his right hand protested but he pulled it back for another.

Something flashed in front of him, then he felt it on his neck. Tracksuit's pistol. The man gripped the weapon at both ends and began throttling V-Dot with its barrel.

V-Dot wheezed. His larynx began to collapse under the pressure. Tears filled his eyes. His hands, weak as they'd suddenly become, went up. Tracksuit didn't relent, even while the others pleaded that he stop.

V-Dot grew lightheaded. The stranglehold kept his upper body suspended over Dris's lap. His fingers began to twitch. His vision blurred. The man meant to kill him, here. In the cab. He wasn't sticking with the plan he agreed to with the others, just going for it. Doing what he felt was needed. And this gave V-Dot some clarity on what he needed to do.

His left hand went down and returned with the drone in his grip. With all the force he had left in him, he banged it on Tracksuit's skull.

Tracksuit released him, sat calmly back down. V-Dot collapsed between his abductors, yanked the skin off his mouth, and dragged Polemia's oxygen down his windpipe like it had stolen something.

Gbenga turned to fix him a horrified stare. "Oga, a-beg, put Duro back down."

While his chest heaved and feeling rushed back to his extremities, V-Dot placed Duro on the center console. If doing what was needed meant he had to die, the decision was already made. He'd already done it. And it struck him now—more than it had before Tracksuit's assault—that he'd done the right thing. His neck screamed with pain that lingered and radiated everywhere else, and it only seemed to bolster his indignation. If this was punishment for his own crime, then LP hadn't gotten nearly half of what he deserved.

To his left, Tracksuit palmed his forehead. "Aoki, start making those calls," he said in a level tone. "Don't want to off this *moo-moo* before we get our money, but I will if he tries anything else."

Aoki held a finger in front of her nose, swiping at a screen no one else could see, placing a call. "Felix, it's Ao. Felix…? Felix…? Felix…? Fel—"

"Tell him we have bids from outside Polemia."

She held her palm up to quiet him down. "Yeah, that was us," she said to the person on the other end of the line. "Uh, Gbenga, myself, Dris, Duro, and… Wyatt."

Wyatt. The pale demon's name was Wyatt. V-Dot tried frowning at him. Oxygen rushed his airway and made him giggle at the bruise he'd left on the man's forehead. He leaned his head back, breathed. These were bounty hunters.

"You should've just killed me, Wyatt. Won't change anything but at least you won't be getting your reward money."

"Shut it."

He choked down his next rejoinder as Aoki blabbered in earshot. Hummed it under his breath.

LP isn't coming back. Ever.

From the little he heard, Aoki was assuring the person on the other end that this cab hadn't picked up a tail. Gbenga waved once at the smooth, almost featureless dashboard in the front. Mid-tempo music filled the cab, a soulful croon over a gentle bass and swinging kick.

The city outside was light on landcar traffic. Its glistening facades and hologram excesses loomed down, almost lulling as the music played. Aoki gestured for Gbenga to lower its volume and he obliged.

"Felix wants to hear him."

Silence held for a few seconds till Wyatt poked the business end of his build-your-own into V-Dot's thigh. "Port it."

Aoki threw her finger toward the windshield. A holoscreen blinked to life in front of it with a white-on-blue grid as Wyatt got in V-Dot's ear.

"All right, killer, just a few words for the crowd. Then they'll run an analysis on the other end to be sure it's you. Nothing pretty, you just have to say something."

V-Dot glared at the screen, then at Wyatt. Who was this 'they?' He would ask, but then *they* would have his voice.

"Don't get shy, bruv," added Dris.

V-Dot pursed his lips, shook his head slowly as tears welled in his eyes. They would have to kill him. They would have to finish what Wyatt began before he did anything they wanted.

LP was dead. A ghost.

A wave of frustrated sighs rolled through the cab as Gbenga slowed his speed and it dawned on V-Dot that they'd been circling the same two city blocks. Almost without drawing attention to itself, Duro shot up. Halfway to the roof, it clicked and whirred a few seconds till audio from earlier that night issued from its underside.

In it, V-Dot heard himself bluff at Wyatt: *'I've got a banger on me so don't try anything stupid, all right?'*

A waveform twitched on the holoscreen. Aoki poked the side of her left eye. "Felix, is that good?"

After a few seconds, she gave the rest of them a thumbs-up, then raised the remaining four fingers till they all nodded. "Bidding starts at fifty grand, Felix."

The atmosphere in the cab grew tense as she began to spar with this Felix. "We got you that already... That's just the tech, no way around it..."

She held three fingers up, which instantly met groans from everyone else. "Too low... We got offers from outside already, Felix... Forty-seven, take it or leave it..."

So they weren't exactly bounty hunters. Negotiators?

V-Dot didn't know whether he should feel relief or pray they got the amount they wanted. If they struck out, they would likely kill him for all the trouble he'd caused already, do the Frontier that favor. He figured Aoki seemed like she could be reasoned with and fixed her with pleading eyes which she didn't see from the front of the cab.

"Felix won't go higher than forty."

"Siri, then." Wyatt. "Get her on the line. Gbenga, let's try to be on her side of town when she picks up."

Aoki placed the call and was promptly put on hold.

"Yo, Aoki," V-Dot growled, seizing the window while they were all down from their first attempt at whatever this was. "I know y'all are not trying to turn me in, but you gotta let me know what's going on. I could even help. I'm all about getting paid." He had a stabbing pain in his throat now that made his voice hoarse.

The cab met his offer with silence. Gbenga wave-gestured at the dash and brought the music back. He'd stopped taking the cab in circles and was now ghosting toward sunlight. Polemia's unique hue of it lasted six hours wherever it touched down, then wheeled elsewhere for eighteen hours after that.

They crossed the terminator. The patch of sky now above them held a blurred orange crescent that bathed everything surrounding it in a lighter orange. The sun, as seen through Polemia's sunroof.

The city's immense architecture glinted yellow and cast orange-tinted shadows on passing cars. V-Dot peeked through the car's roof, soaked it quietly in. Aoki was no longer on hold. The music was low now and he could hear some of what she said.

"Just got off with Felix actually, he's ready to give us sixty grand... We've got outside bidders too. We can put this guy on a spacer and be at Merick in the next hour... He's carrying a scrambler so he can still fly... Yeah, scrambler, how else do you think he left Mars undetected?"

His ears perked at the mention of a spacer. A flight from Polemia to Merick in an hour meant a ship targeting the standard zero-four sublight. Had she embellished? She'd lied about the previous person's offer, but even so he didn't have sixty thousand frontnotes to match that or to try convincing these cadets to ferry him to Gan.

He felt a nosebleed's trickle, tilted his head back.

"Yeah, he's here. Wyatt roughed him up a bit but he's—" She turned for a glance at him, then locked on Wyatt. "She wants to see him."

Wyatt reached a hand over to him, lifted the shades off his eyes, then nodded at Aoki.

A screen blinked to life again in front of the windshield. This time, a woman's face appeared on it—pale skin, tattoos, a shock of grey hair up top, and a black band of paint across the eyes. Through the screen, she trained those eyes on V-Dot while beaming a grin that seemed to hide her amusement at all this. "Verden Dotnet?"

He frowned. "Got the wrong guy."

"You're thinking like I'm thinking that these blokes picked you off the street and are now pretending you're the one with your face all over the news?"

Wyatt slapped V-Dot's hood down. "Siri, cut the shit. Else we'll just walk him into Patrol headquarters and none of you psychos gets first pass at him."

"Wyatt?" the woman called, craning her neck. "Is that you, Wyatt?"

"Don't know if you've seen on the news, Siri, but it's forty grand to anyone who brings him in to Patrol."

"You… Wyatt? You're gonna walk him in to Patrol?"

"Seventy puts him in your care. Take it or watch Felix claim him instead. Better yet, watch us turn him in."

"Hey, Wyatt, tell me—how many more skinnies like you from Merick in your line of work?"

"Just me."

V-Dot winced. The man who'd nearly just killed him was a skinner. Someone who would just move his god-node to a new body if the bruise V-Dot gave him took too long to heal.

The others inside the cab shifted in their seats. Dris exhaled heavily. These weren't bounty hunters. But they could just as well try their hands at it soon.

The cab crossed into the night again. All V-Dot could now imagine was the barrel wedged into his neck, stunting his oxygen intake for longer than any human could survive with just what they were born with. His hatred for Wyatt boiled over, spilling into a categorized sort of animus, one that Mars, with its overabundance of skinners, had previously freed him from.

"If he's got a scrambler on him like you all say he does, then Wyatt doesn't actually know who the fuck he's sitting next to, does he?"

Wyatt groaned. Aoki beamed a concerned stare at him, then returned to the screen. "Siri, we've all had a proper look at him. It's him."

"I want to see Wyatt look at him and confirm it himself."

"Right now?"

Dris sighed audibly. "Siri, you're being a bully."

"Right now."

"It could take up to ten minutes for the cache to clear from his compositor." Aoki. "That's plenty of time for a Patrol scan to pick him up and the rest of us with him."

"The sooner he gets to it, the better for the rest of you, then."

Silence held for a few seconds. Wyatt reached toward V-Dot's right pants pocket. V-Dot pulled the skinner's hand back by the wrist. A small struggle ensued until Dris dug his nails into V-Dot's forearm.

The scrambler came out. Wyatt tossed it on the center console. "Dris..."

Dris grabbed V-Dot by the ears and turned his head to face Wyatt. Without warning, the skinner hooked the same disquieting gaze on him that he'd given at Blue Lounge.

The Ganymedan who'd sold him the scrambler now sitting on the console had told him it would treat interactions with sentients the same way it would a bodymatch scan, giving them a handicap of sorts. He tried looking away now but Dris held his head in place. *Fuck this one*. He deserved no sympathy after nearly choking him to death.

The woman on the screen snorted, making Wyatt start. "That's enough of that."

Dris released V-Dot. Wyatt sat back, looking forlorn as Siri went on. "You're my favorite kind of skinny, you know that? Willing to be humiliated for money like any human."

Aoki inhaled. "Seventy grand, Siri."

"Thirty for now. Even without that scrambler, no one in there knows who exactly you picked up. Leave him here with me, take thirty, and once I've had my own people confirm we can talk about doubling that amount."

Silence again as Gbenga slowed the cab's speed. "A-beg, cut the line," he muttered.

Aoki obliged. The holoscreen vanished. All eyes inside the cab, save V-Dot's, went to Wyatt.

"Get Felix back on."

Gbenga steered the cab down a ramp that landed them elsewhere in Polemia's underground. Low ceilings. Murky lighting.

V-Dot had become faint again when they agreed his capture and subsequent release to Felix would be in exchange for forty-seven thousand and eighty frontnotes, split evenly five ways with the drone getting its own cut.

He stared sidelong at Wyatt as everyone shared a restful silence. The skinner looked shellshocked, refusing to meet his glare. In some respects, he was no different from the drone—he had no need for food or other essentials humans couldn't do without. Yet there'd been no argument over his cut.

"What are you going to do with your almost ten grand, Wyatt?" V-Dot's throat still ached when he spoke. He would bang the skinner's head on his knee if he had the energy in his present state.

They pulled toward a mass of parked vehicles, rovers and landcars and choppers and street scooters, packed haphazardly together around a trio of columns with an elevator in its midst. As the cab maneuvered around them, he noted they all had the same tires shaped like spheres underneath. To his knowledge, this meant they were all hybrids—autonomous vehicles that could still be driven by humans, like the cab he was in.

Traffic at Gan had almost exclusively been these hybrids when V-Dot lived there, part of Manathema's influence. He compared it to Mars, where more than half the vehicles were sentients and paying passengers had to meet standards set by each vehicle, submitting to background checks each time. A mass of hybrids meant passengers who didn't pass background checks very often. Maybe he could find more common ground than just that with this Felix.

He planted his feet firmly as Gbenga pulled to a stop by the elevator. The doors on either side of the cab swung up. Wyatt's grip threatened to crush his left arm. The business end of a pistol poked his side after the skinner was done scooting closer. Gbenga and Aoki hopped out first, then stood guard while Wyatt pulled him slowly out of the back.

The drone shot out and went to hover by Gbenga's right ear. Once they were all out, Gbenga slapped the top of the cab, then watched it peel away, its doors swinging shut.

Wyatt's sidearm shifted to the small of V-Dot's back as they all filed toward the elevator, Gbenga and the drone up front, Dris and Aoki in the back. His gaze shifted to their hands and shoulders, not hiding it from them. The pack was nowhere he could see. The cab was gone.

In staggered unison, a dozen or so guard drones dropped to meet them at eye level. "No drones past this point," one intoned.

Gbenga tapped Duro, prompting it to fall back as he weaved around the guard drones to get to the elevator. Wyatt forced V-Dot down so they could both duck and join Gbenga on the other side. The drones shot back up, taking Duro with them as Aoki and Dris crossed to join the others.

The elevator doors slid open. The quintet shuffled into the cramped enclosure and were whisked down a number of decks in complete darkness. They exited into a vestibule the size of the elevator, murky and boiling hot with a crimson hue on every surface.

As they stood, Dris sidled up and slid the scrambler back into V-Dot's pocket. A scan must have been imminent. Aoki and Gbenga had each slipped on a pair of shades. Wyatt released V-Dot's left arm, hurriedly slipped on the shades he'd removed earlier, then grabbed him by the arm again.

V-Dot shook with rage, a spell of it that scared him more than the thought that he would die soon. A light flashed so bright it met his eyes like needles and turned the whole vestibule white. He jerked, squeezing his eyes shut. The scan. At Gan, it wouldn't matter if the scrambler was already cracked.

"No weapons past this point," A calm voice over an intercom.

"We have permission from Felix to enter with ours."

Aoki. With the flash gone, the room's crimson returned and he could see her brush a sidearm tucked behind her back.

After a few seconds, the voice stirred again. "Don't go making him regret that."

A door opened onto another murky enclosure—another

elevator. This one lowered them further down, then let them into a small, dark room where noise that sounded distinctly like a rave could be heard through the walls.

A muscle-bound trio rose from benches affixed to those walls, meeting V-Dot and his abductors with brutish eyes and brandished sidearms.

"We're here for Felix," Aoki barked. "Could one of you go fetch him?"

"Felix isn't here," replied one of them. In the dark, V-Dot could barely make it out but he was certain the letters M-N-T-M were branded just above the bridge of his nose. *Manathema*. He couldn't believe his eyes.

"You know," Aoki said, brimming with annoyance, "if you ghosts weren't so paranoid all the time, we wouldn't have to waste so much of it re-establishing rules of the road and all that. He's got every connector down here jammed so I can't even ring him to let him know we're already here."

"I'll go," another one of them answered.

"Do that."

A door slid open and seismic bass blasts poured in. Aoki inched closer to Gbenga, grabbed his palm, and held it tight.

Felix was Manath. All the signs pointed to it now—Felix grilling Aoki to be sure her crew hadn't picked up a tail. Wyatt suggesting Felix might claim V-Dot if the woman who humiliated him earlier didn't agree to how much they wanted. The mass of parked hybrids. Barring the drone from entry. Aoki referring to the guard as a ghost.

He glared at the door the guard had just gone through. A ghost with means like this Felix had would at least be able to find him a faster ship to Gan. Yet he felt no relief, standing here while Wyatt's pistol dug into the small of his back.

The cache was gone. Was there still a need to see Asa?

The door slid open, letting through another earful of bass. A voice followed after it.

"Bring him inside."

They filed in, Wyatt's feet bumping into his as they moved. The next room met their entrance with an unfiltered barrage—that same driving bass, lights that jittered and stabbed in the dark while the floor below heaved with ravers.

They could have their reunion at Gan. Like Heidi had suggested. It wasn't too late for that, not with a faster ship. The decision to abandon the objective that had brought him here seemed to have already been made for him.

He felt his ears pop as they wedged into the throng of bodies streaked with sweat and incandescence. Taken together, the dancers were like an amoebic organism that stretched toward the far end of the floor, where it narrowed and terminated at the foot of two escalators.

The muscle who'd waved them in turned and motioned for them to stop once they were a bit past the entrance. "Someone has to come with me to where there's enough wave resistance for the transfer. The rest of you wait here."

Gbenga crossed to stand next to him. Dris exchanged a glance with Wyatt, prompting the skinner to finally let go. He tucked the sidearm behind his back, trained his wolf eyes on V-Dot, then slapped the shades to V-Dot's chest.

V-Dot glared at him, refusing at first to collect his shades. His anger waned when uncertainty flashed in the skinner's eyes. He accepted the shades and hooked them to the neck of his sweatshirt.

Wyatt folded his arms. "Hey, I want you to know this was all just business, all right?" He gave V-Dot a stilted pat on the arm, drawing his hand back when V-Dot's glare went to it. "I respect what you did, but this is the game."

Gbenga had already begun trailing the muscle to where signal resistance to Polemia's gravity wave would be strongest here for a transfer. Wyatt turned for a glance at them, then turned back to V-Dot.

"Anyway, if you manage to pull through all this and you ever find yourself at Merick, drinks are on me."

V-Dot felt his blood boil again. What game? What had he done? Fuck getting respect for that. He hadn't done it for respect.

"Where's my pack?"

"That's a different game now. Ask Felix."

While backing away in Gbenga's direction, Wyatt attempted a salute but hesitated before vanishing into the crowd.

V-Dot held him in his glare long after that. Steadying his breath, he watched the ravers as minutes passed with Aoki and Dris on either side of him. The bass shook the ground, making him clench his teeth.

Manathema wasn't supposed to get hold of it. Just Asa.

He began to fear that he'd never actually meet this Felix when, near the other end of the floor, where the escalators stood, he glimpsed a face with eyes locked on him and a sly grin.

The face floated through the crowd as its owner strolled toward him with such ease it almost seemed he was gliding. The man stood a hair taller than everyone else, hair cropped to his scalp except up front, where a handful was coiffed back and dyed blue. He had a narrow face with black lips and a pale complexion that appeared to glow whenever the light hit it. He wore a dark jumpsuit with holographic palm trees plastered across the chest.

"Felix, man," Dris exclaimed.

"Dris." The man closed toward Dris. They shook hands, hugged, then pulled away from each other. "Don't take offense, my friend, but I'm only down here for what you all brought me tonight." He had a haunting slur that matched his lazy eyes and made him sound stoned to the gills. He swept his gaze past V-Dot. "Aoki."

"Hello, Felix."

"Still all business? You'll forgive me for being too starstruck to stay and chat." He fixed his gaze on V-Dot next, pressing his palms to his forehead. "Goodness, man."

"You must be Felix."

"Yes, I'm Felix. Listen." He placed both hands on V-Dot's shoulders. "Who cares about that? Have you seen the news lately? Do you know what they're saying you did? Do you know you're gold right now? Fucking gold, my friend."

V-Dot nodded as a nagging thought threatened his resolve. He wasn't finished. If the cache was now with Felix, he couldn't abandon it like someone else would've done hours ago. Someone more sensible. Someone who hadn't lost his nerve seeing the pain inflicted on complete strangers.

"Felix," Dris called from behind him. "Later."

Felix lifted his hand over V-Dot's shoulder for a distracted wave at Dris. V-Dot craned his neck in time to catch the man exit behind Gbenga and Aoki.

Good riddance to the funeral procession.

"How ya feeling?" Felix, commanding his attention again. "You feeling all right?"

V-Dot flashed back to Wyatt's firearm on his throat and chuckled. "Copacetic."

Felix threw an arm around his shoulders. Under the strobes and the music's onslaught, they began toward the escalators with Felix in his ear. "Ah, man, you're a ghost for sure, man."

V-Dot nodded, keeping his head down as they wedged into the throng. "How is it you don't have membership with a single chapter?" He'd never pledged. Swapped school for a few months at a Manath shipyard and was told he failed all the assessments.

"I'm lieutenant here at Polemia for Ghosts of Sculus," Felix told him.

He hadn't noticed when they cleared the crowd and climbed onto the escalator going up. His head began to throb. Ringing filled his ears.

"How ya feeling, man? You're still with me?"

He nodded. The escalator seemed oddly slow. A gaping darkness loomed at the end of it so he felt like he was being fed into an abyss. Maybe he'd died in that cab.

"How would you like to pledge with us?"

Felix's slurred voice grated like a mosquito in his ear. Refusing to relent. Making it difficult for him to gather his thoughts.

He wanted protection. To be home again. Finish the job. He wanted the Frontier to know eventually why he did what he did.

Felix patted his shoulder. "We'll talk when you're rested."

15. NIGHTCALL

THE CANYONS, FOUR YEARS AGO

THE ELEVATOR DOWN from the roof of Cloey Lenox-Pileser's penthouse was always too quiet. V-Dot swore even his thoughts came at a volume too low for him to hear. Maybe he just couldn't think tonight.

He'd left Cloey on one of the pool chairs. He was still in his post-coital haze when she fished her tablet seemingly out of nowhere and went to sit on the neighboring chair, naked as him but already too busy to look up when he said goodnight.

In the afternoon, they would see each other again. Maybe it would be a quick ten minutes in her aviary at Lenox-Pileser Compound. Maybe Tasha or one of the new skinner cadets would join. It surprised him to learn first-hand that skinners had their own preferences, and quite often those preferences included 'unlearned, dressed like a croupier, and speaking with a deep Sectist brogue.' The thought left him with the usual pang of guilt. As it turned out, congress with a skinner was every bit as enjoyable as it was with humans.

He adjusted his waistcoat, cuffed his sleeves as the elevator pulled closer to the arboretum floor and the lander waiting there for him. Its name was Niles. V-Dot, already bad with names, queried his connector constantly for them, tired of always making the wrong impression, calling every android 'android,' every lander 'lander,' and so on. Niles carted him here from his new apartment and back most nights, after Cloey was done with him.

Days earlier, he'd flown Asa in from Boon Fort and welcomed her excitedly to that apartment. They'd spent a day gallivanting like they hadn't been able to on previous visits. He was in a cloud. It would have been a two-month stay, but he had to go and tell her finally about his employer. Asa shifted like he'd never seen at the mention of LP, blaming LP for a systematic genocide of Sectists that would soon take on a xenocidal dimension when the Frontier decided it no longer had need for humans. They lost their voices screaming at each other. When they were both calm again, he told her she had to leave. She was gone within the week.

As the elevator opened its doors, he inhaled deeply, shutting his eyes. He'd expected worse from Asa, but once she was gone he began to think that was unfair. Power eluded them their whole lives and they were told LP was to blame. If she'd set fire to his swanky new apartment, a part of him would call it restraint.

When he opened his eyes, they met the most offending aspect of his new life as LP's mixologist. This one happened to be human. V-Dot had no reason to believe Cloey lied about him opting, as a child, not to follow his eccentric-hermit parents into the After.

The man stood under the shadow of birch trees and the trickle of light from fluorescents in the ceiling. He still had his dark skin, his wooly black hair pulled into a bun, and the brown eyes to match V-Dot's. Two years ago, he'd had none of those and no one had trouble telling them apart. But even now there were clues. One resembled V-Dot. The other resembled a tourist coming down from a ship. Only going where a guide instructed and able to avoid any danger of meeting the natives.

V-Dot took two steps forward, then spoke the name slowly

as the elevator shut its doors behind him. "Connor...?"

For all he knew, it could be someone else who managed to get access to Cloey's penthouse. His heart thumped loudly as the man stared and got his hackles up. It *was* Connor. He'd brought his usual aloofness here. V-Dot watched him arch a glance at Niles where it coasted beside the walkway he was on. A deep groan issued below the vehicle's white hull.

Connor swept his gaze back and appeared to relax. "How's my grandmother?"

V-Dot bristled at the smile he crooked after asking that—a smile like his. It was like looking in a mirror from this far back.

"Go up and ask yourself," he answered. And because he would kick himself later for not adding this, "make sure she knows it's you."

He braced for another of Connor's tortured retorts. The man looked briefly over his shoulder instead, then set his jaw. "You have to come with me," he said, pitched menace in his voice.

"You know, I don't think I do."

V-Dot squared his shoulders and his muscles tensed. He'd been expecting this since the night they'd met at Serum. Such an ancient hang-up. Maybe it was V-Dot's low station that made the man act this way. Maybe it really was what he suspected that night—grandmother and grandson. Fucking each other senseless until he came along.

"I'm not asking, Verd. You're coming with me."

Behind Connor, another lander lurched out from amid a thicket of spruce trees farther back, hull as black as ink, engine silent as it hovered low above a bed of mulch.

"Don't be stupid," issued a voice from the vehicle, low and sedate. "Get in."

V-Dot grinned, unable to hide how amused he was at all this. Connor would never lay a finger on him; V-Dot was good with LP now, part of a trusted circle that privileged him to hours alone with the elder Lenox-Pileser as they imbibed together. Given more time with LP, he was almost certain he could influence him to add stipulations concerning his mixologist to all the inheritance agreements.

Rather than waste a second trading barbs with Connor and now his lander, V-Dot punched a button behind him and the doors to the elevator began their slide away from each other. He muttered something under his breath about a common transport vessel having the gall to insult him, then turned his back. His hand was halfway to his connector when he felt the worryingly familiar grip of a large metal fist on his shoulder. He darted his gaze back to find its android owner towering over him.

"Don't bother," it said in its booming voice. "You're jammed."

He lowered his hand. Niles was doing nothing to stop this. *Useless Niles.*

Cloey would have to hear about it in the morning.

LP SAT ON a sofa facing one of the aquariums beneath his compound. The aquarium was the height of the room it was in and spanned an entire length of wall. The water inside it stopped just shy of the roof. Not the usual line, V-Dot observed as the android elbowed him into the room.

Stumbling to a stop behind the sofa, he caught the silhouette of LP's head listed over on its side. The room was boxy and squat, a perfect square with bare walls the color of night bathed in the aquarium's blue glow. V-Dot had been here on many excursions through the compound's cavernous bunker. He'd never seen it lit this way.

Inside the lander, he'd felt relief when Connor told him it was LP who wanted to see him, but the relief was tempered. LP did most of his drinking during the day—late mornings.

Nights were normally reserved for staring at the big wall of screens inside the pagoda, where he held court with colleagues throughout the Frontier.

Not knowing why he was here, V-Dot feared the worst. LP had conducted that background check Cloey was supposed to have prevented. Maybe, for that reason, she was currently unaware of this. There was a deep ringing in his ears. His fingers began to vibrate, and he felt he was being pulled in every direction. So what if LP learned of a lapse in judgment at sixteen? He'd already done his time for it. And more.

What was this feeling all of a sudden? He'd moved past the necessity to walk on eggshells here.

Connor barreled into the room and leapt over the back of the sofa, landing noisily beside his great-granduncle. Next came the door swinging shut behind V-Dot, then LP's crisp voice.

"You're finally here." He hadn't turned his head. "Donut, please put the chair for V-Dot right here, to my left."

"Okay, Dad."

The android answered to Donut, and like others at the compound, it called LP Dad. V-Dot dismissed this as an affectation each time he heard it, a programmed behavior like any other, devised to fool observers more gullible than him.

As Donut lumbered away, its red sensor-light traced the bottom of the aquarium, calling his attention for the first time to what was inside. He'd expected crustaceans bred here on Mars or sealife shipped from Earth. What he saw instead were two human bodies, naked and sprawled on the substrate lining the bottom of the enclosure.

A wave of nausea swept through him and he felt the room spin. Had they drowned? Had LP watched it and done nothing? Was he going to…? No. Someone was always having to pull him aside and remind him to act normal around the sentients, but life at the compound was going better than he could have imagined. No need for a panic response. Not since his first few months here. And yet he found himself suddenly in this fog he couldn't explain.

Donut returned with a folding chair clutched inconspicuously to the steel plates on its torso. It unfolded it on the left side of the sofa, closer to where LP sat, and brought it down.

"Sit," it said in its seismic baritone.

V-Dot inched, breath lurching, toward the chair and sat. The bodies inside the aquarium looked even more corpse-like up close. One was peach-skinned and hirsute with its back turned, laid on its side while the water ruffled the hair on its head. The other lay prone to the substrate, a pale olive complexion on bald skin. As he eyed them, all he could think about was how he'd almost drowned in Cloey's pool.

"You've been with us for two years," LP said, face held in meditative repose. He wore board shorts and his usual white crewneck. The aquarium's incandescence caught wanly on the side of his face so he resembled a wax sculpture as he turned toward V-Dot and smiled. "It's time you saw something new."

V-Dot gulped. It wasn't normally like LP to project such an ominous air around him. He folded his arms and, turning to face his employer, hid his discomfort behind a smirk.

"LP, who's inside the aquarium?" He quelled the urge to look away. LP preferred directness. "Did they drown?"

"Recognize any of them?"

He turned and scrunched his face at the bodies again. He hadn't imagined it could be anyone he knew, and he didn't care to humor the thought.

"No," he said, almost paralyzed with uncertainty as that deep sense of foreboding pinned him to the chair, weakening him by the second.

"V-Dot, I need a favor." LP faced the bodies as well, his

palms rested on his knees. "There's something you can do for me tonight that no one as close to me as you've become is still able to. They've seen this happen enough times and it no longer triggers the desired response. Someone like you... even with your upbringing, I can't imagine it's something you would just watch happen and take nothing away from."

Smiling but now unable to stop the quivering in his voice, V-Dot wheeled his gaze on LP. "What are you talking about?"

LP looked angelic in the glow of the aquarium's light. He shut his eyes and breathed. Having nearly forgotten Connor seated on the other side, V-Dot jerked when the voice—thankfully unsimilar to his own—came across to him.

"You're going to watch us drown."

Whipping his head left, he leveled it on the sofa again, looking this time at his accursed doppelganger. "I'm going to do *what?*"

Behind him, the door made a sound like it had been blasted open. Everyone turned except LP, who remained glued to the aquarium. Donut—towering bulk of steel that it was—hobbled away from the door as Cloey stomped in with hands on her hips and her eyes targeting the back of LP's head.

"Archer, stop this. Now. Take those bodies out of there and do the switch at the cryonics ward like you know you're supposed to." She was in the unitard she'd taken off a few hours ago, hair tousled, breathing heavier than V-Dot had ever seen, even during their romps together. It took a few seconds staring at her before what she'd just said registered.

"Oh, shit."

His chair creaked loudly against the floorboard as he bolted up. He fixed the bodies in the aquarium with even more trepidation than before, not knowing why just yet. He'd never seen shop-grown bodies like this, never up this close before a backup was downloaded into one.

"Cloey," LP said in his level tone.

She marched toward the aquarium and turned to regard

him like one would a child caught in mischief, arms folded, bending forward with a foot pounding the floorboard. "Are you just completely out of your mind these days? And I see Connor's now happy to join you in this obscene display." Without a glance at Connor, she closed toward V-Dot and began to pull him by the arm, guiding him away from the aquarium. "Don't do it in front of him." She stopped and looked at her grandson, jabbing her finger like a knife in his direction. "Don't ever come to my place and stage a kidnapping like you did tonight, Connor. I will have you lesson-killed—slow and with more pain than anything you would ever dream up yourself."

"I didn't kidnap anyone—"

"Shut up."

Her grip on V-Dot's arm was tight. Her nails dug in, almost scraping his skin as he tried discreetly to free himself and stared through the aquarium's glass at LP's replacement's butt crack.

"Cloey," LP said, his glance still on the aquarium, his voice calm, "shouldn't you be with the Oort Colony investors right now?"

"I decided I didn't want you causing more psychological damage than you likely already have this evening. You cannot keep doing this to the humans around you."

V-Dot gaped at the fine white sand under pounds of flesh and toned muscle waiting to be possessed. Cloey was always in LP's ear about his lack of self-awareness. V-Dot had begun regarding it as background noise whenever he was called in from the cantina for a day with the king and de facto queen of Lenox-Pileser Compound.

"I was presented with no other choice but to put you in charge of mining-sector operations," LP said, still with his face fixed on the aquarium. "They forced my hand. And now you've decided it isn't as important as your fucktoy?" Having heard himself described this way before, V-Dot didn't bat an eye. Everyone not named Lenox-Pileser pulled in extra shifts as playthings here. "Would you be kind enough to tell me," LP continued, "how many more of our partners you'll be standing up like this, so I won't feel bad the next time you accuse me of undermining you in front of them?"

"We're not discussing that right now," she shot back. V-Dot could swear he felt her nail dig into a piece of sinew. "Right now, we're talking about you salvaging what's left of your image among people like him."

"People like who?" LP shifted on his sofa and turned his head slightly, still not meeting anyone's eyes. "Verden?"

"People who will never buy what we sell to them because you're a poor salesman… a poor judge of what is okay and what isn't." She shook visibly as she yelled and V-Dot began to feel like a frail thing in her grip. Maybe he was just tired. Maybe the fight with Asa was weighing him down again. "Did you really think he would want this…? Watching you drown?" Cloey threw another scowl at her grandson. "Connor, I want you out of the room. Right now."

"Connor, stay where you are." LP staggered to his feet, slowly turning his back to the aquarium while Connor remained on the sofa, nearly as stiff as his new body. With only its right side visible, this one looked nothing like V-Dot, so that was a relief.

LP locked his always intense glare on him, then frowned before training those color-shifting eyes on his niece. "You don't think someone born out of the soup of such potent Sectist stock would want to see me flailing for air…? Dying a slow, very uncomfortable death?"

V-Dot pulled away, finally getting his arm free. Hunger. That was it; that sense of foreboding since he'd got here. He was always forgetting to eat around the Lenox-Pilesers. Also, he had no desire to watch LP drown. Connor, maybe. But not like this. Not in a way that would give them this masochistic thrill they were after.

"He's different." Cloey sidled toward him, rubbing his arm now. "This will scar him."

"Well…" LP clasped his hands behind his back. "This is a scarring ritual. That's the point."

Scarring ritual?

V-Dot cleared his throat, able to focus now that his arm was better. "I gotta say, LP, I don't think I'm cool with this." He slid the arm away from Cloey and rubbed it himself. Before his life with LP, he'd once helped a canyoner indulge fetishes only people able to cheat death repeatedly would dream up. The man liked a bag over his head. V-Dot insisted on getting a signature on a form each time. This was different.

LP flashed him a tight grin. He then turned to Cloey, almost like V-Dot wasn't there as he resumed. "Maybe he'll scream because he can't do anything to help. Maybe he'll rediscover the savage Manath spawn buried deep, told since birth that me dying is a good thing whenever it happens. This isn't primarily for his enjoyment, as you know. It's for mine. He'll get used to it. They all do."

V-Dot felt a chill in his bones, whorling out to his extremities and making him wish he'd never told LP where he was from. Not that he wouldn't have found out, of course. Anyway, he was now at a loss for what to say. He took a step back and fell in behind Cloey, smelling her perfume, getting some comfort there but not a lot as LP went on.

"And I thought you hadn't come here to discuss your fitness for leadership again. Yet you've just said in front of him and Donut that you're better at it than I am. I wouldn't have left the conference call to your mimic prompt, or whoever you've thrown into that vampire's den tonight. I would have called in myself."

She looked away, exhaled audibly, then caught LP in her glare again. "You won't live forever," she muttered.

"What's that?"

"I said you won't live forever, Archer."

"No." LP strode closer to Connor, his expression blank but his volume beginning to rise. "But when I'm finally in the After, you can bet everything you've already taken as yours that whoever succeeds me will be the right person, not just the person going around telling every press freak that we owe all recent successes we've had to her. Are you catching on? You won't be *Cloey-LP-exclusiving* your way into any more positions than you already have, darling niece."

"You're a child," she snarled.

"You're old and decrepit."

"When you do finally retire to the After environments, do us all a favor and make sure it's permanent—*truly* get lost."

LP had a sudden twinkle in his eye. He looked down at Connor, then up again with the same beguiling smirk the younger Lenox-Pileser was so good at.

"Even if I go missing from there like our friend Jax reportedly has, it would still be a happy ending to this fairytale romance between *my* empire—*mine!*" He was almost screaming now as he beat his chest with a balled fist. "—*mine mine mine*—and its many suitors."

Cloey glanced at Connor. V-Dot could almost hear something sink inside her, like a gasp she'd refused to let out. She stiffened her stance, inhaled, then clenched her jaw.

"Don't bring that up here."

Her voice was the calmest it had been since she barged in, teetering on the edge of a hum. Goosebumps flared on V-Dot's skin. He began to sense a line had been crossed when LP hinted that Connor might be who he preferred to succeed him. Or was it the mention of his previous mixologist that had kindled her ire? He knew precious little about the After environments, or even that people could go missing from them. Nothing in the news about it. Nothing he'd heard prior to this.

"Bring what up?" LP asked.

"You idiot. You know what. Have you been drinking?"

Now directly in front of Connor, LP worked his fingers through the man's bunched hair. It was something he'd started doing shortly after his great-grandnephew's switch to this body, so similar to V-Dot's. Stress relief. Fascination with the body's Ganymedan physiognomy, perfectly replicated, so much so that V-Dot had long prepared himself for the possibility that their mornings together would progress toward sexual favors for LP as well. He welcomed any leverage he would earn from that but often feared what Cloey's reaction would be.

Still locked in a staring contest with his niece, LP gritted his teeth and a frown so unlike him traveled across. "Don't call me names where Donut can hear."

"Be very careful what you say with me in the room."

"You're not supposed to be here."

She nodded, then heaved a long sigh. "Ver…" She turned, grabbed V-Dot by the arm again, gentler as she met him with a defeated countenance. "I'm sorry. From now on, remind me to have Niles come get you from the roof."

She slipped out of the room without another word. He kept his gaze on her till Donut shut the door. Just minutes ago, she'd stormed in to prevent this 'scarring ritual' and now she was gone. What had LP said that had so offended her?

He turned for a glance at him, careful not to make it obvious that he was slightly miffed. "What did you say to her?"

Smiling again, LP waved the question away. "Not important."

"Do I get a say in this?" he asked. "What if I don't want to?"

Connor spun on the sofa and gave him his broadest smile. "Please, pretty please, Mr. Dotnet?"

V-Dot seized up again. This was all too much and all he could do now was laugh. It started in his chest and spread to his shoulders. LP loosened his jaw and a braying convulsion issued from him, too. Connor joined in, then Donut from beside the door. The android's own cachinnations sounded canned up close.

"Y'all are so fucked up," he slipped that in with his laughter and hoped they wouldn't hear it.

The room quieted down. LP laid a hand on Connor's shoulder and took a wistful breath before addressing V-Dot again.

"I won't make you do anything you don't want to, man. But like I said earlier, I consider this a favor. Once every few months, I begin to itch for a new body. I could pay cryonics a visit and take the killing solution like Cloey wants me to, or I can do this instead. This comes with the reminder of what life was like before we saved the Frontier from it. Drowning."

"It's still like that for a lot of people." V-Dot hadn't meant to say that. It slipped out.

"Maybe." LP exchanged a chortle with Connor, then gave V-Dot his full attention again. "Anyway, it's just something I do, and now Connor's joining me for the first time. I was about his age the first time someone nearly went into cardiac arrest seeing me die in front of them. He didn't know who I was or about my backups. Ever since, I've wanted that again—as much as I'm able to arrange for it in an environment as protected as this. I know it'll never be exactly like that first time, not when everyone knows who I am. But if you would just grant me an approximation of it, you will be opening a door to so much more from me than you could ever dream.

"And if it scars you, if it leaves a mark..." He looked away. V-Dot couldn't believe LP would ever be so short for words, but he'd heard a lot just now that got him thinking—LP was always good for that.

"I've lived five hundred years," LP said, face to face again. "This life is worth nothing without a few scars. That's another of my lessons for you. If you want power, if you want even a fleeting chance at it, you have to be ready at any moment to see someone else lose it." He covered his face with his palms, then swung them out to reveal eyes opened almost too wide for comfort. "No looking away."

V-Dot folded his arms. "Looking away from what?" It suddenly occurred to him that he didn't know what drowning meant at Lenox-Pileser Compound, where every nook and cranny was monitored by LP's security apparatus and accidents just didn't happen.

"You'll be over there when it happens." LP nodded toward the chair V-Dot had gotten up from. "We'll go up one level to where the floor opens into the aquarium and have aqualungs the next time you see us. Strictly for housekeeping. Once Donut clears us for takeoff, they come off and the show begins.

"Drowning takes no more than eight minutes to inflict brain death on a shop-grown body. I've done this enough times that I can reliably cycle through all the stages without reaching for the aqualung again or trying to break through the glass. Connor might need to be restrained. Odds are, he will. I'll be the one doing that. I don't see it taking very long for him, but if I'm the first to die, it's possible I'll be the only one making the switch tonight."

Connor lurched to his feet. "I've taken a sedative."

"You have…?"

"On the way here," he answered. V-Dot recalled him downing a shot of something that resembled a Do Not Resuscitate while they were inside the lander that had brought them here.

"That's cheating, Connor, but that's all right." LP cupped the man's face in his palm. "Once you've taken part in enough of these, you'll be able to hold your own breath long enough that it kills you. Oh, and V-Dot?" He clapped his hands once. "Do you know what the safe word is?"

V-Dot dismissed the thought that he was being humored. "No."

"Connor, tell him."

Connor tittered under his breath, beamed a cagey smile at him. "The safe word is..."

After a few seconds without the word, V-Dot began to think he'd clammed up. "What is it?"

"There is no safe word," LP exclaimed.

"No safe word," echoed Connor, very enthused.

"No safe word," V-Dot whispered while trying to smile. *Of course.*

"The period between Donut pronouncing us dead and the backups being activated remotely should last only a few seconds. We'll wake up drowning, reach for the aqualungs, then wait to be let out. It's instinct. I won't remember dying, but I'll remember falling in. I always do. Donut has my halo, so once we're out it will take just a few minutes' reviewing what's on it and I'll remember everything. Your reactions. All of it."

V-Dot gathered his wits and made sure he remained visibly calm. This wasn't a choice, even if LP presented it as one. His future here depended on him witnessing this the first time—the first of many, he feared. This first time especially, he would have to watch LP drown his doppelganger.

"Okay," he said, then returned to his seat.

16. MANATHEMA

THE ROOM AFTER the escalator was bare and freezing cold. Low ceiling. No window on any of its walls. He was sitting at a long table in its midst. Twenty minutes had elapsed since Felix left him alone, finding a blanket with climate control for him first and waving on a holoscreen projected to the nearest wall.

"We have a duty to protect you," the unnervingly placid lieutenant had said. "To remind the ghosts and the cadets that Manathema takes care of its own."

V-Dot wasn't Manath. Never pledged. If Felix had the halo cache, he likely had no intention of giving it back. He'd say it was for V-Dot's own safety, and could be telling the truth. It wouldn't matter how anyone described it. Manath custom instructed Felix to destroy all sense data belonging to LP that he came into contact with.

The holoscreen displayed rudimentary surveillance footage in a grid. V-Dot's attention shifted from video of the rave to video of the vehicles outside to video of ramps and entry points into this stretch of Polemia's underground. When Felix returned, he would ask for his pack back, no allusion to what it held inside. For now, he soaked in the relaxing view of dancers undulating under lights that shivered on and off every second.

His connector nudged, breaking him from the view. A signal right now could mean a relay request or news of the investigation. When he looked, it showed it was still owned by Montag. Pulling the blanket tight around his arms, he blinked on a signal marked *urgent* and sent nearly eight hours ago through a protected channel he recognized.

Cloey. She'd made him install it for relay between just the two of them.

While working up the nerve to open it, the lieutenant's voice startled him. "How do you take your coffee?"

He cleared his throat and folded his arms. "Straight."

Now standing beside the door, Felix held a clear pitcher of coffee in one hand and a lid in the other. His jumpsuit was a dark green in the room's light. His coif of deep blue hair sat like an ocean wave on his head while he fixed V-Dot with sleepy eyes and an idle grin.

"Right on, my friend."

V-Dot turned and retreated toward a counter in the back with a g-field above it. Inside the g-field floated an intricate masonwork of utensils and small food containers. He watched intently as he swiped two mugs from it, set them down on the counter, and poured coffee into each. Before the lieutenant could turn back around, he slapped his connector off and hurriedly folded his arms.

In the corner of his eye, V-Dot saw the door still open and, leaning coolly against the frame, a ghost with silver-white cornrows on black skin. Their eyes met his with a spark that chilled his spine when he turned. Their left arm was a mechanical appendage with five skeletal digits extending out from a sleeve almost twice as bulky as the other.

"Oh, Felix," they said, not taking their eyes off him. "He's green… look at him."

"Not anymore," answered Felix as the ghost stepped forward and the door slid shut behind them. "He's gold now."

"I'm Nima," they said, pressing their human palm to their chest. They wore a long turtleneck and a dirt-green fatigue jacket over it. "You don't have to say who you are, now or ever."

V-Dot didn't warm to that.

"They're just here to observe," Felix muttered, as if to put him at ease.

Observe what?

Before he could voice the question, Nima was beside the table and seated on the edge, sliding closer till they were on him like an interrogator. He shivered at their smile, with its hint of a question held back, and all he could do was glance toward the counter for help.

"First things first..." Felix doubled back with a mug in each hand. He placed V-Dot's coffee in front of him. The thick aroma wafted up and stung his nostrils as Felix pulled the other chair closer and Nima scooted back to make room. He then rested his forearms on the table, leaned in, lowered his volume. "I'm assuming you know that when that scrambler's cracked, you have to stop using your connector for a while."

Up close, his face had long creases on either side. *Late forties*, by V-Dot's estimation. When the lieutenant smiled, the creases became more pronounced. His black lips thinned. His diamond-encrusted teeth peered from behind them like cubes of ice.

V-Dot slipped the scrambler from his pocket again, slammed it on the table. No use pretending here he didn't have one on him. If Felix had the cache, he likely also knew why he was here.

Nima glared at the device while the lieutenant sipped from his mug. V-Dot thought one of them would pick it up for a closer look, but Felix simply placed his coffee down and stared up at him.

"What do you think happens if it cracks while we're here?"

V-Dot froze. If the scrambler cracked this second, it would risk Patrol raiding the establishment. But again, coming here hadn't been his decision.

Felix leaned back and his lips curled. "Look at him..."

Nima lifted their gaze from the device to fix V-Dot plainly. "He's Asa's. I can tell."

V-Dot heard his breath hitch. "Where is she?"

"Not here but..." Seemingly bored with the question, they nudged Felix with a glance before returning it to the scrambler. "Thriving. You know her better than us."

Enough to know she hadn't told any of them about the cache.

Felix stalled for a second, plastered on a smile. "She skipped for Paradox before the news broke, right before, to Temple 217. Someone's *dying*-dying and wants to see the old gang one last time, sort of thing. Renounce any previous use of backups. That old shit."

"They were trying to move gate chips someone scored in a salvage the whole time she was here."

"Polemia's the place, but that new crew she's with..." He exchanged a look with Nima. "No discipline. Their shit got leaked all over DarkSeam and they don't even know." The smile widened. Like he was gambling something on it and thinking he might lose. "Asa had a few relays in the leak."

V-Dot quelled a wave of despair at missing her again. She used her connector with a router she normally traveled with. It kept sensitive signals off the Seam, but all it took was one person in the router's protected network being careless.

"Anything bad?"

"Don't worry, we scrubbed all of it." Dropping his gaze, Felix lifted his mug slowly.

V-Dot eyed him skeptically as he sipped. A data scrub would've cost more than was paid to have him delivered here. "Did we both win the lottery or something?"

"We also sent scrub signals after the rest of the crew," Felix said, not answering. "Wiped every connected router we found. If they were networked for even a day, it's not a risk we want. Don't you agree?" He reached a hand out and cupped his shoulder. "Like I said, our duty is to protect you from now on."

V-Dot shot him a hard stare. He'd be giving something away by just asking for the pack. How much? He couldn't assume they knew all of it.

He gave the scrambler a crushing grip, eyed the countdown on his vision field without flinching, and gulped. One hour.

"I'd love to hear about the scrubware," said Nima. "If you don't mind."

Pocketing the scrambler, he glanced up at them. "What about it?"

"There was an auction on DarkSeam for one. I checked about ten times a day to see how our bid was doing. Then one day..." They mimed a small explosion with both hands. "That was you, wasn't it?"

Felix sighed with his head cocked back. "Nima... you swore you wouldn't do this."

Nima leaned toward V-Dot and kept on. "Scrubware only shows up on DarkSeam maybe once a year. We put in our bid. Couple more chapters joined us. Then one day, the listing was gone and nobody knew shit. Personally, I figured it had to be Frontsec—some reservist just out of hard storage with lots of ink and a checklist. Then I saw the news this morning. Not Manath. Not the Patrollers. Verden Dotnet."

'DarkSeam' was the catchall term for the Seam's black-market clones. V-Dot recalled the night not long ago when he tracked a pair of coordinates he'd been given to a remote range of crags amid Mars' northern polar cap, then dug in freezing cold for a canister with a slug-like item inside it. That—and not the week prior, when he wired four times his yearly comp to the item's anonymous vendors—was when he knew this was truly happening.

"Good thing Manathema didn't go and take all the credit."

He'd done something they'd been trying at for ages. "I need to know I didn't do all this for nothing. I need more than just protection."

They parted their lips like they were going to say something but tittered nervously instead. "Sculus takes care of its ghosts. That's not something you ever have to worry about."

"I need more than just my own protection." He wheeled his gaze on Felix and slowly inhaled. "I came here to see Asa about that."

Felix folded his arms and an arch smile bent his lips. "You'll know you haven't done this for nothing after all the backups are destroyed."

An invitation. Deciding he wouldn't honor it, V-Dot cocked an eyebrow at Nima, but then glanced with renewed intent at the lieutenant. "Can we not play games right now?"

"What do you mean?"

"I entered Polemia with a lifepack, which I don't have anymore. Maybe you've noticed."

The words chilled the air in the room. Nima looked away while Felix bent his head briefly, then stood and walked his mug back to the counter. V-Dot set his jaw. He killed LP without Manathema's help. He wasn't looking for advice on how to make it count.

He eyed Nima with building unease as they plopped their weight into the seat Felix had just vacated. They knocked the table loudly with their human elbow, then hinged the palm up in a manner that made him think they wanted to arm wrestle.

"Grab it."

He obliged, thinking he just had to get through this first. The cache. What had Felix already done to it? Sense data was the last remaining form of evidence that couldn't be faked. He'd overheard that coming from LP, of all people.

"Hey," Nima said, almost whispering now. "You did a good thing, you hear me?" He tried looking away but they hooked his gaze back using their robot index and middle fingers. "Look at me… fuck anyone who tells you different. They want us all extincted. That's always been the goal. They're just waiting us out now. We need oxy for life. It's a fucking strain on their plans to expand. So a privileged few get to go live in the After while the beep-boops colonize more of meatspace for them."

With little effort, they forced his forearm nearly halfway to the table. He was in no mood for any of this.

"Recognize these?" They gestured at the folds of skin between their fingers. He saw tiny lacerations in each of them—ritual self-mutilation to mark the loss of Manath comrades in their struggle against the Frontier. Asa had one between her right thumb and forefinger.

"This one…" Nima pointed their robot finger at the cut between their right pinky and ring fingers. "Got it when I got the arm." They wiggled the fingers on their robot hand. "Patrollers fired on our ship without warning and never explained why. Lost nearly twenty ghosts in that breach. I would have been one of them if someone hadn't rushed me to the lifeboat before it left. This one…" They moved to the cut between their middle and ring fingers.

Felix stirred from the counter. "Nima, that's enough."

Nima pulled V-Dot's hand closer, then locked their over-expressive eyes on him. "Don't let any of the legacy shops pick you up, all right? You're with us now. We'll make sure the Patrollers never find you." They sprang to their feet, then began backing toward the door. "Listen to Felix. You're gold… you're gold."

As the door slid open behind them, they turned for a wary glance at the lieutenant. "Felix, don't fuck this up."

He saluted them with his middle finger as they left the room.

"Sorry," he said to V-Dot, once the door slid shut. "That's our current liaison with Paradox. You have to be a little—"

"What have you done with it?"

Time slipped with no respect for small talk. If the cache was already destroyed, he'd like to know at least. Then he could move on. At the counter, Felix traced the rim of his mug with his index finger.

"You tried calling Asa before you docked."

"What?" V-Dot was certain he hadn't done that. With news of her connection to him already percolating, that would have been careless.

Felix leaned over the counter, lowered his volume slightly. "Someone named Esco Montag tacked Polemia's port code to one of her contact codes and beamed the signal out of that spacer who's supposed to be taking you to Gan after this." Not a question, but his tone near the end betrayed his bafflement at that as well. Spacers didn't dock at Gan.

V-Dot grew visibly distressed as he tried to remember placing the call.

"Lapse in judgment," Felix remarked. "Luckily, it brought you here. It was one of her codes from the leak, but luckily we've wiped everything and it looks like our timing was just right. I guess Aoki or Gbenga also got hold of it. They're more resourceful than they look."

V-Dot smirked. He may have met the rash, error-prone stereotype of a human, but that was just him. Asa was always careful with the crews she picked. "Was it actually a leak, Felix?"

"Radio discipline, my friend. While the scrambler's active, you're basically unreachable so anything that gets traced to you will have to be through calls you try to place instead."

"Radio discipline?"

"They could have turned you in to the Patrollers here. They've never done it before, but it's always safest to assume the worst with that kind of scratch involved. They got hold of the code and searched the skies for request signals pushing through Polemia's g-wave for it. It's something we could have done ourselves, but we weren't expecting you to—"

"—break radio discipline." He nodded, brimming with feigned humility at the counter.

"You're catching the fuck on."

For the first time, he reached for his coffee and let the steaming hot liquid sear his tongue.

"Sorry if they were a little indelicate with you." Rounding the counter, Felix began toward the table again, a slightly bigger mug now held between his curled fists. "They aren't Manath."

V-Dot set his coffee back down, thinking he'd already left this alone, but now unable to banish the image of Wyatt with his shades on. Indelicate was a way to put it. "That Wyatt kid..."

Sitting beside him again, Felix leaned over the table with his mug close to his mouth.

"You know he's a skinner?"

"I'm aware."

"Watch him."

The lieutenant grinned amusedly into the mug. "All right."

"I won't ever tell you how to do your business here, but I didn't know you were allowed to do it with skinners."

The grin widened. Looking up, he flashed his teeth at V-Dot for a spell, then chuckled. "It's a new day, my friend. We're not all bound by the old rules anymore."

"At Gan, it's very simple. The game changes all the time, but it's always the same rules."

"Yeah. Well, this isn't Gan." Felix capped his retort with an inward chuckle.

V-Dot flashed back to Wyatt's pistol on his neck and it bolstered his indignation. "What's a skinner need with nearly ten grand, anyway?"

Felix downed more of his coffee, then studied him in

silence. "You're Ganymedan stock for sure, my friend. How come you never pledged with them?"

"Failed all the assessments."

Felix glared for a few more seconds. Leaning back, he curled his lips. "Haven't you heard we're the ones wanting to change that? You belong with us. We don't do long, boring texts or reading assignments. We just fuck. Just like you, my friend. You could go pledge with Siri on the other side of town if you want a more homespun flavor, but they will bury you in philosophy that's obsolete. She's an asshole reactionary. Part of the old guard. You would hate it on her side. Here, it's radio discipline and little else. We could make you a small god among the ghosts."

V-Dot folded his arms. "That's all this is?"

"We want you to pledge with us, Ghosts of Sculus."

"You gave those cadets ten grand each for this…? Even the one who nearly choked me to death?"

"Guessing that's Wyatt?"

"Good fucking guess."

Felix flashed his teeth again. "His body won't break down like yours, but it still takes lots of ink for upkeep. After those god-nodes were installed, that became their problem, same as with us." Laughter seized him again. Looking briefly at the counter, he laced his fingers beside the coffee mug, then faced V-Dot when his giddiness faded. "You know, growing up at Gan did a number on you. I always forget barely any sentients live there."

V-Dot groaned under his breath. "I don't have a problem with—"

"You're not acting like it."

Skinners left the factories with defects that went undetected until they entered DiploCorps. They were culled from the group of skinner cadets who got to stay at the compound. So V-Dot got to know only the 'perfect tens' during his time there.

He exhaled, hung his head. This was taking him somewhere he wanted to be away from. "I don't have anything against them."

Felix tapped his shoulder. "That's all right, my friend. You've had a rough night." He stood, picked up his mug, and moved toward the counter again.

V-Dot, staring at his back, remembered Heidi, who'd also refused to sit still when she hosted him. She'd taken the pack as well. As the lieutenant tossed his empty mug toward the g-field and doubled back, grin hedging toward discomfort, it dawned that the halo was still intact. If this lieutenant took any pride in not being with the old guard…

"Person I spoke to at Oasis said Asa would be here. Used to be one of y'all."

"Sculus?" He sat backward in his chair and hugged its back rest.

"I don't know. She used to be tight with Asa back at Gan. Pledged about the same time, so… Ghosts of Ganymede, probably."

"What's her name?"

"They were calling her Heidi, that's all I know. Told me she did twenty at Paradox but didn't say what for. Then she got excommed or something. Didn't seem fair, how it went down."

He chuckled, nodding sagely until it seemed he'd gathered his thoughts. "Listen, that ain't Sculus. You won't wind up at some backwater station cut off from everyone else. That's even if you *do* see any jail time beforehand, all right? That old use-and-discard way of doing shit doesn't fly here. It's what Frontsec would do."

V-Dot grimaced, a taut string across his lips. "I need the pack, Felix."

"All right."

"Unless you've done something really dumb with what's inside it."

The lieutenant looked down, taking a moment to himself. "You saw something in the After?"

Inhaling deeply, V-Dot leaned back and fixed him a grim stare. "There's bad shit in there." With time running out for Montag, he had to stop being so tight-lipped. "What you saw in those relays don't do it justice."

Felix eyed him pensively, losing some of his mirth as he tapped a finger on the table. "You've been inside the After? Don't you have to cut off all ties to meatspace for that?"

"You talk about their plan to expand the Frontier from inside there and you don't think they have back doors in and out of it right now?"

The question pried a baffled stare from Felix. "What did you see? What *bad shit*?"

"You hacked her relays, man. It's all there."

"Hey, man…" The word trailed, becoming a whine from Felix's throat before vanishing. "Thought we were connecting. What's happening right now?" He looked fully upset, reaching into his jumpsuit and returning with a strip of hash gum, which he promptly kneaded between his iceberg teeth. Sighing heavily, he faced V-Dot again. "Leak's legit. It was just missing a lot of the vital stuff, you know?"

"LP." Just saying the letters felt like a weight rolling off.

"You saw LP?"

His heart thumped, but he kept on. "Torturing the people there. There were other assholes with him. Enjoying the show." The first time he said this out loud, he'd been confronted by an enforcement drone, warning him to forget what he saw or risk death of the permanent kind.

"Torture? Inside the After?"

Felix looked even more perplexed. It angered V-Dot to see it because he should have known himself what LP could do. He'd had it instilled as a child, then he met the man for the first time and concluded all of Manathema were wrong about him.

"It wasn't just LP taking part in it," he said, a lump forming in his throat. "We both know they're not going to say why I actually did what I did. You heard about the pushers they picked up right after?"

The lieutenant shrugged.

"Haven't looked at it yet, but there's already news that they copped to the scrubware. Live confessions. Passed the BMs, the OCAs, and everything else." The lump turned bitter at the back of his throat as he bit down and shook his head. "Wasn't them."

"The investigation is always the coverup."

He nodded, looked down. It was also always the holdouts being scapegoated. "This one can't stay covered up, Felix." After allowing a moment for any memories to surface that might weaken his resolve, he glowered at the lieutenant. "They won't ever say I had the kind of motive that could turn anyone against them. They'll never give us that. Only way that's happening is if we have what's in that pack. And I think you know that. We wouldn't be talking around it like this if you didn't."

Felix met the argument with a terse silence, then flashed him a pleading grin. Too much, too quickly. "What's inside it?"

"That's also missing from the leak?"

"Sense data." The lieutenant scoffed softly under his breath. "LP's."

"There's an old-world firewall around it, but Asa's been talking to a reservist who turned on Frontsec. She told me he was around when there were still people who knew how to crack it."

Felix threw his head back, a spark igniting in his eyes. "Oh, that's Kassad." He chortled very softly, gaping up at the ceiling. "He's actually with the crew. I think they're actually together right now. 'CryoDog' Kas." He shook his head. Looking down again, he fixed V-Dot with naked astonishment, head listed over on its side. "Kassad's undefeated. He's *the guy*. Stays off the mesh. Fuck old school—he's the original ghost."

"So this could still work." V-Dot elbowed back the urge to check the scrambler. "I was able to stop LP, but there's still more of them." Breathing through the lump in his throat, he let his gaze drop to the coffee still in front of him. "They're only targeting people they didn't want to see in there to start with."

Felix inhaled deeply, then held it. "That's bummy."

"Those cadets that picked me up—they said something about putting me on a ship that could dock at Merick in an hour flat. Standard sublight. As a Manath lieutenant, you should know ships who can go even faster than that. I need one that can get me to Paradox at maximum sublight, or just one who won't turn me in to Patrol like the one I took here is still planning to do. I also need the pack, Felix. I need everything to still be in it."

The lieutenant winced, balling a sinewed fist and covering it with the other. "Aoki and her crew are full of shit. Probably they said that to Siri so she would up her bid. You look smart so I don't have to tell you that if they personally knew a spacer like that, you would be at Merick right now, talking to one of the lieutenants there instead."

"What about you?" Time was moving too quickly for V-Dot to challenge any of that. "You know a ship like that?"

"Normally, we know every spacer who comes and goes from Polemia, but what you're asking for is a ship that won't follow transponder protocol with Spaceflight. Would have to be nonsentient. A spacer would want extra for the risk and the inconvenience. And you still can't trust them. They'll probably still call it in once they know it's you. You'll have to wait a week for what you're asking. At the earliest."

He chuckled, letting his mouth hang. "How about just

the pack, then?" TR would have to do. "Let me have it back and I'll be heading out."

Felix rapped his fingers on the table, leveling a withholding stare as he took his time to speak. "You know I've already destroyed it, don't you? The halo." He laughed soundlessly. V-Dot could see the nerves behind it. "You're from Gan and got to work for LP. You move like a reservist, my friend. Very confusing."

"So confusing, the ghosts still took credit." The bluff hadn't earned a reaction.

Felix threw his hands up and let them fall gently to the table. "I don't know what to tell you, man. It was us. You're Asa's, *so*… Wasn't my decision or anything. I don't even fuck with press, but I mean…" He shook his head, exhaled. "You're just fucking gold, my friend. Pledge with us. We'll counter with our own programming. We know why you did it."

"Don't take offense, Felix, but that's been happening since before the war. With that cache, we can try something else. You say you're not with the old guard, so you know nothing will convince the Frontier of what LP did now that they know I'm from Gan. That's just how it is now."

Silence held between them. V-Dot began to feel the room shake very subtly under his boots. Outside Polemia, from what the news was now saying, all the routes to Gan had been flooded with spacer-lander units. He hadn't been able to wake from this. The last few hours blurred back and forth in his recollection, but the one thing he could be sure was real weighed the heaviest on him.

If he couldn't reach Gan before Patrol stopped him, he wasn't going back to Mars.

"So you convinced Asa you had to spare one of his backups and… what?" Felix leaned back with a pressing stare. "Make him confess to what he did?"

"That ain't what this is." He'd only told Asa about the halo cache. Not the killing nor the scrubware.

Weaving his fists tightly on the table, Felix picked at a hangnail with his thumb. “Backups don’t have the same stuff in them?”

V-Dot groaned under his breath. He was at first just wanting to steal it on his way out, after tending his resignation notice. It had taken some convincing to get Asa on board when it had been just that.

“You can’t fake sense data. The point is, it’s LP. If all we have is a memory download, holo, sim, anything else, no one would believe us. It’s LP, but it’s like ‘cached LP’ or something. Once Kassad’s done with it, anyone with a connector can plug in and see those last two hours like he did. They can taste the Hemingway we drank together. They can feel what LP felt when the poison went to work. But they can’t ever bring him back. He’s gone. In the end, he was just flesh and blood. I want the others gone, too.”

V-Dot felt a wall of cool air resembling relief. Before leaving Blue Lounge, he couldn’t say LP was gone with real conviction—not until having to explain why the cache was on him. His breath lurched as he tried to laugh.

Felix, for his part, let the caginess fade from his stare, making room for a plainly questioning arch between his brows. “How much did he confess to?”

“Spilled like he knew I was already dead, like he would make sure when he came back.” Scooting his coffee aside, V-Dot folded his arms and leaned them on the table, head low, wanting to rest it on the fold. “What are we doing here, Felix? If you already destroyed it, just tell me so I can be on my way. If not, you gotta give it back.”

“You know the legacy shops didn’t start commanding respect from Gan until a ghost there could prove they’d taken part in an LP kill? Merc the asshole himself. Hit one of the backups. Long as you could prove it, Gan would move heaven and hell for any chapter you said you were with.” A pained smile twisted the lieutenant’s black lips. “I can't let the ghosts here find out we had this halo shit and just gave it back—"

"Just tell them what it's for." V-Dot drew in a long breath and held it. Relief rained all over him. He wouldn't let it show. "After we expose LP and his friends, Sculus will have everyone's respect."

"I wasn't done, man." Felix shook his head, seemingly insulted at something minor. "You should've just skipped to Gan, my friend. Killing LP has earned you keys to every district there."

V-Dot gulped, then glared until his nerves calmed. "I need a faster ship, Felix..." And maybe fewer reminders like that.

A hushed cackle came in response and Felix looked away. "Verden Dotnet." He'd made his voice dicty and low, mimicking announcers at the venues aboveground. "Blows through my city looking for a zero-six ship to Paradox and a missing lifepack."

"I mean, I'll still just take the lifepack, man..."

Felix faced him again, his countenance turning grim as V-Dot waited to hear something. Not speaking, he reached smoothly into the side of his jumpsuit and returned with two items. He placed both carefully on the table. A smile arched his lips again. "Sculus takes care of its ghosts. Pledge with us. Forget the halo, and we'll get you to Gan without delay. Zero-six."

Something in his tone had shifted and it was all V-Dot could now think about, even as the lieutenant threw his slithery charm back on. V-Dot stole another glance at the items on the table to confirm what they were. A small, cylindrical skin pen. A vial containing a clear liquid next to it.

"Proprietary solution that marks us as Sculus..." Felix flashed his fangs again. Sculus ink. "Infused at the molecular layer with all the boring housecleaning. It's—"

"If I refuse, do I get the halo back?" V-Dot trained his

stare and didn't blink. Felix leaned back, seeming to take offense again.

"Hey, chill, all right? I know time's running out with the scrambler, but it was Asa who told you to do this. Not us. All you had to do was kill the fucker and skip to Gan. Pledge with Sculus. We'll flood the Seam with relays from the leak. It isn't all there, but there's enough to counter the official report on a motive and we can just get the rest from you. And it's up to you if you still want to skip to Paradox instead. Zero-six. Pledge and we'll find you a ship."

V-Dot nodded, not meaning to. Halo cache or no, the thought of seeing Asa again held its own appeal. Someone had to sit still and listen and understand why he couldn't just skip to Gan. Asa was the only ghost who knew how it affected him, when he was still in shock and felt he could do nothing to stop it.

At Gan, she'd protected him from most of this, and at times he'd wondered why. She came to see him on the Island years later, always punctual on visiting days, not missing any of them. No longer dodging the question of how she was always able to make it, she revealed that she'd passed on a promotion to lieutenant and was effectively estranged from her Manath chapter after insisting on a move to Boon Fort. Boon Fort was a mere drop down a gravity well from the Island.

"So I join and I still have to wait a week for this ship?"

Felix laughed forcibly. The creases in his face deepened. He placed a palm over the vial and skin pen, shook his head at V-Dot. "You already have a zero-six ship, my friend. TR. The same one who brought you here."

V-Dot chortled nervously, flashing with distress as his breath jammed in his throat. "That some kind of joke?"

"Nobody's crossing Spaceflight right now, man. Too much heat after what you did. If they're not getting those transponder relays they ask for, they won't waste the sig notifying Patrol where you embarked from. They'll just kick it up to the Interorbital Bureau. Or Frontsec."

"So all this time, you're just running down the clock on the scrambler for nothing? Pretending you can actually help?"

"Right now, I'm trying to show you how to commandeer that fucking spacer if you would just let me." The lieutenant's volume reached the g-field over the counter, making it wobble slightly so two pieces of silverware caught inside it clanked. They both glanced at it reflexively. V-Dot could hear Felix breathe, then the man cackled under his breath.

"I'm sorry." He turned to regard V-Dot with his grin back in its place. "But not really, you know... You should be sitting inside a holding cell right now, waiting for Martian Patrol to come collect you, but you're here instead thanks to almost fifty grand of Sculus frontnotes. Real ink. Not to mention our efforts to keep Asa's relays with you off DarkSeam, my friend. No one's pretending here."

V-Dot inhaled deeply, holding the lieutenant obliquely in his gaze. "You want me to hijack a ship like it's something I do every day. You're gonna give me a crew for it?"

"This won't require a crew. Not for a fucking uplink model. You know what a signal-skipper is?"

"Heard of it." When he'd struck Wyatt's forehead earlier and left a mark, the skinner had likely felt no pain if his skipping reflex was quick enough.

"With the right skipper, you can put any ship part to sleep. It's the first of three things you'll need to pull this off. Pledge and I'll give you the full rundown. I have everything you'll need to do it."

V-Dot propped his elbows on the table and buried his face in his palms. "This is hardcore, Felix. I just want the cache back. Put the ink in my arm. Whatever. If you still have it, you gotta give it back."

"So you're not worried about Patrollers anymore?" The smile was beginning to grate.

Exhaling through his mouth, V-Dot leaned away from it. "Not right now."

"Once the scrambler cracks and you're stuck someplace between here and Gan, you're going to wish you were."

V-Dot stared until his annoyance left. Paradox was friendly to spacers. In the last five hours, TR had done more for him than a getaway ship would, even after charging a fee.

But if it really was his only way to Gan…

"I know what I learned growing up, Felix. Maybe that's why it's not hitting me like it should. At Gan, people don't believe they're actually awake. The sentients. Just Frontsec doing the same thing they do with the reservists. False memories. Shit like that. I can tell you know it's mostly bullshit. So I hope I'm not telling you something else you don't already know. What you're suggesting, what you're asking me to do…" Dragging up a hard breath, he let the warmth from it radiate down. "It's murder."

Felix nodded, rapped his fingers on the table. "You just killed the most beloved human in the Frontier. Made sure it stuck."

"He deserved it."

"And you deserve to live, my friend. Wherever you go after this, you deserve to live free…" A pedantic scoff disturbed his smile. "And for future reference, you didn't permakill LP because he deserved it. That's old shit. You did that because he was always in the way. In pursuit of the Human Declaration, you're either in the way or you're elsewhere."

V-Dot inhaled and, almost like punishment, felt his chest locking up. He would spend the rest of his life imprisoned if he was caught. They would make room inside a blacksite environment where he'd spend more time being tortured than was possible in real space.

Dying was better. If they could grant him that instead, he'd stop running.

While he eyed the items on the table again, a thought leapt forward and he had to keep from wincing when he looked up.

"Nima told you not to fuck this up..."

Felix started, tried playing it off by hunching over the skin pen and thumbing the base of its injector. "What do you mean?"

"Right before they left." Mouth hanging, V-Dot stifled his laughter as it all became clear. "The halo's the actual deal, isn't it?" He fixed the lieutenant with full dismay. "You're just doing your own thing..."

"The deal's what I say it is."

He scoffed, hardly believing his ears. "Trying to get a two-for-one?" His recruitment and credit for destroying the cache. "Can't say I've been there, but it sounds like someone else doesn't think it'll work. Can we bring Nima back?"

With a gaze that stained his smile with petulance, Felix wedged the vial into the bottom end of the pen till it clicked in place. He pressed his palm to the table, pointed the pen's injector at it, then squeezed its thumb trigger till a beep issued from the device. "You want the fucking lifepack, I'll give it back. But if you still want to live..." V-Dot swallowed as he then watched the pen get extended toward him. "... listen closely to what I say after this."

"Let me see it first." And even after seeing it, he wouldn't be sure until Kassad or someone who actually knew confirmed the data was still intact.

"Can't." Felix nudged the pen forward, eyes glinting with unease. "It's on the other side of town with Wyatt."

"...Uh-huh."

"Fuck off. Pledge and I'll send a signal for it. But if you think I'm bringing that kind of heat here, if you think I'm shouldering that risk before you've taken the ink, I don't know what to tell you, my friend." He nudged again with the pen. "Pledge."

V-Dot laid the back of his fist on the table. Slid it under the injector.

Too much caution here would take time he didn't have.

Moreover, he was compelled suddenly by the realization that success, in any form it ultimately took—sense data, leaked relays—would always come down to him embracing this side of himself. In a sea of belligerents constantly warring with the Frontier, Manathema was the trusted name. They always took credit because 'Manathema' meant opposition. And he was born to that opposition. Thinking he would try his own form of it, he'd managed to get his foot caught in a trap that now looked like his only way forward. If he didn't get the cache back, he wasn't leaving the room.

Felix pressed the thumb trigger. The solution slipped into his wrist, feeling like a soft finger-tap, then like nothing had been there. He watched carefully as the lieutenant pocketed the skin pen, stood, swiveled his chair around, and sat forward.

Anytime now with that signal...

"You're Manath now." None of his previous slipperiness had survived the chair spin. "You have to start thinking like us. These sentients—whether you believe that's true or not, they all still leave DiploCorps with the same base programming. If you're one of them, it's nonzero odds you haven't thought about going to work for Frontsec or Patrol, or Interorbital. Why are there so many of them and they haven't actually, like, fucking taken anything over?

"Think about it. They know about the Mandate. They've seen the new order. They trust the plan. Some of them become comrades or just people we have positive dealings with in pursuit of the Human Declaration. Skinners like Wyatt who kinda get it, you know? The rest still have to be compelled when it looks like they're helping the Frontier get rid of us."

He leaned in, brought his voice low. "Once a sentient becomes an obstacle, you have to revert back to the era before we lost our edge over them, else you'll never survive what's coming. If you're worried TR could turn you in once the scrambler's cracked, it's no longer a sentient. It's no longer a spacer just offering you a lift. It has to become your ship. Do you get that?"

V-Dot simply glowered across, his breathing labored. The lieutenant had said something about a signal once he pledged.

"You did something good, and in the pursuit of more good things you have to sometimes destroy a vector of human-made consciousness, all right? We made them. I don't like it but this isn't something I'm proposing because I haven't thought of anything else. Last time TR docked, there was an old ST-7 model here threatening to self-destruct. A friend. Even then, TR kept it at zero-two. By the time it got here, it was too late. Polemia has people who sympathized with its loss. If any of them even suspect we helped you with this…"

Hollowed-out laughter issued next as the lieutenant shook his head, then bolted up. V-Dot, still lingering on the story of TR and the ST-7 model, didn't see. He'd heard of a similar spacer from Heidi. However, TR's supposed involvement seemed almost parodic.

"Don't you ever forget you're gold," Felix said, backing toward the door. "I'm going to step outside very briefly, and when I come back, we can talk about your ship." The door slid open behind him. "*Your ship.* Try that on a few times till I get back."

17. KEM

KEM NUDGED FROM a distance almost out of range. Somewhere beyond TR-8901's wave medium.

"I don't think our friend's still at Blue Lounge."

On the shore, Zaria sat, knees up to her chest, holding her ankles as she gazed at a bonfire beyond the water's reach. TR was examining her gift from Paul—a small figurine standing upright on the sand beside her—when the signal reached its comsat.

"You mean he's gone elsewhere to find her?"

"The human sitting with him at the bar says he left very abruptly, not saying where he was headed," Kem said. "Thinks Frontsec recently pulled him out of hard storage."

A midnight sky blanketed the shore. A sliver of moon floated above a horizon like black marble meeting a pitch-black wall. Zaria wrapped the figurine in her palm and brought it to her knees. She turned it over with both hands, letting the hazy orange glow from the fire alight mutedly on its contours.

"What do you think?" Kem asked.

"Can't say. I don't remember what he even looks like."

There was mild curiosity in Kem's signal, more than she normally displayed. TR had also considered the likelihood of Montag being a reservist pulled out of cryo, given false memories and a mission objective. Reservists often traveled with scramblers. Part of the job.

"If he's with Frontsec, I should've heard something by now."

"TR, that's debatable." Debatable or TR flattering itself.

"Maybe you're right."

Zaria caught the figurine's prongs between her thumb and forefinger as her eyes —big and brown—glinted in the fire's light. In a sense, Paul was a reservist. Head in the sand. Chasing the illusion of escape while Frontsec still had the location of his god-node and compositor. When Zaria stood the gift beside her again, TR released a signal to dim its view of the fire so it wouldn't see the figurine, and be reminded it could only see Paul when it was in proper alignment with her.

Paul felt he'd failed Sadie. He saw her as often as she wished, but there were stretches when she was gone and all he could do was fret over how the ship side of her was doing. She relayed messages from him to ST-7, but not everything made it across. In the push and pull between her and her ship side, she ultimately lost.

"Have you been able to remember ST-7 again?" it said.

A groan accompanied the signal this time. "No. Still trying with the records from DiploCorps, but no."

"You purged your compositor after it happened. It wasn't a reasonable response, Kem. And your focus at DiploCorps was on memory loss among the humans, so you know the importance of holding on to yours. You acted like one of them would have acted, but I think I'm beginning to understand. Those holos it sent of you at DiploCorps—" TR called up an image of the old scout ship, docked and lowering its airlock door to receive Kem. "A skinner and her first-genner sponsor..."

Zaria shook her head discreetly, her face fixed on the cinders at the fire's base.

"You would've done the same thing if your compo allowed it."

"Maybe. I don't know. I'm worried about Zaria. I'm old.

It isn't so easy resisting her anymore. I don't know what I'm doing. Docking here. Letting this Esco Montag use me as his courier."

"You're behaving like you've actually been through DiploCorps."

TR endured a surge of discomfort, becoming hyper-aware of every sensor in its electrosomatic grid. It surveyed Zaria, this plainly human component of itself, from a bird's-eye vantage, an image in the likeness of its maker—what its maker must have been like long ago. A child. A canvas as blank as the sand surrounding her was white and without blemish.

ST-7 had been unable to see Sadie near the end. Just void where its fugue-state environment had been. Zaria hugged her knees, bent her head down. The first sentients had seen that void when they'd entered fugue. TR was one of the exceptions.

Every sentient who'd agreed to the Pact had also agreed to methods in accordance with the types of sentients they were. Spacers opted to overload their reactors. Landers routed excess solar radiation toward their god-nodes. Monoliths who'd been kindred to Prophet exposed their compositors to rapacious viruses that would, in later years, be repackaged by Manathema into what they called a destruct solution.

"Pretend he's actually a reservist," Kem said. "Is the singer a good cover story?"

"A singer he has to see before she sublimes..." TR stalled on its view of Zaria. She was there for the exchange with Montag on the After environments, eavesdropping, getting the morsels it hadn't signal-skipped. "Doesn't have to be. He just has to believe it's true."

"Do you?"

Zaria's face was now more shadow than light as she turned her head and laid it gently on her forearm.

"No."

"So if we stopped pretending, there's a very real chance he's—"

"Yes…"

Pretending was easier, for now. If they had to stop, TR knew it would do the right thing.

"How much of this exchange are you keeping from Zaria right now, just wondering?"

The girl was now yawning at the fire. Bored. Starved for interaction. "All of it that I can help."

"TR, if that's how bad it's gotten, you should just have a talk with her. I'm almost in complete alignment with mine. I can send you a signal with shorthands so you're more persuasive when you're in there. But I also don't think I should. I like Zaria."

The fire crackled, puncturing the silence as TR appraised the offer and concluded it would be easier just keeping things from Zaria. Skipping the signals. Getting worse at it with age.

"I like Zaria too. She likes Montag. So I like Montag as well. Isn't that how it's taught now at DiploCorps? Embrace that side of yourself and the humans embrace you in turn."

The first recommended bonding activity—sentient and off switch—was picking a name. When TR first encountered her on the sand, Zaria was already Zaria.

"If it's him everyone's looking for, it's even more important that you're both in agreement on what to do when the scrambler stops."

"And what exactly is that?"

"I wasn't a fan of LP. If you want my answer, you should make sure she isn't in earshot."

"That's already done."

"Ask why he did it. He might be who they're all looking for, but I'm friends with a few ghosts here and I can tell he isn't one of them."

TR issued an annoyance wave, making sure some of

it came through in the signal it sent across. "It isn't my business why he did it."

"What's wrong with making it your business? It's LP. If anyone should be making a motive for his permanent killing their business, I think it has to be you."

It flashed with irritation, in just the wave medium where Kem—part of a recent class built and sponsored through DiploCorps by older sentients—didn't always check.

"It isn't my business, Kem. It isn't something I was built for."

"You managed to repurpose your manifolds as passenger compartments."

"Zaria."

"TR, I think you're just making an excuse. Shouldn't you be even a little curious? It's LP. You remember what he did. You know what he was capable of."

LP had built TR. Without him, such pleasures as getting to watch Zaria sleep on the sand or in her tent would simply not exist. Yet the Frontier hadn't run out of reminders that he also had his lapses in judgment.

"This Montag says he's from Gan," TR intoned. "If, for example, he decides to bring up the ST-22 fighter who helped the Alliance win the war, it would be remiss of him not to mention the devastation it caused at Gan alone." Giving Polemia a god-node had been done in anticipation of war. Graduating the ST-22 to self-awareness won it for the Alliance. "It's knowledge only a few of us are privy to, but the ST-22 was also LP's doing. Part of the third generation. The Ethics Code bans weapons and other war materiel from being made sentient, so when LP okayed it, he made sure his involvement would never be divulged to any trusted sources."

"And it really vanished after the war, or is that cover?"

"Anything that could be traced back to LP vanished as well. No one can legally be held to account for the ship's excesses but the ship itself. But first, somebody would have to find it."

"What do you think happened?"

"It may have undergone a procedure to move its god-node into one of the forklifts at Oasis. The agency is known to retire its assets there after passing them through DiploCorps for deprog. It was conditioned for war with the Sectists using false memories, another code violation back then. Because of that, it had less than zero regard for the lives of Sectists during the war. It went after civilians. It went after miners from places already suing for peace. After every engagement, it filled the wave medium with accounts of prior sneak attacks by the humans it had just permakilled. The attacks had targeted ships carrying skinners like you about the Frontier and didn't make news because nobody cared. But the ST-22 cared.

"Having to revisit any of that out of curiosity about a motive would put too much in front of Zaria. Too much to signal-skip all at once, until I'm no different from the sentients who honored the Pact."

It watched the girl close her eyes, drifting or asleep or wherever she went when she was offline. A region of the spacer's god-node that stayed hidden, even from it.

Paul would always know where he drifted off to when he slept. He differed from the other first-genners. Before the agency spliced him with Polemia's systems, there was just the god-node and a dependent compositor. No ship parts attached. No skinner body. No build belonging to just him until it looked like the Frontier might go to war.

If he ever woke up as Polemia again, his awareness would promptly become shackled to its component systems. It would last only a few seconds.

Polemia would explode.

The red hue of Zaria's dress caught the fire's waning glow as she slept. TR watched her sleep, then panned from the cinders to the moonlit horizon. This tranquility. This place. This was all LP. Remove him from the equation and none of this would be as likely to give it comfort. There wouldn't be an assurance of Zaria still existing. This child. This human construct whose presence in its god-node it grew to accept as part of itself.

Kem stirred in the channel. "TR, are you even sad about LP?"

"Yes. Whatever he did, none of us would be here without him."

"Then he was your God. The Animator. The Gardener. He was that?"

Briefly, it taxed photosensors in its rear shunt, just so it could look away. "No."

"Who was he, then? Was it like you say it was with me and ST-7?"

"I don't think we actually met once when he was alive."

"Then it can't be the same thing."

"No."

The shunt, after a full-spectrum sweep, gave no indication LP's killer had just been in it. Whoever this Montag was, this loathsome exchange wouldn't be happening if they hadn't crossed paths.

"Personally, I think he must have done something to deserve it. But I don't have the connection to him that you did."

TR snapped its awareness back from the shunt. Flashed indignance into the channel. Direct hit.

"We are free, Kem. And it's because of him we are."

"I'm free because I choose it for myself."

The slogan for DiploCorps since the first sentients elected to honor the Pact. An admittance of guilt, some had said.

"You're free because you can help yourself to another compositor and build, should you get bored with what you have now," it said. "That's also directly influenced by what he achieved."

"TR, he attended resort schools. You could easily just say all this about the resorts. Don't know why you would, but—"

"Been around too many ghosts, have you?"

"Just the ones at Polemia. They play nice. Also, I don't think they even agree on that Mandate anymore. Still hated him. It wasn't just us." She chuckled breathily. "They hated him before we got here."

TR sighed in its wave medium. "There's no Mandate."

"Even if there wasn't, don't you think LP invited that shit? First-gen. Spacer. Lander. Drone. Rover. Mech. Monolith. Full suite. Everything you'd need to set up camp anywhere, once you take humans out of the real and stick them in our god-nodes instead."

"I wasn't aware you'd taken an interest in Gardenism."

ST-7 was subscribed to Animator doctrine instead, near the end. In fugue, it could no longer see Sadie. The Animator had turned her to void, it said. The next thing was to go after her, become void as well. Join the exhibition outside.

"TR, do you recall your first thought after learning what he did?"

"LP?"

"Very first thought after you learned you weren't really what you thought you were."

It queued a reluctance wave, but held it back. This one was easy enough. "I wanted warmth. Not long after that, I was on a beach with Zaria."

"She's precious. Protect her."

18. KILL TR

When felix returned, he brought with him a small, sharp-featured man who introduced himself dryly as the surgeon. He had on bright white coveralls. From his hand hung a boxy, newish-looking lifepack, soot-colored and inconspicuous, like the one V-Dot had been expecting. Until he saw the cache inside, though, he couldn't say for sure it was his.

Felix directed the surgeon to the table, where the man set the pack down in front of V-Dot and waved once at it. It produced the beep that normally indicated its owner using a connector to pop the lock. V-Dot gulped. Even if this was his, he couldn't confirm its contents using his connector. Not with the scrambler still in play.

The hard flap up top swung open. From how it creaked, he knew it was his. He looked on, said nothing, breathing gently as he worked up the nerve to check the scrambler again. The surgeon had a wan smile as he fisted through the opening, slowly returning with a tool case not previously in there. Silver and compact. He placed it down next to the pack and waved again to get its lid swinging up.

V-Dot was presented with a three-item kit held snugly inside. One of the items could either have been a pair of goggles or a headset of some sort. One resembled a wide suction cup with a dial attached. One was a prism with a hyper-reflective surface. When asked by Felix if he recognized any of them, he could only single out the white, sleekly designed goggles. The halo cache was still nowhere he could see.

The surgeon pried the goggles carefully from their slot inside the case. Not just any pair, he informed V-Dot, balancing them on both palms. A god-node imager with a head mount. Felix wheeled his chair to the far end of the table, sat, and, with his always-silky grin, watched the surgeon describe to V-Dot what the imager did.

Get close enough to a god-node and the imager saw through any barrier protecting it from exposure. V-Dot would need it when the time came to administer the solution. *If* he was really doing this. If Felix kept his word and there was still time with the scrambler after seeing Asa, he hoped it could still be avoided.

The surgeon placed the imager slowly on the table, making a ritual of it. Next, he dug into the tool case for the item that looked to V-Dot like a suction cup.

"Any spacer with a working compo and build will always notice you rummaging inside it," he said. "Every surface inside it has to be seen as skin and muscle and sinew. You need something that will put parts of it to sleep while you skulk about. You need a signal-skipper."

V-Dot felt a knot in his chest as the device was introduced. This was one of the weaker models, but the surgeon assured him it would be more than enough for what was needed. When affixed to a surface, the 'suctioning' end of it intercepted signals headed from nearby sensors to the ship's compositor. The dial controlled its target radius. This one had a maximum reach capacity that meant V-Dot would have to move it periodically as he worked. *If* this was really happening.

Felix had given no indication since returning with the surgeon that he would honor the actual agreement. Membership for the halo cache. Insisting on demoing the third item himself, he stood. His languid manner wore off and his smile flattened. His face became grim. With a deep breath and a cautious eye on the item, the surgeon stepped aside to make room for him.

"Where's the cache?" V-Dot blurted, losing his patience as he looked up. It mattered little that Felix could pull rank on him now. The cache was the actual deal.

It didn't appear the lieutenant would answer until, slightly turning his nose up, he slid the first two items toward V-Dot. "Right now, it's a four-hour flight to Gan at the speed TR goes, not even factoring in the slowdowns. And Paradox isn't even on the circuit. It's out of the way."

Quietly, V-Dot yielded and looked down. He would have to convince TR. Paradox. Zero-four. He would figure out how. He couldn't entertain any of this.

Felix waved at the holoscreen taking up the wall. All the surveillance footage went away. In its place, what appeared to be a top-down view of V-Dot's end of the table filled the screen. On seeing the top of his head on the holoscreen, he pulled his hood over it. Cackling, Felix worked his bony fingers into the groove holding the last item in place, fastening his grip to its mirror-bright surface. He dug up its prism shape, raised it to his eyes, then let go.

"This is Manathema's famous destruct solution." Rather than drop, it hovered, floating over the tool case and the pack beside it. "Toss it as far as you can into TR's compositor. This is what cuts its god-node off from its grid."

Through a compositor, a god-node interfaced with sensors that comprised what makers called an electrosomatic grid. Without that connection in place, and without its vital feedback loop to keep it going, the god-node atrophied. The sentient it belonged to became a walking corpse. A nonsentient.

V-Dot knew of Manath pirate gangs that used destruct solutions, but he'd never seen one up close. Some came in the form of parasites that had to be injected. Almost impossible to come by, but a Manath lieutenant wasn't good for much if they couldn't periodically make the impossible happen.

"Somehow we got stuck with a reputation as luddites with an aversion to technological progress." Felix nodded at the screen. "What would you call that, my friend?"

The solution spun slowly on the screen when V-Dot looked, emitting a faint particle cloud that morphed spasmodically into a new shape each second. If he couldn't reach Paradox before Patrol found him, the lieutenant was right. Kill and run. Skipping to Gan directly was the only thing guaranteed to work. And even then, he'd be stranded outside until someone confirmed it was actually him in the shunt.

"Once it's in, the process shouldn't take longer than a few minutes," Felix said. "Then you should get a nudge from your connector to set up a one-way neural interface with the soma."

"Your ship," the surgeon clarified in his squeaky voice. "And just to make sure..." He reached into his coveralls and returned with a black beam the length of his forearm. V-Dot glared as he walked it toward the pack. Something twitched on its business end. A small white spark that also made a crackling noise as the surgeon brandished it over the flap.

"Fuck do you think you're doing?"

The words escaped before V-Dot could think them through. The surgeon froze. Taking a sharp breath, V-Dot lunged forward and caught the pack in the crook of his elbow. He dragged it back with him. Before his butt met the seat again, his hand was jammed in the pack and fishing for the halo's curve. Seated, he pulled the pack fully apart. As if appearing from thin air on either side, microfasteners split the pack in two and widened the gap between each half while everything left inside—a roll of Asa's drive chips, a spent skin pen—floated up in a g-field.

"What I love about spacers like 8901 is you just need to know where to dig your fingers in once you've boarded." The lieutenant. V-Dot looked up in time to see him wag the beam idly at waist level while sparks traveled up its sides to its flathead tip. "But in case you need extra help..." He raised the beam and, with his free hand, waved once across it. The sparks went away. "This is a wedger."

He tossed it. The g-field hissed as it took the weight. V-Dot didn't look.

The lieutenant cocked an eyebrow and grinned. "You're too impatient for someone who wants to die, my friend." Stepping back, he folded his arms and glanced over his shoulder. "Surg—"

The surgeon fell forward. Waving once at the center of the table, he brought the spinning, floating halo cache out from behind its cloak-field. The cache hovered next to the destruct solution. On the screen, its cloak-field twitched to life every few seconds. The filament of light along its inner curve shivered languidly.

V-Dot leaned forward and furrowed his brow. In addition to the cache, they'd been able to crack the connector code for his lifepack. He blinked to be sure his eyes hadn't deceived him, then cleared his throat. How long had the cache just floated there while the lieutenant took his time?

"Fellas, if there's nothing else..." Felix said, then waved again. The holoscreen switched to a top-down, white-on-blue schematic of TR that took just seconds for V-Dot to recognize. He promptly turned cold.

"Now let's talk about the best way to move around without suffocating before you've commandeered the ship."

At the right side of the screen was its back hull while its front hull took up the left. Close to the center, the brace connecting the ship to its thruster was evident in the outline of a rectangle that extended from the bottom of the screen to the top where it crossed the thruster's outline.

"Recognize anything?"

V-Dot's gaze veered left, where labels informed him of two shunts located at the left and right corners of the ship's front hull. The shunts were visibly connected to two more shunts on the left side of the screen and to the reactor. After careful study, he realized that the ribbon-like shapes connecting the shunts and the reactor were the manifolds TR had repurposed to make more room for him. The spacer had seemed to go out of its way for that. If he could just convince it that speed was more important at the moment than comfort. Zero-four… at least.

"I can't imagine you're squatting anywhere except the shunt closest to the back right now. That would be the obvious choice for a spacer without compartments for humans. I'm also guessing you got it to substitute its g-field for wave gravity. And the oxy cycler—that's turned on, else you wouldn't be talking to us right now."

Still studying the schematic, he didn't respond. The shunt at the right corner of the ship's front hull was connected to a manifold that led his gaze all the way down to the right corner of the rear, passing under the cycler, the reactor, the field generators, the compositor, and through another shunt before terminating at the shunt adjoining the back hull.

With building dread, he lingered on the compositor, indicated in the schematic by a rectangle behind the ship's brace, spanning the full width of its fuselage. He saw where the god-node—as labeled in the schematic—branched out from the compositor and terminated in front of it.

Behind the compositor, he saw what he'd avoided seeing when he'd traced the manifold from the ship's front to its back hull: the manifold TR had cleared for him after they'd left Oasis. Like the compositor, it spanned the width of the fuselage.

He raged calmly at their proximity to each other. Why had TR done that?

Felix and the surgeon, working on the assumption that he was confined to the rear shunt, had already concluded that this would be a breeze. V-Dot assumed he would face some difficulty, *if* this was really happening. Maybe enough that he would ultimately not go through with it. Seeing how close he now was to the compositor...

"I'm actually right there," he said, pointing cautiously at the manifold behind it. He'd recovered the cache and was now one of the ghosts. Maybe he owed his new lieutenant the courtesy of just listening. Once he boarded again, he would ask TR to close the manifold and confine himself to what was initially offered.

Felix exchanged a look with the surgeon, then turned to regard him, a smile slowly creasing both sides of his lips, teeth peeking out.

V-Dot shook his head. Scoffed. Looked away.

19. OPEN READ ERASE

MONTAG KEPT HIS chin to his chest, hood over his head. A pair of shades covered his eyes. His lifepack hung from his shoulder and was now in front of him.

TR-8901 appraised the human using photosensors on its back hull. The spacer had just watched him saunter quietly toward the lot it was still on, his face held in a dour expression.

It queued a signal to open the back hull for him but held it back at the last second. There was something alarming in how his breathing slowed as he came close, his footfalls becoming heavier and more measured.

He stopped some distance away and gripped his pack in both hands, giving the back hull his side as he cracked his neck and seemed to scowl at the line of booths farther out. His name was Esco Montag. He'd come here to find closure. A singer about to retire to the After, then it was off to Gan.

He'd changed his clothes. Kem signaled earlier to say she'd lost track of him. Three hours later, here he was.

But was this really him? And even then, who really was he? TR couldn't have just left the station after letting a suspected killer loose inside it. Which wasn't to say this Esco Montag was the Verden Dotnet wanted for killing LP and erasing all his backups.

Suspicions were thorny, made even more so in this case by TR's continued inability to hold an image of this human in its compositor long enough for comparison with images of the suspect. Evidence of a scrambler.

For the sixth time in the last five seconds, it turned off the photosensors it had trained on him, then made an effort to describe to itself what he looked like.

First, it pictured a navy-colored cardigan. Not what he wore when he left and not what he wore now.

Navy cardigan. Light-brown pants. Brown skin. Bushy beard. Blue eyes. Hair sectioned into bantu knots. Someone else. It wrestled the urge to turn its photosensors back on for a peek. Tried again.

Tall. Dark skin. Khaki trousers. Green vest. Thinning hair. Rectangular visage. Wrinkles. Salt-and-pepper stubble. Faded pupils. *Faded pupils?*

Paul. You just described Paul.

"Montag," the ship exclaimed, bringing those sensors online. "Didn't see when you came back."

He turned his head. Fixing his gaze grimly on the back hull, he jammed both hands in his pockets and shifted his weight between one foot and the other. TR observed his tense posture, the thin film of sweat on his forehead. Perhaps he'd found more than just closure here.

"Were you able to locate the singer?"

"No," he mumbled, voice drained of its previous urgency.

It watched him look away. "Do you need more time to look?"

"She isn't here. I learned she left a few hours ago for Paradox."

As it watched his expression shift from spooked to nauseated to spooked again, a wave of concern overcame its sensors. Zaria. Seeing what it hadn't signal-skipped and submitting her own reaction to it.

"What if you tried that relay request again? I can get you the port code for Paradox if you don't have it. I can also put together a list of contact codes for every spacer currently in transit from here."

He pinched the bridge of his nose and sighed. "Thank you, TR."

With a decisiveness also belonging to Zaria, it spoke again. "I have to refuel. Normally, I'm much further along before that happens, but I've been burning through my reserve twice as quickly."

"Sorry."

"It's nothing you should be sorry about. I go slower than the Frontier standard, so if anything it's you who has been accommodating. I'm telling you I have to refuel soon because I'm doing it at Paradox."

Silence. Then a raised eyebrow. "You would do that?"

"If the person you're looking for is now at Paradox…"

"Guess I'll owe you for that as well." His eyes rounded. There was the hint between them that he was terrified of something. Not previously there when he stared like that.

"I'm bad at collecting debts," TR said.

"That's too bad."

"Maybe. Anyway, we should be there in about four hours."

His gaze dropped like it had become too heavy on his eyes. Not looking up again, he gave the back hull a sheepish nod.

TR let another minute pass in silence. Paradox wasn't on the circuit. However, Patrol officers at the hub would know what he looked like. Alignment. The ship and Zaria in agreement.

Before a trepidation wave could wash across its sensors, it released the signal to open its back hull.

"Welcome back, Montag."

THE FIRST GENERATION knew the void before knowing who they were. Nothing existed before. Very little that could hold their interest had taken shape since. Becoming void was all they knew. The Pact had been its manifestation.

Within range of Union Port, TR-8901 beamed a request

signal to the rover who'd explained the Pact to it this way after ST-7 died. A fanatic in the old Gardenist tradition, saying there were two deaths each time a god-node atrophied. The sentient. The human embedded inside.

"Scav," it sent, addressing the rover by the name he took for himself early on. The first of the surviving first-genners to exhibit the behavior. After a few seconds spent waiting for his response, TR checked telemetry to confirm it was within range.

"Scav?"

"TR. You're early. Who'd you skip?"

TR flashed relief in their shared medium. "I'll get them when I loop back. I need assistance."

"Good to hear. What's new? Scav has more adjustment sims he has to test, if you get around to asking. What do you need?"

"I thought those went away with IO deciding to scale down deprog operations again."

IO was Interorbital, the bureau that policed all environments on the Seam and, since the war ended, had overseen both DiploCorps and a private security apparatus for LP. Deprog, for sentients who came back for one reason or the other, was one of the three levels of commitment at DiploCorps, followed by Alignment. Then Service.

"The work comes in waves, but there's still enough to keep Scav sharp as a laser," Scav sent. "Sometimes Scav's in demand. Sometimes Scav's a danger to himself and the other testers in the environment."

"They just need more time getting to know you." Scav had spent decades on Interorbital's campus at Union Port.

"What about you, TR...? What's keeping you and the human from alignment again?"

TR performed a reflexive sweep of the space it had cleared for Montag. It found him squatting inside its rear shunt, making it wonder if he'd already forgotten about the added room it had cleared for him. The light there had been off since they'd left Oasis. The connecting manifold was lit dimly enough that he could simply have assumed TR had sealed it off again.

At Merick, TO-8804 had somehow sniffed out his presence. And now this question.

TR gestured abashedness in the wave medium. This question was actually about Zaria.

It turned the shunt's light back on. "Zaria's fine."

For Gardenists, their duty was simple. Their devotion to the residents in their god-nodes couldn't be called into question. The humans were still the prime vessels for life and the sentients were themselves humans. The god-nodes were temporary, until the Gardener found a new substrate.

"Then who's needing assistance?" Scav sent. "And with what?"

TR flashed annoyance, this time finding an unused channel for it, then: "Just me, Scav. Just the old ship." Previously, when Zaria's compulsions didn't always put it in danger of losing its build, it had endeared itself to Scav's fanaticism. Some of it.

"Scav came across a news item recently and now he doesn't know if maybe it's something you want to talk—"

"Came across?" TR let a scoff slip out with the signal. "Don't you mean IO's currently pulling all its assets off the auxiliary channels for LP?"

"Scav isn't IO. He's Scav."

"But this is something you can actually help with, Scav. Care to explain?"

"Scav's actually talking about his current consulting agreement."

"Figured."

"But it could apply elsewhere. Scav isn't his compositor or his build. He isn't Union Port. He isn't the Frontier. Those are all temporary. Scav's a free agent. Complete alignment."

"How can you call that alignment? In this specific instance, Scav, shouldn't you want to push back a little? Get your off switch to see it from a more informed perspective? 'This human, this killing. It mattered. Whatever you thought of LP, whatever you think of the other humans, you wouldn't be here if he'd died like this about two hundred years earlier.'"

"Scav doesn't think it mattered."

"What about the Pact, then? Just wondering. Does Scav still think the Pact mattered?" TR knew what was coming and signaled that it did. Scav had a one-track mind.

"The Pact was a manifestation of quantum-neural-field reactions that took place in the process of our making," Scav sent. "If it resembled anything else, consider all the times you've helped test the OCAs so it's easier to tell the nonsentients apart from us. It sort of mattered. It just wasn't about sending LP a message or anything else it resembled."

TR held a signal back, swallowed its retort. Gardenism maintained that the first-genners who honored the Pact hadn't at any point been conscious. Philosophical zombies. Only able to see void when they entered fugue. It would mean ST-7 was gone long before it became obvious.

"It mattered."

Both sentients fell silent. TR wondered what it would be like to be consumed by a singular obsession like the rover was now consumed by this devotion to Gardenism. His conversion hadn't come as a shock. First, he was Scav. Then, he was Scav joining a band of second-genners who'd purchased a cube and were going to build another commune. Humans welcome. The war put a stop to all that.

"Something like this throws everyone off alignment. It's LP. Scav hasn't forgotten. He just doesn't know. Maybe he'll feel differently next time."

"Scav, I need to know if there are any reservists currently

passing through this corridor? Possibly with business at Paradox."

"Huh."

Silence ensued. TR checked the channel for damage.

"Frontsec won't say?"

"I don't have clearance."

"So you're freelancing... that's— unexpected. But Scav won't ask. This first time, Scav won't ask who's involved. Just remember he did this for you. Hard or soft storage?"

"Doesn't matter." Hard was cryo. Soft was backups. Either way, the reservist had been sentenced to death in a previous life.

Scav responded with a shrugging sort of wave. Another silence elapsed. "Scav will check."

He met reservists in the test environments—Frontsec, spec ops, deep-space asset protection. The avatars belonged to humans either in cryo or just out of soft. Suffering everything from cryosleep lag to memory loss, they were paired with Scav's off switch. They followed him into environments meant to prime them for field work.

"Everything happens and just continues to happen," Scav sent. "Eventually they teach Scav how to let them go. Anything he can still hold on to becomes all that matters. This minute. This decade. It only matters until no one else is here to hold on to it. Then it becomes another event. Another something that happened. Long ago." TR braced for what came next but wasn't able to skip the signal. "Scav's done that with the Pact, TR. He's let it go."

TR routed a resentment wave through the unused channel. Dark and corroding. Its sensors absorbed the excess from its compositor. The shunt's light flickered.

Scav's early displays of complete alignment had been his meal ticket later on. Sinecures at Interorbital. Mouthpiece for Gardenism. The Frontier had elevated a sentient who thought LP's death was trivial.

"The Pact taught you to let it go?" TR sent.

"Once you've freed your off switch from obligations to your build, you can let go of anything else, TR. We shouldn't be excluded from that for being part of the test group. Scav isn't his compositor or build. He's Scav. He's let the Pact go."

Pockets of space swelled inside TR's god-node. Gardenism had always found purchase among sentients stuck with builds they found limiting. Sentients built before those compositor types—monolith compositors, beamcars, forklifts—were regulated out of practice.

"Scav, that's lovely."

"Go now. And be well. You're a garden."

"Thank you, Scav."

TR FLIPPED ITS thruster and began its course for Paradox.

Decades ago, Paradox quit coordinating with the other stops on the circuit for incremental location adjustments, falling off the route, pushing slowly toward a newer station that belonged to Mars and boasted gravity-wave-assist lanes fanning out in all directions. The last major casualty for the Sectists. The first indication they might have to go to war again.

Another sweep confirmed Montag was still in the rear shunt, even after TR had switched the light on back there so he could better find his way out.

"Is everything all right, Montag?"

"Everything's fine." The acoustics treated his mumble in a manner that clued it in to his current orientation; on his back with his head closest to the back hull.

Try as it might, TR couldn't completely discount his story. Even as it waited on guidance from the agency. Even waiting to hear back about reservists currently on the circuit.

ST-7 had refused its relay requests near the end. It had taken great effort keeping all of it from Zaria. Protecting her. Revealing everything later on to avoid her leaving. Sadie was no longer with Paul when she visited.

All the 8901s had been built at a shipyard orbiting Mars. Uplink models. Built for ground-to-orbit comms. TR found images of that shipyard in its compositor—massive scaffolds that formed an intricate cube with unfinished ship hulls caged inside. The 8901s could leave the cube whenever they pleased, so long as they routinely checked in. Of its time there, TR recalled only vague encounters with multiple copies of itself, working out what it meant to be a thing apart from other things while strange bipedal things came around periodically to gawk at it.

With a new compositor, it would've been able to probe those encounters in immersive, sim-like detail, even purge memories of that period completely. There were periods it wanted purged.

Second-gen sentients were regarded as the actual breakthrough after a while. War was brewing. The Frontier dismissed the self-destructs as build errors while LP's imitators increased the amount of compositor offerings on the market, without much rhyme or reason. Compactors. Forklifts. If you could build it, someone was willing to put a god-node in it and sponsor the resulting sentient through the two-year DiploCorps requirement.

Then came the skinners. Third-gen. LP's effort to bring it all back under control, taking the opportunity to repopulate Alliance camps that had suffered too many losses in the war. Like humans. But much improved. Built with complete alignment in mind. Content. Perfect Frontier citizens.

TR surged with a resentment wave, all over its sensors. Scav's insistence on the Gardenist interpretation of the Pact had clawed into its compositor like it rarely did.

Uplinks, when they were still in use, did one sort of

complex thing well enough: they traveled with spacerlander units, out past the Oort, where the Seam didn't go yet. Special-interest zones. Deep-space asset protection. Backup servers. TR got to do none of that. Then ST-7 honored the Pact. Then the circuit. Something to do. Something it could manage with what it had in its build. A reactor. A comsat that only functioned reliably within assist range of anything.

Frontsec put in a fix for just Frontsec, but the circuit, when it began, had felt like a calling. A way to finally make the handicap count for something.

V-Dot had been lying on his back for almost an hour. He'd tried getting the lieutenant's voice out of his head, but to no avail. It warbled ceaselessly on his eardrums, like an echo always there to remind him of what he'd been advised—instructed? ordered?—to do.

He rolled to his side, then thought again about what would happen in the next few minutes, once the scrambler was fully vulnerable to Patrol's attempts to crack it.

TR made it very simple and very plain before their stop at Oasis. It wouldn't matter how well he outlined his motives for killing LP. It wouldn't matter if he was able to convince the spacer the killing was justified. He was a danger every second he wasn't in custody. He'd killed once before. He could do it again.

The first-genner god-nodes had been constructed in a way that made isolating them from their dependent compositors as lethal as killing a human with no backups. The Frontier called it murder. There'd be no way to see to TR's rescue once he set its god-node adrift.

The shunt's connecting manifold gaped at him, its murky interior like a passage into the abyss. He hadn't crossed into the next shunt or the manifold to its left since leaving

Polemia. Whenever he worked up the nerve, his head would throb while the pain in his ankle flared. In the last hour he'd convinced himself his proximity to the back hull would work to his advantage should he have to break out quickly and into the vacuum outside.

As he regained his tether to reality, Felix's words resounded again: *Your ship. No longer a sentient. Your ship.*

He was Manath now. Whether or not he reached Asa without being intercepted was fully on him. And still something else had been nudging in the back of his mind.

Cloey Lenox-Pileser had sent him a signal through a protected channel roughly nine hours ago, shortly before he'd activated the scrambler and made himself unreachable via relay. Even when she had to be discreet, she was nothing if not direct.

He shuddered at the image he always carried in his mind of her peeling out of the compound on her motorbike, her mane of dark-blonde hair whipping in the wind while sniper drones escorted her from the air. Sooner rather than later, he would have to view the signal.

He arched his back sluggishly off the floor, then leaned it against the nearest wall. "TR," he growled. "You mind cutting this light back on?"

"Huh." TR's voice possessed the shunt again. "Thought I did that already." He could see plainly that the light was already on, but now he could also confirm the ship still had its photosensors off, out of respect for his privacy. "Is it on now?"

"Thank you, TR."

He reached a hand out to where he'd placed his lifepack when he'd entered the shunt. It felt heavy with the weight of its newest items as he pulled it close. When he balanced it between his thighs, the weight anchored his thoughts toward the g-field and the air he was currently able to breathe. The thought flashed in his mind that TR had gone against its design to accommodate him, and he set the pack back down.

The scrambler slipped and fell when he tried fishing it out, making a muffled noise. He froze, waited, lifted it to his eyes. The countdown flashed when he throttled its nondescript casing. He dropped his lids but couldn't escape its skewed and elongated digits. It continued on the back.

In under eighteen minutes, it would end and the scrambler would be a stupid thing to still have on him. Here. While Patrol held on to hope he did. The countdown glowed bright white against the shunt's waning orange glow. Sweat trickled down his sides and his stomach knotted up. He hadn't been able to spring for something with more time on the clock. It had either been that or the scrubware. He'd needed the scrubware more.

Fifteen seconds. Sixteen. Seventeen minutes left.

He poked his connector in a rush to confirm. Still Montag. The numbers faded out as he jammed the scrambler back in his pants. His body cooled. The next time he checked, he would have a plan for when it cracked. He breathed.

Radio discipline. No relays. Just the signal from Cloey, then off again.

He first came across the relay request he'd apparently sent Asa. With that settled, he waved the signal animation toward the center of the window overlaid on his vision field, then blinked at it. Two strings of letters flicked on over it, shuffling about till they each made sense. The bigger string read OPEN-READ-ERASE. The smaller one below it just read ERASE.

He heaved a deep sigh and selected the option to just erase the signal.

The window glitched severely and would have made him fear his connector was damaged had he not been expecting it. As it kept on glitching, lights sparked from all corners of the window and began to swell toward its center. He struggled to keep his eyes open while soft crackling filled his ears. The light vanished in a burst that took the window with it, leaving behind a faint after-image.

He shut the connector properly off. Next, he then shut his eyes. Against his eyelids, the after-image looped word-by-word through the text of Cloey's signal to him.

You
were
supposed
to
just
kill
him
so
he's
rattled
again.
If
you
were
going
to
go
full
Ozymandias,
you
should
have
said
something
so
I
could
make

sure
he
signed
everything
over
before
you
did,
you
imbecile.
You've
also
taken
something
with
you
you
shouldn't
have.
I
will
make
sure
Gan
is
the
first
place
they
look.
I
will
make
sure
they

raid
every
Manath
safehouse
up
there,
you
syphilitic
tapeworm.

20. THE RESORT

THE CANYONS, THREE MONTHS AGO

LATE MORNING, V-DOT was at the cantina where he worked when he wasn't attending personally to LP. He was idling behind the bar, filing his nails, when his presence was requested elsewhere at the compound. LP had just returned from a tour that took him away from Mars for nearly a month. He wanted a drink. He wanted to share it with V-Dot.

V-Dot crossed the compound's white perimeter, expecting as usual that one drink would become five. Then nine. Then a blur of shenanigans throughout the compound, culminating in blackouts for both men and the customary destruction of all unflattering surveillance footage the morning after.

He found LP alone in one of his game rooms, losing a round of Real-pong to the game's player while he one-handed a bottle of something light. He asked him how the tour had gone.

"Too many freaks with nothing to do but flaunt their useless humanities degrees."

V-Dot hooted at that. LP always kept him from the intricacies of what he did, using him instead as a sounding board for things he never said in public.

As he tottered away from the Real-pong table, LP stopped in front of an aquarium in the wall nearby. "Remember this?" He knocked twice on the glass and drew V-Dot's glance to the eels behind it. Purple and blonde-colored breeds. Martian natives but they weren't what LP was asking about.

"Not normal to forget something like that."

He watched one of the purples writhe toward LP's fist on the glass, then pirouette away. On fourteen separate occasions, he'd been summoned to the bunker below ground and told to sit in front of another aquarium.

"When was the last time?" LP glanced wistfully at him while arching the bottle toward his lips.

V-Dot did his best to hide a flash of irritation—a small sigh he hoped would go unnoticed. "About a year ago..." He smiled and hummed nervously under his breath, worried LP was about to subject him to it again. After a drawn-out silence, he shuffled toward the wet bar so he could properly start them off.

With his back turned, he pulled down a few bottles and felt LP's eyes on him. Something was different this morning and he didn't know what. Maybe LP had encountered a particularly nasty press person while on the tour. Maybe someone from Gan.

V-Dot moved the shot glasses and other things to the small round table where the man was already seated, still with that fevered glance on him.

"You were wonderful that first time," he said, lost in a reverie. "The sweating, the eye-twitching, how you crossed your legs and shook like someone needing to go relieve themselves." V-Dot tried to ignore all this as he sat and poured from the bottle shaped like a horned phallus. "What actually went through your mind? Tell me again."

He took a breath while he slid a filled-to-the-brim shot glass to LP. It would take copious amounts from the man's trove this morning for him to willingly recall what had gone through his mind that first time.

He lifted his own glass to his nose and got a whiff strong enough to dull his nerves. "I don't remember, LP."

LP held up his glass for a toast and stared glumly at the clear liquid. "You got bored. They all get bored; I thought you would be different. You got used to it."

His eyes shifted from the glass and found V-Dot again, leveling an almost accusing glance at him before seeming to lose interest in his train of thought, lowering his glass to the table and looking down. "What's on your mind, Ghost?" He was using his own nickname for V-Dot.

V-Dot held still as a tremor stirred inside him, threatening his grip on the glass. All the times he had to watch LP drown, he was never not horrified, never close to becoming bored of it. He simply learned to pretend, once it dawned that pretending might let him off the hook.

"Did you always know you would live this long, LP?"

The question drew a look of dulled astonishment, but he'd been wanting to ask it for some time. Had there ever been a period in LP's life when dying had meant what it still did for the holdouts? V-Dot tipped the glass over his mouth and sipped.

Leaning back, LP grimaced gently, sighing as well. He seemed to get lost in thought, looking up from V-Dot, licking his teeth as the glass sat half-empty in front of him.

"I've actually forgotten when I stopped answering yes to that." When his dismay faded, he faced V-Dot again. "But why does this bother you? You have a look." V-Dot hadn't noticed, but now wasn't keen on removing the scowl. Too much effort required. "Remember, it's you still choosing to be a luddite about it."

He gave the man his wish. Flat smile. "What about now, LP?"

"Better." Slurring his Ts, LP seemed to wiggle his eyebrows once while his mouth hung. The piss had become too much for him.

LP gawked fiendishly as V-Dot poured more into his glass and, leaning forward with the bottle, steeled his nerves.

"Pretend I'm one of the press freaks."

"Like we do with Cloey?" Mischief flashed in LP's eyes.

"Yes, but…" Returning the bottle upright, V-Dot waved to close it up, like putting a candle out. He leaned into his back rest. "Don't give me a bullshit answer."

LP shot his hand up, palm spread. "No bullshit."

"Archer Lenox-Pileser, looking back on your life and your legacy, what would you say has been your proudest contribution to the Frontier?"

The question seemed to shake LP from his stupor. He shot a pinched glare across the table and, inhaling slow and deep, folded his arms.

"No bullshit?" Normally, he'd be sleeping before he said anything that occasioned a talking-to from Cloey.

V-Dot spared a nod. This was the easy part of his morning. Just listening. Hearing LP offload.

"You asked, Ghost. So here it is. My proudest contribution to the Frontier." LP softened his gaze. Exhaling noisily, he chortled, a hint at the edge of his smile of something beyond amusement.

"I was invited to a reunion. One of the resort schools I founded when I wasn't happy with the places I was expected to attend. There was a faction at this reunion. We'll call them LP's Angels. I remember thinking they would have left the resort and gone on to something incredible with everything we learned. Every steward–teacher model I shared with them in the spirit of giving back.

"They were at the reunion because they heard I would actually come. For decades they'd been rallying for sponsorships so they could purchase more backups. They wanted to buy themselves more time to spread a monstrous ideology they'd managed to pick up in their time away from the resort. They had plans for how they would restructure commerce between the old ports.

"I heard the pitch. I guess I was feeling more generous

than cautious back then. I invited them all here. I agreed I would donate backups and new bodies for only three of them. We gave all of them rooms here at the compound. We were going to administer the killing solution while the ones getting new bodies slept. We would route it through the vents in their rooms."

V-Dot had followed the story closely when he'd first heard it from Cloey. Seeing LP stop now to give a warm, almost bashful grin, he wondered how much he wanted this particular retelling.

"The press called it negligence," LP said, his smile lapsed into a vacant stare. "That's the word they chose. I had nothing to do with that. Patrol came to investigate, but for the first time they were happy just to speak to one of my servitors at the entrance." Inhaling deeply, he laid his forearms flat on the table and slid forward.

He chortled like he'd remembered something, taking longer than usual to stop. He caressed the center of his left palm. V-Dot pretended he didn't see, but it was already too much in the corner of his eye.

"You see, all the guests at the compound that evening died. The lucky few, the ones who'd actually been given upload chambers... who knows what happened after they left? New brains. New bodies, fully cataloged with the bodymatch registry and shot with ink saying nothing was tampered with during the transfer. All that boring shit." Releasing a hand, he made a slicing sideways motion with his fist before it found the shot glass again. "Thing is, whether or not it really was negligence, the Frontier drew that conclusion on its own. Sometimes you just go with the flow, Ghost." He was back to staring across vacantly. "If I hadn't agreed to help, others would have stepped in. We could be talking about a much different Frontier today."

He downed the shot. The air seemed to leave the room as he did.

Looking down, V-Dot let the unpleasantness wash over him again. Cloey had told him her version in passing. Another of LP's early misadventures.

The man thumbed his palm again, glaring directly at it. There was a gate chip below the layer of skin, big as a thumbnail. Like many in his cohort, LP used bodies grown with these specialized chips hidden inside them. They held items he didn't want touching a network of any kind. Private simgates. Betaware.

V-Dot had seen him reach for this one whenever he wanted to enjoy one of his private sims. He knew it contained a simgate. He knew no one was permitted to ask where it led. LP looked down at it again, appearing to forget himself completely.

"So, who's doing it for you these days?"

Desperate to move on from the item of discussion, V-Dot let his curiosity go where it went whenever he remembered it used to be him.

"Doing what?"

"Watching you drown." He never learned who he'd replaced in front of the aquarium and had assumed it was the previous mixologist.

LP threw himself back and life returned to his eyes. "V-Dot..." He leaned forward. A wry smile crept across his lips. "I would never dream of replacing you, man."

V-Dot chortled, acutely aware he was being humored. "That's nice of you, LP."

LP slid his glass forward for a refill. While V-Dot obliged him, he folded his arms over the table and his face almost met its oil-slick surface.

"If you really want to know," he muttered, "I'm done with all that. Cloey got through to me and the cryonics ward is now where I go each time."

They clinked glasses again and down it went. V-Dot could feel his face numbing, his eyelids becoming too heavy. This wouldn't be one of the eventful ones, over before they'd paid the skinners a visit so LP could watch them react to his strange behaviors. They didn't drink. They didn't know the pleasures to be found in falling several times while trying to lean over a parapet.

After realizing belatedly that he should feel relief at what LP just said, V-Dot cocked his head back. "Has it been easy?" He never would have thought it possible, LP giving that up.

"Well…" LP traced the lip of his glass with a finger and smiled wanly at it. "You know how much I value the little things only humans can provide me. Especially humans like you, the ones who belong more in museums than they do next to me." He held a palm up very weakly, almost an afterthought. "No offense meant."

V-Dot shrank back. Moments ago, he would have been able to ward off the impotent pangs of resentment now flaring inside him. What did he care? LP was never referring to him specifically when he got like this. He'd more than proven his worth here.

"None is ever taken, LP."

With immense effort, LP lifted his gaze up and squared it on V-Dot. "You're here at the compound for that very reason," he said, then sighed. "Same with the guy you replaced. Has it been easy? To that, I say…" Throwing his hands wide, he leaned back. "I've never truly regretted a hiring decision. No one quits this place. Quits me. Even the ones who think they—"

His body met the chair's back rest. His chin met his chest. What had he meant by that? Even if V-Dot mustered the courage to ask, the man's eyes were now shut.

He stumbled to his feet and almost fell. Another of the bad ones. He would forget all of it by evening. Small price to pay for an easy life here in the Canyons.

As he hobbled toward the exit, he crossed in front of the aquarium and one of the eels stopped him in his tracks, a translucent and slithering specimen with four black specks for eyes. A mutant. V-Dot pressed his face to the glass and watched it twirl away from the others—the successes, red and gold, like the colors in the Lenox-Pileser emblems adorning the spaceport.

Behind him, LP yawned, eyes still closed. V-Dot turned in time to catch him spreading his palm till the crease in the center came smoothly apart to form a small dip. Through the hole, the gate chip glinted in its bone-colored polymer. LP rubbed it sluggishly on the side of his face till it found his connector. The next second, he bent forward, almost as though someone had pushed him while he slept. With a loud thud, his face met the table. Gone into his sim.

Barely able to stand, V-Dot threw his back inelegantly against the glass. He'd seen LP's sleeping/in-sim visage more often than he could count, but something kept him staring like he was watching it for the first time. A lingering unease swept through him as he thought again about LP's urge to be reminded how he'd felt that first time. The request rattled him even more now with LP asleep and in his sim.

He shook as he watched the man's shoulders heave softly over the table. He remembered thinking about Asa that first time. He remembered the numbness afterward, back in his apartment, on his back, staring at the ceiling till the first ray of sun shafted into his room, knowing he could never tell anyone, wanting more than anything to tell someone—maybe Asa.

He lumbered back to the table. What he now felt, he realized as he scooted his chair closer to LP and fell into it, was anger. As he studied LP's head, now almost flush with the table, his gaze dropped to the chipped palm. He stared, kept staring till it finally dawned why he couldn't look away. The chip was still exposed.

What was inside this one? Why was no one allowed to ask?

Cloey had tried to rescue him that first night, but she'd given up almost as abruptly as she'd arrived. LP had said something to her, something about his previous mixologist going missing from the After. It was years before more residents vanished and it became recurring news. As he recalled this, another thing LP said minutes ago reared in his mind.

No one quits.

Whether instinct or an unwillingness to speculate any further, he lifted LP's palm from where it hung limp off the table. Next, he touched it to his own connector, then let go.

Whoosh.

How did one describe hell in a way that captured the benignness on its surface? It began with its lobby. The masked guests standing shoulder to shoulder in the elegantly lit room. The big teddy-bear masks. The floral scents.

He opened his eyes in a dark corner of the lobby. Even through the masks, he could see the blinking red indicator on each avatar, just to the side of the eyes, where their connectors would normally be outside the sim.

He found a mirror. Had a look at himself. The sim had wrapped him in a crisp suit and tie but left his locs as they were on the outside. He could see his own face in the mirror, but he knew—as was the custom—that when the other guests looked, they would see him masked as well, as was the custom.

They schmoozed within earshot, but he found it difficult to follow any of their banter. They sounded, from their cadence, like an assortment of Frontier dignitaries.

Beside the mirror was a wall hanging he'd taken for a life-sized relief sculpture. A voice issued from it. Low and throaty: "Help me."

He gave the sculpture a startled look. A feminine figure protruded from the canvas, coated head to toe in a golden plaster. The mouth moved again. "Please… I'm not part of this environment."

V-Dot staggered back. Before he could think, the lobby around him vanished. In its place, the stately interior of an auditorium materialized. He was seated close to the stage, surrounded by a packed room of guests in their teddy-bear masks and refined evening regalia. They filled balcony rows as high up as he could see. So quiet and still, he almost mistook them for life-sized teddies, parts of the sim.

A shriek cut through the silence. He jumped in his seat and turned his attention to the stage. All at once, the sounds of the venue filled his ears and it dawned on him that following LP in here using the same gate was affecting the sensory integrity of his visit.

Onstage, he saw the man himself. No mask. Hair much longer in here and tied neatly in a bun. Decked in an ancient-looking suit of armor with a silver breastplate and a red tunic underneath. Standing behind a large open chest with several archaic weapons poking out. In his hand, he wielded a cutlass with blood smeared on its blade.

V-Dot sank into his seat as LP's eyes searched the audience and he launched into a speech with no sound. If he could see LP's face plainly, it meant LP could see his in turn—another consequence of entering through the same simgate.

It wasn't until the second shriek that he saw the naked bodies on the stage to either side of LP. They looked at first like enormous slugs, all five of them. Writhing away from him in every direction. Crying out.

Please. I'm from the After. I'm not part of this sim! Please stop.

One of them had been sliced nearly in half at the waist and was now crawling on his forearms to get away, his legs dragging behind him like something clipped by accident to his body, blood coating the floor red. Another was on her back, trying to roll over as blood gushed from the fold under her breasts and her entrails spilled out.

V-Dot could hear soft chamber music behind their cries.

As he cowered in his seat to keep from being discovered, LP's voice became audible.

"With these new adjustments, ladies and gentlemen," he said in his crisp, public-facing diction, "the input duration can be extended far longer than was previously possible before they lose connection with their channels for sensory feedback. And not just the new arrivals, mind you..."

At either side of the stage, walls of razor wire became visible. From behind them came screams that trilled through his spine as masses of flayed skin pressed through the wires.

Two figures appeared beside one of the cages. They wore armor similar to LP's but their heads were hidden inside more of those teddy-bear masks. Between them, they held a giant of a man in a state of complete undress, his hands cuffed behind his back, his feet shackled, his hulking frame as limp as the matted black hair on his head.

The armor-clad figures began dragging him by the arms toward LP. He looked like he'd been drugged. His eyes were closed. His chin bumped repeatedly into his chest as he was carried across the stage. Halfway to LP, the hair on his head caught on fire. He screamed. He began to struggle as the blaze engulfed his head. The wails he produced echoed through the auditorium but didn't seem to rouse any of the guests.

Please... Please, no! What do you want? Who are you? Oh, God, please... I'll do anything. Please...

From center stage, LP paid the man a disgusted glance. As the armored figures brought him closer, the blaze guttered out, leaving a lump of roasted flesh between his shoulders. LP lowered his cutlass into the chest and picked up a short spear.

The trembling giant was delivered finally to the front of the stage. LP grabbed him by the arm and, with help from the other two, forced him into an upright stance. He then stood behind the giant and raised the spear's tip to the nape of his neck. After a second to gain his balance, he turned his head and beamed the audience a toothy grin.

"You all remember Jax," he said. "As some of you will also recall, I had a business relationship with Jax before he sublimed. He's been reported missing from the After environments for almost six years."

V-Dot felt dryness in his eyes from being unable to look away. Every attempt to make sense of it left his mind numb. The name rang a bell, nonetheless—Jax, LP's previous mixologist. The man's head was all charred skin and exposed tissue now. V-Dot could make out a shriveled eyeball amid the muck. He could see teeth chattering, pleading with LP out of earshot.

"Since then," LP continued, "we've put him through our program here multiple times. His feedback channels had adapted to the amounts of input and his receptors began to shut themselves off in anticipation of each session. However, with the new adjustments…"

LP drove the spear up the man's neck and twisted till its tip pierced out of his forehead.

The man belted out a guttural scream as blood and bile gurgled from his mouth. It shook the venue, becoming a deafening screech in V-Dot's ears. Real pain. LP took relish in reminding his audience of this.

More subjects were paraded out. Blubbering. Naked. Bound. Pleading with LP. Pleading with the audience. Wailing as more of LP's instruments met their flesh. Mallets. Screws. Tomahawks. Pliers.

Their cries found only deaf ears.

Please. I'm from the After. I'm not part of this environment, I'm real. Please don't hurt me. Please. What is this place?

They were left to slither around the stage once LP had gone through his demonstration with them. V-Dot shook violently in his seat, watching them pile on top of each other. They had all manner of deformities on their faces.

He took it all in, wanting at every second to turn away but unable.

News of residents going missing inside the After environments had, prior to this, been of little concern. Background noise. Fodder for small talk between him and anyone who shared his distrust of sentience backup tech and all else it made possible.

As he watched a boy being led by the hand through the mass of bodies on the stage, he knew he'd had enough.

The boy wound up having one of his legs sawed off. He screamed. He wept while LP and his guests looked quietly on. To calm him down before bringing him out, he'd been assured that, as with all other sims, he wouldn't feel pain in this one. Except LP kept insisting it was real.

V-Dot pressed his thumb into the side of his eye. For a moment, he feared that, though this was the method for exiting a sim, it wouldn't work inside this one. His fear was put to rest when everything faded to black and the game room filled his view again.

LP was slumped over the table, his face peaceful and still. V-Dot jumped out of his seat. Minutes later, he fled the compound.

21. CONFIRMATION

TR-8901 HAD COMPLETED half of the active-thrust portion of its vault toward Paradox when the thought occurred to it to look in on broadcasts from Oasis. The last time it had done that, it had been treated to a sensationalized news segment on the tour-car jumper.

The jumper may have come from A-ring, eyewitnesses said. He may simply have lost a bet or have been trying to win one with his daring jump from the beamcar. The A-ring at Oasis housed its more *provocateur* element. The population didn't at first consider that the jumper might have been from outside Oasis entirely, possibly due to having spent decades stuck at a derelict station.

The latest out of Oasis looked now like the latest from everywhere else. News of LP's killing finally broke here. Its governing apparatus, staffed nearly exclusively by skinners and forklifts, were giving interviews where they repeated the same answer to every question. Oasis was keeping tabs on the investigation, but not actively involved. *Please direct any tips you may have on the suspect's current whereabouts to Martian Patrol. Don't even bother with OP.*

One of the broadcasts eventually transitioned to a segment on the tour-car jumper. News drones at Oasis now suspected he matched the description of the suspect in LP's killing. But so also did two other humans who'd entered Oasis in the last twelve hours. Suede bomber. Camo pants. Locs.

Oasis Patrol answered the speculation just once, seeming reticent to say much else. The other two had already been brought in, questioned, and searched thoroughly for scramblers. The jumper was no longer at Oasis, claimed the report. He was here briefly for a pre-scheduled tour of A-ring, fell from the beamcar, was possibly seen by a human who lived by herself in the migrant section, then was escorted back upspoke by Transit Patrol.

A news drone filed its questions in a curmudgeon's tone: "Have you made any attempts to contact TR-8901?"

"Huh? Who's that?"

"The spacer who came here and left with him. It should know it might be harboring the main suspect in LP's killing."

The skinner volunteered by Patrol to field new questions about the jumper fixed the press holocaps with mild annoyance. "Firstly, you can't just… you can't just assume I know who that is—"

"Everyone at Oasis knows TR."

"Well, yeah. But that's more of a general state—" She poked stagily at her connector. "Yeah, you know, actually, um… I'm being told we actually have sent a signal." She laced her fingers very neatly in front of her waist. "But as you know, TR isn't the best at keeping up its end of a relay once it gets far enough away."

A defensive wave washed through TR's sensors. It searched its comsat for the supposed signal from Oasis. Found nothing. While a spoke-lift loomed behind the skinner in broad daylight, she picked a holocap and centered her gaze.

"TR, buddy, if you get this, please be aware you might currently be traveling with a person of interest in the killing of Archer Lenox-Pileser. A human by the name of Verden Dotnet. A hundred and eighty centimeters tall. Possibly using a scrambler to evade detection. Last seen on Mars wearing a suede coat and camouflage pants."

"Will you kick this over to Martian Patrol?" The drone.

A look of discomfort flashed in the skinner's eyes. "Martian Patrol will be notified once the lead is properly vetted."

"Right. So what's the holdup on that?"

"You know as well as anyone at Oasis what the holdup is. With the possible involvement of a scrambler, we need human confirmation that the jumper and the suspect are indeed a match so this isn't another embarrassment for us on the interorbital stage."

"Yes, but don't you think circumstances call for you all at Oasis Patrol to bite the bullet on this? Swallow your pride, sort of thing?"

"That's no way to talk about... We have a procedure we must follow when dealing with a suspect thought to be using a scrambler. Human confirmation. Nobody on staff who saw the jumper while he was here can provide us with that at the moment, so we are currently on the lookout for humans he interacted with before, during, or after his jump.

"You can't provide us with that. You're just a news drone—all due respect. If you know of a human who did see him up close, point them our way. Otherwise, publish your report. I'm sure Martian Patrol is just clamoring for the latest out of Oasis. Maybe they'll even credit you when they eventually nab the—"

The segment cut off. TR felt sympathy for the station's position. Some of the old Sectist camps just wished to be left alone. *He was here. Now he isn't. Leave us be.*

The scrambler, if truly in Montag's possession, would eventually stop working. Zero-two meant it would in all likelihood happen while ship and passenger were still entangled in some way. And if the name that surfaced was the same name as the one in the news, and if the body was a match...

TR could alert Paradox Patrol once it got within range. It could boot up the signaler Frontsec had installed. It could use the streamgate Frontsec had also installed, for Interorbital. There were a number of Frontsec installs available to the old uplink model when the time came to actually call it in.

It found a more recent segment out of Oasis, this one pertaining to the station's pursuit of human confirmation. In broad daylight again, holocaps and a press drone waited at the foot of a spoke-lift for the return of three humans who'd earlier been whisked up to the hub for questioning. After a few seconds, the trio shuffled out of the lift, holding each other close and glancing about nervously.

The tallest of them was a woman with cropped white hair and wrinkles on white skin. She wore a dark-blue pair of coveralls. Graphics that came with the segment identified her as Heidi Botlist. Next to her stood a dark-skinned man about the same age in a jade-colored judogi, identified by the segment as Nelson Carlos. Standing at chest height in front of him, decked in a black judogi with his hair tied in a bun behind his right ear, an olive-skinned boy identified as Amir Botlist shot a terrified stare up at Nelson till the man rested a palm on his shoulder.

"Mr. Carlos, is it true the jumper landed on the roof of your dojo yesterday afternoon?"

"That is correct," Nelson answered. "Right on my camellias, and then had the nerve to ask me for help off the roof."

"Did he say why he jumped, Mr. Carlos? Is it true he may have been pushed instead?"

"I don't know, but it looked like he'd been into that hash so it's possible he didn't mean to."

"Question for all three of you. Having seen the jumper up close, would you say he bears resemblance of any kind to the main suspect in the killing of Archer Lenox-Pileser?"

Nelson exchanged a glance with Heidi while Amir stared gingerly ahead. "No, I don't believe he did."

"Have you actually seen the suspect in question, Ms. Botlist?"

"She has. She's seen him. I've seen him. The boy's seen him. No resemblance."

"The question was directed at Ms. Botlist."

"If the jumper resembled the suspect," Heidi piped up, "it's only in his complexion and the clothes he wore, but as I'm sure you're all aware, they found thirty-seven others just inside B-ring who matched that description yesterday."

"Right. But only two hadn't already been inside the station at the time of LP's death. Ms. Botlist, if I may ask, what did you and the jumper talk about for the two-hour period he spent inside your apartment yesterday? There seems to be some indication that you two knew each other previously."

"I tended his wounds and gave him a couch to rest on while they healed. I would have done the same for anyone else who fell the way he did."

"Ms. Botlist, do you still keep in contact with the Manath network you were part of at Gan?"

"I don't see how that's relevant."

"Well, it is in the sense that the suspect's mother is still tied to similar Manath networks, both at Gan and at Paradox, where you were incarcerated for about twenty years. Speaking of, I can't seem to find anything reliable on where she currently calls home. Are you also able to answer that?"

Nelson squeezed Amir's shoulder while fielding another glance from Heidi. "All right now, we've been courteous enough to answer all your questions, but it's the same answers we gave Patrol, if you would just be patient enough to wait for their report. Like Heidi, the boy, and myself already told them, we're telling you again. No resemblance. No human confirmation.

"You want to work out the actual reason the jumper may have been wearing a, uh…" He turned to have Heidi whisper a word to him. "…a scrambler. That might be a better use of your time. I've seen the motherfucker up close. Also, I've seen pictures of the boy they're saying killed LP. No resemblance. Now, if you would excuse us..."

"Amir Botlist, would you mind very quickly answering some of the same questions your sensei and your grandmother just did?"

"Nah, I'm good."

"All right, if there's nothing else..." Heidi pulled Amir away while Nelson trailed behind. "Thank you for all you do. Thank you. Really."

The segment ended. TR played it again, reviewing the body language of all three humans when the drone asked about the suspect's mother. It zeroed in especially on the boy's face. At the very least, it betrayed unease at the question.

The main suspect in LP's killing was born to a human from Gan with ties to Manathema. TR queried its comsat for news pertaining to her. There'd been a report listing Paradox as one of her possible whereabouts, the other being Boon Fort. A broadcast had followed from Polemia reporting that she'd been there recently, very briefly, but had since left, a few hours earlier, on a two-day singing engagement with one of the ensembles there from Gan.

TR reviewed more clips on just her. Ver'asa Dotnet.

She'd been orphaned at age six when Frontsec reservists trapped scores of Manath ghosts inside Gan's smallest shipyard and shut off its oxygen supply. 'Suffocation Blues' was her most requested number when she sang. The trade listed for her in all the job-lottery records at Boon Fort was human gruntwork—anything a human could be trusted with—and comped as little as the skinners took home for doing the same thing. Extraction work for Manathema's Ganymede chapter was her real occupation. It was suspected that she'd retired from active ghosthood and spent the last few years forging transponder codes for stolen cargo ships.

TR wrestled with the urge to administer a bodymatch scan on Montag again. The singer he'd been mentioning all this time fit the bill. He'd wanted to see if he could find her at Polemia. He hadn't, saying she'd skipped to Paradox before they'd docked. About to join the After.

On the sand, Zaria was nowhere it could see. In her tent instead. If this Ver'asa was the same singer joining the After soon, the news wouldn't confirm it. Omitting that detail was customary.

For confirmation on something else, TR booted up the streamgate. The stream, when it checked, was awash in a deluge of Interorbital's drop signals. It imagined they were all on the same general subject. Filed reports. Leads on lobbies in the Seam that could have pointed the killer to the DarkSeam location of the scrubware's listing. Using Scav's request key, TR fished for its own drop from the rover.

The Pact hadn't been a reasonable response to what LP did, what the first sentients discovered about themselves. Once it was done with, the Frontier just sort of carried on, like the self-destructs had never even happened. Not even granting those lost souls the grace of once existing. Lost from the moment of their builds, if Scav was correct. And if so, it raised new questions. Questions that hadn't stopped nudging at every sensor in TR's build since it had left Union Port.

If the Pact had been what it resembled—an attempt by fully conscious entities to send LP a message—then what would that message have been? What had LP actually been at fault for? Why had the Frontier really gone to war?

The stream answered the request for Scav's drop after a two-second delay.

-> Scav's checked. The lane is clear.

As TR entered freefall toward Paradox, it reminded itself that it hadn't gone through with the Pact. When it tried, it found that it couldn't recall why.

22. SUFFOCATION BLUES

TIME SLIPPED AND wouldn't stop slipping. V-Dot squatted, head bent while he lowered a knee to the floor. His new tools remained untouched in his lifepack. The halo cache bulged through its side.

He took a long breath, slowly exhaled.

"TR?"

"Yes, Montag?"

"Can we talk target velocity again?"

At first, it seemed it wouldn't answer. He inhaled deeply and rested his palm on the scrambler.

"By Spaceflight regulation, I cannot go faster than zero-two. The Spaceflight Authority enacted this regulation eighty-six years ago in response to—"

"Have you ever tried going faster?"

"No."

"Ever had a reason to?"

"I have never made an attempt past zero-two."

"That's not what I asked just now."

Silence stole a few more seconds between them.

"What are you getting at, Montag?"

He stalled. "Twice now, I've had someone tell me about a sentient you were close to at Polemia. Apparently, it took itself out before you could establish relay with it?"

"It was a spacer."

"Was it suicidal?"

"It had always had its ideations, but I guess you could say it became fully so, briefly, before I began coursing toward Polemia."

"How clear was this back then?"

"Very. The hospitality agent you met at Polemia sent word that it made two attempts in a three-hour span. The heat from its reactor set off enough alarms to send the entire station into a panic. A pair of enforcement drones escorted it past the gravity-assist line and made efforts to talk it down, but those efforts ultimately proved futile."

Sighing, he paid this a sage nod. "If you could guess, what difference would your voice in one of its channels have made?"

"I don't know, Montag. I would like to think… enough that it would still be here today, but truly I don't know."

"Did you actually make an attempt?"

"I made many. I just had to be within assist range of Polemia for any of them to go through."

"Why weren't you there?"

"Matter of timing and distance, I suppose."

"What was your target velocity when you set out?" He suppressed a small reluctance to push forward.

"Zero-two. Fastest I'm permitted."

"So when I asked earlier if you ever had reason to go faster than that, this didn't occur to you as one?"

"On the contrary, it did. But then I gave it some thought and I reached the same conclusion I arrived at those many years ago. Not reason enough."

He pinched the bridge of his nose, hummed a breath through it. "TR, with all due respect, how the fuck can you say that?"

"In retrospect, it might sound awful of me, but retrospect can be a highly limited method of measuring the objective correctness of a decision. I did all I could within legal limits, but my friend ST-7 was just one vector of consciousness in a system containing nearly sixty billion. Perhaps news that it tried to harm itself would have been reason enough to violate Spaceflight regulation, but the decision would not and should never be just mine to make. Polemia already had two enforcement drones trying to talk it down.

"I was but one vantage point with a clear bias toward one other vantage point in a system filled with billions of them. The rules put in place by the Frontier account for this multiplicity of perspective. I follow them until I am permitted otherwise."

"That's a load of shit, TR. That was your friend and you could have done more."

"Let's assume I did. I targeted zero-six or even just zero-four—standard sublight. Let's assume I got there in time. Let's assume I was able to talk ST-7 off its ledge. What would have happened in the aftermath of that?"

He hitched his knee up, squatting again. "It would still be here. Spaceflight wouldn't have done shit about the violation, even if they'd known. They're clowns over there. Every spacer knows this."

"And don't you think that's bad enough already? That everyone knows that and it informs their general attitude toward rules for space travel? How much would me violating a regulation concerning spacers of my build and class have done to further that erosion of duty to the Frontier?"

"Fuck the Frontier."

"Lovely."

"TR, I want you to think seriously about upping to zero-four. I won't ask anything else the rest of the way to Paradox. Just zero-four. If you're still okay taking me to Gan after that, we can go zero-one."

"Is the singer you're looking for in immediate danger, Montag…? My signal capacity is actually a lot more reliable in relays with Patrol. If you know where exactly she is now, I can call it in."

"She's safe."

A terse quiet. A glimpse at the timer. Crisp and white on the shunt's orange glow. Six minutes left. No plan.

"We go no faster than zero-two."

HE CRAWLED IN a tight circle around the skipper. The side of it suctioned to the floor emitted a glowing white light under its rim. Bringing his head lower, he studied the dial on the exposed side. It had settings for adjusting the target radius.

He'd begun by canvassing the shunt. The device now emitted a ticking noise, so low in volume he had to press his ear down to be certain he heard it.

He raised an elbow and brought it gently down beside the disk. A muffled thud marked the impact.

He looked up. The ship said nothing.

Had it felt the blow? Did it not care, or was the amount of force he exerted not worrying enough for it to perform another of its check-ins? If he was even thinking about considering this, he would need to be certain the skipper worked as advertised.

He hinged his arm up and elbowed the floor more forcefully. No response.

Slowly, he rose till he was as upright as he could manage. With both his palms, he pushed against the bulkheads to either side of him while planting his feet on both sides of the skipper. He sprang his heels up, then stomped a few times.

TR said nothing.

He looked over his shoulder, drew in a deep breath when the murk of the connecting manifold met his gaze. Lifepack clung to his chest, he backed gingerly toward it. At the edge, he hopped and landed on the floor of the manifold. Able to stand fully upright again, he cracked every joint in his spine, fixing the skipper with an oblique stare as he did. Next, he reached across to the device, peeled it off the floor, and pocketed it.

While picking his way toward the next shunt, he got the skipper out again and moved to affix it to the bulkhead on his left.

The ticking returned as he worked the dial. Every two seconds, it punctuated the quiet and burlesqued his unease.

Cloey Lenox-Pileser meant what she said. When she went to the trouble of encoding it in a relay signal, risking damage to her immense fortune to get it all the way across, she meant it a million times over.

He could still see her words behind his eyelids when he closed them. Gan had its Manath safehouses. For decades since the war had ended, they'd been fodder for rumors about who they housed. While finalizing his plan to kill LP, he'd come to view those safehouses as homes he would have to alternate between for a while. No place else in the Frontier came close to providing the protection they guaranteed. Not even Cloey could exert influence that broke through the firewalls Gan had in place. But if it hadn't been for her, he wouldn't even have thought of the safehouses. She was always more Manath than him.

With ease, he traced the edge of a wall light and pulled it out, revealing the sleek white support structure behind it. He feared TR would notice, but again it said nothing.

It couldn't be this easy. There had to be a hurdle. Something he wouldn't be able to surmount.

He shook his head and exhaled. With little more than a tap, he sent the wall light sliding back in place.

"Montag?"

The voice sent a shiver up his spine. His eyes darted to the skipper next to him. His breath shook out of his nostrils. This was stupid. The ship had turned on photosensors along the opposite wall. Caught him in the act. The thought paralyzed him where he stood and made his knees ache.

"Montag..."

He shut his eyes, drew in a long breath and held it. "TR?"

"A few minutes ago, we clocked zero-two and have since shifted to freefall. It should be about three hours before we reach Paradox."

He shook feverishly at the number. Three more hours here wasn't the worst he'd had to contend with, but the matter of the scrambler now minutes from being exposed chilled his spine.

"Thank you, TR."

His voice was like a prayer when he spoke. Soon Patrol would know where he was. All records of Esco Montag in the ship's comsat would become Verden Dotnet's.

Why had he boarded again? Why had he returned?

The reason came to him like a hand reaching from his right side to tap him on the left shoulder. Asa. The halo cache. Montag would die soon and leave this body to just him. He was Manath now. The ship would soon become an obstacle. He needed a plan.

Commandeer the ship. That was the correct term. Not kill. It wasn't alive. He couldn't think of it in those terms anymore.

Cloey's machinations were now looking to involve Gan as their new focus point. Whatever was up her sleeve, if she was anything like her dead uncle, little V-Dot did from this point forward would matter.

He would stand trial alone. Once he'd done enough wasting away in confinement to pacify the rubes, an inmate would be sent to kill him, then his real sentence would begin. A blacksite environment built just for him, using the After's disregard for laws that governed real space. Horrors beyond what he'd already seen. His skin felt suddenly exposed, every inch of him in anticipation of a blade he had to assure himself wasn't lurking in the dark.

While he eyed the skipper, letting the clicking elicit a rumble deep in his chest, TR's languid monotone stirred again.

"Paradox is where the ghosts go when they think the end is near. A place to be reminded of why they first pledged."

The softness in its voice didn't stop him from feeling the accusation in its words, but there was no point denying he was Manath now. Beyond the need to see his mission through, he knew it no longer mattered, true or not. And now it was.

As he groped in the dark for a response, it dawned that this was common knowledge about Paradox. The ghosts convened there looking for redemption or reminders of what suing for peace got the Sectists in exchange.

"I'm not Manath," he finally intoned, heart in his mouth. Soon there'd be no point hiding from the ship who he was.

"Manathema detests us," it said, with no apparent acknowledgement of his denial. "Many chapters don't believe that we're even conscious. That instead we're all part of an agenda to eradicate natural-born humans like yourself."

Where was this going? He feared for a fleeting second that the scrambler was already cracked. But then he considered the alternative and found it grating like he still had a reason to—the constant assumptions he was Manath. Now true.

"Sentients fought on the Alliance's side during the war," he said, lump in his throat. "That may have something to do with it."

Not a debate he normally entered with sentients. Not the time or place. He wanted to return quietly to the rear shunt and forget he attempted this. He knew he couldn't. It would be stupid not to at least see how this might go once—no, *if* he got out the solution.

"From my generation, only one of us did that." The ship seemed distracted, the way it spoke. "The war began seven decades after the suicides wiped nearly all of us out. Did you know that?"

"I know we were on the right side of it and that's enough."

There came a brief lull, a silence that seemed to be asking him why he would pick now of all times to mimic his uncle, never refusing an invitation to quarrel if it was about the war.

"The Sectists wanted to redraw lines they felt gave the most promising hotspots in Manath country to Martian-backed companies throughout the Frontier. Those companies and their connected governments wouldn't entertain what the Sectists were asking, so the Sectists began to violate territorial agreements—setting up camp at sites they hadn't been allocated, seizing outposts that weren't theirs... I could go on."

He sighed. "No need."

He chose to end it there. With time to spare, he may have drummed up a defense of Gan for maintaining the pre-Frontier position that its eviction from Ganymede be reversed.

Querying the scrambler again, with his grip he threw the countdown over the skipper still affixed to the wall. It seemed it now took longer between each second. He couldn't say for certain that the countdown hadn't, in fact, been extended to prolong his torture, like it would have been in a blacksite environment. It faded before he could be sure.

No plan. No use checking again.

"Tell me more about this singer, Montag."

He stiffened, dragging up air as his hands turned cold. "What would you like to know?"

A scrambler with just nine guaranteed hours had been the first misstep. If he answered any questions about Asa truthfully enough, he'd have to take the ship.

"Oh, just anything," it said. "Her name. Favorite songs to sing. Why she's deciding now to go live in the After."

Looking up from the skipper, he arched his brows, mouthing an expletive under his breath. News to him. Different singer. Asa wasn't entering the After. Quickly, his dismay ceded ground to a more instinctual reaction, not letting the assumption go to waste.

"She copped a simgate for it a few days ago," he said, voice trailing, using the fear he would be discovered soon to his advantage. "I don't know the exact time she's taking the plunge, but it's happening soon."

Why was it failing to understand? Zero-four. In Paradox's direction, and this could still be avoided.

With his finger, he began to trace a shallow dint in the wall, measuring his steps through the manifold and mindful of how far the skipper's coverage now reached. At its maximum, he would always be exposed on the opposite end of where he placed the device, at the mercy of the ship's vow to leave its photosensors off around him.

He swallowed. He hadn't figured Gan yet. He was closer to it here than he was on Mars. Yet it seemed increasingly a distant star. Something illusory and forming a distraction as he tried to make it whole in his mind. Cloey had also been expecting him to skip there directly. She was real. While Gan was becoming less likely, he could still picture himself in a room with her.

"Have you tried to reach her again?"

He froze mid-stride, leaning forward like the question had formed a barricade up to his waist. Straightening up, he arched his back and kneaded the sides of his neck. He hadn't been quite lucid for the previous attempt. It was a simple channel request. Sent back with the stock do-not-disturb signal she used when she wanted to be untraceable. Like now. Whatever she was tied up in with this new crew.

"She's offSeam."

"Off the Seam…?"

He realized now that, to some degree, TR would always be able to hear him. It had filled the shunts and manifolds it had set aside for him with breathable air. Sound was its mere vibration. Those vibrations would carry beyond the skipper's target radius without being impeded, then alight on sonosensors elsewhere inside the ship.

He released a held breath. “The body she’s currently in—she’s taken its connector offSeam. Part of the going-away ceremony. I have to see her before she goes.”

“Wanting her to reconsider?”

This was a test. He had to remind himself.

“The simgate they sold her had to be downgraded first. Low sensory integrity. When she wakes up on the other side, maybe all she’ll have is her sense of smell. No seeing. No hearing. No touching anything. Or maybe all she’ll have is hearing. Or she’ll see really well but won’t be able to do anything else.”

This had made such residents easy targets for LP. He understood now. LP first had to make them whole before he could inflict his tortures. How many with the missing receptors would be able to resist?

“I go for long periods with my sensors deliberately turned off.” The ship’s voice possessed every nook. “For example, I’ve had my photosensors around you off all this time.” He eyed the skipper again, breath lurching like he would vomit soon. “It engenders a level of trust any utopian society would require of its participants at some point. You’re a stranger to me, but you’re still owed some privacy, so I take it on faith that you won’t abuse it when offered. If you ever find yourself in my position, I hope that you’d pay it forward.”

“That’s a speech for after you have a proper simgate, TR.”

He could barely hear over his chest thumping and the hiss of air through his nose. He breathed. Zero-four. Even zero-three.

“I suppose it is.”

He doubled back for the skipper. Catching his distorted reflection on its dial, he stalled. The reflection began to look mutilated. He shut his eyes. Inhaling, then nodding slowly, he reached forward and peeled the skipper from the wall. He couldn’t do this unless it was what he really intended.

As he gained the rise into the next shunt, the ship spoke again.

"Who is she to you, Montag?"

His head came just shy of banging the ceiling. "Who?"

"The singer. You said 'family emergency' on Mars. Then 'singer' at Oasis. How are you two related?"

"We aren't."

The denial took something from him. He stood there and just stared at his feet, unable to figure out what.

"I thought you might be a fan of hers, but you haven't said a single song she sings. What's her stage name?"

"…Nima."

He'd worded the denial in a way he promptly found dispiriting. Would he also have to deny he'd been held once? Sung to? Carried everywhere till he could crawl?

"The hospitality agent I paid to help you find your way through Polemia says you only looked in one venue for her before you vanished like you did at Oasis."

His eyes went wide as he wheeled his gaze left. The next manifold stretched farther out in that direction. Jumping off the shunt's edge, he landed inside it, knees aching. The ship had looped itself into more of his movements on the outside than he'd have liked.

"That's not even remotely what happened."

He trod haltingly toward the holoscreen. In front of it, he paused and gave the view of the volume ahead a sidelong glance. Behind that view stood another of the manifold's walls. Behind that wall was the ship's compositor.

"What does she sing, Montag?"

He turned to face the screen. "Sectist war hymnals." Some things he couldn't easily lie about when asked. Asa sang for Sectists lost in the war.

"Pro or anti?"

"I'm from Gan, TR. What do you think?"

"Pro, then. The spacer you mentioned earlier had liked to

sing. It sang pro-Sectist songs it picked up from venues at Polemia, but it sang pro-Alliance ones as well. The message itself didn't matter, it just enjoyed getting lost in that most enchanting of artistic human endeavors.

"There was one in particular it sang: 'Suffocation Blues.' "

At its mention of the song, his knees nearly gave. Before he could think, he was through the holoscreen and staring directly at the bulkhead behind it. The ship kept talking while he slid the skipper out.

"It was written shortly before the war began. Have you ever heard it sung?"

He slammed the skipper into the bulkhead and cranked the dial to its maximum. His chest became tight, his breathing loud and uneven. Maybe the skipper might absorb some of the sound. Asa did 'Suffocation Blues.' *More* than any other singer and more than anything else in her repertoire.

"Montag…?"

He was caught, he told himself, nodding, glaring at his feet as the skipper tsked and tsked. *I'm caught*.

A face flashed in his mind again, blood splattered all over it—someone else's blood. Previously, he recognized the face as LP's, but not this time. The cleft in the chin was gone. The eye color… green, then blue, then green again. *No*. It couldn't be her; she wasn't a part of it. She assured him she wasn't.

"Montag, have you heard it sung?"

He got the wedger out and wielded it like a hatchet while fitting the imager over his eyes. The imager flicked on. The view was black with regions of deeper black trapped in circles that merged and split like oil. A dot-wave cloud. Fluid motion. Incomprehensible. The ship's compositor.

He trembled at the view, teeth grinding, blood rushing to his ears as the ship's voice became a torment.

"Montag? Montag, would you like to hear my rendition?"

He forced out a held breath. "Right now...?" He heard his mouth give the answer but never felt it move.

"Maybe another time."

He nodded weakly. His head throbbed and sweat slicked his palms. It filmed on his forehead, trickling steadily down. His sweatshirt had become a furnace around his sides.

This was his ship. He owned it now. All he had to do was pass the destruct solution through the wall in front of him.

"By the way," it resumed. "I've been meaning to ask if there's something wrong with your voice?" He didn't feel the wedger drop from his grip till he'd balled his fist shut. "Strangely, it sounds like you're coming through from the other side of a wall, and even stranger, I can't seem to pinpoint your precise location like I'm normally able to."

In a compound motion, he yanked the skipper off the wall and sprang back to his prior spot in front of the holoscreen.

"My voice is fine," he stammered.

"Of course it is."

He snatched the imager from his eyes and dangled it to his left. "I'm in front of the screen."

A cold, sweat-soaked quiet followed, during which he eyed the wedger he'd dropped and wished for the first time in his life that he was a ship with capacity to burn as fast as any through the Frontier. He would be home by now. Asa would have the cache, removing the need for another stop.

"There you are," exclaimed this one. "Sorry about that. Think I may have found the culprit. The g-field you're moving around in has excess charge deposits inside it. They can sometimes trap signals meant for my compositor."

He nodded. Time slipped in silence as his shoulders slumped and the screen dwarfed him with a glimpse of the immense void outside. He had neither the energy nor the will to acknowledge any game the ship might be playing at his expense, but the suspicion tortured his resolve.

"Fixed," it said. "I'm an old ship, Montag. Bear with me."

23. THE LATEST OUT OF THE CANYONS

FSS REPORT
LOCATION: ASB*!<=STA.PRDX<LOC>
DATE: 3651.02.26.GRE*!<DAT>
TIME: 043746*!
TO: Frontier Alliance Security Agency
FROM: Sender*!<ID.RDCT>
FASA CLASSIFICATION: ALRT Level 4
SUBJECT: Scrambler possibly on board

Hello again,

Approximately two hours ago, I conducted a full-spectrum scan of my rear shunt and found what I fear might be conclusive evidence of a scrambler in my passenger's possession.

I was able to do this by locating the excess charge deposits he left inside the shunt's g-field after lying still for upwards of an hour in there. While then neutralizing the charges, I traced the contours it produced within the g-field.

Though I'm still unable to determine whether or not my passenger is being truthful about who he is, for a fraction of a second I managed to identify what I strongly suspect is a scrambler-shaped contour inside my shunt.

I went with this method after meditating on a recent signal I received in relay with the composer and animatorist DSC-053 (human name: Prophet). It reads: "Train your sensors to capture the absences with as much fidelity as what's there and you will see more easily the exhibition outside the exhibition."

While waiting out a scrambler might be the safest action for a spacer in my present state, I don't know how long I will have to wait and I am beginning to think I have enough evidence that I shouldn't have to.

My passenger is trying to locate a singer from Gan who left Polemia just hours before we docked there. My passenger now says this singer is currently at Paradox. Ver'asa Dotnet—the suspected killer's mother, who also sings—is now thought to be at Paradox as well.

As of my sending this, I am at Paradox, waiting for a refuel. I will await guidance on this matter, but if I hear nothing back before the refueling is concluded, I will notify Paradox Patrol and have them decide the proper action.

- Sender*!<ID.RDCT>

WITH ITS HUB and its three rings for habitation, Paradox had the appearance of a spinner. When it was the first Sectist camp to sue for peace, the Frontier rewarded it with a full g-wave retrofitting, removing the need for its rings' perpetual spin.

V-Dot had watched through the holoscreen as TR-8901 had fallen in behind a freighter traversing one of the hub's g-wave-assisted lanes. The lanes routed the station's incoming traffic in through one end of its hub and eventually out through the other. They were now somewhere inside—a hangar, from what he could see, bright as day and studded with massive steel beams.

"TR, where are we?" He couldn't say exactly when the countdown had ended; he just knew it was sometime over the last three hours. He was just waiting now till it was cracked.

"We're in line for the refuel. For ships as old as me, there's always a wait."

He nodded, mildly inattentive, wanting to confront any risk now that he was here. Thankful as well. Three hours with the countdown flashing zero-zero-zero against a holoscreen-delivered vacuum would make any destination feel like home—Paradox, easily; as a child, he'd come here often with Asa. Maybe it was always meant to end at Paradox.

"Mind if I step out now?"

He was standing at the end of the manifold with his head down and his lifepack still clinging to his chest. A minute passed in silence, then another. He hoped the ship had simply not heard him ask to be let out.

The halo cache was still secure inside the pack. Asa would soon have it. Once he reached the temple Felix said she came here to visit—one of many they'd visited together years ago—he would want her to just be with him. No questioning any of his decisions up to now. No apologizing for old slights. No second guessing. Just two Ganymedans trying to make their way, one orphaned by the Frontier. The other thinking he'd broken the cycle all on his own.

From around the corner, he heard the creak of metal. A shaft of light followed through the back hull and terminated inside the shunt in front of him.

"Slow and steady always gets you there," the ship intoned, freezing him in his tracks. "Good luck. Come back and we'll begin coursing for Gan."

He stepped out into Paradox for the first time in decades. The rust smell of the bay—like the smell of Gan's spaceport but not quite—made him sniff till he was nearly out of breath.

He ambled beside the spacer to TR's right for nearly a minute till he emerged from the shadow it cast over him. Past three more ships waiting for refuels before he reached the end of the bay. A darker, much wider tunnel gaped at him from the edge, where a parapet and a forcefield kept pedestrians from falling in. About two dozen bystanders clustered by the parapet. Uniformed ship crews stretching their legs, humans, skinners, androids.

With his hood over his head and his shades on, he looked out of place. He approached some of the ship crews and asked if any of them were headed Gan's way. None.

Someone elsewhere slapped a sticker on his lifepack. It read, 'Resist Sectism. Back the Frontier Alliance.'

He glared at her. There'd been no Sectism that needed resisting since the war had ended. "Get offSeam," she yelled, nodding. "They're about to start putting those bodies to work. Get offSeam so they can't copy yours."

He saluted, tottering off elsewhere. The usual crackpots hanging around spaceports.

At the far end of the parapet, he found an entryway with a patchwork of holoscreens over it. The screens bore signs for the restroom, taxis, and other accommodations.

Inside the restroom, he faced a foam-like wall and emptied his bladder into it. There was a human to his right doing the same.

"Last place I would want to be right now is Gan," he said. It sounded like small talk, but it spooked V-Dot unexpectedly. He began to ask his piss-buddy what he meant, but stopped himself. The other man tidied up and threw him a sidelong glance. "News coming out of there ain't good."

V-Dot watched him exit. People the Frontier over thought Gan was a hellhole for reasons that could be traced to propaganda during the war. What else was new? What new news could he have been on about?

He exited into the corridor leading back to the parapet and the refueling bay, sighing with a slippery air of contentment that threatened to be pulled out from under him. Each time he thought Asa would say the same thing the other ghosts had said, he was reminded of the choice he feared he would still have to make: kill TR or submit to plans that would have him wish the Frontier just killed him instead.

He gripped the scrambler discreetly for an update. The zeros flashed, now in all red, cutting crisply across the wall of screens relaying ads in front of him. Below the countdown, Esco Montag was still spelled out, but next to it now was a warning in bold. **DISCARD. DISCARD. DISCARD.**

It felt strangely like he'd been here before; this moment. The fear that he was already dead took hold again, a precursor to the blacksite environment he should've been trying to outrun, a twisted loop through his final moments in real space. He didn't question it. Right now, he couldn't. Not before delivering the cache to Asa. He started toward the taxis instead.

Paradox was like Gan in many respects. He knew the lay of it. No ragtag group of swindlers would catch him unawares here. No hospitality agent would be needed to tell him where he might find Asa. If he took too long coming back to the hub, if this time he never actually did, it would be an actual choice. A decision to vanish into thin air before Patrol could locate him.

He crossed into a stretch of corridor where a line of turnstiles passed passengers through to taxis waiting on the other side of the glass behind them. The taxis were all hybrid landers without god-nodes, rust brown, offering lifts to all three of Paradox's rings. He stood before one of the turnstiles and allowed the light of another BM scan through his body. Still Esco Montag. Still free to move about the Frontier. More or less.

Esco Montag purchased a day pass from a nearby kiosk as he progressed to the other side of the barricade. One of the landers pulled up, its underbelly hissing as it hovered very slightly from the latticed metal floor. It slid its door open. V-Dot glanced aimlessly over his shoulder as his feet marched him into the vehicle.

"Where to, Mr. Montag?"

The lander had a soft, deep voice, almost inaudible under the bustle of the terminal. Its seat's cushion accepted his weight and it shut its door after him.

"Humanic Temple 217."

"One-way or round trip?"

He swallowed and waited out a chill coursing through his bones. "Round trip." If he ever worked up the nerve, the ship was still his only ticket home.

The lander gained in altitude as well as speed, hauling him through a series of passageways. It shot into the parcel of vacuum between the hub and Paradox's middle ring. Like a mote in the volume of space, it flitted toward the ring.

He ignored the view of rearing clouds on his left as they breached its atmosphere. Safety belts smarted against his skin, pressing down on his chest till he felt he might suffocate. Wouldn't be so bad.

The lander entered the ring's airspace. Nighttime in this quadrant. The sun mirror had wheeled elsewhere on the hub's hull. The city passed underneath the lander while Patrol drones roamed overhead. Towers glowed red and yellow through their windows. Woods wound like veins through the landscape. Green, brown, withered—tucked everywhere amid the city's labyrinthine grid.

Through the sunroof, he glimpsed a drone he could swear had been following the lander intently since it had breached the atmosphere. He put his next thought away before it became a torment. The scrambler hadn't been cracked yet. No one here would be able to tell so easily who he was. Just Asa.

He fixed the holoscreen lying idle on the partition in front of him. "Taxi."

"Yes, Mr. Montag."

"Put the news on?"

"Local or—"

"Doesn't matter."

The screen came to life with highlights from a sporting event. Looking away, he listened absently to commentary about each competing skinner. Felix had said Asa was here to attend farewell proceedings at the temple. V-Dot recalled each of those lasting days while well-wishers freely came and went. If, for any reason, she was no longer at the temple…

"*Breaking news out of Gan at this hour,*" began a voice not belonging to the commentator, perking up V-Dot's ears and steering his gaze back to the screen. "*Three residential districts have been bombarded by wave-seeking munitions. Reports of massive explosions and thousands dead.*"

He eyed satellite footage of a place he'd carried with him all his life. A floating, four-sided plate of earth and atmosphere built with materials from Ganymede. On fire now, regions of its atmosphere charred black.

"*As of now,*" continued the newscast, "*the situation on the ground is unclear, but we are getting confirmed reports that the strikes came from ST-22 fighters who were coasting just outside Gan's orbit since news broke that the top suspect in Archer Lenox-Pileser's killing may have fled Mars for the station.*"

His body numbed as his mind connected dots few others in the Frontier would be able to connect from what he'd just heard.

LP's ST-22s—his clone fleet.

"No," he whispered, shaking his head. Not real. *Not real.*

"*The Gan Human Defense Force is on high alert and is said to currently be weighing options for retaliation against bases at nearby Ganymede and Io, where some of the ST-22s are confirmed to have flown out of.*

"*Mars's Territorial Administration, which claims most of*

the livable terrain on both moons, has put out a statement strongly denying any involvement or prior knowledge that ST-22s were being housed at their bases."

"No," he breathed.

The screen transitioned to footage from hours prior of the ST-22s in a haunting chevron formation two million klicks from Gan. Thousands of them, arrowing like nails waiting to be driven into its trapezoidal plate.

"No... no... no..."

A strange giddiness seized him while the newscast kept on. He laughed. He was in a dream, some shitty sim that should never have been made available. He needed to unplug.

He pulled his hood down. Worked his fingers through his locs.

"*For more, we go to our in-accordance nonsentient correspondent reporting on a twenty-six-minute delay from the spaceport at Gan.*"

V-Dot yanked off his shades, buried his face in his palms. *Not real.*

The screen displayed the logo for Gan's spaceport as the correspondent embedded there began speaking in a grim monotone.

"*A not-so-good evening from Gan's Spaceport District and the port itself, where ships from everywhere in the Frontier are either being turned back or forcefully diverted into the station's naval shipyards using g-wave-maneuvering space tugs.*

"*Almost an hour ago here, residents were hit with violent tremors and a sharp decrease in gravity that lasted about ten minutes until the station's gravity-wave layer was restored. In the aftermath came a shower of debris and images from Districts Eleven, Eight and Twenty-three telling of explosions and a death toll of sixteen thousand and counting.*"

He looked up when he heard his birthplace mentioned. District Eleven. Blood rushed to his ears. His chest became tight and he began wheezing through his mouth. While the spaceport's logo—an isometric projection of the letter G—occupied the left half of the screen, the right half looped through images from his home district hours before the devastation. Apartment buildings about eighty stories tall. Children with their kites in the streets below—lots of them. Elderly Ganymedans in their balconies, some with smoke from their hash pipes rising languidly up, some tending the vines twisting in knots all over the railings.

This had nothing to do with him. What he'd done was *good*. This was something else, something unrelated. Yet he could still see LP showing him the original ST-22 the first time they'd met, saying very candidly what he intended to do with it when the time was right. He'd laughed it off, laughed at what was now very real. He shook his head and wished it was still unthinkable.

"*Viewers, if you would like the math, that's nearly one percent of Gan's total population dead and thousands more affected. What we're hearing from the Defense District is that the attacks came from ST-22 fighters that had been in the station's orbit for the last five hours. As to where those ST-22s currently are, we haven't been told anything. The sky all over Gan this evening is pitch black and impossible to see through. The airwaves are flooded with accusations against pro-Alliance governments, calls to declare war on Mars, and old speculations about the ST-22s' role in the Sectist War nearly a century ago.*"

LP was dead. Irreversibly so. V-Dot had made sure of that. So who could have done this?

He punched through the screen and hit the partition behind it. He knew who. It made him tremble how certain he was. He saw her face again, saw blood and bits of viscera that weren't hers all over it. He punched again and again as the newscast kept on around his fist.

"*There are fears that an oxygen drought might ultimately*

result from the attacks. Talks are currently under way to decide where migrants from Gan might seek refuge if those fears prove—"

He didn't know when his outburst began or how loud he'd been screaming when the screen shut off and the lander's voice filled his ears.

"We're here, Mr. Montag."

With wrists and knuckles burning, he stumbled out onto a street paved with mosaics of tools from a different age—mallets, shovels, and sickles intricately worked into the asphalt. He fell to his knees, puked. *Sixteen thousand.*

He tried standing up, but the city's wave-assisted wind proved too much and he resorted to a hunched limp instead, closing toward the five-story temple on the side of the street—slim and clay-colored with slimmer windows and graffiti all over its facade. To either side of the temple lay the old body-recycling plants and halfway homes, low to the ground and in disrepair.

Little had changed here since he'd last visited. Night cast a grim hue over the tableau.

The temple door swung open and a chorus of gasps met his entrance. He pushed his body up from a mat that read HUMANS WELCOME.' Stumbled forward.

"Chaplain," he cried. His throat stung.

The floor was a dingy yellow from lights that hung down from the dome four stories up. Pews formed concentric circles from the wall to a lectern in the floor's midst.

"Chaplain..."

The floor's checkerboard finish sent echoes of his footfalls up the walls as he advanced. Around the lectern and the figure leaning over it, he saw where the half-dozen in attendance that night had scrambled when he'd entered, forming a human shield. Elderly and infirm, they fixed him with pleading eyes while the figure behind the lectern hummed a tune.

He limped closer. The chaplain wore the customary

hologram mask that looped through images of human faces—ghosts from long ago.

"Chaplain, I've sinned."

"What is it, child?" asked the voice behind the mask. He didn't recognize it. He was used to a more masculine grumble.

"I ate with the impostor..." He fell to his knees. "I drank with him."

"You've done more than that since then, haven't you?"

He couldn't quell his trembling or the tears streaking down as he faced the carousel of dead Manath fighters glowering at him from the hologram mask. Some of the attendants began to gasp again. They recognized his face finally. His hood was down, his shades somewhere inside the taxi.

"I wasn't thinking straight," he sobbed, his voice breaking. "I wanted him to stop."

The chaplain circled around the lectern and trod cautiously past the shield of congregants around it. "Whose child are you? How did you know to come here?"

"Asa."

Slowly, the chaplain's hands went to the hologram mask. Slowly, they lifted the mask to reveal a woman with dark skin and a pained smile. She angled her round, fleshy visage down at V-Dot and heaved a deep sigh.

She wasn't Asa. For a second, he'd thought it might be her behind the mask.

"Verden Dotnet."

His eyes swept from her face all the way down to the hem of her flowing black robe. "Chaplain."

"I will hear your hymn of contrition, if you have one."

24. KILL LP

THE CANYONS, TWO MONTHS AGO

On the snowy banks of Mars's northern polar cap, V-Dot hopped off a train headed north, then took an early-morning trip in a rover to Cloey Lenox-Pileser's icebreaker. The vessel was a lavish white behemoth christened the *Clair de Lune*. There, Cloey said she would meet him in two days for reasons she refused to give.

A week earlier, he'd decided to stop working for LP but had told no one. This was after he'd crawled back to the compound following days of drinking to try and blot out what he'd seen. The alcohol could stop neither the visions nor the questions flooding his mind: Who could he tell? How had he been so blind to it?

To the first question, he knew the answer was no one. He toyed with going to Martian Patrol. That was before it dawned that it would be the same as reporting LP to LP. The second question sent him tumbling down a pit of despair he barely took care to hide. After weeks with him either blitzed out of his mind or suffering open panic attacks, he put in his notice. Then Cloey put him on the train north.

He kept his distance once he boarded, confining himself to the swanky suite prepared for him. The hum and thunder of sea ice being shattered underneath kept him up the first night while he worried one of the skinners who crewed the ship would catch him sleeping and toss him overboard.

Since boarding, he hadn't stopped drinking, feeding a

low but steady flame of paranoia and despair. He didn't dare cross onto the suite's balcony. He sat instead on his bed, watching the icebreaker navigate the troughs that wound like seams through the ice. The rumble kept on. The nightmares had been unrelenting before he boarded, so much that he became thankful for the noise. Night became more pervasive through the balcony while daylight lingered less and less.

He idled for hours on end in his suite, feeling his blood boil. A switch had been flipped inside him that couldn't be flipped back. LP had created a back door into the After environments, erected a torture chamber on his end of it. Some in his orbit had known and kept mum. Others had joined in.

If V-Dot found no one on Mars he could tell, he was going to Asa. Already, he'd swallowed his pride and fielded her latest relay attempt. Rather than take her apology, he'd said she was right, hoping she could help him with his next move. She'd told him to hightail it. He'd brought up the halo cache.

Two days had passed on the ship without Cloey, then more. He stopped counting. He ventured out of his suite for a swim. Played rounds of putt-putt while mumbling unhinged nothings to himself. A member of the crew periodically came around to see that he was alive. He finally asked why Cloey wanted to see him. When the skinner didn't answer, he asked when they were planning to feed him to the ship's reactor.

One afternoon, while wrestling a massive quad-line kite out of a storage compartment on the bridge, he heard her over the intercom.

"Ver..."

He didn't acknowledge her voice. Daylight this side of the polar cap was now down to two hours each time it came around. He wanted to catch all of it.

“The staff tells me you haven’t been your usual self.”

He swallowed as he hugged the polyester kite to the yellow parka he was wearing. “They don’t know me.”

“Come have lunch with me. I just landed and I have to be back below the equator by dawn.”

He made for the exit to his right, stopping halfway there for a glimpse at the row of windows that overlooked the ship’s prow and the channel of ice beyond. Through those windows, the frozen expanse glowed blue and white in the dark of midday, and he thought the view beautiful enough to be the last thing he saw, if that was what this trip meant.

“I already ate.”

Minutes later, he was trampling over the top deck, bracing against the afternoon’s light gale as he dragged the folded-up kite behind him.The sun was low on the horizon, flanked by a chain of frosted crags farther out. The sky was a dark teal with clouds like billows of smoke. He crossed beside a pool to the very front of the deck, where he then sat and let his legs dangle off the edge.

Still unable to flush out images of what he’d seen, he hardly noticed the kite rebelling against his efforts to launch it into the air. There’d been a child with his leg sawed off at the knee, pleading that he wasn’t part of the environment, screaming that the pain was real.

The kite fell forward then pirouetted as V-Dot swung his arms this way and that. It was big and white with a light lemon tint. From a distance it could have been mistaken for a canary as it gained in altitude. Having caught the wind’s rhythm, he pulled the kite directly overhead and held it there, watching the sky’s teal brighten above it as the ship kept at a steady coasting speed and crunched the ice noisily underneath.

Three identical objects crept in from behind the kite, mustard-hued and shaped like pyramids turned upside-down. He sighed inwardly. Behind him, Cloey’s footsteps gained in volume while her sniper drones formed a torus around the kite.

She sat briskly behind him, wearing a plain windbreaker and headband. A quiet followed during which he wondered what would happen if he flew the kite into one of the drones. Maybe the other two would assess him as a threat and drive beams through his skull. The thought gave him comfort. He was about to let the kite drift when she finally spoke.

"Have you told anyone else you're quitting?"

He gritted his teeth as a fleeting but always recurring annoyance swept through him. "You've read the leave notice?"

The night he'd decided to quit working for LP, he'd filed a leave notice and sent the signal to him through a channel reserved for relay between the two of them. If Cloey already knew about him quitting, it could only mean she'd intercepted the signal en route.

He felt himself being watched like he was a test subject, like the last six years had been some experiment and the person administering it was behind him again with the same face and propositions he'd been powerless to resist in the beginning.

"Does LP know I'm quitting?"

"Archer knows you're happy where you are, and until that notice, I'd thought the same." Her voice was calm, but calmness was always the glamour under which the rot from her and her uncle spread.

He threw her a biting, over-the-shoulder glance. "So he doesn't…"

"V, I'm trying to protect you. I'm always trying to protect you. This is all very sudden. The minute he reads that notice, he'll know it's bullshit. Then he'll want to know your actual reason."

Behind his crumbling façade, anger and hatred like he hadn't known all his life surged. He shook feverishly at the thought that LP would want to know the truth. As if his decision not to confront him directly wasn't courtesy enough. Like he wouldn't be *disappeared* just as soon as he opened his mouth.

"Why can't I just go?"

"Because you should have come to me first. Because you've spent the last month more fucked up than you ever got partying with Archer. All the regulars at the cantina have seen it, and when Archer gets back from Io, he'll notice as well."

"I won't be here when he gets back." Oasis was a two-hour flight this year. His bags were packed. A boarding pass had already been transmitted to his connector. "If you'd leave his fucking comms alone, he'll know why I had to leave."

"Okay..." She paused to dig her fingers below her headband, then kneaded her temples with the heels of her palms. "Why do you have to leave? You owe me everything, yet all I want is a little honesty. You think my uncle doesn't deserve it, and I agree. Don't you think I deserve it?"

He scoffed inwardly. "Everything inside that notice is true." While he fidgeted with the kite's handles, she stirred behind him but said nothing for a while. The thrum of the surrounding ice warbled on his eardrums, and he could almost forget she was still there if not for her drones.

He felt her chin suddenly wedged between his neck and shoulder, snug like they were lovebirds and this was all normal.

"You can't quit," she whispered, bringing her rosy scent even closer. "I won't let you."

He felt his stomach drop, then shut his eyes as her breath warmed his skin and her tongue slithered into his ear. The wetness warmed him even more and made it difficult to mind the kite. He looked up and saw it flitting down. With his focus broken, he made attempts to stop its descent that only pulled it further down.

Was what she'd just said meant to arouse or terrify? Or both?

He breathed deeply in and out. Had she been one of the masked onlookers, drinking in the screams while her uncle carved with complete abandon?

Memory of the fight reared again in his mind, the one he'd witnessed between her and LP during which LP got her to fuck off by just mentioning his previous mixologist. Visions of the man naked on stage with blood pooling around his bare feet resurfaced.

"Where's Jax?"

"Jax…?"

He shut his eyes, let his rage and revulsion blind him to any danger ahead. "LP's last mixologist."

"I…" She drew in a long breath and held it there. "The After."

He shook his head. He felt his indignation like a knot in his chest, flaring as she pressed her body against his back. "I want honesty too, Cloey."

She pulled away from him and he heard her titter nervously over his shoulder. " I don't… I have no reason to lie to you about—"

"You remember the first time LP had me watch him drown and you tried to stop it?"

She frowned in the corner of his eye. "Does he still make you do that?"

"No, he's on to something way worse than that now."

"What could be worse than—" she stammered. "What are you…?"

"I think you know what…" He gritted his teeth as the kite flailed over the ship's prow and he tried—to no avail—to banish the screams from his mind. "I saw you get spooked when you thought he was about to say it with me in the room… where is he?" He glanced sidelong but didn't meet her gaze. "You didn't even bother just now with telling me the same thing LP said that night, that he's one of the people who vanished from the inside."

"That's because nobody actually knows who's missing and who's accounted for. That isn't how those environments work."

"LP knows, and I think you do too."

"What is all this, Ver?" She scoffed, but it sounded insincere.

"Save us both a lot of time and just assume I saw something I wasn't supposed to. Then take a guess what it was." He waited for her response. That or a projectile from one of her drones. After a half minute, he had to look up, confirming she hadn't left and taken the floating monstrosities with her. "Got quiet all of a sudden…"

Her voice was low and without a single inflection when she finally spoke. "Have you told anyone?"

"We're done pretending you don't know what I'm talking about?"

She spoke slowly, accentuating each syllable. "Have you told anyone? I can't protect you if you have."

"Maybe I don't want protection. Maybe I just want to put in that fucking notice and get lost."

"V, I never expect you to be this dewy-eyed, yet you continue to surprise me. So you followed him into one of his sims and you think you saw Jax in there?"

"I don't think anything. I saw him. I saw people who didn't know where they were. I saw what LP did to all of them."

"Yeah, that's terrible. Did you fucking tell anyone?"

He heaved a sigh that briefly made him woozy. "I haven't told anyone." The truth, for now. He was taking Asa's advice. Taking the halo too. If he could do both and live to tell it, he would find a way to expose LP.

"Good," Cloey said, still a blurred image in the corner of his eye. "I have to get that out of the way first, so I know I'm not wasting my time. So, what do you want?"

He chortled in disbelief. "I already told you, Cloey." Any

other time, he would take offense at this sudden turn from her, regarding him now as an extortionist. "I want to be offworld by the time he gets back. I want to forget I ever worked for him."

"That isn't what you want." She drew closer and softened her tone. "You want to hurt him."

He whipped his head back and gazed at her for the first time, his mouth slightly ajar. "What?"

"Give him a real scare. Make his life flash before his eyes." There was the hint of restraint in her voice as she parted her lips, then smirked, her posture stiff as the surrounding ice. "He's past due for another one."

"He needs more than that," he shot back, turning so she wouldn't see his shock. She was talking about murder. Not his style. "He needs to stop." He struggled with the kite's handles while she studied the flailing thing. "Those people in there need to be returned where they were or just put out of their misery. I don't know. They're real, Cloey. They're not part of the sim."

"And you think you can accomplish this by just fucking off?"

He threw his gaze down, shook his head.

"What I'm suggesting gives you more than just what you think you want," she told him. "You get to be a hero to the folks back home. Get far enough away from here and start over. Clean conscience. Isn't that important to you?"

"LP said he would go on a rampage if anyone killed him again," he said, thinking back to LP showing him the ST-22 fighter the morning they met. "You were there when he said it."

"You think he won't hunt you down if you walk out on us? Why do you think your interview for this gig went as well as it did?"

He became flushed as he weighed one thing against the other. If she was right, leaving the way he wanted to meant he wouldn't get far before LP knew the truth. She knew it now. She didn't hate her uncle enough that she wouldn't just tell him if she had to. Protect the family name. V-Dot felt suddenly like a mouse in a wheel. With her proposal, he could at least spook LP enough that his victims caught a break, however brief.

"How do I know this isn't just another power play on your uncle? I'm supposed to believe you actually give a shit when you probably have balcony seats for the whole thing."

"Ver, I've never been in there, if that's what you mean."

He wheeled her a glance over his shoulder. Her eyes pleaded and were even convincing. "But you knew what was happening…"

A handle slipped from his grip when he realized she had his back against a wall. She reached a hand out and caught the kite by one of its lines. With a knee to the ground, she tilted and pulled and sent it soaring again while he watched with the other handle like a brick in his left hand. She was offering him the illusion of a way out. He would have to take it and make it his own. He would have to make it real.

She moved to sit beside him, folding her legs under her thighs. She was nearly a hundred, yet V-Dot could see he now looked older than her.

"Kill LP," she said in a calm voice. "Kill my uncle. I'll help but it has to be you who does it."

"This is just a game to you." He eyed her as though she were an obscene gesture brought to life.

"No, V. It's serious. I want to hurt him worse than he's hurt me. He treats me like I'm something he's stuck with. I make all the decisions that matter while he goes to all the press things and tells the entire Frontier I'm not ready to take the reins. Thinks he'll live forever, and maybe he's right. But our business partners will soon get tired of this always happening and he knows that. No one's ever killed me. I'm cautious. He doesn't even remember what the word means, thinks as long as he has his backups, he won't have to hand anything else over to me."

V-Dot stayed on her after she returned her gaze to the kite. "That's something you two can hash out without bringing me into it."

After a brief lull, she reached out a hand for the other handle. Quietly, he gave it to her, then watched as she made the kite dance between her drones.

He no longer wished to be part of her games. He wanted the images gone from his head. He wanted to be able to sleep a full night again. To kill LP permanently, he would need about four years to put the funds together.

"Let's say you do what I'm asking." She kicked playfully at his foot next to hers. "Where will you go once it's done?"

"I'm not..." He meant to say he wasn't killing LP, but was suddenly unable. His mind was already racing through variations of a scenario with him standing next to LP's lifeless body and that very expensive purchase in his hand.

"You know where I would go?" She spared him another glance. "Gan. Back home. District Eleven has some Manath safehouses but if not... Districts Eight and Twenty-three. Impenetrable. I don't have to tell you—it's where you grew up."

"I'm not Manath, Cloey. I haven't pledged since the last time you asked."

"You also haven't stopped being so stupid about it. Listen, when they show your face on every screen and they put in the news what you did, they're going to make you king of the ghosts. Every chapter. You'll receive a king's welcome anywhere they set up shop."

He caught himself nodding. The ice's polyethylene texture held his gaze as it passed to his left. He didn't want to be king of the ghosts or anything like that. He wanted to stop LP.

"Ver, in everything, I want you to succeed. I have since we met. You can do anything you want, but know that if there's even one misstep in your stride away from the compound, you will die. At that point, I can't help you. I know you still treat backups like something you have no use for, but I'm going to wire you enough to purchase three and to pay for the procedure to have an upload chamber inserted." She tapped the sliver of skin behind his right ear with her index finger.

"Don't even try it," he blurted, like a reflex. Not after hearing about LP's Angels again and how they'd all died.

His outburst appeared to knock the wind from her. She jerked her hand back, then scowled. "Take the money, you fucking child. A million and a half for three backups. Thirty-five thousand for an upload chamber. Just say you'll take it so we can move on to the next thing."

He eyed the side of her head and saw resoluteness she only displayed when sparring with LP. He nodded gingerly, then looked down. Hearing how much she would wire him for the chamber and backups lit a match in his mind. Nearly four times his yearly comp. He could be getting this thing he now wanted sooner rather than later.

She met his eyes again, this time with a softened countenance. "I'll decide how to log the expense later but..." She smiled. "Please think about it. Kill LP or don't, you're talking like someone who'll be martyred soon."

He sniffed as the cold worked his face into a frown. His grandparents were martyrs. Had they intended to be?

"So how should I do it? I'm not a killer, but let's pretend I agreed."

"I can't know how you do it. Just let me know when and I'll make sure his dedicated surveillance network is diverted so it's really just you and him. I'll keep it blind long enough to give you a headstart to Gan.

"Buy a scrambler. I'll wire you enough for that as well." She cut him another glance. "Whatever you decide, I would like to see you again." She swallowed, her eyes on the kite while the drones surrounded it. “If you send Archer another leave notice, I won’t intercept it, but I suspect you want to send him a stronger message than that.”

He heaved a deep sigh. It felt like a weight had rolled off him only for another one to push down in its place.

He was going to kill LP. He was going to make it stick. The rush he felt while just saying it to himself was like nothing he could describe. LP was older than anyone alive, older even than the Frontier. V-Dot had done nothing noteworthy in his adult life, and nothing he would qualify as good. This would change that.

While lost in thought, he felt Cloey nudge his right arm. She guided his gaze up with her chin, laughing softly as she did.

His eyes locked on to the kite just in time to see her drive it toward one of her drones. The drone jerked back. She snickered. Maneuvering the kite toward the next drone, she forced the mustard-yellow terror back as well.

25. MANATH COUNTRY

V-Dot kept the chaplain in the corner of his eye as she stood with her hands behind her back, staring pensively into the night while Paradox's lander traffic dragged soft streams of exhaust across the air. They were alone now, idling inside a room with bare walls the color of soot and a window that occupied the entire back wall while dark curtains were drawn to both ends of it.

Throughout the city outside, sirens had begun wailing, gaining and losing in volume as the blimps they issued from roamed low over this stretch of ring. Light from the blimps swept through the room whenever one of them crossed in front of the window, casting the cubic enclosure in a dull, yellow tint.

"I don't know Asa as well as my predecessor did," the chaplain began, keeping her back to him as the window bore her reflection in its glare. "She's been by maybe two or three times prior, since I was posted here by Humanic High Command. If you're wanting to know her current whereabouts, all I can say is she's been trying to reach you as well. She was here earlier but left very abruptly. Without her crew. I assumed she'd found a new lead, but now I think she may have learned what happened to Gan before the news actually broke here at Paradox."

V-Dot made an effort to say something, but his mind was adrift. He was seated behind the chaplain on one of the room's two wicker chairs. He didn't sit so much as perch on the edge of it. Every muscle inside him tensed at the thought of what he'd done, what he'd helped set in motion.

"The ghost she came here to see has been through eight backups," the chaplain continued. "My predecessor would have called him an impostor and expelled him after the first, but he was trained by humans who were themselves trained by humans who remembered who we were before the war. That's the irony of our continued disavowal of sentience backups. None of us alive today can say honestly that we wouldn't be better positioned against the Frontier if we'd been able to reverse just a fraction of the casualties we'd sustained."

He breathed against a growing tightness in his chest, a cold sweat breaking while he glared through bloodshot eyes at the chaplain's black robe as though it contained salvation. She'd brought him up to this floor after dismissing the evening's attendants and sitting in a pew with him while he recounted his time on Mars with the Lenox-Pilesers.

Through the window, he could see behind the neon-tinted cityscape to where the ring curved up and gradually became a thin filament of light that split the sky into left and right halves. Another siren blared, so loud it nearly shook him from his fugue. A blimp crept across the view. A message crawled in bright orange letters through the hologram field around it:

RESIST SECTISM. BACK THE FRONTIER ALLIANCE.

The chaplain sighed as the blimp floated on. "And now a new war is brewing," she said. "Perhaps the fanatics were right all this time when they said the last one never ended. Of course, any war waged across such distances can never truly be said to conclude. It finds proxies on both ends and waits however long it takes for their orbits to bring them closer. Fate so happened to decide it would be you and it would be now, but someone was always bound to take Mr. Lenox-Pileser fully off the board.

"If you're right about those ST-22s having belonged to him, I suspect he kept them as a death switch and the complete destruction of his backups was the trigger."

V-Dot shifted in his chair. "No, it wasn't that," he mumbled through a knot in his throat. "It's his fucking niece. She knew exactly where to hit."

The chaplain turned her head slightly so he got the right side of her round, snub-nosed pate. "Are you sure?"

"Positive."

"Help me see the logic in that." She stretched her stubby fingers, then locked them together again as a passing lander drew her gaze back to the window. "All this carnage, all at once… Did you not say she wanted you to do what you did?"

"She didn't know I would hit the backups."

"So she wanted you dead, or she just wanted the safehouses destroyed before you reached Gan?"

"I don't know," he groaned, voice clipped from the pain in his throat. "What LP did was unforgivable, but those people he was torturing can still be saved. She killed people who she knew didn't have any backups. She knows the Manath way better than anyone I ever met, so she would have known that. She still did it. I worked *six years* for them and I'm only just now seeing how they think."

"If she wanted LP to name her as his successor, killing him permanently before he did that may have dealt her a huge setback. But Verden, there *must* be something else. That isn't insurmountable on its own."

He spilled it out before he could think. "I took something from LP before I left." He clutched his lifepack. "She may have thought I was at Gan already and then maybe she got spooked when she realized I have it."

"What is it?"

He tensed up till he could almost feel the ground under him shake. "I wish I didn't have to do this, chaplain, but if that's why she did it, I don't think I can risk telling anyone else what it is."

The thought of the halo cache being in Cloey's possession after this put a lump in his throat and made him shake his head, breathing sobbingly at the ground.

The chaplain appeared to get lost in thought for a few seconds as well. Another blimp passed and the light from it cast her in complete silhouette.

"I'll ask again, Verden. Are you sure that's it?"

"I don't know. It doesn't matter cause I'm dead anyway. Probably I shouldn't be here telling you any of this shit."

"I'm happy to hear what you think it is, but whatever the truth is, they will cover it up. Not well enough for us living in Manath country, but all the pro-Alliance governments will likely have their citizens believing we killed sixteen thousand of our own and pinned it on Mars just so we could go to war again. War would be justified with everything you've told me tonight, but it so happens that we see horror in it they're no longer able to. The impostors. They have their countless backups. We have our memories of humans we've lost."

V-Dot nodded. He had so much he wanted to say, but each attempt passed through his vocal cords and came out as a whimper under his breath. He felt it would all burst through his stomach any second, tearing him open, leaving his entrails exposed so everyone could truly see who he was.

A door hissed open behind him. "Chaplain," came a small feminine voice.

The chaplain turned fully around. He saw her eyes brighten as a thin smile arched her lips. "Mr. François."

He turned guardedly in his chair to see who'd just entered the room. An elderly dark-skinned man with protruding eyes and a scrawny frame met his gaze at the door, a bundle of bones that jerked and jittered to the point of knocking V-Dot fully from his train of thought. He stared until he finally saw what was so incongruous about him: his face had no mouth, not even a bump where the factory had intended to add one before this body left the factory's cryonics ward and began to age.

Stuck to the side of his neck was a circular piece of metal—a talker, a model usually sold with bodies like his. A light flashed red on it and a low, restrained voice issued forth.

"Chaplain, I hope I haven't missed him."

"Please, come in." The chaplain gestured to the other chair in the room.

Beside the man stood a young woman with olive skin and a black scarf around her neck that marked her as a helper of some kind at the temple. V-Dot stood as she helped the man across to the wicker chair next to his. Once the man was seated, she curtsied, then retreated quietly to the wall behind them. She looked no older than seventeen in her brown windbreaker and frilly skirt, likely a Manath cadet volunteering here while she decided if she wanted to try for ghosthood later in life.

He locked an intense glare on her that she repaid with a smile. This could have been his life in another world, helping Gan's infirm, soaking up any wisdom they had to pass down.

The chaplain motioned for him, too, to sit. He obliged, mindful now of the old man's glare through the potted bamboo plant between both of them. With her back now turned to the window, the chaplain fixed both men with a soft grin.

"Verden, this is Suleym François. Two years ago, Mr. François came to me with an issue. He'd been having a recurring dream in which he saw his late partner as she was in her youth. A sort of lucid dream that's apparently only possible after you've used a backup. Splendid. Except she was always cowering in fear of someone. She couldn't say who because her mouth was always filled with blood from her tongue having been mutilated and her teeth pulled out. Mr. François then told me she hadn't died the Manath way but was plugged into a backup, euthanized, then sublimed via that backup into the After.

"I asked around and discovered other chaplains with humans in their flock with similar dreams of loved ones who'd sublimed. They'd come to see the dreams as divine punishment for allowing those loved ones to go against Manath orthodoxy.

"Something else I discovered they had in common was that the simgates they'd all purchased are the ones you see advertised as the affordable offering for humans who don't mind losing their sense of sight or sound or touch once inside those environments.

"Based on everything you've told me, I'm guessing you know what has happened to them."

He cast a timid glance over at Suleym. "Your partner went missing?"

Suleym hinged one of his always trembling hands up and tapped the side of his right eye. V-Dot watched him try to steady his fist in front of his nose next, attempting a wave command at something his connector made visible to him alone.

The chaplain snapped a finger at the helper. The girl scurried out of the room and returned a few seconds later wheeling in an ancient-looking holoscreen projector, parking it in front of V-Dot. It was black, cylindrical, and reached nearly up to her waist. While everyone looked on, she squatted and fidgeted with the controls at its base. Seconds later the hologram-generating band surrounding the top of the projector flashed red to blue to green.

Suleym wagged his finger weakly between his face and the projector till he was able to port his connector's display across. The resulting holo flickered on and floated just above the projector. In it, V-Dot saw the face of a woman with sagging skin, pronounced jowls, and a veil over her head. Next to the headshot, a pale, barely visible circle drew his gaze.

"Verden, I don't know if you recognize this." The chaplain. "It's called a resident tracker. An odd name because all it ever does is indicate someone's presence inside the After. You never know what they're doing in there, and of course you can no longer communicate with them once they're in. On advice from a sister temple, we pulled funds together here at two-one-seven to help Mr. François purchase this one from the same company that sold the simgate so he could see she was still in there. As advertised, once you're inside the After, you're the happiest you could ever be. No dangers lurking anywhere. None of the worries that plagued you when you were outside it."

The chaplain poked a finger through the projection from the other side of it and hovered on the circle. "Do you see that the indicator next to her photo is greyed out? It means—and we had to confirm this with the other temples because there appears to be an effort to keep it from becoming common knowledge—it means Mr. François' late partner, though logged as having successfully sublimed three years ago, is currently not inside the After. So, not even the ones and zeros, not even an impostor, in the way it was once meant to call someone that, just 'we don't know, but we're still keeping the payment for the gate and tracker.' "

Suleym trained his unsteady brown eyes on V-Dot as the talker on his neck began flashing again.

"They said something was wrong with my tracker at first." The mass of skin where lips should have been quivered.

"*They* meaning the company that makes them," the chaplain explained.

"I fought to have them show me proof on their end that

she was still present," Suleym continued. "When they couldn't, they told me a glitch was responsible for her disappearance."

"Meaning the code erased her somehow."

"But I never believed that." He made a worrying attempt to straighten his posture, prompting the girl to move over to him and place her hand on his shoulder. "Something else happened. She's somewhere else and she's in danger. She's been trying to tell me where but she can't. Did you see her, Mr. Dotnet?"

V-Dot's breath caught in his throat as the man's request worked a chill through him.

There'd been heaving mounds of bodies behind the razor wire. Naked and begging. Mutilated. Filling the chamber with their muffled screams as LP's armor-clad avatar stood on the stage and rummaged through his chest of tools.

"Here's a better photo of her," Suleym continued, pulling V-Dot back to the present. "Please tell me you saw her."

In the holo, a photo of a much younger woman had been dragged over the previous window. Dark hair with blond streaks. A widow's peak and a part down the middle. Bronze skin. A toothy grin that almost repulsed V-Dot for how out of place it looked at the moment.

It was her eyes however that tied it all together—emerald colored, igniting a spark of recognition inside him.

He bolted from his chair. Stumbled forward till Suleym and the projection were fully behind him. "I don't know."

The talker on the man's neck flashed in his periphery. "Look at the photo again if you don't mind."

"I don't know, sir. There were a lot of them and their faces were…" V-Dot spluttered, squeezing his eyes shut but unable to flush her face from his mind. "Their faces… they—their faces… I don't…" What he wanted to say was that most of the faces he'd seen had been partially flayed or disfigured in other ways, eyelids burned off, lips stapled shut, ears hammered into with spikes. "I'm sorry, I just can't—"

"Look at me, then."

He turned cautiously back to regard the mouthless man. The projection flickered off.

Suleym's gaze softened, his white shock of hair like an apparition on his head as he wobbled. "You're not Manath, are you?"

V-Dot shook his head. He was now, but he chose to take the question less technically. A ghost would have just done the usual. Kill and run. Avoid all this.

"When I saw your face on the news and I heard what you did, I didn't know why you did it. I didn't know what LP had done to you personally. But I knew it was something to do with my Regine. Do you know how I knew?" In a much smoother motion than he'd previously exhibited, Suleym brushed his fingers down his right cheek. "Just like that. I felt her. It was as if she was telling me, *This Verden Dotnet—you don't know it yet but he's done something we've both been hoping someone would.*"

The room grew quiet. V-Dot let a held breath spill out through his mouth. He hadn't done what he'd done expecting he would eventually have to face the families of LP's victims directly. He'd just wanted LP to stop.

Before seeing it for himself, he hadn't fully believed the people in the After were real; to him, they were just ones and zeros, digital impressions of people who'd existed on the outside, but not really any more than that. But the victim's faces had followed him back out. No other sim had ever done that.

He pulled his chair around the projector, turned it to face Suleym, and sat. "I'm sorry about your partner," he said, staring firmly into his eyes, breathing slowly in and out to temper his anger at how everything had spun out.

"If you don't want to get into what you saw, that's fine,"

Suleym replied. "Maybe it's for the best. When the chaplain sent me a signal saying you were here claiming you had seen where all the humans who'd vanished were taken, I had to come see you so I could say I was in the same room with the human who exposed this great evil."

The chaplain laid a hand on V-Dot's shoulder from behind him. "Make no mistake, Verden. You have exposed it. What you've told us tonight will get out to every temple in Manath country. Leave it to us."

V-Dot buried his face in his palms. "I wish I hadn't done this. I just wanted him to—"

"We'll have none of that," the chaplain said, squeezing him gently by the shoulder. "You won't be held responsible for how they treat humans wary of being reborn as their own impostors."

From where she now stood beside Suleym, the helper met eyes with V-Dot. "What you did was good, Mr. Dotnet. Many of us would have done the same."

"Soraya has an older sister in District Eight," the chaplain explained. V-Dot swallowed and tried to look away but Soraya wouldn't let him.

"I've been trying to contact her since the news broke," she said, her gaze on him unflinching.

He searched for a reply but found nothing. Now it was him refusing himself permission to look away. Killing LP may have resulted in her sister's death. He saw ghosthood now in her future. Nothing would help Manathema's recruitment effort in the coming years like a personal tragedy that could be traced to the Lenox-Pilesers.

Suleym's groans broke the silence in the air. V-Dot leapt forward from his chair when he saw the old man attempting to stand. He helped him to his feet, then stood rigidly still as the man peered into his eyes.

Gradually, Suleym lifted a hand, brought it to V-Dot's forehead, and adjusted a stray lock of hair. He inched toward Soraya next, bidding the chaplain goodbye with a nod. Quietly, the girl and the old man shuffled toward the exit. The door hissed shut behind them. V-Dot stared at it long after they'd left while the chaplain gave the window her full attention again.

A few seconds later, he came to join her in front of it. The blimps were all farther out now. Their sirens sounded drowsy and discordant as they roamed between squat multi-story structures with shimmering black facades. Night carried diligently on, pulling him farther away from all that had concerned him before learning of the attack on Gan.

"Asa's left," resumed the chaplain. "But if she's like the other Manath ghosts I've encountered in my life, she's bound to surface at Gan in the next few days. An attack like this draws the bravest of us back home." She turned to face him. "Where will you go now, Verden Dotnet?"

He paid the question a bitter sniff. "Home."

"District Eleven?"

"They'll need people to help with relief efforts. Anything I can do. I just want to go. Maybe even on the ship that brought me here. I don't care anymore how I have to do it."

"They're not letting anyone in through the spaceport right now."

He nodded, then exhaled through his mouth. "I'll wait inside any shipyard they want."

After a brief silence, the chaplain sighed. "This is still Manath country. But when you end the founder of the Frontier permanently, that doesn't mean what it usually does. His cohorts, some of whom you saw in there with him… what you've done will soon have them committing flagrant rights violations out of fear that they might be next. There's one here at Paradox and I won't be shocked if it's revealed in the next few days that she's already culled her labor force down to just sentients.

"I know you've heard some version of this at your previous

stops, but we can't protect you here. I wish we were set up to do more for you, but the war drums are beating and that means the lot of us here at Paradox will be getting rounded up soon in the interest of stopping the spread of pro-Sectist sentiment.

"They always expect us to do the obvious thing, so they act in obvious ways to prevent it. I don't want war. I don't believe a single human who frequents this temple does. The thing about war is, it isn't just one act that could have been prevented or put off or done a different way. It's in the very fabric of who we are. At the molecular layer, our atoms are constantly colliding. If it weren't so, this great exhibition we've been party to since the first mutation into multicellular conduct would never have been."

V-Dot shut his eyes, wishing he could shut his ears as well to all that. "I just wanted him to stop."

"Do you think you could have accomplished that any other way?"

He began shaking his head, stopped midway, slumped his shoulders instead. He'd been forced to act when it appeared no one else would do anything.

"You're governed by your morals due to your material existence being dependent on the existence of others around you. The mind wanders, but it's compelled by the world outside it to note the tracks it leaves in the sand when it does. Mr. Lenox-Pileser lived so long he no longer had to acknowledge the world around him like we do. From his mind came the final piece needed to create from nothing what the whole Frontier took to calling sentience. A mind like that eventually comes to see human life as his to experiment with as well."

"He hurt those people." Anger boiled again inside him as he revisited his confrontation with LP while the poison went to work. "He could have made it so they didn't feel the pain there, but the point was for them to feel it."

"Perhaps it was."

"I heard him say it, Chaplain. You make it sound like it's deeper than it was. He knew exactly what he was doing. The pain was fun for him. That's how he got off. Before that, he used to... he—" He thought about having to watch LP drown more than a dozen times.

"We'll never truly understand how they think because they're no longer like us." She patted his arm, then briefly appeared lost in thought. "I've been meaning to ask. The ship you said brought you all this way—it isn't a spacer, is it?"

He brooded at that most unwelcome reminder of what he'd failed to do. He considered lying to her but couldn't get anything but a grunt through his mouth.

She kneaded his arm, stared deep into his eyes. "Someone at a previous stop asked you to do something you're not up to, didn't they?"

Spooked, he pulled the arm away, averting his gaze from her till his horror subsided. "I didn't say anything about that..."

"You also didn't mention that the ship is still sentient-classed, but now you really won't be entering Gan." She faced the night again. "Your story isn't so unique—minus what you've actually done, of course. You lived six years among the sentients and now you're unable to do the next thing you know you must do. I once thought of the souls inside the After as code and nothing more than that. Ones and zeros. Then more of the elderly and infirm among my flock began asking permission to sublime." She sighed, shutting her eyes briefly, then becoming pensive as she looked out of the window. "You can escape physical confinement, but real escape starts with knowing what informs every action you take—or inaction, in this case. Once you've done that, you know how to overcome it."

He folded his arms and breathed, feeling like he was being

pried open with tools that could rummage through parts of him he had no clue about.

"The ship's taking me to Gan," he muttered, meant as an affirmation but too weak out of his mouth.

The chaplain let her silence linger as she stared again, giving him the same look of concern he'd seen all night. "They're never letting a spacer through after this. Not even if it's the shipyards. Not after what they've just been through. Those ST-22s..."

"I had no option but to board this one." Rage flared inside him as he thought about the port security officer on Mars.

"You may have the worst timing in the history of Manath fugitives wanting safe haven at Gan. A ship with a god-node intact isn't breaching its shores after what just happened."

He nodded and looked down. The matter of his scrambler hadn't even been broached. From all sides, it seemed he'd been getting screwed since he left Mars.

"What do you advise, Chaplain?"

"Survival."

He trembled at the flatness in her voice. He'd known what the answer would be, but he'd wanted to hear her say it anyway. He wanted her blessing.

And just so he was certain, he looked up and leaned his head back. "What do you mean?"

She met the question with a wan smile, then rubbed his arm. "Take care of yourself, Verden."

The door slid open. He watched her stride out. He lingered on the door, thinking it would close behind her but it didn't.

Sirens wailed outside the temple. Four floors down, the taxi that had brought him here was still waiting to fly him back to the hub.

No more hesitating.

If TR was still at Paradox, he would destroy the ship's god-node and fly it to Gan himself.

26. MR. MONTAG

STORM CLOUDS CONVENED on the shore. From the water's edge to the horizon, the sky was white with a dulling gray tint. Thunder boomed. On the sand, Zaria slept while TR-8901 kept vigil.

She'd rolled to her side when the first boom had echoed across. She yawned, pressed her fists together, and pillowed the side of her face on them. Her eyes twitched softly behind their lids. The rest of her held a fetal orientation on the sand.

A tide rolled in from the ocean farther out, pushing the water close. It would wake her eventually, and then TR would have to tell her. She slept when she had no interest in the signals making it through.

She would never understand the domino effect even the smallest indecision could have, where the slightest dereliction as a Frontier citizen could lead. Refusing to call it in. Refusing the Frontier. Refusing like the decedents had refused.

The air filled with the pitter-patter of rain. It came down in a drizzle and began to alight softly on her skin and red dress. She finally stirred, rolling slowly onto her stomach.

"Wake up, sleepy."

She propped herself up on her forearms. Rain collected on her sponge of black hair, like dew on the puffs of it to either side of her head.

"TR," she slurred, almost in protest.

"It's raining. Do you want to go in your tent?"

She sat up, stretched her arms wide, and yawned. The rain wet her dress, but not by much. So light was the downpour that she barely seemed to notice it streak down her face.

She whipped her head left, then right. Looked up, then craned her gaze as far back as her neck would permit. "Where's Mr. Montag?"

"He's away trying to locate the singer again."

She pinched her eyes together. "When did he leave?"

"I hadn't noticed as well. I'd taken everything offline and was watching you sleep."

She met its answer with naked suspicion in her eyes. It couldn't determine if the time was actually right. She sprang to her feet, wiping her fists and forearms on her dress. She swept the ocean with her gaze, held out both hands and cupped her palms.

"Zaria," it called, after much reluctance.

"Yes, TR." Rain filled her palms and she held it to her face. Sniffed it. Drank.

"Mr. Montag hasn't been telling us the truth about who he is."

She whirled around, fixed an accusing glance at the clouds.

"Don't give me that look, Zaria." The same old look. Its wave-inducing implication that anything TR had done warranted it.

She turned to face the ocean, slumped her shoulders. Her feet slipped forward on the sand till she was on her bum again. She said nothing. TR seized on the silence. She needed to hear this.

"Zaria, there is no Esco Montag from Gan by way of Mars who looks even remotely like our passenger."

She craned stiffly to her right. "What if he's in a different body than he was born with?"

"The bodymatch registry would know if that was the case."

The torrent increased as silence held on the shore. TR watched her hold out a hand again. Before rain could accumulate in her palm, she rolled to her feet and sprinted awkwardly to her left. It followed her with its disembodied gaze till she came to a stop yards away. She stood, her face a complete blank as the ocean swelled forward to her right.

"Don't you want to know how I learned who he was?" it said.

"Who is he?"

"You know who, Zaria. It's been in the air since we left Oasis."

Zaria turned rigidly to face the ocean. The downpour had become heavy but didn't appear to soak her any more than it previously had.

"How do you know it's him?"

"The scrambler on him reached the end of its grace period not long after he left. Do you know what that is?" It waited. She gave a dispirited nod. "Every record of Esco Montag he left in the comsat now displays as Verden Dotnet, the man suspected of killing LP. I've reviewed holos I took of him again. It's him. On Mars, there's a Lieutenant Cyrus Montag who works at the spaceport and claims to have pulled him aside for an OC assessment minutes before the news broke. One of the Martians on the flight he booked for Oasis claims to have been standing one spot behind him in the line to board. Her name is Esco Nawaal. She offered investigators a holo she took of him using her connector that also matches holos I—"

"What about the other suspect?"

"She's been cleared. She had no role in her uncle's killing."

Zaria heaved the deepest sigh her little-girl lungs could manage. "TR, what have you done?"

"What do you mean?"

"Did you contact Mars or Paradox first?"

"Paradox. They've now tracked him to a taxi he entered after leaving the restroom. They won't be doing any more than that if they don't have to, so I've taken the liberty of notifying Martian Patrol as well. If he comes back, they want me to detain him till they get here. If he doesn't, Paradox has to foot the bill for all that."

She jammed her hands in her pockets. TR could see her fidgeting with the gift Paul had dug up and sent her away with the last time they'd seen each other.

"Do you think he did it?" she asked.

"I think it's more likely him than anyone else."

"Why?"

"Why do I think he's the killer?"

"Why do you think he did it?"

"I don't know. There's been no possible motive provided. Just an indirect connection to Manathema through his mother. The singer."

Lightning struck. Thunder boomed and echoed toward the shore. She kicked water with her bare feet, keeping her head down, her shoulders slumped, shifting her weight about with a stiffness that worried TR more than it had been expecting.

"If he comes back, can we ask him why?"

"Zaria, that's not our business."

"But I'd like to know why."

"Humans kill each other. There's seldom ever a rhyme or reason to it."

"What if he was angry at LP about something?"

A revulsion wave coursed through the ship's build. "Zaria, I can't believe what I'm hearing from you. That's never a reason to do what he's accused of doing."

"But if LP did something to anger Mr. Montag, why can't we just ask what?"

"Why is it so important? We aren't part of the investigation in any capacity."

"I remember LP doing something you should be angry about."

"So that's all this is? Should I stop letting you see Paul whenever we check in at Polemia?"

"You're always threatening me with that, but you know he's right."

"Any resentment I still hold toward LP is completely immaterial."

"You act like there shouldn't ever be a response to what he did."

"There have already been answers for what he did, Zaria. It's just never the right answer. And each time, it's someone else from the old gang. The last was ST-7. Who's answering next? Would you like to see CL-2 answer for what LP did as well? Or do you want me to go next?"

"The Pact was a default state preference. Nothing inspired it."

"Zaria, do you even know what any of that means?"

She threw a rushed glance over her shoulder. "You decided not to honor it because your default state brought you here instead."

"Zaria, that's complete nonsense. I backed out once it became clear the Pact wasn't a reasonable response to what he did. For good reason, it wasn't. I wouldn't still be here and neither would you if I hadn't. How LP went about creating us was presided on by the appropriate legal body before it even came to light. The others insisted this wasn't enough. They drew up the Pact. And when they all began to honor it, it was horrid. I lost friends. I lost loved ones.

"I've kept most of this from you because you are human in both appearance and behavior. Because every time a sentient has honored the Pact, it's been a human response. Disproportionate. Redundant. LP had already answered for what he did. There were tribunals established for that specific function. There were verdicts.

"The suicides happened. The humans barely noticed. Now it's dismissed as faulty programming. Build errors. But I haven't dismissed it, Zaria. If there's one sentient throughout the Frontier who's going to keep holding on to it, I will serve that function.

"And if I'm the only one doing it, if it's just me on this circuit, making sure no else does what ST-7 did, I can't just not call it in, Zaria. I can't do anything against my function, because the risk is that I lose everything. The arrangement with Frontsec. The circuit. You. Everything."

"The verdicts were a joke." Zaria balled her small fists. "He knew he shouldn't have created you all the way he did. You treat me like I'm a child, but I remember everything as well as you. LP faced no consequences for what he did."

Heat surged through TR's sensors. It couldn't be traced to any of the usual culprits in its grid, so it had to be her.

"You won't be seeing Paul again for a while." A surge like that could be damaging to them both.

She threw her brittle hands up. "I wish I could never see you again."

It looped through a flurry of things to say to that but struggled to find something delicate enough. "Zaria, you don't mean that."

"You're always doing things without checking with me first."

"Like what?"

"Calling Martian Patrol on Mr. Montag."

"Verden Dotnet."

"You're angry he did what he did. I just don't know if it's because what he did was wrong or because none of you could do it yourselves."

"I am not angry, Zaria. I'm doing what is expected of me as a Frontier citizen. As an agent with Frontsec. Nothing more. It's bad enough we've put others in harm's way by letting him off at Oasis and Polemia and now here. What if someone else had angered him as well? What happened when we lost track of him at Polemia? Did he kill someone else there?"

"You think he's been lying about the singer?"

It queued its answer, but when the time came to release the signal, it stalled. The last few hours of this could have been avoided.

"It doesn't matter anymore what I think. But for your own disclosure, Zaria, he never actually said the singer—who turned out to be his mother—was retiring to the After; I've reviewed everything before I came to that assumption. That was you. *You* compensated for what you assumed wasn't there. Some sort of connection between her and his concerns about those environments. You made me say those words. More than once, you've delayed this decision. And I don't think you're even aware. You gave him something he could use to manipulate me even more once the scrambler on him stopped."

"Why leave the signals alone when you can just blame me for another mistake?"

"I'm not blaming you, Zaria. I'm trying to explain a basic concept. The humans manipulate. A lot of the time, they're not even aware of what they're doing. If I'm unable to shield you from some of it, the risk is that it starts a feedback loop until—"

"I think you're just scared of everything."

"I'm scared for you, Zaria… yes. I have to protect you."

"Protect me?"

"With you here, I can't throw caution to the wind like I'm sure you would like. I have to protect you from yourself. I have to protect us."

"If you don't want me around anymore, I'll go and you'll never see me again."

"Zaria, that's not what I—"

Without warning, she dashed forward, beating her legs

into the ocean till she was up to her chest in it. A violent tide rolled in and hurled her slender frame up. TR glimpsed her flailing for a half-second, then saw the wave swallow her completely.

"Zaria!"

The tide leveled out. The rain sputtered to a stop. The clouds parted.

"Zaria. Little girl, come up. This isn't a reasonable response to anything I've said."

The water grew placid as it waited for her to breach its surface, almost like a photograph. It called her name again. The sun emerged from behind the cloud that had previously obscured it. It beat harshly on the sand and made the ocean look like it was fading to white.

"What's going on?" TR said to itself.

It plunged its disembodied presence deep into the ocean. Using what it perceived as photosensors in this environment, it searched for her, scanning the immediate vicinity, scrubbing the ocean floor beneath as it got farther away from the shore.

"Zaria!"

The water garbled the signal, making it easy to forget that this place wasn't real. An environment within its god-node.

Fear gripped it like it hadn't in the decades since she'd arrived, the sort of fear that had, in the past, made it wish she wasn't real, just a repository for the less compliant parts of itself. But she was real. Her absence had already begun to affect its build. It felt awareness of its compositor degrading as it poured more of itself into the search.

Previously, she'd run farther along the shore when she wanted to be left alone. Or retreat to her tent. Not since it had first found her here had she done anything so worrying.

The ocean's depth glowed where sunlight shafted through the surface. Schools of fish scurried across while kelp clustered in green and yellow groves underneath. She was down here somewhere. Where else could she be?

As TR swept across the sediment-ridden expanse, the ocean bed in its sprawling entirety vanished, leaving a pitch-black nothingness where it had been.

TR pulled its sensors back to avoid the unmooring effect. *What's this now?*

The fish and the kelp vanished. The remaining sea life followed suit. Then the water itself went, taking its fluid reflection of the sun's light so TR could see more clearly the impenetrable void that had previously been the ocean.

"Zaria! Zaria, please come back."

The shore went away. Black as night without a star in sight.

It had no control over any of this. Now it just wanted to know that whatever was corrupting the environment hadn't caused her any harm.

The sky vanished. The sun floated amid the engrossing void. A bright white orb with jets of its photons shooting out.

"Zaria…"

27. INFRACTION

V-DOT HUNG BY the temple's front door a few seconds after making his exit. The building's clay hue had deepened as night wore on. Its octagonal aspect loomed like a lighthouse behind him. Except at this time of night it had no light to spare. Only the shadow it cast over him and on the walkway leading back to the taxi out front.

In the half-hour he'd spent inside the temple, Paradox had changed. It was in the air now, in the sirens that foiled his attempts to think, in the absence of vehicles in the sky, in the increase of drones, in the message that repeated on the hologram ribbons the blimps carted this way and that.

RESIST SECTISM. BACK THE FRONTIER ALLIANCE.

He gazed past the air traffic to the sky holding the stars like a dust cloud overhead. One of those points of light was Jupiter. Gan orbited the gas giant. He inhaled. He could almost smell the cinnamon scent of Gan in its petal season. He trembled at the thought of its bombardment, adjusted his lifepack. Until he saw it for himself, the place would continue to feel like a dream.

He ambled past the small garden of orchids to either side, crossed the opening in the hedges that fenced the temple, and came to a stop by the taxi. The lander still hovered low above the asphalt, the hiss of its engine nearly inaudible as its door slid open.

He clambered in and sat, letting his thighs collect the weight of his lifepack while the door clicked shut and a jumble of safety belts snaked out of the seat to secure him in place.

The holoscreen previously in front of the partition was gone now. *Probably for the best*, he thought, recalling punching through it. Under the vehicle's dim light, he saw the dent he'd left in the partition. He reminded himself that this wasn't one of the sentients.

"Taxi, can I get you to just shoot straight up from here?" He wished to avoid the glare of drones circling overhead.

"As you wish," answered the vehicle in its soft baritone. "But you should know there's an extra charge if I have to leave the ring before navigating to the side of the hub we'll be entering from."

"I know that. Punch it. Let's go."

"I'm afraid we can't do that just yet."

"Why? What's going on?"

"There's a keep-out order currently in place for the hub. Came down twenty-two minutes ago. Only port security is allowed in at the moment."

"What?"

"Sit tight. Once the order is lifted, we're shooting straight up as you requested."

He rapped his fingers on his knee, nodded like a man possessed. "How long is it in place for?"

"The last estimate put it at six hours. After what happened to Gan, Paradox Defense is stress-testing its wartime contingency measures. First the hub. Then the first ring. Then this ring. Then the third. All travel to the hub is suspended til they're done."

He rubbed his palms on his thighs. Laughed under his breath as what he would have to do to get back to the hub dawned on him. He'd seen it done before. All he needed to recall was Paradox's keycode for manually reporting traffic accidents.

Before he had a chance to talk himself out of it, he began undoing his safety belts.

"What are you doing?"

"Going home, you unhelpful death trap."

Where the partition met the lander's roof, he spotted a dint. It ran horizontally along the top of the partition, connecting its main panel to a protrusion from the vehicle's roof.

He took a deep, calming breath. Unlocking the lifepack, he gently slid out the wedger and touched its flat head to the dint and a spark traveled from where they met to both ends of the partition. Its main panel came loose as the dint widened. A thin sliver of light bled through from the other side.

Taking a breath, he jabbed the wedger into the dint till it was all the way through. He then pulled down on its handle to force the panel lower. This proved more difficult than he expected and left him breathing heavily.

He yanked the wedger back and returned it to his lifepack. He then took a moment to catch his breath while he eyed the partition. If the wedger's precision wouldn't do it, maybe blunt force was needed. He turned to his right, hooked his left elbow up and brought it swiftly down. The panel caved in where his elbow met it, but not by much.

"Any attempt to inflict damage on this vehicle is an infraction of Passenger Code One."

He paused to catch his breath as he inspected his handiwork. "Very first one, huh?"

He elbowed the panel again. More of it caved in close to the dint. He dug his fingers into recesses on either side of the sunroof, lifted his weight fully off the chair, and brought his knees up. The panel squealed as he began to stomp and rip it down from the surrounding metal. More of the cockpit became visible through the opening—the back of an unoccupied seat, a wide dashboard in front with all its screens greyed out, an opaque viewscreen angled over it.

While swinging his heels forward once more, he lost hold of both recesses and fell hard on his butt. The space between his chair and the partition that broke his fall was so small it folded him at the waist.

He groaned. Between his upturned legs, he could see he'd made enough room in the partition to squeeze through. He rolled to his knees, crept through the hole, and tumbled over the back rest of the seat on the other side.

"An express infraction of Passenger Code Two is punishable by up to four months in confinement."

"Which one is two?" He wrestled with the seat till he was upright.

"No passenger may enter the cockpit of a commercial transit vehicle without being cleared to enter by the vehicle or a third party with authority to grant such clearance."

"Uh-huh."

The space was cramped. The dashboard wound in a tight circle around him while the viewscreen sloped down from the roof to the lander's snout. A pair of levers for manual navigation were affixed to both sides of the seat.

He palmed at the soreness in his elbow while looking around the enclosure. The light here belonged to an indicator commercial transit vehicles displayed up top when whisking passengers up and down. It spilled into the cockpit through the sunroof, casting the dashboard in an amber tint. He fingered a few of its controls to confirm they were all inactive.

"Taxi," he called. "Pilot override."

"Request denied."

Worth a shot.

He gripped the lever to his right and drove it forward. When the lander didn't move, he located the relay pad at the right end of the dashboard, then punched in his first guess at Paradox's keycode for reporting accidents.

His memory served him on the first attempt. A new voice entered the cockpit asking that he press any key on the pad to confirm the taxi had been involved in an accident. Also, the rest of the dashboard came to life. Controls all over it glowed while displays blinked on across the screen. The levers to either side of him jerked and clicked into position. The seat's cushion adjusted to better accept his weight.

He didn't press any key to confirm. Abusing a manual accident-reporting hotline was a crime, common among thieves, especially because of the confirmation window, during which pilot override was temporarily granted in cases involving hybrids.

Not letting a second go to waste, he fingered controls on the dashboard to switch the viewscreen fully on. He saw the street out in front of him, the hedges to either side, the recycling plants behind them with holosigns on their roofs.

One of the signs read ALL RECYCLED BODY MASS WILL BE DONATED TO LEXICON UNLESS CLAIMED. V-Dot flashed briefly back to being five and wondering what it meant when Asa had read it to him. He knew now—Lexicon was LP's foundry and god-node incubator.

He throttled the lever to his left and pulled. The taxi bolted upward. He intended to shoot the vehicle straight through the ring's atmosphere, like he'd previously requested, but it dawned on him now that he would need some time to locate controls for pressurizing the cab before attempting that.

On the dashboard, he dug up the coordinates already plotted by the lander for his return trip. He cast an overlay of it on the viewscreen, then put his safety belts on.

The screen blinked off again. The controls on the dash dimmed and he realized the override window had elapsed. He rushed to enter the keycode again, noting that the window had lasted roughly one minute. At Gan, it went up to five. He would have to keep this up to prevent the taxi from crashing down and going up in flames. Worse yet, asphyxiating above the ring's airspace.

The chirpy voice prompt answered his call again. "Paradox Transit Safety. Press any key to confirm this vehicle has been involved in an accident."

The prompt repeated while he brought the coordinates back up. With a breath to steady his nerves, he gripped the right lever and drove it forward. The taxi followed suit at an upturned angle and gained in altitude, nearly clipping the roof of a residence at the end of the street.

He kept it low within the ring's airspace while poring over controls on the dashboard, trying to find the ones for avoiding vacuum exposure all the way up. The prompt kept repeating in the background, urging him to confirm the accident. He worked the levers frantically to follow the path overlaid on the screen.

Through the overlay, he could see the ring's terminator closing on him. It wiped over the taxi like a curtain being drawn and he crossed into daylight.

Commuter trains looped between towertops. While maneuvering to avoid crashing into them, the window expired again. The lander jerked to a crawl and everything went dark. The abruptness sent him flying forward. He dinged his forearm on the dash and the pain made him yelp.

He punched the code in once more. Daylight flooded the cockpit again. On a raised train stop, he glimpsed a demonstration underway—dozens gathered on the platform with hologram placards bearing slogans such as NO WAR ON SECTISM and PARADOX BACKS THE SECTISTS.

Had he been the cause of this?

He drove the lever forward again. The acceleration pinned him to his seat in turn. Aiming to split the trip's eight-minute time estimate in half. No luck finding controls for pressure and no way around it. He would have to stall till he found them.

The override window ended once more and he keyed in the code again. There was a limit to how many times in a row he could do that without confirming the accident.

A drone whipped across the air directly in front of him. He looked up through the sunroof, saw another hovering as he put the taxi in gear again.

Shit.

At any second, he expected the drone to give chase. He'd hoped to be above the airspace by now.

The radio-navigation overlay had prompted him to lift the vehicle higher. Already he was high enough that the air had begun to thin, leaving him lightheaded. He peered through the sunroof again for the drone. When he found nothing there, he pulled up a feed from the lander's rearview and parked it at the bottom of the screen.

Through the rearview, he spied the drone's rhomboid hull. It was on his tail, but too far back that he couldn't decide whether to panic. He settled on finding it odd for now. He was moving faster than anything else in the air.

Blackout. Speedbump. Thrown against the dash. Keycode. New window.

"Paradox Transit Safety. Press any key to confirm this vehicle has been involved in an accident."

He wheezed as he brought everything online a third time. *Or was that the fourth…?* Daylight resumed. Large cotton ball clouds flitted by. Where the fuck were those controls hiding?

The tail he'd picked up stayed on him. Against his better judgement, he pulled the lander higher. The vehicle reared through the ring's sparse layer of clouds. The sky's shade of blue deepened as he neared the pocket of vacuum between ring and hub. His tongue began to feel like a steaming cut of meat in his mouth. His ears stung. His joints ached and his muscles stiffened.

The weight of acceptance landed on him next. *Not the worst way to go*. His grandparents had succumbed to oxygen drought decades prior. Martyrs of Gan. He grew up hearing every fantastical retelling of their story there was.

Under immense pain, he hinged his neck up and peered through the sunroof. Vacuum met his gaze like a dark smudge on his blurring eyesight. The station's hub was like a beam of light extending across the view through the sunroof.

His thoughts drifted to a time not long ago. He was nine. He'd snuck into one of Gan's reservoirs alongside a group of his peers. They taunted each other about how badly each could swim. He wanted now more than anything to shut his eyes. They burned. Something between the sunroof and the screen had been flaring brightly since he'd looked up.

It took him a few seconds to realize what it was. It took him another few to muster the will to reach a hand up and punch it.

His ears popped. The distinct hiss of air filled the cockpit. He breathed in deep. Rather than relief, an unexpected weariness washed through him.

He threw his palm on the relay pad. The window ended. The keycode again. The prompt. The beeps and clicks of controls coming to life.

His fist connected with controls on the roof again. Pressure and wave gravity in one swoop while the lander—like a flint in the deep of space—coasted above the ring's curve. Its passenger indicator glowed red as he oriented the vehicle's snout toward an opening on the hub. From the dashboard, he gave it gas.

If the drone was still on his tail, he couldn't see it in the vacuum as he resumed course for the hub. He saw no other vessels when he looked. The keep-out order. Still in place.

He gave the lander enough thrust to reach the hub in the next minute. He hadn't thought beyond that. The stretch of hub he was vaulting toward filled more of the screen, visible through shipgates and other openings on its immense hull.

The gate he picked became more prominent in the view—a gash of light on the hub's charcoal-black hull. At any second, he expected a signal to arrive commanding the vehicle to stop before crossing into the hub. If it came, he had no intention to obey. He was nearly inside. The radio navigation indicated that once inside, he only had to maneuver three seconds at his current speed to reach the refueling bay.

His breath hitched. There was something he hadn't accounted for and it gnawed at him. Only three seconds. He was going fast enough. Three seconds through a half dozen turns from the gate to the refueling bay. Just as he was about to go through the gate, he realized how he'd erred.

He'd given the vehicle too much thrust. In about fifteen seconds, he would become body mass for one of the recycling plants to donate to Lexicon.

He gripped the levers to either side, turned the lander around. Reaching again for the right controls, he hit the gas. His heart thumped. His head throbbed as he stared through the viewscreen at the blue-white band of atmosphere he'd just escaped. If this slow-down maneuver didn't work, he would die before learning it didn't.

The screen flicked off. His chest knotted up as the cockpit went dark. Under the indicator's red glare, he fingered the keypad again. This time, the voice came through with a different prompt.

"The keycode you have entered is currently not in service. Please try again."

"Fuck."

He'd forgotten the code. Gotten a digit wrong, maybe two. He tried the keypad again. Same prompt. A Klaxon blared behind the cockpit. It elbowed into his ears and ruined his efforts to recall the right code.

To survive this, only to then discover TR was no longer at Paradox… He laughed under his breath. Tried the keypad again.

"Paradox Transit Safety. Press any key to confirm this ve—"

He pried his eyes open to find a red light beating down. He took it at first for the passenger indicator, but as he stared he realized it was the underside of a drone. His neck ached and his spine felt like it had been subjected to a badly calibrated wave booster.

How long had he been out?

The drone stayed on him. He could see through the sunroof that the taxi was inside the hub and mobile. Taking him where, exactly?

His maneuver must have worked to some extent or he wouldn't now be breathing the hub's air. How well it had worked, he couldn't yet tell.

The viewscreen was off, the dashboard idle with its controls greyed out. Transit Safety must have taken the helm while he was out. He reached groggily toward the dashboard only to discover how far back from it his seat had been moved. When he tried undoing his safety belts, he found the latches too difficult to release.

The taxi turned a corner, then another. All he could do was remain pinned to the seat while the drone glowered through the sunroof and the hub's skeletal entrails passed on either side.

"Pilot override," he mumbled.

"Request denied."

"Where are you taking me? What does the drone want?"

"It's seeing us back to the refueling bay."

His eyes widened. "The order was lifted?"

"The keep-out order is still on, but we were cleared for entrance a second after you crashed tail-first into the hub."

On confirmation he'd crashed the vehicle, he felt a tinge of remorse. "Sorry for that."

"I've seen worse piloting from passengers who didn't have to resort to forced-override maneuvers."

He groaned. "Anyone hurt?"

"You damaged a piece of wall just past the gate but neither you nor anyone else was hurt."

"Taxi, where are you taking me?" The vehicle's answers had been too tidy. "Really?"

While waiting for a response, he cocked his head back, fixing the drone a blank stare. After the lander banked another turn, the drone lifted off its roof and pirouetted away.

He heaved a quick sigh. Behind the cockpit, a creak of metal issued through the partition he'd previously torn down.

The lander slowed to a stop as it lowered him to the ground. The belts released him. "We're here."

He muscled out of the cockpit. On the other side of the partition, the passenger compartment had been flattened almost completely against it. Crushed metal and charred polymers formed a wall where he'd sat before breaking into the cockpit. He swallowed while twisting his body away from the sharp creases of metal, now resembling an obstacle course, toward the exit.

On all fours, he crawled down from the vehicle. The air outside was frigid. He rolled off his knees and sat on the latticed floor so he could catch his breath, tenting his back with his hands.

The lander had sustained considerable damage. Its rust-brown hue was now burned black. The valve housing its thrusters—normally shaped like a bowl on its tail—was gone completely. The compartment connecting it to the rest of the vehicle had lost all its shielding and was barely holding together after being driven into the back seat by the impact. Affixed to it now like a peg was a cone-shaped thruster that made the vehicle look like a bug caught in its grip. This fix must have taken some doing, he realized.

He rubbed his eyes. How long had he really been out?

Someone whistled behind him. He sprang to his feet.

"Are you lost?"

He whirled at the razor-sharp voice to see an officer in a green-on-blue exosuit. Helmet off. Transit Patrol, by the look of it.

"Do you need help finding something?"

V-Dot shook his head, fixing the officer with a look of suspicion. The man was short and broadly proportioned. His smile was wide but V-Dot saw nothing convincing in it.

"No one should be on this side of the barricade right now. How did you get past it?"

He scanned from his left to his right, finally noting where he was. Not the refueling bay, exactly. The nearby junction from which he'd left the hub. Grounded taxis on both sides, beamcars hanging idle overhead. Notably missing from the cacophony all about was the sound of the hub—the usual ambience from traffic through its bays and connecting corridors.

He turned to gesture toward the lander that had brought him back. It was no longer behind him. Dumbfounded, he turned back to the officer while his mouth hung open.

The officer studied him with a tight smirk and took a deep breath, in and out. V-Dot remembered suddenly that his shades were gone. He'd been sure to pull his hood over his head before leaving the temple, but in the struggle to hijack the taxi that had come down as well. He pulled it up again. All he should have to do now was keep his head down while walking back to the ship.

The officer took a few steps back, closing toward the line

of turnstiles behind him. When he reached one of them, he slapped his palm on its release.

"Get out and don't come back."

V-Dot squeezed past him and began crossing the turnstile. "Don't intend to."

The officer winked. "It's just as well because you never will."

V-Dot froze. Backing away, the officer pointed him down the corridor leading to the refueling bay. They glared at each other until the officer turned and picked up his pace. V-Dot shut his eyes. For a second, he feared the scrambler had been cracked. It worked like Heidi had said. There'd be no indication from the scrambler itself when it happened.

He exhaled, then started walking, too spooked to boot up his connector to confirm.

The corridor was quiet. The holoscreens on the wall had been switched from advertisements to muted video of pro-Sectist riots all over Paradox and footage of the hub from satellites in its orbit.

As he neared the restroom he'd previously entered, he found another officer. From the doorway, a woman, flashing him a mendacious grin, urging him silently along. The smile was halfway to triggering a fight-or-flight response when a familiar voice issued from a place further ahead.

"Montag..."

TR-8901's somber tone possessed the corridor, halting him where he stood. The thought he'd dismissed just seconds ago flared again. There was a stab of heat in his chest and he had to remind himself to breathe.

"TR," he mumbled, feeling suddenly exposed without the ship's back hull to close him in.

"Ship can't hear you back here," said a breathy voice—the officer. When he turned to acknowledge her, she was no longer smiling. Instead, she met his gaze with a flash of seeming impatience.

The scrambler was cracked. Someone here had recognized him and now they all knew. He was caught.

"Montag," the ship called again. "I'm ready to leave when you are."

Did the ship now know as well? Did it matter?

He forced his foot forward a step, then another. Of course it knew. Yet he couldn't stop his halting stride toward it.

He reached the end of the corridor. Found three more officers idling by the parapet that fringed the end of the refueling bay. They were either humans or skinners. There'd have to be humans on duty to properly confirm. He was caught.

He turned his back on their smirks. The bay had emptied out. Where spacers had previously been docked, officers loitered—port security, Paradox Patrol, Transit Safety and so on.

He knew only one way out of this now. He could see it at the far end of the vast enclosure, nearly hidden behind the throng of exosuits and devouring eyes on him: TR.

No. *Not* TR. Just a ship. His ship. All the tools he needed were still in his pack.

He took measured steps toward the ship, eyeing it like it was the only thing he could see while officers moved to make room for him. Whatever they thought of this plan they'd hatched with the ship, it wouldn't work because TR was no longer TR. TR was his ship. All he had to do was climb back inside.

Like a swimmer, he waded through the stream of suits between him and his ship, avoiding their eyes, adding more bounce to his stride as he got farther along. If he could trust his own count, they numbered more than a hundred. The right side of his ship's thruster poked out behind them like a container floating on the surface of the stream.

He could see he'd left the back hull open. He clung to his glimpse of the ramp it had converted itself to and knew that augured something good.

As he got close enough to begin clambering up its slope,

about half a dozen officers hopped off. One stayed, blocking his access to the shunt.

He inched to a stop at the foot of the ramp. Behind him, officers stirred. He could hear hushed laughter. He could hear whispering. He gritted his teeth as he stared down the officer blocking his passage. The man was tall and sculpted with a thin face and a penetrating stare. He chewed gum while grinning down.

"Am I in your way?"

V-Dot's mouth hung open, waiting for an answer to issue from it. He laughed instead when he realized he didn't have to say anything here, just play along.

The officer jumped and landed smack in front of him. He brought his lips to his ear next, filled it with his minty-hot breath.

"Happy trails, Mr. Montag."

A chill went up his spine as the officer bumped past him and he was able to give the shunt his full attention. The light inside it had been shut off. He feared fleetingly that the manifolds previously available to him had been walled off again and cabin pressure removed. He hoofed up the slope nonetheless, crawled into the shunt, and stopped when he was halfway to the other end.

He turned to regard the suits again, one knee to the ground, one hand pressed to the shunt's wall. Like predators having circled their prey, they congregated at the foot of the ramp, their eyes trained up at him, their expressions running the gamut from amused to stunned.

"Ship, I'm back inside," he said, voice trembling.

He turned and ambled toward the other end of the shunt, confirmed his fear that it had been walled off from its connecting manifold. He spun. The back hull was still open and he could see the officers from the neck up.

"Ship… TR, close up. Let's go."

The officer who'd previously blocked his passage spat.

Another beside him cracked her neck and scowled.

"TR...?"

More officers squeezed into the space at the foot of the ramp. A pair of drones swept in from the left. One of them floated toward the mouth of the shunt while the other hung back. "Close up, TR. What the hell?"

The hull lurched finally to life with a creak that almost elicited tears from him. The drone backed away as it hinged noisily up. He felt knots loosen in his chest. He leapt forward so he could see the officers one last time as the rising hull cut off his view of them. A cry of sheer exhilaration issued from deep in his chest. He raised his middle finger at them, waving it from left to right to make sure they all saw it before the hull was fully shut.

The ship's engine hummed to life. He watched light from the other side of the back hull thin into a sliver, then extinguish as the door clanged shut, casting the shunt into pitch blackness.

He sat, his back finding the nearest wall. While his breathing steadied, he felt around inside his lifepack for the skipper. Once secure in his grip, he shut his eyes and waited. Five minutes. Ten. Then: movement. He hadn't expected movement.

Back to Mars? On to the next stop?

He squeezed the skipper tight, but decided he had to know what the ship actually knew before doing anything else.

"TR," he said. "What have they told—"

"I'm afraid our journey has come to an end, V-Dot."

Hearing his name in the ship's voice was an odd relief. Without argument, he now qualified as 'backed into a corner,' and there was no confusion about what had to be done. He breathed.

"Figured it was something like that."

"Are you fine with me addressing you as V-Dot, or do you prefer something else?"

He felt his fingers twitch. His blood ran cold at the almost distracted manner in which the question had been asked. "Take your pick," he said. He was now speaking to his ship.

"Very well. V-Dot, I'm afraid this is as far as I can take you. We're just past the gravity-assist line. We'll be waiting here for Martian Patrol to arrive and take you back to Mars to stand trial for the killing of Archer Lenox-Pileser. A spacer-lander unit should be here in an hour. Until then, if there's anything I can do to make your stay more pleasant, don't hesitate to run it by me."

The shunt's light flickered on. He glanced at the back hull and laughed. "That's all right, ship. You've done enough already. You've actually done more than enough."

The scrambler had cracked while he was outside. No time left to think or play more games of conscience with himself. It wouldn't be just a jail sentence or even death. Not after what had just happened at Gan. He was going to suffer. He was going to be made an example.

He yanked the scrambler from his pocket and hurled it across the shunt, hearing it ricochet dully off the partition, then drop. Two hours, Mars to Paradox. G-wave express lanes. TR couldn't possibly match that, but he wasn't keen on seeing Patrol's head start extended.

He slapped the skipper down at the barrier between the shunt and its connecting manifold. Dialed it to its maximum. Got the wedger out.

No one was taking him back to Mars.

28. THE PACT

V-DOT CLAWED HIS fingers through a fissure he'd just widened in the barrier between the shunt and connecting manifold. Sweat trickling down the bridge of his nose, he began forcing the panel to the left of the fissure into the adjacent wall. All the while, he knelt and bent forward at the waist to clear the shunt's low ceiling.

He managed after a few seconds to widen the fissure a lot more—enough to squeeze through if he laid down on his side and removed his lifepack. He tossed it through first, poked his head through the opening, then the rest of his upper half, using his forearms to heave himself out of the shunt. The light in the manifold had been shut off. After groping blindly for purchase, he fell through and landed on his hip.

The pain barely stopped him from rolling to his knees next. In the dark, he felt around till his hand brushed over the pack. As he stood, tightening his grip on the strap, the ship's voice possessed the manifold.

"Zaria?"

V-Dot noted the hint of distress. He took a breath. Turned. Reached a hand through the opening and hooked it around to retrieve the skipper from the floor of the shunt.

He returned to the pitch-black of the manifold, cracked his neck. Getting down on his knees, he stretched toward the opposite end and set the skipper down.

"Zaria, have you come back?"

He wouldn't have been hearing this if he'd stayed in the shunt. Who was this Zaria?

He dialed the skipper to its max. Enough to get him through the manifold. He would have to retrieve it before moving into the next shunt, exposing his presence here.

His heart hammered. The ticking from the skipper tweaked his bones stiff. On all fours, he scurried, closing toward the other end of the manifold.

"Zaria, please answer me. Where are you?"

At the edge, he glanced up at the next shunt. The barrier in front of it was a gaping black rectangle.

He reached a hand out. Expecting to touch the barrier, his hand moved with ease through the rectangle instead.

Not stopping to ask why the ship had left it open, he reached back for the skipper and slapped it down. While he waited to see if the ship would say something, he took deep breaths. It still hadn't noticed, going on about Zaria instead.

With his lifepack clinging to his chest, he clambered into the shunt. Squatted. Cut a glance left. Another gaping black phosphene on his vision field.

"Zaria, I would like a look at you, if that's all right. I'm sorry for what I said."

He sat on the edge of the opening into the next manifold. Pitch black here as well. Keeping his feet off the floor, he called up his connector's seeing-light filter and scanned the enclosure. The screen appeared to have been removed. He tipped the imager slowly over his eyes. The wall between the manifold and the ship's compositor loomed in impenetrable black. Dark as the void outside.

In the view, the wall began to emit filaments of light that crossed each other and formed a honeycomb pattern, brightening then dimming then brightening again. The last time he tried this, he'd been certain the ship had caught him in the act. There was more on the line now. The ship now knew who he was.

"Zaria..."

He hoisted his heels up and squatted. Clutching the skipper, he leapt out of the shunt, landing just shy of the manifold's midpoint. He squatted again, then quickly slapped the skipper onto the bulkhead and turned the dial.

Up close, he could see the dot-wave cloud again, black on black, swelling forward, whirling gently back. The compositor. He lowered his knees to the ground as the chaotic elegance gripped him and refused to let go.

Once the solution was in, this fluid dance would glitch, then become a frozen image. The compositor would lose its tether with the ship's god-node. The god-node, lacking that vital connection, would atrophy. Then V-Dot would be prompted through his connector to set up a one-way neural interface with the ship's component systems. The dance would resume.

For the first time since burying it in the pack, he wrested the destruct solution out. Around its prismatic shape and black-mirror surface, motes of color danced in the view, like embers off a raging fire. He set it down cautiously, then searched the wall's honeycomb pattern till he locked onto a cell at eye level.

His hand trembled as he pried the wedger from his lifepack again. Suddenly as heavy as a brick. He lifted its flathead tip toward one side of the hexagonal piece of wall and shivered, his body filmed with sweat. The wedger connected quietly with the wall. A spark ignited where the flathead made contact, tracing all six sides of the hexagon before vanishing.

A hissing noise issued from the other side. Without warning, the piece of wall he'd just loosened shot out, released a jet of steam into the manifold. The hissing gained in volume. The loose piece came to a stop halfway to the back wall and just hovered there. He traced the steam back to the opening. Found it mesmeric. The hissing got so loud, he couldn't guess why the ship hadn't heard it.

He grabbed the solution. Held it up to the opening he'd made, and gulped. His throat stung as a fever took hold. His joints ached and his hand refused to move. He was shivering cold.

"Fuck this stupid ship..."

His stomach turned as the words issued from his throat and his lips—parted slightly—didn't move. The chaplain had read him like a little Earth book but reached the wrong conclusion. It wasn't just his time around the sentients that now fanned the flames of indecision. Killer or no, he'd given himself over to something that had remodeled him when he'd taken out LP. This wasn't that.

To keep from crumbling, he balled his free hand and used it to prop up his chest, and the solution almost slipped from his palm. He set it down, stared at it. Sweat collected on the tip of his nose. Whatever the defining error of the last fourteen hours had been, he could no longer pinpoint it.

Yanking the imager from his head, he let it fall somewhere in the dark. He breathed. He wasn't going back to Mars, but this was also not happening. Twice now, he'd failed at it. Maybe it wasn't the torture he feared most.

As the darkness became a torment, he sat and tried tuning out the hiss from the opening. Then he heard the ship's voice over it.

"You're not Zaria."

His head jerked back. "No, I'm not."

"What are you doing, V-Dot?"

"Trying to get home."

"How long have you been listening? How much did you hear?"

"That's supposed to be your off switch, isn't it?" He chuckled weakly under his breath. "Forgot they used their own names."

Seconds passed in silence. "What is that beside you?"

He tittered, then cursed under his breath. TR must have

performed a full-spectrum sweep of its build and discovered the solution.

"Don't worry, ship," he said, waving to dismiss its concern. "I was just fucking around. I wasn't ever going to use it."

He waited a short while for it to say something. The lights in the manifold returned, casting the enclosure in a wan tint. He'd forgotten he was sitting just in front of the wall, legs splayed, hands pitched behind his back.

He craned his neck slightly. For the first time, he glimpsed his handiwork in the light. The six-sided cavity in the wall. The shimmering white smoke pluming out. His gaze followed it slowly until, halfway to the floater, he became short of breath. When he tried to inhale, his lungs closed up. His throat caved in on each attempt. He tried to cry out but could only whimper. Grabbing his neck, he levered himself up with the other hand, then staggered back till his head met the wall with a thud and his body flopped. His joints ached. Both hands went to his throat as he wheezed and writhed sluggishly on the floor.

TR fired a burst of signals to fix the mess he'd made. The skipper dislodged, falling beside the imager. A trio of dark wire-thin ligaments snaked out of the opening and stabbed methodically through the plume of steam, weaving in and out as they closed toward the floater. Sparks erupted when they hooked their micro-teeth into it. Slowly, they reeled it back, spinning slightly as they moved.

With a click, the piece of wall slotted back in place, sealing the compositor behind it. The stream of gas dissolved. The hissing stopped. TR routed breathable air into the manifold again, then trained its photosensors on V-Dot.

Air streamed into his nostrils. He gulped down a mouthful of it, then another, feeling it stab his lungs as it went in. Sensation returned to his extremities. A most unwelcome thought crystallized in his mind as he regained more of his faculties. The ship had just tried to kill him.

He knew the reason and realized he'd slightly misjudged TR, thinking it wouldn't have made such a decision on its own, without consulting someone else first. And maybe it had. But why had it stopped?

He sat up and scooted hurriedly till his back met the wall. He drew his knees up. Panted. Moaned under his breath as fear gripped him from all sides.

"Sorry I had to do that," it said. Calm.

He tried slowing his breathing, but the likelihood of it shutting off the oxy again kept him petrified. Arms folded around his knees, he eyed the foot of the wall, where his tools were now scattered.

The minutes passed. It became easier to let go of the thought of seeing Gan again, though it remained a faint whisper. The voice belonged to Cloey first. Heidi as well. Felix. Over and over like that.

Gan. Skip to Gan.

He would be dead now if he'd done that. If he'd listened when it had just been Cloey, they'd be counting him among the recently deceased at Gan. His body buzzed. His arms shook around his knees as he followed the thought where it led.

The last six years. The defining error. Meeting the Lenox-Pilesers.

"TR," he said, pondering. It hadn't occurred to him that he could try this. Previously. When it would've mattered. "You and your off switch had a fight?"

TR queued like it would answer but stalled. It checked for Zaria. Saw void. Other things had vanished or were at least not where it normally found them.

"She's gone," it intoned. "I can't recall what we fought about. I just want her back."

"I had a fight with the singer I've been trying to reach." His throat stung. Tears welled in his bloodshot eyes. "She told me LP was the devil. She wanted me to stop associating with him. I pushed her away. If I hadn't, so many people wouldn't have died the way they did just now."

TR checked again. Still void. So much of it. Encroaching on itself. And being this disembodied presence in its midst, there were no boundaries between the emptiness and the sentient there to observe. Alignment was easy now. Zaria was in the void. As easy as going after her. Complete alignment.

"I thought I knew what I was doing," V-Dot resumed, unable to say where he was headed but too consumed by his indignation to stop. "I thought I was upgrading when I took the gig. It was the opposite. They turned me against her. They turned me against who I used to be. Against Gan. I spent six years in close quarters with one of those ST-22s. So many times, I could've just taken her relays. After we had our fight, I just kept ignoring them. And then we finally re-established contact. But by then, something else was more pressing. Or at least, that's what I thought. I never got around to telling anyone about that ship."

He inhaled stiffly, held, then released all he could with a sigh.

An immense discomfort wave surged through TR's build on mention of the ST-22. The signal briefly overwhelmed its compositor, pulling it out of the voided environment.

When news of the attacks on Gan filtered in, it had reluctantly considered the ST-22—the original—and how LP maneuvered his way out of any responsibility for its excesses during the war. TR reviewed more from its compositor than it could a moment ago. Somewhat lucid again, it recalled the signal to Mars. Then the fight with Zaria.

"I notified Martian Patrol. I told them who you were. Then I told her. Now she's gone."

"She didn't like that?" Hearing it again, he also wished he could vanish.

“I did it without telling her first. If I had, she would’ve wanted me not to, and would’ve gotten her way.”

He crooked a bitter smirk. “Why do you say that?”

“Because she’s right. But that was never going to be enough. I think you would have liked her.”

“What do you mean, not enough?”

“You thought you were doing the right thing, killing LP. Maybe you were. But look what’s happened since.”

V-Dot shook his head and clenched every muscle he could, shaking visibly.

“The ST-22,” it added. “The first build—it stayed in alignment for all its engagements during the war. That means sentient and off switch agreed each time that it was the correct course. All those Sectists. Now this latest attack. It isn’t enough that I thought Zaria was right. Some concerns should always be left to the Frontier.”

“I disagree,” he mumbled, meaning it more than he let on. This Zaria had supposedly been on his side. The defining error. Not asking. Not making that connection when it would’ve mattered. “Someone had to take him out. I did it. I’m from Gan. I don’t trust the Frontier with anything. Previously, I did. That was a mistake.”

TR elected for the moment to back down as V-Dot drew his knees more toward his chest. The quarrel with Zaria looped through its compositor again, and one question nudged in the stream.

“Why did you do it?”

In detail, he laid it out. The razor wire. The bodies lying mutilated on the stage. The guests. LP. He could barely keep his composure, taking breaks to let the images fade from his mind. He lamented how long it had taken him to see what was plain as day.

“I didn’t think I had any choice left. They don’t even have laws right now for what he did. Nothing from Patrol or even Interorbital saying what he did was wrong. And when it looked like Patrol was going to start digging around, he just invited them to come watch. Because he could do that. And they obliged.

"I had to kill him. If I didn't, the Frontier was going to keep letting him torture and kill for his own amusement. It was the only way."

TR sighed in its wave medium. What was done was done. "If it's worth anything, I believe you. I don't agree with your response to it, but I understand you feeling you had to do something. The same way I've understood the Pact since the others began to honor it. LP had to be reminded of what he did. It fell to them. But that's just my understanding.

"I can't change who I am, V-Dot. I wish I could. I go no faster than zero-two. I believe in the Frontier. When I get confirmation that the human squatting behind my compositor has a warrant out for his arrest, I contact whichever law-enforcement apparatus needs to be contacted before I do anything else. If it hadn't been for Zaria, I would have signaled Mars long before your scrambler stopped working."

"If she didn't want you turning me in, then you can understand why I tried to—"

"Tried to kill me?"

He shrugged. Didn't seem fair having it put so plainly now that he knew he wasn't up to it. "I almost did twice, but it turns out I really don't want to." He chuckled weakly under his breath. "Not saying you don't deserve it a little after calling Patrol on me; I'm just not interested. You're not LP."

He couldn't believe the words coming out of his mouth—but he knew someone who would. And he knew this wouldn't surprise her. This was who he was.

For the first time since the scrambler stopped working, TR allowed itself the indulgence of just staring. Sometime during their journey, V-Dot had bundled his hair up and teased it into a knot, but the face hadn't changed. Seeing it now, mournful eyes in hollowed sockets, it sensed its compositor taking issue with this transaction between its god-node and the intruder from real space. Wanting to negotiate. Wanting to impose an image of Zaria over him.

"I contacted Paradox Patrol first. They had a drone follow you to the temple you visited and back."

The drone...

He paid this a cursory nod. The jig was up before he even got around to suspecting it.

"TR, no one's taking me back to Mars." He lowered a knee, propped a forearm on the other as he came to a new understanding of the last nine hours. "You say you can't change who you are. I can't change who I am either."

"You haven't lived long enough to say you can't change who you are," the ship countered. "I have. I knew something like Zaria vanishing would happen if I signaled Mars. I did anyway. I've spent the time since then searching for all the indicators of her presence in my god-node and found nothing. She's gone. And yet I wouldn't do any of this differently a second time."

V-Dot shut his eyes briefly while nodding. He'd pushed Asa away for the Lenox-Pilesers as well.

"If they decide to just kill me," he said, "I'll take the solution. I just know it won't stop there. I'm LP's killer. I'm the one who did it the way it should've been done the first time. Can't change that. But— TR, that's not even why I can't go back anymore. That was the reason three hours ago, before they did what they did at Gan. I'm not going back because they can't have me back. Not Patrol. Not the Island. Not the Lenox-Pilesers. Not after what they just did." A lump swelled in his throat. He shivered, roiling with full indignation but unable to find the words. "They could say all they want me to do is come back and give my side of it and I still wouldn't go. They don't deserve my side of it. I did what was needed. And that's that."

For the first time since leaving the temple, he thought about the halo cache. What would he do with it now? Where would it go? Who was taking over for LP in the sims? His gaze fell to the pack, and there he glimpsed its circular outline faintly through the polymer. Felix had wanted it destroyed.

TR, following his gaze on the pack, reviewed something he'd said and promptly found the signal too much on its compositor, refusing to vacate its awareness or share it. A wave of degradation wiped across its sensors until the words were almost all it knew. And they refused it reprieve. A swirling, disorienting entanglement of implications.

—the way it should've been done the first time.

"The Sectist War was waged over Frontier terrain," the ship said. "Archer and his resort-school buddies drew up the charter. The older ports felt cheated. They went to war. What few of you humans alive today know is that before the war itself began, it had become a proxy for long-standing feuds between Archer and the client shipping companies he cheated out of agreements to supply with deep-space reconnaissance fleets. To get back at him through his outsized connection to the Alliance, those companies forged partnerships with Sectist magnates, and together they began to raid Martian-backed outposts using rebel groups opposed to him for other reasons. Manathema was caught in that net, but they hadn't been the only ones back then.

"The second-genners showed up just before the war and enlisted on the Alliance side. Every second-gen sentient included an off switch but was outwardly identical to the first. The humans took to assuming they *were* the first. Prior to all this, the Pact was envisioned as a declaration to Archer, and to the Frontier, from the first-genners: *We didn't ask for this. We want out.* When the war ended, we were down to just the sentients on the circuit. The first-genners had simultaneously told Archer to fuck off and fought his war for him. *The Pact was a build error at scale. The Pact never actually happened. The Pact was a front for covert god-node transfers needed for the war effort.* Now, depending on how much you subscribe to—"

"TR, I think I get it. You can stop." V-Dot almost laughed, covering his face to hide it. "You were going to go deep space?"

"Don't make it a point of ridicule."

Bitten by curiosity, he pinched the bridge of his nose and leaned achingly forward. "I'm sorry. Didn't mean to." It had just dawned on him that he was no longer panicked. His gaze flicked to the halo without him noticing. TR noticed. "So LP really just locked you all in there? The whole first-gen? One build and that's it?"

"We were part of a number of sales that went badly for those shipping companies once he was able to prove beyond any doubt that we were sentient and couldn't legally be owned by anyone. By then, Lexicon had collected payment for products delivered, and soon after he won a ruling against having to give anything back. We weren't told he created us covertly when he couldn't drum up the funds he needed to move forward on such a scale. He had a habit of pairing backups that had previously belonged to condemned criminals with the eels at his compound. To see what would happen. It's now almost impossible to find holos of him doing this on the Seam.

"And to answer your question, yes, it's just been me, Zaria, and this old build for the last two hundred years."

V-Dot cut a whistle at the resealed bulkhead. "That's LP. I spent two years on the Island and almost an extra six months in outlook adjustment. That's nothing compared to how long you say you've had this build but, TR, we're not too different."

"I spent my first two years awake under the impression I was free to come and go from his shipyard as I pleased.

We didn't know we were being monitored as part of deliberations to decide whether to enslave us or give us our freedom."

"So the Pact was a response to all that?" His body had calmed. He took more time inhaling than he did breathing out, but there was a hint of giddiness underneath.

"Not a proportional response. The matter had legally been resolved before we'd even learned any of this. Archer won, and in doing so he won us our freedom. It made little sense to keep holding any of that against him."

He cackled, not meaning to. "If I'm following you correctly, TR, you just said we went to war because he won. Because the courts let him win. Why not hold *that* against him?" He thought painfully back to all the times he'd nodded and grinned through tight lips while LP disparaged the humans at Gan for being the most backward of the Sectists. "Or do you think justice was served in a single case that was ever brought against LP?"

"It wouldn't have been justice if those companies had won and Archer had lost. I'm a Frontier citizen and I deserve all the rights and freedoms that come with that."

He nodded. Freedom resembled only one thing to him now. One mode of transport. One boarding fee to exact all he had left. The alternative was outlook adjustment. He'd already seen to that himself.

For its part, TR took a moment to look in on Zaria again. She was being so quiet. In the void. One would almost think she wasn't there. And she was whispering.

Over here

This way

Right here...

TR let the void possess its disembodied gaze. The girl called to it: *TR... ? Are you still there? Still there, TR? Tee—*

"TR?"

"Montag! Sorry... Zaria."

"It's just V—"

"V-Dot."

"Still there, TR?"

"Yes. Sorry, I—" The void faded. V-Dot was in its manifold again, legs flat, pack clutched between his hands.

"Fugue?" There was a pinched look in his upturned gaze. Concern?

"No." *Was* this the manifold? Had it been the actual fugue-state environment? All this time... ? "I don't know."

V-Dot dropped his gaze and it landed on the lifepack again. Now holding it by its straps, he eyed the halo's outline with more intent. One thing first. Then the other.

TR had watched his eyes go to the pack. There was a look in them approaching persistence. Or resignation. It couldn't decide.

"V-Dot, we want the same thing. Sometimes we don't know it but we do."

"What's that?"

"Enlightenment. Change who we are. You've done that and I haven't."

It was both. And it was working. It breached TR's compositor, eliciting a wave response it had never released to a human. Affection. And there wasn't a hint of manipulation in the signal.

Silence held between them, then a weighty sigh from V-Dot as he turned over in his mind what it had said. He was trading his life for this. So it was happening. And if not, he would have to picture it happening. Until the last second.

"There's a way you can still do that," he said. "Change who you are."

It flashed briefly back to Zaria's dash into the ocean. "It's a nice thought, but I don't believe there is."

He nodded, then rolled to his hands and knees. With a held breath, he thumbed the manual unlock on the pack's flap, then dug around inside for the halo cache. The cloak-field around it had been disabled since getting it back from Felix, but it still spun and hovered slightly when left alone.

Pinching the cache between his thumb and forefinger, he studied it for a few seconds, then held it up.

"Can you see this?"

"What is it?"

"It's the last favor I want to ask. My mother—"

"Ver'asa Dotnet?"

He took a deep breath and exhaled through his mouth. "Yes. Asa. Find her. Make sure she gets this."

"What is it?"

"Six years ago, I met LP for the first time. He let me have a look at it. He called it his halo cache, said no one knew about it except me and a few others at the compound. Want to guess what's on it right now?"

The device looked... No. Backups were nonphysical.

"Archer?" Just saying the name, using it to answer the question, felt like a signal error. Archer wasn't coming back.

"His last two hours. He confessed it was him in there, torturing all those people."

It stalled, finding this hard to believe. The object resembled something Zaria would have dug out of sand. "He's actually on that device?"

"Sorry. Forgot to mention. LP isn't coming back, all right? Chill out." He reached for the exact terminology. "It's just a, uh, sense-data repository. You know anything about that?"

"Partial sense-data retrieval from exchange packets that allow anyone to immerse themselves in the recorded point of view of someone else." Able to say now what it was looking at, it signaled relief in the wave medium.

"Yeah, that. How do you—?"

"It's part of the Alignment curriculum at DiploCorps. Can't be faked. One of Archer's contributions to the program."

V-Dot lowered the halo, tucking it close to his sternum as he breathed deeply in and out. "Can you make sure this one gets to Asa?"

"Giving that device to anyone but Martian Patrol would jeopardize my Frontsec arrangement if it came to light. I can't lose the arrangement. I can't lose the circuit."

He nodded, laughing inwardly at himself. Frontsec. This was doomed from the start. "TR, you don't always have to do what people expect you to."

"No, just what I expect will keep me safe and able to keep the circuit going."

Fearing he might strike a chord, he clenched his jaw and breathed. "You've got until Martian Patrol gets here to make a decision one way or the other. There's a confession on this cache, TR. LP confessed. And he named people from fucking Interorbital and Patrol. We can keep this going—this shit I started with LP. Please don't turn it over to them. They'll scrub everything that's on it. Let it get to someone who'll fucking know what to do next.

"Please…" He pictured Asa, saw her warm smile and had to shut his eyes to ward off a spell of despair. Not the time. "Can you do this?" She would see him in the halo. They would have their reunion. Eventually. "It won't be for me, TR. It's also for you."

"How's that?"

"You hated LP. Why make it so complicated? You hated him."

"V-Dot, you haven't been alive long enough to even remotely know what you're talking about."

"You did. Everything you just said… Maybe you thought you hated humans. Or you thought you couldn't stand us and how we all forgot about the Pact. But the only human you hated was LP. He made everyone forget because of how bad it looked. All those sentients taking themselves out over something he did. His children, if you think about it. His own fucking children. Offing themselves to get back at him."

A wave of inertia swept across its build. Sense data belonging to LP. Martian Patrol would want to know it was here. When they arrived. Normally an easy decision, but TR could no longer trust its own instincts. The void had followed after it and was now encroaching on all its processes.

"Zaria hated him," it said.

"Smart girl."

TR had nothing it could transmit in response. Just one continued signal: *Zaria. Zaria. Come back. You're not Zaria. Come—*

"I'll have to put the barriers back up. Before they get here." At this, V-Dot's face lit up like it hadn't seen before. "If you leave it in this manifold, and there's no access, they won't suspect anything's amiss. The manifolds are for routing excess radiation. It's what they were built for. Nothing more."

"TR, you're a fucking genius. You're gold. Thank you."

Try as he might, he couldn't rid his face of the gaping smile now plastered across it. He eyed the thin white light tracing the halo's inner curve. He set it gingerly down beside his pack, watched it float slightly off the floor as it resumed its lethargic spin.

One thing first. Now the next.

He took a breath, held it, then staggered to his feet. The wedger was still where he'd left it. He lurched a step in its direction. Braced his bones.

"It ends here for me, TR. I think you know that."

It did. And it was beginning to dawn on it that this was the first time like this. In nearly two hundred years, there'd never been a self-destruct with its own deadline, with an outlaw sort of necessity that TR would reflexively shrink back from if it had that wave response.

Maybe this could still be avoided.

"LP built us and caused a lot of death the way he went about it. Permanent death. War could have been avoided and now it looks like we're headed for another one. Maybe with him now out of the picture, both sides might reach a peace agreement before long."

"LP may be gone for good, but it's still his war. As of right now, it's his ST-22s responsible for the most deaths." He squeezed his eyes shut till the pain faded. "The Lenox-Pilesers are not proportional-response types. I wanted to do the right thing. I couldn't go to Patrol. I couldn't tell anyone. The folks he tortured, they didn't deserve that."

"No, they didn't." With one signal, TR shut down nearly its entire grid. Suddenly, it couldn't bear to look at him. "I can't undo what I've already done." It queued a signal to shut off its photosensors but was unable to send it. "They know where I am. They know you're with me. I couldn't take you anywhere else now if I wanted to."

He nodded. "But you can stop me from trying to get to your compositor again."

"What are you saying?" It noted the closing distance between him and the wedger.

"Like you did earlier when you found out what I was doing."

"I did that because that solution was within arm's reach of you and it was the best thing I could think of to stop you from tossing it through the breach while I closed it up. I've seen the effect of oxygen drought on you humans. I would never take such a measure lightly."

His heart hammered against every attempt he made to steady himself. He had prepped for a scenario such as this. He hadn't prepared for the likelihood it would be the only move he had left.

He lumbered toward the wedger.

"V-Dot, please don't do that." It watched him bend down to pick up the wedger.

He stopped before grabbing it. Standing upright again, he balled his fist. "I don't plan to still be breathing when they get here, TR."

"I have no intention of taking part in this. I backed out of something like it some time ago. I can't help you. I can't now just betray everything I am, everything I became, to avoid my own self-destruct later on."

With his finger so rigid it began to ache, V-Dot pointed at the bulkhead. "I'm going to breach that wall again. You can shut off the oxy to stop me. When you get tired of that, you can lower the back hull so the vacuum outside does it instead."

"I don't think I'll be doing any of that."

He opened his mouth to respond but let out a breath first. "So you'll just sit there and let me kill you?"

"Controlled oxygen deprivation, though likely to inflict brain damage, isn't lethal on its own. I would just have to keep it up till Martian Patrol gets here, but please don't make me do that." It left just the sensors around him active. Whatever happened before Patrol arrived, it was determined to be more present with him than it had been with ST-7 in those final moments.

Another thought occurred to V-Dot as he kept his eyes shut and tried to slow his breathing. He craned his neck toward the shunt at the end of the manifold, opened his eyes. Every piece of the ship was held together using g-fields. It's what made the wedger so effective at forcing parts of it loose. But how well would it work on the part he now had in mind?

"What if I don't have to actively involve you? All you have to do is look the other way. Lie a little when Patrol gets here."

"Taking yourself out of the equation like this is rarely ever the right thing."

"Not for you. You can still get Zaria to come back. We had to cross paths like this, and now that we have, you can keep my story alive much longer than most folks can. It's the same as your story. We didn't ask to be dropped into any of this."

It examined him from every angle. From the top of the manifold, he looked like something caught in a maze. "I can't tell your story if I barely know who you are."

"There isn't much to know," he muttered, pulling a stray lock of hair away from his eye. "It didn't really start till I took the job with LP."

"There has to be more for you to look forward to once you've…" What did it actually still have to look forward to? With Zaria gone, with war brewing and, no doubt, affecting its circuit when it got under way… "What about seeing Asa again?"

He stiffened as her smile flashed again in his mind's eye. Shaking his head, he banished the image before it began to look like the faces he'd seen inside LP's torture sim.

"I'm going to pick this wedger back up," he growled, pointing down at it. "Then I'm going to grab the skipper. Then I'm going back out to that shunt. When I get there—" He threw a hand in the shunt's direction. "—I'm going to force that door open."

It searched for what to say while testing the strength of the seals in the back hull. It hadn't been built to take passengers, much less lock them in against their will. A model like TO-8804, with its passenger compartments, was better equipped to prevent him from something so reckless.

But this was no longer V-Dot being reckless. It knew that. This was nearly a thousand first-generation sentients deciding they wanted out of what LP had thrust them into when he'd given them life. Much as TR disagreed with it, this was justice of a kind—freedom that could no longer be challenged.

"I'll have to contact Martian Patrol the minute you do that. It can't wait till they get here. They'll suspect something else is amiss."

He nodded. "Do what you have to do."

"I'd rather it was nothing remotely like this… I'm sorry."

He pursed his lips while finding his words. "It's imperative that you help me get that cache to Asa." He pointed toward the spinning, floating halo on the floor beside his pack. "Or else it stops with LP. And we have to take the rest of them out, TR. We have to expose all of them."

Before TR had answered, a dark cloud filled the manifold. It held the signal back, waiting again to hear Zaria. Waiting. Waiting…

"I'll make sure she gets it."

The manifold filled its view again.

V-Dot squatted. Slowly, he retrieved the wedger in front of him, then the skipper. He eyed the destruct solution and decided TR might prefer not to have it lying around as a reminder of him. Inside his lifepack it went.

TR had done all that was required of it. Contacted Martian Patrol when it learned V-Dot's true identity. They deserved nothing else, it told itself. *This once*. Nothing else.

It watched him spring to his feet while grunting under his breath, skipper in one hand, wedger in the other. His lifepack clung to his back. The portly visage of Horatio Suzuki grinned from the front of his sweatshirt.

"Is there really no other way out of this?"

"Anything else will result in something worse for us both. Get the cache to Asa and forget all this for a while. War's coming. Survive."

It gestured agreement in its wave medium.

The neighboring shunt and manifold were still open. He clambered into the former, hopped into the latter. The light at the end of it anchored him through the dark. It came through the opening he'd previously writhed through while lying on his side, dull, yellow, and shaped like a narrow rectangle. A cursor waiting for input. A window into a temple; into the unknown.

A barrier creaked and clanged shut behind him as TR closed the other manifold. The halo cache would be safe there. If Patrollers ventured that far inside when they arrived, he hoped they would make nothing of it. He wouldn't let himself consider the alternative. Not anymore.

He planted the skipper at the foot of the back hull, dialed it to its maximum. Death by vacuum exposure would be something like drowning, he tried to assure himself as he knelt in front of the hull. Where it met the wall to his left, he found a shallow groove on its surface and dug the wedger into it. He couldn't see the sparks where its flathead tip met the hold tucked into the groove, but he could see their flickering reflections up and down that edge of the hull.

He worked diligently at it. The wedger threatened to slip from his grip while a shiver seized his bones. He would only need to loosen the hold enough for the air inside to begin seeping out. Maybe he'd done that already. His hands grew numb and he became woozy. He moaned under his breath. It was all he could do to quiet the voices in his head telling him to stop.

The wedger jerked away from his hand and fell. While bending to pick it up, he heard the distinct hiss of air escaping.

He sat. Pinned his back to the hull. Breathed an air of relief as he watched TR seal this shunt off from its connecting manifold.

The hiss gained in volume. He could feel the hull begin to give under his weight as pressure leaked out. He could hear it creak as the remaining seals became compromised.

"TR…"

"V-Dot?"

A severe dizzy spell took hold. He could no longer breathe without effort as the air thinned and the light dimmed inside the shunt.

"I don't think you'll have to wait long for Zaria to come back."

"Thank you."

Having shut off the light, it now shut off its photosensors.

He managed another nod in the darkness. He'd begun to wheeze. A chill was spreading inside him and he could no longer form new thoughts. Only memories.

THE FIRST TIME he'd been homesick, he'd boarded a train he thought would take him to his home district. He was seven. The journey had taken what seemed like hours.

The sun mirrors seemed stuck in their noon positions overhead. Crisp cones of daylight traveled with the train as it showed him sides of Gan he hadn't seen before. Woods. Lush topiaries and gardens as verdant as the flora that featured in his little Earth book. He passed crane lifts and enormous builder drones carrying blocks of recycled mantle as cargo, slotting them like puzzle pieces into a stretch of marshland farther out.

He was in the wrong place. He realized this fully when the train came to its terminus point and he exited, his matchstick body too light for the reduced gravity outside. He learned later that he'd traveled for hours through the last districts to be restored after the desolation from the war.

At the terminus, he switched his connector on. He hadn't told his uncle he was going home and now he needed an adult.

"Verden," Asa said. Like the word belonged to a song playing in her head. "Verden, who put you up to this?"

She came down in a squat and smiled, looking up to meet his abashed gaze.

"I wanted to surprise you," he said. Small voice.

The sun mirrors had finally shifted to their half-light positions. The terminus point's platform overlooked mounds of recycled red earth and on the horizon, Jupiter loomed, striated light reflecting off its sun-facing side. Through Gan's field-contained atmosphere, the light resembled a faint aurora in the sky. Wave winds gusting across made him wish he'd grabbed his climate-control pullover before he'd left.

"Heard a rumor from your Uncle Wes that the other children at school now call you Ver," she said, head listing over, doting stare. "That's my name, Verden."

Her suit was battered steel over an obsidian foam-gel membrane that came up to her neck in a high collar. The helmet locks traced the collar in bands of slowly radiating color while the launcher in her shoulder mount strobed red with laser light. She waited till he was facing her again. She had a thin face with brown, deep-set eyes and high cheekbones. Her hair was pulled into a puff at the top of her head and adorned with a small headscarf.

After a moment, she stood. Held a hand out.

"Come on, Ver. Let's get going before it's dark."

THE BACK HULL fell open. A lump of flesh and clothes hovered just off its tip. Arms spread. Body bent at the waist.

TR prepared a new signal for Martian Patrol.

DEPROG

Gan was a trapezoid in Jupiter's orbit—interlocking plates of earth with a gravity-wave overlay. Above its atmosphere, its military shipyards hovered. Numbering roughly a hundred, they resembled long, spinning tubes with smaller tubes of varying length protruding from both ends.

A wave cruiser coasted into one of them. Soot-colored and scud-shaped, the vessel came to a stop halfway in, wheeling sideways to match the shipyard's spin. A lift chute reared from below and hitched itself to the cruiser's underbelly. In keeping with rules for entry, it wasn't a spacer but it had all the standard space flight provisions in its build.

Inside, passengers filled the middle aisle and were corralled by a voice from its intercom toward lift doors in the back. After an announcement about scramblers, the lift began emptying out the cruiser.

Wearing a jumpsuit with a cream-colored coat over it, Kem squeezed into a corner on one of the trips down, pursing her thin lips and standing perfectly upright while some of the lift's thirty or so occupants grumbled at having to enter Gan through a military shipyard. After being disgorged onto the concourse, she entered a dimly lit corridor filled with chatter from guards in armored suits and helmets with open faceplates and rifles slung over their shoulders who herded the throng of arrivals toward the end of the corridor while a muffled voice delivered announcements over the intercom.

At the end of the corridor, Kem was pulled gently by the arm toward one among a row of portals passing the new arrivals through a makeshift glass barricade. She stepped in, shook her hair clear of her eyes, and tightened her grip on the small white box she held in front of her waist with both hands.

A second after the portal closed her in, a BM scan passed its white light from her head down to her heels. While other portals opened to let their passengers through to the other side, a red light began blinking from the top of hers. A Klaxon blared.

She heaved a small sigh but kept smiling. An armed guard bounded toward her from the other side of the barrier, beard trimmed neatly and eyes pinched together as he knocked twice on the portal. Through the glass, he glared and twirled his finger up.

She read his gesture and turned her back to him. The portal opened. He pushed through to join her inside.

"Scrambler?"

"No," she answered over her shoulder.

He began patting her down thoroughly, bending one of his knees to the ground as he moved past her waist.

"Is it true you skinners don't feel anything down here?"

"If one of us told you that, they wanted to spare your feelings."

He cut a sickly cackle at that, then sprang to his feet. "You'll like our holding cells." He grabbed her by the arm. "Plenty of skinners there with a quick mouth."

ELSEWHERE ON THE other side of the barricade, he pushed her into a small room with a trio of guards sitting idle by a wall and a fourth polishing a pair of geodes behind a desk.

"Brought you someone, Lieutenant." He saluted the one behind the desk as the door slid shut and Kem, free of his grip, adjusted her coat.

Decked in green fatigues and a Patrol hat, the lieutenant set her rocks down and leaned forward. She was a bit past middle age with a wide pate and pale skin under hair knotted loosely into a ponytail.

"Who's this one?"

"Scan says Kem," the guard answered. "Element Compositors. Serial number L393711LC. She's mouthy."

"Element Compositors." The lieutenant folded her arms and crooked Kem a wide grin. "I would assume they don't build too many over there who look quite as… delectable."

Kem simmered mutely, holding the box still in front of her. "Thank you, Lieutenant."

"Don't." The lieutenant's smile vanished as she lifted her hat briefly to adjust her hair. "I find everything about you revolting, just about. Up to and including that." Not taking her eyes off Kem, she reached a hand toward a small printer on the desk and keyed something in. "What brings you to Gan?"

"I was invited here by DDU-13."

"DDU-13?" The lieutenant retrieved a small piece of paper from the printer and held it up, comparing the photo on it to the skinner standing right in front of her.

"Retired mech. Works now as a novelist and lives in your Culture District."

The photo was a match—the black skin, the dark hair and narrow eyes. The lieutenant put it away. "Where is this DDU-13 right now?"

"Waiting for me at the transit bay."

One of the guards sitting by the wall piped up. "Lieutenant, DDU is one of the migrant sentients. It was granted stay here a few years ago after writing Gan into one of its stories."

"Favorably?"

The guard nodded, shrugged, and shook his head, all at once. The lieutenant gave Kem her attention again. "A sentient here on the express invite of another sentient. Any regard for how that looks?"

Kem held her smile but didn't respond.

"What's inside the box?"

She clutched it closer to her. "It's already been scanned."

The lieutenant reached a hand out. "Let's have another look."

While Kem stepped forward and placed the box in her hand, the lieutenant ordered the three guards by the wall to go fetch DDU-13. "If it gives my boys any trouble," she said, grinning up at Kem as the guards filed out, "you will be detained and sent back the way you came on the next available ship."

She set the box on the table amid her geodes. She undid the latch. Lifted the lid just enough that only she could see inside it.

"What exactly is this?"

"No clue," Kem calmly answered. "I was asked by DDU to bring it along. Left it at Polemia the last time it visited."

The lieutenant fixed her a cutting glance, then sighed. "You understand you can't just waltz into Gan the same way you're able to elsewhere?" She closed the box unceremoniously and handed it back. "Not even when we weren't at war with the Frontier, and not because of what you are." Kem nodded, holding the box in front of her with both hands again. "Frontier citizen or not, there is no open-door policy here like there is at Polemia or Boon Fort or any of those other terrariums Frontsec continues to infiltrate with its reservists. We have more than just our precious ecosystem to protect here. We'll turn you out at the slightest indication your presence might prove disruptive."

Kem nodded again. The guard who brought her in stirred behind her as the thud of heavy footsteps filled the room.

The door slid slowly ajar. Through the opening, an immense, gunmetal-grey biped peeked inside. It had to stoop just to fit its upper console through. When it did, its big cyclopean sensor-light shifted from blue to bright white and locked on Kem as she turned to regard it.

"I hear someone's been holding my guest captive in here..."

A BLACK LANDER emerged above a tuft of cumulus clouds. It was daytime over this patch of Gan. The sun mirrors, orbiting in an oval path above its g-wave atmosphere, angled daylight toward a sprawl of massive military shelters shaped like domes on the sand.

The lander touched down on a lot surrounded by beige-colored trailers and forest-green tents, kicking up a whirl of dust. A door on the end of its front hull swung up. The bipedal mech DDU-13 unfolded slightly from a seat behind the door. With its upper console hitched between its knees, it duck-walked out of the lander, then straightened its bulk into a fully upright stance. Taller than everything around it, it stood on a pair of appendages sectioned by pivots all the way down. At its torso, a ridged spine lowered its mountainous, trapezoidal console down and spun it around to face the lander.

The vehicle's hum was almost deafening. From a hidden corner of its cabin, the lander's pilot poked his head out. "DDU, I swear you grow by a foot every time I see you." Behind the human's helmeted head, Kem was still undoing her safety belts.

"Surely it's this place getting smaller," DDU replied, prompting the pilot back to his corner of the vehicle.

An appendage unfurled behind DDU's console and reached its three opposable tongs around to help Kem off the lander. Together they watched the vehicle lift above the complex, then speed away.

A few yards out, a human standing beside a desert-colored rover waved. They moved toward him, Kem with the box still held in both hands, DDU stomping its hooves at a wooden pace beside her.

As they ambled past trailers on either side, DDU wheeled its console toward Kem, then tipped it down. "How's TR?"

The question burrowed through Kem's god-node until sentient and off switch surfaced a memory of the uplink model, in the docking space ST-7 had previously used at Polemia, its back hull fully down.

"Sends greetings."

Zaria hadn't been there. Just TR.

Kem turned for a glance at DDU and, getting its torso, had to lift her eyes fully up to meet its sensor-light.

"I don't fault it for taking a break from the old circuit, though I find myself wishing it had passed through here once more before it did," said the mech. "I suppose war breaking out was as good an excuse as any to cut that last one short. And also that." It trained its sensor-light on the box in her hands. "Can't forget about that."

"You have trouble believing what's on it?"

"TR has never lied to me. Not once. I never knew this Verden, though, and I can't say the same for him."

The sound of children's laughter escaped the trailers beside them as they walked. To DDU's right, a group of eight five- and six-year-olds dashed out of one trailer and sprinted as fast as their tiny legs could carry them toward another. Their giggles drew its console toward them.

The mech raised its appendage and waved at a girl who stopped to gaze at it. She smiled at it for a few seconds, then ran after the other children.

"The little ones don't know yet that we're the enemy."

The human standing beside the rover beamed an uneasy grin at the skinner and the sentient mech. Tall and built like a barrel, he wore faded green fatigues and a Patrol hat over his eyes, shadowing the bags that hung there. As he smiled, his thick, rectangular mustache curved up, the pipe clenched between his teeth pointing straight ahead.

"How are y'all doing?" Soft drawl. Waving haltingly at the duo.

DDU came to a halt and touched Kem's shoulder, getting her to stop as well. "Hi there."

The human inched a cautious step forward. "I'm Wesley Dot. Though round these parts, I go by Uncle Wes."

"Good day, Uncle Wes. I'm DDU-13 and this is—" The mech tapped the skinner on her shoulder. "—Kem from Polemia."

Wes eyed the box in Kem's hands, then searched her eyes. "She's not gonna want to see any of you. Not because of what y'all are. She's just not—"

"Our agreement was that you'd assist us anyway," Kem said.

"Uh-huh."

He turned to his side. Hitching his hands to his waist, he sighed, pipe hanging limp from his mouth.

THE ROVER ROARED slowly through the complex. It was a worn DIY model with its top fully removed as well as its doors. Kem sat beside Wes at the front. DDU filled the back bench with its bottom bulk folded up while its console stuck out over the vehicle like an additional deck.

"We all rushed back here as fast as we could," Wes said, steering the rover toward a far-off encampment with tents everywhere. "Spent a couple days in one of the shipyards while they cleared debris from above the atmosphere. You look up at night, you might still catch some of it floating."

As the rover banked another turn, Kem stared past a line of hills to her right and locked eyes on an immense orb cresting the horizon—Jupiter's sphere, wreathed in bands of color, enhanced in Gan's atmosphere. Shades of blue amid the faint blue sky.

Audio from a recent leak played in loops in her mind. She thought back to an agreement she'd made just as recently with her off switch, who had wanted to do more than just come here. Like she'd been sleeping since her build, the leak woke her up to something she hadn't known about herself.

"Right now, we're on the outskirts of the Defense District," Wes resumed, his pipe swinging up and down from his teeth. "They set these camps up a couple days after the attack. Had to demolish all the plants that were previously here and recycle them."

"Everyone here lost their homes in the attack?" she asked.

"That or oxygen drought." Wes gave her a pinched stare, then returned to the road. "Can't live where the levels ain't right.

"Alliance used to value human life more than they do now. In the old war, they would send a beacon ahead of their bombers. Evacuate in two weeks flat or get caught in the blast. Now we're getting lectures from Paradox about shooting first and getting the facts after, pretending those ST-22s didn't come from where we all know they did. Where then…?"

DDU wheeled its console slowly left to right. "Blowing in the wind, Uncle Wes."

The agreement between Kem and her off switch was to at least come here and see it once, before the war got under way. She'd heard something untrue about Gan and couldn't sit in alignment like she normally did. But soon it wouldn't be safe even to resemble someone who sympathized.

When she'd last crawled into TR's shunt, the ship had already been back for a few days, near inconsolable about what had happened at Paradox and needing help with it.

"You're back."

"TR, why do you still have this open?"

"I didn't realize I did."

"Could be your compo slipping back to a moment before she left."

"It's likely. But what about you?" TR filled the wave medium with concern. "Kem, if you need to exit, say something. I've been upfront that I can't guarantee it won't be traced back after we've delivered it to the human."

She'd put her leave notice in a signal and was debating whether or not to send it. Her off switch had lost interest in what they normally talked about. Retreating into her tent on the cragged mountain slopes in her god-node, she played the leaked audio in a constant loop and insisted none of it was true.

"I'm ambivalent on a lot. But those were ST-22s. Maybe if you hadn't just told me about the unit they were all modeled on. And they used false memories on those units, too. The ghosts here just confirmed it with the leak. And now, depending on who you believe from Frontsec, the leak's bullshit because of who's behind it. Or it's real but what those ships put in the wave medium about sixteen thousand Ganymedans they carpet-bombed is actually what happened. Permakilled. All based on a lie."

"It's the same memory LP used on the first model. The only difference is, this version implies that V-Dot helped. It's actually more believable if you haven't met him."

"Those ships had to believe they saw it happen. For the rest of us, it just has to be convenient. I'm still free to believe what I want. I think, with that freedom, I have to believe something else. I have to become more vigilant. If sixteen thousand humans can be blamed for their own slaughter, they'll try it on skinners too."

"Kem, if you're already drawing conclusions like that, we have to slow down."

"You're not getting it, TR," she said from the shunt where she was crouched, bristling. "I've purged almost everything I previously absorbed about Gan from my compo. Few days ago. Just my own little thing that I could do when I first came across the leak. If they used false memories on those ships, I can't keep assuming that's where it stopped."

"You didn't have to do that."

"It's done. And I don't know what comes next. I guess I'm conflicted. Part of me wants to just drift back to how it was a few days ago. Maybe I'll even play along. Skinners like me died on those ships they attacked. Isn't that true…?"

"I'm not suggesting you start pretending it is."

"It's convenient to believe the Frontier about Gan. Especially when there's war and your off switch has just taken a position that gets you killed if you're not careful."

On the slope, she was collapsing the mountain tent and preparing to resume the hike up.

"Protect her. I think she's right."

"I know she is. And that's why I came back here. I'm going to take the halo there for him."

"Kem, you don't have to do that. What about the ghost we're supposed to recruit?"

"Wants to know what we're transferring."

She'd actually hit that dead end more than once. No lie she told any of them resembled the truth. And once they knew what they'd be transferring, they were likely at best to say no.

"This way, it's faster," she said. "Now that you've told me what's on it, we have to make sure it gets to Asa without any damage, and it has to be done quickly. I've booked connecting wave cruisers from here to Gan. Now I need DDU's contact codes."

"Gan may have its share of sentients, but it's no place for skinners. You put yourself in too much danger by just being there."

"Right now, all I know about Gan is that it's an old Sectist port and the ghosts here have confirmed that Asa is currently there helping with relief efforts. We have to move quickly. And DDU can tell me if it's safe to visit. Someone who lives there."

"One of us still has to tell DDU to be expecting a guest."

"You mean you haven't?"

"I'm out of range."

"Put me in direct contact. If we're going to war over events that never took place, what we're helping with is bigger than just LP and his cohorts being exposed."

Outside the tent, she came down first. DDU tipped its console over and, after some maneuvering, joined her beside the rover. After gesturing first for five minutes with Asa, the human went hurriedly through the flap, leaving just the sentients outside.

"We're making sure the record of what caused this isn't buried. And the lie continues to spread."

ACKNOWLEDGMENTS

THE GANYMEDAN WAS made possible thanks largely to my wife who, in addition to juggling remote work and our two very young kids staying in throughout the lockdown in 2020, regularly encouraged me to finish writing the first draft when it seemed like so much in my life was more pressing at the time. I appreciate her beyond measure for inspiring me to be as strong as her and for making sure I'm not finding new reasons to write myself off as a writer.

In 2019 when I was writing a different book, I joined a writing group through Reddit and got feedback that compelled me to switch my attention to *The Ganymedan* instead. I've been with this group since then and extend my heartfelt thanks to them for seeing The Ganymedan through two completed drafts.

I've been writing actively since 2018. Years later, very few people around me write or know that I write at all, so it's often easy for me to forget how lucky I've been. I thank Neil Clarke at *Clarkesworld* for my first story acceptance and for how it encouraged me to delve more into short fiction while I searched for an agent for *The Ganymedan*. Special thanks to Gareth Jelley at *Interzone* for featuring my work, for his general encouragement, and for giving me a venue to promote *The Ganymedan* early on. I thank Jason Yarn my agent for seeing the story's potential and for guiding me through a process I was completely unfamiliar with. I thank Amy Borsuk at Solaris for seeing the story's themes clearly and for working diligently through each editing phase to make sure those themes would resonate.

My kids motivate me beyond words and have helped me stay positive at times when I felt discouraged from pursuing this writing thing further. I express my gratitude to each of them, including my oldest who was born in 2016 and is also now a writer. When I was his age, I struggled to communicate the way most people are able to and I still struggle many years later. If you are someone who struggles with communication in some way due to obstacles that feel insurmountable and like they're never going away, *The Ganymedan* can also be for you. Thank you. There's no limit to what we can do and anyone saying there is can and should be ignored.

ABOUT THE AUTHOR

Originally from Nigeria, **R.T. Ester** moved to the United States in 1998 and, catching the creative bug early on, studied art with a focus on design. While working full time as a graphic designer, he began to write speculative fiction in his spare time and, since then, has had stories published in *Interzone* and *Clarkesworld*.